"Faith and love triumph in this small-town story of overcoming the past and finding hope for the future. *Leaving November* gently plays the heartstrings and embraces the spirit in the name of love."

—Linda Windsor, author of WEDDING BELL BLUES
and FOR PETE'S SAKE

"Deb Raney's books have been an enjoyment and inspiration for me since her first, *A Vow to Cherish*. She has again touched my life with *Leaving November*. A gifted storyteller, she also has a way of having her characters learn to lean on God that causes me as a reader to relearn that same lesson. I highly recommend *Leaving November*."

—Yvonne Lehman, author of 46 novels and director
of the Blue Ridge Mountains Christian Writers Conference

"I loved *Leaving November* by Deborah Raney! Raney's books always touch the heart in deep ways that keep me thinking about the undercurrents long after I turn the last page. The Clayburn series is a keeper!"

—Colleen Coble, author of ANATHEMA

Leaving November

a clayburn novel

Award-Winning Author

Deborah Raney

HOWARD ®
Fiction
A DIVISION OF SIMON & SCHUSTER
New York   London   Toronto   Sydney

Our purpose at Howard Books is to:
- *Increase faith* in the hearts of growing Christians
- *Inspire holiness* in the lives of believers
- *Instill hope* in the hearts of struggling people everywhere
Because He's coming again!

Published by Howard Books, a division of Simon & Schuster, Inc.
1230 Avenue of the Americas, New York, NY 10020
www.howardpublishing.com

Leaving November © 2008 by Deborah Raney

First Howard trade paperback edition March 2008

In association with the Steve Laube Agency

Library of Congress Cataloging-in-Publication Data
Raney, Deborah.
  Leaving November / Deborah Raney.
    p. cm.—(A Clayburn novel)
  1. Homecoming—Fiction. 2. Adult children of alcoholics—Fiction. 3. Coffeehouses—Fiction. 4. Art galleries, commercial—Fiction. 5. Recovering alcoholics—Fiction. I. Title.
  PS3568.A562L43 2007
  813'.54—dc22

                                                              2007032088

ISBN 13: 978-1-4165-5829-3
ISBN 10:   1-4165-5829-2

10 9 8 7 6 5 4 3 2 1

Manufactured in the United States of America

For information regarding special discounts for bulk purchases, please contact Simon & Schuster Special Sales at 1-800-456-6798 or business@simonandschuster.com.

Edited by Dave Lambert and Ramona Cramer Tucker
Cover design by Terry Dugan
Interior design by Tennille Paden

To Tammy,

with love

Acknowledgments

I wish to offer sincere thanks and deep appreciation to the following people for their part in bringing this story to life:

For help with research and/or proofreading: Russ Buller; my author's groups, ChiLibris and ACFW, who are always ready with expert assistance; Salina Regional Medical Center; Terry Stucky; Max and Winifred Teeter; the kind folks at The Swedish Country Inn in Lindsborg, Kansas, which served as a model for Wren's Nest, and where the ideas for the Clayburn novels were born.

I'm not sure I could have written this book without the help of the ChiLibris Midwest contingent. Thanks to Dan and Steph Whitson Higgins, Dr. Mel and Cheryl Hodde, Dave and Colleen Coble, Till Fell, Judy Miller, and Nancy Moser, who opened her beautiful home for our brainstorming sessions.

Thanks to Pam Meyers for reminding me to be sure Jasper, the resident cat at Wren's Nest, appears in all the Clayburn novels.

As always, special thanks are due my ace critique partner, Tamera Alexander. Tammy, you're the best!

Thanks, too, to my talented editors Dave Lambert and Ramona Cramer Tucker; and to Philis Boutinghouse at Howard Books. My agent, Steve Laube, is always there with encouragement and ideas and extraordinary wisdom.

To my amazing husband, Ken, thanks for making it look so easy to be married to a writer. I know it's *not,* and I love you all the more for putting up with my quirks!

To our children, my parents, my mother-in-law, and all our incredible extended family: what a gift from the Lord you each are. I'm very blessed to have each of you in my life.

Humble yourselves before the Lord, and he will lift you up.

—James 4:10

In his great mercy he has given us new birth into a living hope
through the resurrection of Jesus Christ from the dead,
and into an inheritance that can never perish, spoil or fade—
kept in heaven for you, who through faith are shielded by God's power
until the coming of the salvation that is ready to be revealed in the last time.
In this you greatly rejoice, though now for a little while
you may have had to suffer grief in all kinds of trials.
These have come so that your faith—of greater worth than gold,
which perishes even though refined by fire—may be proved genuine
and may result in praise, glory and honor when Jesus Christ is revealed.

—1 Peter 1:3–7

Her name had to
be on that list.
It had to be.

Chapter One

November

She closed her eyes, inhaling familiar scents. Moldy books. Fresh shavings from the pencil sharpener. A bouquet of wilting chrysanthemums. The *tick, tick, tick* of the ancient grandfather clock in the library's main hall threatened to carry her straight back to her childhood.

The computer fan clicked on and its whirr rescued her, jolting her into the present—not that the Clayburn Public Library had changed one iota in the eight years since she'd moved away from this two-horse Kansas town. But the Internet was her lifeline, tethering her to California. To her future. Adrenaline surged through her veins as she clicked the mouse and scrolled down the web page, scanning the list for the only name that mattered.

Her name had to be on that list. It *had* to be.

One cautious letter at a time, she retyped her name into the search field—Vienne Kenney—and clicked again.

Nothing. There must be some mistake. Staring at the computer screen, her vision blurred and she fought to catch her breath.

She took a sip of lukewarm coffee from the travel mug she'd snuck in, then pushed it to the back of the book-cluttered desk. She'd agonized over this moment for three months, and now it was here. And if this official State of California–sanctioned website was up-to-date, she had good reason to agonize. The site supposedly verified the name of every person who passed the July bar exam.

So why wasn't her name showing up? She glanced at the connection icon on the screen. Maybe there was something wrong with the library's Internet service. Maybe the system was pulling up an old page from when she'd checked earlier today. That had to be it.

She typed in the URL again and entered her information hunt-and-peck style. The page refreshed—with the same results. She slid the pony-tail holder from her hair and combed her fingers through the tangled mass of curls.

She couldn't have failed. Not a second time. A sick feeling settled in the hollow of her stomach. She'd lived through this humiliation once before.

She massaged her temples in slow circles. This was a bad dream. It had to be. She'd done everything right this time. Studied her heart out. Spent money she didn't have on a course that practically guaranteed her success at passing the bar. She'd been *so* confident . . .

How would she ever live it down if she'd flunked the bar exam again? Tens of thousands of dollars wasted on a law degree—money she'd spent grudgingly because of its source.

She lifted her head and stared at her cell phone lying on the desk beside the computer's mouse. Her mother would be calling any minute, expecting to celebrate good news. And Jenny, too. Her roommate had another semester to go, but Jenny was brilliant. She would pass easily. On her first try. Salt in the wound.

Vienne put her head in her hands. She'd probably be fired from her job the minute word got out. And if she knew Richard Spencer, he was probably online at this very moment back in California, checking the results to make sure her name was there. When he discovered it conspicuously absent, he'd no doubt call to offer consolation and a shoulder to cry on.

But he would fire her just the same.

A sour taste filled the back of her throat, and her stomach turned a somersault. She took another sip of lukewarm coffee. At least she wouldn't have to walk in to work and face everyone Monday. But she couldn't stick around here either.

Mom probably had half of Coyote County praying for her. Since the day testing started in July, her name had no doubt been at the top of the prayer chain list at Community Christian, complete with all the gory details: *Please pray God will bless my daughter, Vienne, with success as she takes the bar exam. This is especially important since she flunked—by a margin of quite a few points—the first time she took the exam.*

Vienne gave a silent, humorless laugh. Ironic she would find her name on that dubious prayer list, and nowhere in sight on the list that mattered.

The walls of the library closed in on her. She started to push away from the desk. But something—some misguided sense of hope—compelled her back to the computer. She put her hand over the mouse again. Did this Podunk library even have the right software to display the page correctly?

A glimmer of optimism sparked in her. Maybe she'd just missed it. Maybe she'd been looking at the list from the last exam. Or the postings weren't complete. She'd heard of people who weren't on the list at first, but whose names later appeared, much to their relief. Some glitch must have prevented her name from showing up with the other successful candidates. That had to be it.

The page refreshed, and the ominous message appeared again: *No names on the pass list match "Vienne Kenney."* And this time she knew the truth. She'd failed. Again. Thirty years old and she would never be able to sign her name *Vienne Renée Kenney, Attorney-at-Law.*

Brinkerman & Associates had been forced to keep her on after the first time she'd failed. But without a license, they didn't have a position for her—at least not at a salary she could survive on. Not that she'd consider staying at the firm after this humiliation. And she would not take the test a third time. She'd wasted too many years and too much of her mother's money. Her *father's* money.

She shuddered. It was time to cut her losses and move on. But the job market in Davis was pathetic. Besides, did she really want to face the chance, every day, that she might run into some well-meaning Brinkerman associate who'd feel obligated to pat her arm and tell her how sorry they were and how much they missed her and how was she doing? And was she taking the exam again, etc., etc., ad nauseam?

But where could she go now? She stared at a large painting hanging on the wall in front of her—a misty landscape of gnarled cottonwood trees and a green-watered river. It was probably supposed to be the Smoky Hill that Clayburn was built upon. It was a peaceful scene—and nicely done. But it was *locus classicus* Kansas. And she had shaken the dust of Clayburn off her feet when she left town the summer after high school graduation. The only dreams she'd ever entertained about returning involved thumbing her nose at this hick town and her so-called friends who had made her persona non grata when she needed them most. Surprising that the rejection of a bunch of nobodies could still hurt so much. How her mother could stay here all these years, she didn't know.

Now, thanks to Mom, everybody in town knew about her lofty dreams. Knew she'd graduated law school and worked for a hotshot law firm. Oh, she'd managed to impress a few people. People who'd thought Harlan Kenney's daughter would never amount to anything. It was retribution of sorts, quid pro quo for all the grief this town had given her. She knew it wasn't right, but sometimes it sure did feel good.

But now—now, they'd all know what a fraud she was.

Her cell phone chirped. That would be Mom. She straightened and looked around, hoping the noise hadn't disturbed anyone. But except for the elderly librarian at the front desk, she seemed to be alone in the building.

She didn't recognize the number on the LCD display. Her hopes mounted. Maybe it was about the exam. Maybe there *had* been a mistake. She flipped open the phone. "Hello?"

A brief hesitation on the line. "Um . . . I'm calling for Ingrid Kenney's daughter . . ."

Her pulse jumped. "Yes . . . this is Vienne."

"This is Harv Weimer at Weimer's Food Market in Salina. I'm sorry to call with bad news, but your mother fell . . . out in the parking lot here a few minutes ago. She wasn't able to get up on her own, so we called an ambulance."

"Ambulance? Is—is she all right?" She pushed her chair back and searched her purse for her car keys, almost knocking over her coffee in the process.

"She's on her way in the ambulance now. They're taking her to Asbury . . . the medical center."

"To the hospital? What happened?"

"We're not really sure. A customer found her out in the parking lot. She'd fallen beside her car. She was able to give us your number before she lost consciousness."

"She's not conscious?" Vienne's fingers started to tremble.

"The EMTs seemed to think she may have had a stroke or something."

No . . . not again. Dr. Billings had warned them Mom might not survive a second stroke. Vienne snagged her keys and headed for the entrance, her purse strap lopped over her arm.

Suddenly failing the bar no longer seemed like the worst thing that could happen to her.

5

He was determined
to lick this thing.
And if he couldn't
conquer it here,
then it wouldn't
really be conquered,
would it?

Chapter Two

January

*J*ackson Linder unlocked the door and reached around to flip on the light switch. He stood still, waiting for his eyes to adjust to the bright fluorescent lamps that flickered and droned overhead in the studio behind his Main Street gallery. The alley was black beyond the row of double-hung windows at the back of the room where he'd entered, but the reflection of someone's Christmas lights flickered from the street at the end of the alley. Christmas was over—and New Year's, too, for that matter. Two weeks over. Nothing was drearier than lights and tinsel for a holiday whose expiration date had passed.

He should have waited until morning when the light was better and the wind wasn't so brisk. But he wasn't ready to face the old friends and fellow merchants who were sure to drift in to see him once they got wind he was back in town. Eventually he'd have to face their well-meaning questions. And probably quell a few rumors. Knowing the nature of Clayburn's gossip mill, he guessed the rumors had been far worse than the truth.

Which was bad enough.

The studio was freezing. Almost as cold as the air outside, minus the windchill factor. Maybe he should have stayed a couple more weeks in Florida with Mom. He dismissed the idea as quickly as it had come. He adored his mother, but after two weeks in her cramped condo, they were definitely starting to get on each other's nerves.

Rubbing his palms together, he went to the thermostat by the door that separated the studio from the gallery. The furnace had been set just high enough to keep the pipes from freezing. He cranked it up to seventy-two degrees and closed the door between the rooms.

The furnace kicked on and he pulled in a breath. The boulder on his chest was worlds lighter than it had been when he'd left this place nine and a half months ago. But the weight had never quite gone away altogether. More than one counselor had told him only time could accomplish that. And one man—someone Jack had come to admire greatly because he spoke from sorrowful experience—had warned him it might never go away completely.

Looking around the dusty, austere studio, he put a hand to the back of his neck. It still startled him to have his fingers touch the sun-roughened skin there instead of the knotted weight of the ponytail he'd worn for half his life. Two weeks ago—the morning before he flew out of Kansas City bound for St. Petersburg—he'd cut off his long hair. He still wasn't sure why. Maybe he'd thought transforming the outer man would help complete the rehabilitation of the inner man?

The jury was still out on that. His ponytail and the gold ear stud he'd worn had been affectations anyway. Part of the costume for a role he played—the suave *artiste*. He kneaded the knot of muscles in his shoulder and moved his hand to stroke the smooth plane of his cheek. Maybe his new look was as artificial as his artist's garb had been, although the rough stubble he'd worn back then was more the result of laziness—or a drinking binge—than from any sense of style.

Which costume fit the real Jackson Linder? Or was he someone different altogether? Almost thirty-four years old and he still hadn't managed to discover the answer to that question, in spite of all the hours spent regurgitating his life all over some hapless counselor.

Oppression moved over him like the heavy shadow of a rain cloud over the prairie. His eyes moved to the supply cabinet in the corner. Supplies. It had held his paints and brushes, yes. But it had also been a hiding place for his precious vice. One of many caches. Too many.

The front door rattled, then someone banged on it. Hard enough to make the plate glass clatter. Heart racing, Jack eased open the door to the gallery. The banging got louder.

Without turning on the lights, he picked his way through the dim gallery. Jack didn't recognize the man on the other side of the glass door, but he wore the uniform of the Clayburn police force. The city must have hired a new guy while he was gone.

He unlocked the door and stepped out onto the sidewalk. The frigid air turned his skin to gooseflesh.

The cop stood at alert. "Officer Frank Marren." It was an official statement, not a friendly introduction. "What's going on here?"

"I'm Jackson Linder . . ." Jack put out a hand.

The officer reared back, moving his right hand to the holster on his hip.

Jack quickly dropped his arms to his side and stepped back into the doorway. "I own the gallery." He angled his head toward the stenciled letters that spelled his name on the window. "I just got back into town. I've been . . . gone . . . for a few weeks. Months," he corrected quickly. This was no time to fudge on details.

"You have ID on you?"

Jack looked down at his jeans. "May I?"

Marren nodded and Jack probed his back pocket for his wallet.

The officer inspected the driver's license Jack produced and handed it back to him. "You opening the gallery up again?"

"That's the plan."

"Welcome back, then." Marren gave what Jack took for a smile. "And sorry to bother you. We never got word you were due back."

"Yeah." Jack scuffed the sidewalk with the toe of his shoe. "Well, thanks for looking out for the place while I was gone."

Marren tipped his cap and disappeared into the shadows beyond the street lamp.

Jack locked the door again.

There went his hopes of hiding out for a few days. The news would no doubt be all over town by morning. The thought of facing the town made his stomach twist into a queasy knot.

He shook his head. It still amazed him that he'd been able to live in such denial. He hadn't fooled anyone but himself. He'd talked himself into believing he could stop any time he wanted to. That he didn't need help with what everyone else called his "problem."

For him, it had been a solution. Not a problem. He'd always seen the drinking as temporary. Something he did while he was recovering from the awful thing that happened to him. He *deserved* to soak his mind in a soothing marinade of liquor, to deaden the pain until he was strong enough to deal with it. But two years had turned into three, and still he wasn't strong enough.

Back then, he'd truly believed all the people in his life were worried for nothing—his mother, his friend Trevor, who had such a stake in his sobriety . . . and Wren.

Wren. Who, but sweet white-haired Wren, could have loved him more through all the hard times? Of all the people he dreaded facing in Clayburn, he dreaded Wren the least. She would welcome him with open arms, rejoice with him over one step accomplished, and encourage him to the next.

In fact, before he left, she'd invited him to take a room at the little inn she ran with her husband, Bart. If the offer still held, he could rent out his apartment over the gallery for extra income. The Lord knew how desperately he needed the money. Wren's Nest was just a block down the street. He could have a decent meal once in a while. It made sense. And maybe it would be good for his relationship with Wren. He'd only gotten to know Wren, discovered the truth about who she was, when he was eighteen. He'd gone off to college a short time later, and though he and Wren had both made overtures at having a relationship, sadly, tragedy—and his drinking—had aborted the flimsy start to their newfound friendship. He hoped to remedy that now that he was back.

Still, he couldn't quite picture himself living at the inn with Wren and Bart. Maybe he had to do this on his own. Not alone. This was no time to play Lone Ranger. That he knew. But he had to find out if he was strong enough to make it without some supervisor threatening a Breathalyzer or urine test, or some counselor to check in with every day. He had to do it without running to his mommy. He'd done enough of that when Mom—his adoptive mother—was still living here in Clayburn. Sadly, Mom had been all too ready to make excuses for his vice. His sin. What would be different about moving in with Wren?

No, his next steps had to be solo.

How many more steps would there be? Was he strong enough to finish the climb? Weariness enveloped him at the mere thought. He needed to get upstairs to bed. Shut off all these thoughts of failure.

He started toward the stairs, but his body seemed to be set on automatic pilot, always veering toward that cabinet in the corner. Salivating over the relief he would find there. Thank God there was nothing to be found there tonight. Unless a tube of paint had a measurable alcohol content. He might have laughed at the thought, except there'd been

11

a time he would have considered that a viable option if no bottle was available.

"I'm not a man who does that anymore." He spoke the words aloud . . . a crutch—no, a *recovery skill*—he'd learned in rehab. It was one of the many strategies he'd learned. And it helped. His need was a habit that required breaking. An enemy to be defeated. Not all that different from the dieter learning to resist chocolate or the smoker learning to replace the craving for nicotine with something more acceptable. That's what the counselors had told him. Mind over matter . . . mind over matter . . .

The studio came back in focus, and the siren call of that cabinet grew louder. He bit his lower lip. This was going to be harder than he thought. This place held too many disturbing memories. Maybe it hadn't been a good idea to come back here. Maybe what he needed was a fresh start somewhere else.

But that wasn't possible. He didn't really have a choice. He had a following here, small though it was. The gallery offered his only hope of making a living, of getting back on his feet after the disaster he'd made of his life.

He was determined to lick this thing. And if he couldn't conquer it here, then it wouldn't really be conquered, would it? But it would be tough to change his behaviors now that he was back in this place where it all had started.

He pushed down the fear that clutched at his throat. He was a tightrope walker who'd had the safety nets yanked out from under him. Here he had no choice but to come face-to-face with his mistakes. Both the unintentional—which had wrought unimaginable tragedy—and those he'd deliberately chosen.

He tested his breath again, expelling the air from his lungs easily. His heart wasn't racing. His hands were steady. He could live with what remained. It was an improvement.

He lifted an empty picture frame from a hook on the wall and blew off the dust. Surveying the narrow room, hope swelled inside him. Aside from the thick layer of dust powdering every surface, things appeared pretty much the way he'd left them. He had his work cut out for him getting the gallery back up and running. But that was good. Work would be his salvation—

No. He cut off the thought, corrected it immediately. His *salvation . . .* He blinked back sudden tears and made himself deliberate on each silent word. His salvation had been bought at a price far beyond any labor he could ever endure. He would not diminish the word with such a meager definition.

He looked toward the cobweb-laced ceiling and whispered three words he hoped would never lose their power to humble him. "Thank you, Lord."

He tried to turn on the outside light, but apparently the bulb was burned out. He'd have to unload his car in the dark. Or maybe he'd wait until morning. No sense in getting the Clayburn police force—all three of them—worked up again. If an early commuter reported somebody hauling things back and forth in an alley at four o'clock in the morning, it wouldn't be just the police force that would go on alert.

Leaving the door ajar, he went out and retrieved his small duffel bag from the backseat of the car. The brisk air revived him. Once back inside, he rubbed his hands together against the cold before clearing stacks of cardboard boxes and rolls of canvas off the large framing table in the center of the room. Now was as good a time as any to get started.

He grabbed a push broom from the closet and took it to the floor with a vengeance. There was a ton of work to do before he could open the gallery again. He worked for the next two hours, a long-forgotten resolve building inside him.

Finally, as the first hues of dawn reflected pink off the aluminum paneling of the building across the alley, his eyelids grew heavy. However musty the sheets on the bed in his small apartment upstairs, he doubted he'd have trouble catching a few hours of sleep before he faced the day.

Before climbing the steps, he turned and surveyed the studio, inhaling the heady mixture of canvas and oil, wood shavings, and turpentine that permeated the air. The familiar scents fortified him.

He didn't know why or how, but he felt God's presence here. He couldn't give up yet.

Vienne cringed hearing her childhood nickname. She despised it— Vinny Kenney. The very cadence of it echoed like a schoolyard taunt.

Chapter Three

Hey, Vienne. Where do you want me to put these?" The UPS guy held the back door open with one knee, a stack of cardboard boxes balanced on his shoulder. A gust of icy January wind blew in from the alley behind him even as the sun painted a bright patch of pink on the tile.

"Oh, here, Chuck. Let me get those." Vienne laid her paintbrush across the gallon pail and ran to the door. She was still getting used to being on a first-name basis with the deliverymen, but spying the Crate & Barrel logo on the side of the box, she clapped. "Oh, good! It's my mugs."

He grunted and ignored her outstretched arms. "They're heavy. Just tell me where you want 'em."

"You can set them right over here." She hurried to clear a stack of unread newspapers off the counter.

Chuck slid the boxes onto the faux granite countertop, wiped his hands on the front of his brown uniform shirt, and looked around the renovated café. "Wow! You've done a number on this place. Looks like you're about ready to open for business, too. Got a date set?"

Vienne spun on one heel, panning the space, trying to see it through the eyes of a potential customer. Cardboard boxes littered the floors and counters, and every surface was powdered with plaster dust. But the colorful geometric floor tiles were laid and she'd spent countless hours refinishing the original parquet floor in front of the fireplace. The countertops and appliances were all in place, and there were only a few touch-ups left to be finished on the paint job. She'd bring the old café tables and chairs in from the back storage room as soon as she got the place cleaned up for Mom.

It had come a long way from the run-down café that occupied this spot on Main Street mere months ago. "I'm planning a big open house for Valentine's Day." She heard the pride in her own voice too late to temper it. Tucking a wayward wisp of hair behind one ear, she offered him a self-conscious smile. "Stop by if you have time."

Chuck nodded and walked to the door. He opened it a crack, then paused with his hand on the doorknob. Vienne could hear his truck idling out in the alley. "Maizie over at the flower shop said you moved here from California?"

She chewed her lip and nodded, then took a step toward him, hoping to usher him out.

"What brought you to Kansas?" He cocked his head toward the alley. The wind howled and spit sand and dried leaves at the side of the building. His implication was clear: why would anyone want to leave California for weather like this?

She stepped backward and bit back a sigh. She could only guess what else Maizie had told him. "I grew up here."

"Ah. Back to the old hometown, huh?"

"I guess you could say that. My mom had a stroke. She's in the Clayburn Manor—just for rehab," she added quickly.

"Ingrid, right? I heard about that. She's your mom? I'm sorry. I've always liked her. Hated to see the café close down. She made the best meat loaf in Coyote County."

"Yeah, well, it seemed like a good time to remodel the place. While Mom recovers . . ."

Poor Mom. Vienne had used her mother as her reason—her excuse—for making the move back to Clayburn. "Just until Mom can get back to work," she told everyone. But she'd called Richard Spencer and quit her job at Brinkerman and told Jenny to find another roommate. She hadn't even gone back for her stuff. Jenny had shipped most of it, and Vienne sold the rest on eBay to pay the freight. UPS had just delivered her bicycle yesterday. Not that she'd use it until things warmed up a little here, but Mom would be tickled to resume their evening bike rides come spring.

Her heart twisted. As far as she could tell, Mom was a long way from riding a bicycle. Or from coming home at all, let alone taking over at the café again. Vienne was starting to fear that might never happen. And why would she expect it to? Mom should have retired years ago.

"You've done a great job with the place." Chuck shifted on one foot. His mouth twisted into a teasing smile. "You sure don't look old enough to have a mom in a nursing home. How old is your mom anyway?"

She forced a smile. "She turns seventy this year." If Mr. UPS was flirting—or trying to figure out how old *she* was—he could use some serious tips. And didn't he have other packages to deliver? She opened the door a few more inches—a broad hint—ignoring the debris that blew in. What was another dustpan full of dirt?

An engine roared out in the alley and that seemed to light a fire under Chuck. He opened the door halfway. "Well, I'd better get a move on. Oh, hey . . ." He turned to eye an empty corner where a booth had been. "You've got some extra space. Can I leave a couple packages for the gallery across the street?"

"Linder's? I thought the gallery closed down."

"He's supposedly reopening at the end of the month. I've got some boxes—frames, it looks like—for him. I tried to leave them at the antique shop"—he cocked his head toward the building next door—"but Erma said she doesn't have an inch of storage space to spare."

"I could have told you that. I've never seen a place so packed with junk—" She clapped a hand over her mouth. "Merchandise, I mean."

Chuck laughed. "Nice save, but I think you were right the first time. Anyway, would you mind if I left the boxes here? If he doesn't pick them up in a couple days, I can take them back. I'll leave a note so he knows they're over here."

Vienne shrugged. "Sure. I guess that'd be okay."

Chuck went to retrieve Jackson Linder's packages. She'd had a crush on Jack once upon a time. He'd worked as a lifeguard at the Clayburn swimming pool, and she'd fallen hard for him the summer after her eighth-grade year. When school started that fall, she was a gangly book-worm, a lowly freshman with a king-size crush on him. And he was one of the cool seniors who didn't know she existed. Or if he did, he only thought of her as one of the bratty kids from the pool. Besides, he had a pretty cheerleader girlfriend. Vienne had sulked over him until he graduated and went off to art school in Colorado. She forgot about him when she started dating Rob Parks.

"Okay if I lean them against this wall?" Chuck's voice intruded on her reflection.

"That's fine. You'll be sure and leave him a note?" She was suddenly nervous at the prospect of seeing Jack again after all these years. Silly.

Jackson had moved back to Clayburn and opened his gallery about the time she left for California. Then, last spring, he'd closed the gallery and moved out of state. According to Mom, his mother had retired to Florida about the same time. Mom had never said where Jack moved to, but Vienne remembered her mother saying something about Jack being involved in a terrible car accident. As she recalled, two other people had died in the wreck. Maybe he'd left town to escape the memories.

Oddly enough, she'd heard that he still owned the building that housed the art gallery. And now he was back. Why on earth he'd want to come back to Clayburn, she couldn't imagine.

Not that she had any room to talk. She'd been here since November, and it was beginning to seem as if she'd be here ad infinitum. Maybe Jack was as trapped in Clayburn as she was.

The engine of the big truck revved, and Vienne looked up to see Chuck shifting gears on the brown monster. She lifted her hand in a halfhearted wave and held her breath against the diesel fumes. Dusting off her hands, she started for the door. She had work to do, and it wasn't going to get done standing out here letting her mind wander.

But a squeak of brakes and the metallic slam of a door made her relief short-lived.

"Hey, Vinny!" Pete Truesdell left his pickup running and climbed down from the mud-splattered cab.

Vienne cringed hearing her childhood nickname. She despised it— *Vinny Kenney.* The very cadence of it echoed like a schoolyard taunt.

Pete slapped his engineer-striped coveralls with a grimy billed cap. His gray hair stuck out in fifty different directions. "You 'bout ready to get the café opened up again? I'm sick and tired of the Dairy Barn's chicken sandwich. This ol' boy's ready for some of your mom's good home cookin'."

Uh-oh. "Well, I hate to disappoint you, Pete, but the menu's going to change quite a bit. The café is going to be a coffee shop now, you know."

"I was hopin' you'd tell me that was just a vicious rumor." Pete gave his cap another slap. "So the ol' café's gonna be some la-di-da coffee shop now."

She shook her head and grinned. "'Fraid so, Pete. We'll still have some sandwiches and soups, and Mom's famous chicken and noodles every Friday, but I won't have a full menu. Mom's the only one who could do that justice." Her throat closed around a lump of grief. She missed her mother . . . in spite of the fact that she visited her every night at the Manor. It wasn't the same. *Mom* wasn't the same.

"Oh, I doubt the apple falls far from the tree." The way Pete dropped his head, Vienne knew he meant it as a compliment. "Maybe you'll reconsider about that coffee shop business."

Pete and his generation might prove to be a hard sell. "Oh, I think you'll be pleasantly surprised. And just wait . . . You'll forget all about Mom's meat loaf when you taste my cappuccino."

"Well, I don't know about no crappa-cheeney, but I'll be waitin' in line for the doors to open." He winked. "Now, you offer a prize to your first customer, I'll camp out on the sidewalk the night before."

She laughed. "I appreciate that, Pete." But inspecting his manure-caked boots and grizzled chin whiskers, she realized she didn't appreciate it one bit. Pete was exactly the kind of customer she did not want to attract. The coffee shop would be warm and friendly—the kind of place you'd want to spend the whole morning in—but it wasn't going to be any small-town café. Her shop—*Mom's* shop, she corrected—would be a place where you'd be proud to bring your out-of-town friends or hold your book club or sorority meetings. She'd exchanged grilled cheese for biscotti and chili for borscht on the menu. On opening day they'd be thanking her for bringing a touch of class to Clayburn's Main Street.

Hey. Maybe they could call the place *A Touch of Class*? Nah . . . too obvious.

"How's your mom doin'?" Pete's forehead crinkled with genuine concern.

A familiar nausea somersaulted through her belly. "She's . . . about the same. It's slow going."

"We're prayin' for her—me and Velma. Hope Ingrid can be here for your opening day."

"Thanks, Pete." Vienne bit her lip. She'd given up weeks ago on hoping Mom would be here for the opening. At the rate her rehabilitation was going, Mom would be lucky to leave the nursing home before summer. Vienne had no choice but to stay. She'd take care of the house and get the coffee shop up and running until Mom regained her strength and could take it over again.

She closed her eyes. Who was she kidding? Mom was starting over from scratch. Like a toddler, she was having to learn how to feed and dress herself again, and it was agonizing. Worse, Mom hadn't uttered an intelligible word since that terrible day in November. And the doctors weren't optimistic.

But they didn't know Ingrid Kenney. Vienne had seen her mother overcome far worse than this. She'd be back if Vienne had to supervise the therapy herself.

Eyeing the open door, she gave Pete an apologetic smile. "I'd better get back to work. I've got lots to do before Valentine's Day."

"You go on, then. I'll see you openin' day."

He scraped a clump of mud—or worse—from the bottom of one cowboy boot and climbed back into the cab of his old truck.

As he roared down the alley, her mind raced to think of a way to discourage Pete and his smelly, coveralled buddies from making the coffee shop their regular hangout.

She eyed him like
he might be trying to
pull one over on her.

One corner of her
mouth turned up in a
crooked smile.

"You don't remember
me, do you?"

Chapter Four

amiliar street noises woke Jack just as the digital alarm clock on his nightstand clicked over to ten o'clock. Squinting against the light streaming in his window, he threw back the blankets and eased his legs over the side of the bed. The wood floor was icy beneath his feet. He swept a hank of hair out of his eyes and lifted a corner of the curtain. Main Street was already bustling with Tuesday morning traffic. Well, as much as Clayburn ever bustled.

Most of the stores opened at ten, and it was about time for everyone to be gathering for coffee break over at the café. He looked down the street and was surprised to see four empty parking spaces in front of the little diner. He slid the curtain all the way across the rod and stooped for a better look. Something was different about the café.

The awnings . . . that was it. The tattered red awnings were gone, and the framework of the white building had been painted a creamy green. Ingrid Kenney must have finally decided to do the remodeling she always talked about. But the sign had been painted over. Maybe she'd sold the place. He shook his head. It was hard to imagine anyone else presiding over the local diner. But there'd been a lot of changes in Clayburn since he'd left.

He checked the street in front of the building again. Either the place wasn't open yet, or business was pathetic. A subtle chill went through him. If Clayburn couldn't keep a café in business anymore, what chance did an art gallery have?

He tugged at the sheets in a halfhearted attempt to make the bed. Stumbling in to the shower, he started a mental to-do list. Cleaning up the place was first priority. He wasn't off to a very good start sleeping so late, but at least he'd slept—like a baby. The oppression of last night seemed to have dissipated, too. He felt ready to take on the day.

After a hot shower and shave, he pulled on jeans and a long-sleeved black T-shirt and went downstairs. His stomach growled, reminding him he would need to pick up some groceries before the food market closed this evening.

Thankfully, the alley was empty and he unloaded the car without having to talk to anyone. He walked through the studio workroom to the gallery at the front of the store. The morning sun bathed the gallery in eastern light. Good. He wouldn't have to turn any lights on. Maybe he could keep a low profile for another day or two, get the studio ready to open up again.

Get *himself* ready to open up again.

Two women strolled by on the sidewalk out front, and, instinctively, Jack ducked behind an easel, then felt silly when he realized the women weren't even looking his way. This was going to be harder than he'd thought.

Something caught his eye—a sheet of paper fluttering on the front door. He checked the street before turning the lock, then opened the door just far enough to grab the note stuck to the glass. He locked up again and moved into the shadows at the back of the room to read the note. It was a UPS InfoNotice.

He looked at the date on the slip of paper. They'd apparently tried to drop off his frames yesterday. But the note said they'd left them at an address in town. He looked at the street number scribbled on the paper.

He squinted, trying to read the number over the door of the kids' clothing store directly across the street. Counting down three doors, he realized the address on the note must belong to the café.

There were still no cars on the street in front of the café. Might as well get it over with. He couldn't stay locked up in this building the rest of his life. But the boxes would be heavy. He'd take the car—a good excuse not to risk running into someone on the sidewalk in front of the gallery.

Cruising by the front of the café a few minutes later, he could see ladders and other construction paraphernalia through the plate glass windows. There was a Closed sign in the front window, but it looked like someone was working inside. He hoped Ingrid had his frames.

He turned and parked in the alley behind the café. Peeling the UPS note off the dashboard, he climbed out of the car and went to knock on the heavy metal door. Music drifted from inside—sounded like the stuff that passed for jazz these days—but when no one answered after several minutes, he knocked again, louder.

The door was opened by a pretty girl with auburn curls escaping a blue bandanna. "Hi."

"Hi." He looked past her, curious about the remodeling that was obviously going on. "Wow, they're completely redoing the place, huh?"

She gave him a wary look. "Can I help you?"

"Oh, yeah . . . sorry. UPS supposedly left a package here for me?" He waved the printed slip in front of her.

"Ah . . . yes. Just yesterday. Several of them. Come on in."

As he came through the door, her eyebrows lifted and she took a step backward. "Oh. You're Jack. Jackson . . ."

"You got the boxes, then?"

She eyed him like he might be trying to pull one over on her. One corner of her mouth turned up in a crooked smile. "You don't remember me, do you?"

He considered her again, peering into her eyes, racking his brain. He'd read all the frightening statistics on how many brain cells the typical alcoholic binge killed, but he didn't think he'd lost so many that he couldn't identify an old friend. Still, he was drawing a complete blank. *"Should* I know you?"

She smiled, her lightly freckled cheeks flushing. "Not necessarily. You used to lifeguard at the pool when I was . . . younger."

He tried to translate those burnished curls and blue-green eyes to the image of a young girl. Suddenly things came into focus. "Oh! You must be Ingrid's daughter." He saw the resemblance now to the café's owner. "I'm sorry . . . I don't remember your name . . ."

"It's Vienne. Like Vienna without the *a.*"

"Vienne. That's nice. So is that Austrian? Or Swedish, like your mom's? How is she anyway?"

"It's French, actually. I'm named after some town Mom lived in when she was a foreign exchange student in France. And Mom's . . . about the same, I guess."

He looked up. "About the same? I'm sorry . . . I didn't realize—"

"You didn't know?" Her voice caught and she held up a hand. "Mom had a stroke in November. She's at the Manor . . . just temporarily. In rehab."

He opened his mouth to say, "Well, that makes two of us," but thought better of it, seeing Vienne's eyes mist over. "I'm sorry to hear that," he said instead. "I wish her well."

"Thanks." She smiled, and tucked a curl back under the bandanna.

An awkward moment passed while he scrambled for something to say.

He looked around the café. "You've changed the place. The paint job looks nice—outside, I mean." He motioned toward the street. "I noticed the awnings were gone. And the sign."

"Yeah. There's a new one on order. Should be in next week."

"So you're going to take over the café now?"

"Oh, no . . . I'm just getting things set up for Mom. When she comes back. We figured Clayburn needed a coffee shop."

"Oh, you're adding a coffee shop."

She shook her head. "It *is* a coffee shop now. No café."

"I see." He followed her to the front of the building. The new counter ran the length of the main room and jutted out a good foot farther than the bar had. Plus it was almost chest high with no ledge for stools to slide under—obviously not made for an eating counter. Behind it, under thick plastic covers, was a fancy espresso machine and some other equipment he couldn't identify. He ran a hand over the smooth granite counter. Faux granite, but it looked nice. "So who's doing the work?"

She straightened and narrowed her blue-green eyes at him. "I am."

"No kidding? You've done all this?" He encompassed the room with the sweep of an arm.

Her shoulders sagged a little. "Actually, Buddy Rollenmeyer over at the lumberyard built the counter and put in the fireplace, but I textured the walls and did all the painting and refinished the parquet floor over by the fireplace. It's the original flooring . . . used to be a dance floor."

The rich wood glowed under a thin veil of dust. "Wow. I'm impressed."

"Well, it's not done yet. I still have some trim to paint."

"Looks like it's pretty close to done, though."

She was eyeing him with a look he couldn't quite interpret. He eyed her right back. Not an unpleasant task by any means, but when she didn't say anything, he cut his eyes to the oversized coffeemaker behind her, grappling for something to fill the silence. "So you know how to run that thing?"

She followed his gaze to the stainless-steel machine. "I do. I worked as a barista for a while."

"A ba-what?"

A glint of humor lit her eyes. Blue eyes. Almost turquoise.

"A barista." She gave a little shrug. "I made coffee."

"Oh."

The tables and chairs from the former café were stacked against one wall, but even so, with the expanded counter and the fireplace, it didn't look like the place would seat half as many as it used to. That could be a problem come lunchtime. Of course if the new place didn't have a full menu, lunch wouldn't be a problem. But he had to wonder how Ingrid could make a go of it selling coffee. Unless she charged four dollars a cup like that Starbucks in Kansas City. "Fourbucks," the guys in rehab had called the place. He smiled at the memory. Then frowned that anything about rehab should make him smile. "So what do you do?"

She looked at him like it was the stupidest question in the world.

"I mean, when you're not remodeling cafés for your mom? Where do you live?"

"Oh. Here, now . . . I just moved back from California."

"Really? So you were a"—he fumbled for the word—"barista? Out in California?"

"That's just what I did to work my way through college." She rocked back on her heels, a defensive spark weighting her gaze. To balance the chip on her shoulder maybe?

"I see," he said. "Where'd you go to school out there?"

"UC Davis." She looked away, then stooped to scrape up a bit of painter's tape stuck to the floor.

"Davis? Guess I don't know where that is."

She straightened and pointed to the far corner. "Your packages are over there."

There was a definite set to her shoulders that hadn't been there before. And he knew a dismissal when he heard one.

"Okay . . . I'll get out of your hair, then." He started for the corner, making a mental note of topics not to bring up with Vienne Kenney. "I appreciate you holding these for me." He hefted the first box onto one shoulder. "You might have to hold the door for me . . . if you don't mind."

She padded behind him. "So, you're reopening the gallery?"

Did she want him to leave or not? "That's the plan."

"When?"

"Not sure yet."

"We'll have to have an open house or something. Maybe we can get all the merchants in on it."

He tucked another carton under his free arm, enjoying her attempt at reconciliation far more than he should have. "Yeah, maybe."

She held the door. He felt her gaze follow him while he loaded the boxes into his car. He slammed the trunk and gave a little wave.

"Well . . . thanks. I appreciate you holding this stuff for me. Good luck with the coffee shop."

He climbed in the car and started the engine, not waiting for her reply.

She was not
staying in Clayburn,
Kansas. That much
she knew.

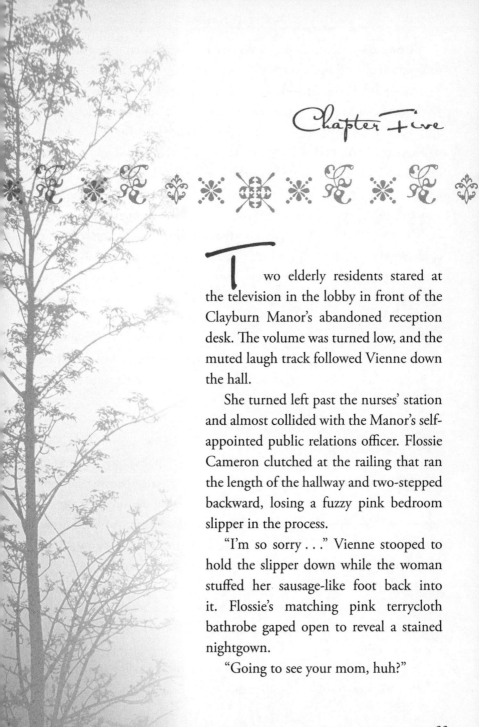

Chapter Five

T wo elderly residents stared at the television in the lobby in front of the Clayburn Manor's abandoned reception desk. The volume was turned low, and the muted laugh track followed Vienne down the hall.

She turned left past the nurses' station and almost collided with the Manor's self-appointed public relations officer. Flossie Cameron clutched at the railing that ran the length of the hallway and two-stepped backward, losing a fuzzy pink bedroom slipper in the process.

"I'm so sorry . . ." Vienne stooped to hold the slipper down while the woman stuffed her sausage-like foot back into it. Flossie's matching pink terrycloth bathrobe gaped open to reveal a stained nightgown.

"Going to see your mom, huh?"

Vienne only nodded, not wanting to encourage the woman. She took a step toward Mom's room.

Flossie did a little do-si-do around her and trailed her down the hall. "Your mom had a pretty good day, but I'm telling you, that speech therapist they've got working with her isn't worth her salt. The girl can't be a day over thirty. You ask me, they need to fire her and get somebody who knows a Sam hill of beans. That girl had poor Ed Bengstrom crying like a baby by the time she was done with him. And he still talks like he's got a mouth full of mush. Well, your mom, too, for that matter, but—"

"Thanks, Flossie." She made a beeline for Mom's room before Flossie could regale her with some other juicy bit of gossip. She eyed the emergency exit at the end of the hall, wishing they didn't have to keep the outside doors locked. Sometimes it would be nice to be able to sneak in without the whole world knowing she was here.

Mom was sitting in a chair, a dinner tray still on the narrow table in front of her. A plate of congealed macaroni and cheese did nothing to inspire Vienne's appetite, even though she hadn't eaten since ten this morning.

She went to the other side of the bed and patted her mother's hands, which were clasped over the bedspread. "Mom? How are you today?"

Her mother's eyes tracked her, her head immobile, as she started her nightly attempt to communicate—a pathetic cross between a grunt and a wail. She couldn't make her mouth say what her brain told it to. Sometimes she shook her head no, when she clearly meant yes. *Aphasia,* the doctors called it. They offered some hope that, with therapy, Mom would regain her ability to speak, but it would take time.

She patted the veined hand. "It's okay, Mom."

Vienne had given up trying to interpret the gibberish. It only frustrated them both and left Mom sobbing—or sometimes, oddly, laughing hysterically.

The heightened emotions were also a common result of a stroke, but it killed Vienne to see her mother this way. "That may not change—or it may lessen after a few months," Dr. Gheren had told her. It was another version of the answer they'd given her to every question she asked. "We don't know. Only time will tell. Every patient responds differently."

This was the twenty-first century. They should have some answers by now. What did all those research dollars go for anyway?

She straightened the coverlet across Mom's lap and went to gather her laundry from the closet. Vienne insisted on doing it herself, even though laundry service was provided for an additional "nominal fee." With Mom in the Manor, Vienne could almost hear the money being sucked from the savings account. She was afraid to do the math. Until her mother was hospitalized, Vienne had never seen her bank balance. She'd been shocked at how large it was. At first she'd assumed the money was profit from the café, but further investigation brought a troubling fact to light.

In the long weeks since Mom's stroke, she'd almost forgotten what her speaking voice sounded like, but now she heard it loud and clear in her mind. *"Don't you worry about the money for college, Vienne. Your daddy saw to it that you'd get a proper education."*

Vienne had always despised the recognition her mother gave Harlan Kenney when it was Mom who'd slaved six days a week at the café, long after she'd reached retirement age. But the truth was, the insurance settlement from her father's accident had provided for them. They weren't wealthy by anyone's measure, but the money had allowed Mom to purchase the café, and it had paid for Vienne's college and law school. But it had left her with a huge debt of guilt.

The money was in that bank account in Ingrid Kenney's name—and in Vienne's. And it was there because her father had the good sense one December night to crash the family car in a drunken stupor, killing himself in the process and thus—after two years of futile contesting by the insurance company—bequeathing a healthy sum to the wife and child he left behind. Sometimes Vienne still struggled not to think of his death as the greater gift to her and Mom. Why her mother continued to canonize the man was a mystery she'd never understand.

She stuffed her mom's wrinkled nightgowns into a laundry bag, stowing the hurtful thoughts away with them. "I finished the glaze on the wall behind the counter this afternoon. It turned out really nice, if I do say so myself." She forced herself to chatter about her day. "I'm anxious to see it in the morning with the sun shining in."

Mom seemed to perk up a little and Vienne imagined she saw a spark of interest in her eyes in place of the desperation she usually detected there. She'd been reading up on stroke recovery and found it encouraging that many stroke victims made complete recoveries from the aphasia and even the paralysis of a severe stroke. She chose to believe this would be true for her mother. Some days it stretched her optimism to the limit, though.

"Oh, hey. You'll never guess who came into the café this morning . . . Jackson Linder. Remember he had the gallery across the street? He's back in town and intending to open the gallery again. Do you remember where he moved away to?" She waited, almost forgetting for a moment that she could wait all night and Mom still wouldn't respond with more than a frustrated grunt or a nod of her gray head.

"It'll be nice to have another store open on Main Street. That much more reason for people to come to the coffee shop, right?"

"Ingrid?" A nurse appeared around the corner, wheeling a blood-pressure machine in front of her. Seeing Vienne, she took a step back. "Oh, I'm sorry. I didn't know you had company, Ingrid. Do you want me to come back later?"

Vienne answered for her, welcoming the intrusion as an excuse to make her exit. "No, it's okay." She leaned to kiss her mother's cheek. It felt dry and papery to her lips. Mom had aged dramatically in the past few weeks. "Good night, Mom. I'll see you tomorrow. Love you."

Shaking off the melancholy that threatened, she slung the laundry bag over her shoulder, hurried past Flossie and the gauntlet of wheelchairs lining the dayroom, and pushed through the front doors into the purple evening shadows. She had to get her mother out of this place.

The air was frigid, and the wind whipped a few of autumn's leftover leaves in frenzied circles around the small parking lot.

She aimed the car toward home. But the thought of the empty house with Mom's abandoned sewing table and silent kitchen caused Vienne to turn the car north and head downtown. She could kill an hour or two at the coffee shop, finish painting some trim, and maybe start the overwhelming job of cleaning up the construction mess. All this grunt work brought back too many memories of her childhood when every spare minute had been spent helping out in the café. Wasn't this part of what she'd left Clayburn to escape?

A knot formed in the pit of her stomach. What if she'd done all this remodeling, turned the café into a coffee shop, for nothing? Was she fooling herself to think that Mom would be able to come back anytime soon? She'd wanted to make things easier. Not that running a coffee shop was a piece of cake, but at least Mom wouldn't have all the cooking to do, the late-night cleanup and 4 a.m. start time. Vienne thought she might even manage to talk her into hiring someone to wash pots and pans. Now that she was done with law school maybe Mom wouldn't feel so obligated to pinch every penny.

Vienne blew out a breath. What a waste of her education this little venture had been. She'd earned a law degree through sweat and tears—lots of tears—and look what she'd done with it so far. It made her sick to her stomach.

"I'm not cut out to be a lawyer." The sound of her own voice filled the car and startled her. She pondered her statement. She'd never admitted it to anyone, let alone herself. But she knew she'd spoken the truth. She'd hated her job at Brinkerman. Every weekday morning she'd awakened with a knot in her stomach that twisted tighter every mile of the commute. She'd been relieved to call Richard Spencer and tell him she wasn't coming back.

And she knew it wouldn't be any different anywhere she went. Why had she ever thought she would enjoy a career in law? She didn't like research. She wasn't an analytical thinker. It stifled every creative bone in her body to be tied to a set of rules.

The air blowing from the heater vents in the car was still chilly, and she reached to adjust the thermostat. Maybe she should start thinking of herself as an entrepreneur. Maybe the coffee shop would start a chain. She laughed out loud at the thought. Yeah, right. She didn't even have a name for the place yet. She'd thought of naming it after her mother. *Ingrid's.*

But Mom would hate that. Vienne could hear her mother now: "What were you thinking, Vienne? Why would I want my name up on that fool sign for the whole world to see?"

The thought brought a smile, but worry lines quickly erased it as she realized how long it had been since she'd seen that spunky side of her mother. She wanted Mom to have a say in things, but that was difficult under the circumstances. Still, she'd explained her plans and made sure Mom understood before spending the money on remodeling. It was something her mother had talked about doing for years, and now the time seemed right. Mom's savings had taken a hit, but you had to spend money to make money, right?

Vienne thought Mom would be pleased with the way the coffee shop had turned out. She hoped so. More than anything, it felt good to be able to give back to her mother a little of the time and energy Mom had sacrificed for her.

One thing she knew: in spite of the fact that she'd enjoyed the remodeling more than she wanted to admit, the minute Mom was able to take over, Vienne Kenney was out of here. Where, she didn't know. What she'd do to support herself she had no clue. But she was not staying in Clayburn, Kansas. That much she knew.

She turned off Buffalo Boulevard and started for home. Main Street was vacant except for a pickup in front of the beauty salon and a couple of cars parked on the side street by Wren's Inn. Vienne had too much California in her blood to feel safe parking in the alley after dark, so she eased her Mazda into a spot in front of the coffee shop.

She let herself in the front door and locked it behind her. Once inside, she breathed easier. As she reached to pull down the blinds, she noticed there was a light on in the window above Jack Linder's gallery.

She started to turn away, but a shadow in the window drew her. She watched for a minute as Jack stood looking out over the street. Her heart lurched when he turned toward her. She tried to duck out of sight.

Too late. He lifted his hand in acknowledgment. Embarrassed, she waved back, then yanked the blinds over the window. Her cheeks warmed as she hurried to the back of the building.

He probably thought she was still some stupid schoolgirl playing spy games. She hefted a can of paint from the shelf and pried up the lid. The smoky forest green trim would be the perfect counterpoint for the counters and shelving she'd already painted a rich autumn gold. She dragged the ladder over and situated the paint can on the counter above her, then dipped a narrow brush into the creamy paint. Steadying her hand against the ledge, she stroked on a swath of color.

She finished the length of the top shelf and climbed down from the ladder. Stepping back a few feet, she squinted, judging the effect. Perfect.

Invigorated, she moved the ladder a few feet and started in on the second shelf. She was halfway across the length of it when a sharp knock on the door caused her hand to jerk. Paint splattered on her T-shirt and left a jagged trail in her otherwise faultless line. She growled under her breath. It was probably one of Clayburn's finest. That first night she'd started working on the floor, she'd told the policeman on duty that she would be spending many late nights here and that they shouldn't worry. Apparently they didn't have anything better to do than harass her.

She climbed down and went to the door, pushing the blinds aside before she turned the key in the lock. It took her a few seconds to realize that it was Jackson Linder standing outside the door. And he was smiling.

She let him in.

"Hi. I saw you were here . . ." He nodded toward the pendant lights that glowed overhead. "I hope I'm not catching you at a bad time, but I wondered if you'd consider loaning me your muscles for a minute?"

"My muscles?"

"I need to move a couple cabinets. They're not that heavy, but I can't do it myself. Scout's honor . . ." He gave a three-fingered salute. "It'll only take six and a half minutes."

That was about the length of their entire exchange the last time he'd dropped by. "Exactly six and a half minutes, huh?"

He grinned. "Give or take. And I'll owe you. You have anything you need done around here?"

"A little quid pro quo, huh?"

He cocked his head at her. "Huh?"

"Never mind." Striking a comical pose, she flexed her biceps—or attempted to. "Sure. I'll help. Just let me put a lid on this paint first."

When she was finished, she followed him to the front and reached for the keys hanging from the door where she'd left them.

"Oh, you won't need to lock up. You'll be back here in a flash. I promise."

She propped a hand on her hip. "You're awfully trusting. For all I know, you have accomplices waiting in the alley and you're just luring me away so they can walk in here and clean me out." Grinning, she opened the door and placed one foot on the sidewalk, but her hand remained on the keys.

He sidestepped around her, laughing. "You've got quite the imagination."

"No. I've just lived in California long enough to be cynical."

"Ah . . . well, suit yourself." He eyed the door handle, waiting. "If you feel the need to barricade yourself in this safe little Kansas town . . ."

"Oh, why not." She let go of the keys. "I'll live dangerously."

He threw her a smug grin and took off at a slow jog across the street, not bothering to go to the crosswalk. She had to hustle to keep up with his long-legged stride.

At the gallery he held the door open for her and gestured toward the rear of the room. "I've got two cabinets back in the studio that I want to move out here."

Vienne surveyed the room much the way Jack had looked over her shop yesterday. Pocked oak floors slanted ever so slightly toward the back of the room and the rafters overhead were exposed. The room had great character, in spite of the fact that it was mostly empty, save for a large front counter and some frames hanging from hooks on the walls. "This is nice."

"Thanks. I've got my work cut out for me getting it back up and running. But then, you know all about that."

His smile was pleasant, and for a minute Vienne let it warm her. "It's been a long haul, that's for sure. Of course, I'm just here until my mom can take over."

He considered her for a moment. "So you said. I hope it won't be long."

An image of her mother, frail and vacant in the hospital bed, flashed through Vienne's head.

"Ready?" Jack's voice shattered the troubling image. "The studio's this way." He turned and led her through a narrow door at the back to a larger room that was equally empty, except for a work-in-progress on canvas perched on a paint-daubed easel. A winter landscape was taking shape—a snowy field with fence posts jutting through at intervals and a faded red barn in the distance.

"So this is where you paint?" She studied the unfinished canvas. She didn't know enough about art to expound, but this piece made her feel happy. "This is nice."

He shrugged and dipped his head. "Thanks. I do my custom framing back here, too—or I used to. I need to get that up and running again. It pays some bills. And I used to teach some art classes. I'm hoping to start those up again soon."

"Really? Are there many artists in Clayburn?"

"I get some in from Salina, but you'd be surprised at the talent hiding out in this little town."

She laughed.

"No, seriously. I've got some swift competition here."

She tilted her head, unable to decide if he was teasing again. She chose not to probe.

He glanced at a stainless-steel clock on the far wall. "Your six and a half minutes is ticking away." He walked to the corner of the dimly lit studio and positioned his hands under the shelf of a tall cabinet. "It's this one right here."

She scrambled over and mirrored his stance on the other side. "I'm ready."

"We may have to lay it on its side to get it through the door."

She followed his lead, determined to bear her share of the heavy load. They manhandled the furniture through the door and set it in place in the front of the gallery.

Jack opened the door of the piece, revealing a series of shelves. "I thought I'd take the door off and use this to display some smaller art—sculptures and batik and such."

"Oh, you do other things besides painting?"

"Well, I dabble. I've mostly done watercolors, but I'm trying my hand at oils right now. And I'm hoping to get some other artists' work in the gallery on consignment." He brushed off his hands and led the way back to the studio. "Okay. Just one more. You didn't strain anything, did you?" he asked, glancing over his shoulder.

Again the glint in his gold-flecked eyes touched something inside her, reminding her why she'd had such a crush on him when they were teenagers. "I'm fine. Lead on, Rembrandt."

He flashed her a smile at that, permanently gluing the whole high school crush thing into her mental scrapbook.

They lugged a similar cabinet to the front, positioning it beside the first.

Vienne backed toward the front door, knowing she should at least make motions to leave, but not wanting to at all. "Well, I guess I'd better get back to work."

"Here, I'll walk you. Wouldn't want you to get mugged on the mean streets of Clayburn. Too bad you don't have that coffeemaker fired up."

"It's an espresso machine. And who says I don't?" She suddenly wanted nothing more than to be sipping coffee with this man.

"Are you serious?"

"Do you have any milk?"

He frowned. "I have half a carton of half-and-half."

"Half a carton of half-and-half?" She grinned. "Does that equal a fourth of a carton? How *does* the math work on that?"

He snorted. "Hey, I'm an artist, not a mathematician. Now, are you going to show me how that coffeemaker works or not?"

Something in the way she delivered that line made Jack think there was still a bit of Kansas remaining in this California girl. Maybe more than she wanted to admit.

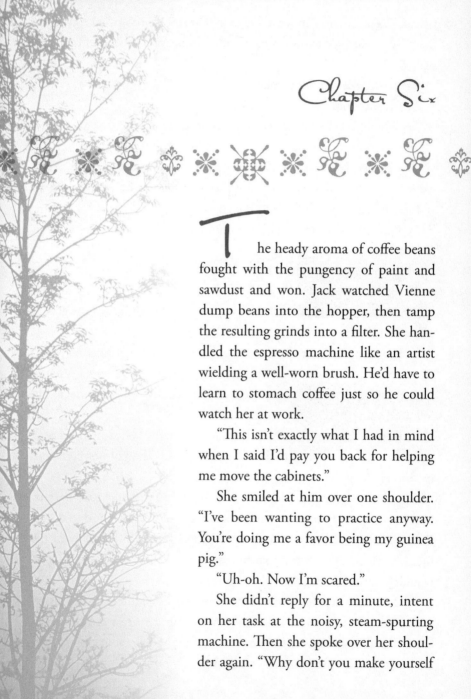

Chapter Six

The heady aroma of coffee beans fought with the pungency of paint and sawdust and won. Jack watched Vienne dump beans into the hopper, then tamp the resulting grinds into a filter. She handled the espresso machine like an artist wielding a well-worn brush. He'd have to learn to stomach coffee just so he could watch her at work.

"This isn't exactly what I had in mind when I said I'd pay you back for helping me move the cabinets."

She smiled at him over one shoulder. "I've been wanting to practice anyway. You're doing me a favor being my guinea pig."

"Uh-oh. Now I'm scared."

She didn't reply for a minute, intent on her task at the noisy, steam-spurting machine. Then she spoke over her shoulder again. "Why don't you make yourself useful? There are some mugs in boxes in that storage room." She inclined her head toward a narrow door. "Grab a couple and wash them for me, will you?"

He hesitated, watching her.

She turned and caught his eye. "What?"

"Nothing. You'll just make a good boss, that's all."

Her eyebrows went up, but she didn't miss a beat. "Thanks."

She turned back to her task and he went to find the mugs. They worked side by side—she at the espresso machine, he elbow-deep in suds at the double sinks behind the counter.

"I knew there was a catch," he mumbled. "You've got me washing dishes. How did this happen?"

"Hey, buster, you want coffee or not?"

Well, not exactly. But he was in no hurry to leave either. He clamped his mouth shut and dried the mugs with the thin dishtowel she offered.

A few minutes later she poured a frothy, dark brew into his mug. "If you want sweetener, I think there's some in the storeroom." Vienne carried her mug to the bar and leaned both elbows on the surface. He followed suit.

"I'll try it this way." He blew a trough through the foam and took a sip. *Whoa. Ick.* This stuff packed a punch. It was the kind of coffee he used to choke down for its sobering powers.

For the first time, he wondered if the pretty girl standing next to him knew his story, knew the mess he'd made of his life. She'd told him she remembered him from high school days. But had she followed his life since then? Had Ingrid told her anything? Probably not, or Vienne wouldn't have welcomed him here tonight.

The thought depressed him. Sometimes he just wanted to wear a sign with big letters that said, "I'm totally messed up. Don't say I didn't warn you." The thought wasn't fully formed before he felt the strong tug on his heart. *You are fearfully and wonderfully made.*

He ran his finger along the rim of the mug, acknowledging the quiet whisper inside him. When he'd started the long, slow slide into addiction, he hadn't for one minute thought about ever coming out on the other side. He hadn't wanted to live with the knowledge of what he'd done, what he'd caused. Maybe things would have been different if he could have seen the future. Grasped the consequences.

He looked up to find Vienne watching him, head tilted as if waiting for an answer. Had he missed a question? *Shake it off, Linder. You're ruining a perfectly good conversation with a very nice girl.*

"Well?"

"I'm sorry? What did you say?"

"The coffee. What do you think?"

"It's . . ." He cast about for a reply and settled on honesty. "It's good and strong."

Her face fell. "You don't like it."

He cleared his throat and curbed a grin. "I don't much like coffee, period."

"Huh?" She threw up her hands. "Why didn't you say something?"

He shrugged. "I thought maybe yours would be different. Isn't that what guinea pigs are for?" He scooted his mug as far away from him as his arm would reach.

Vienne threw her head back and laughed.

"Sorry." He tried to appear appropriately chagrined.

She took his mug and walked around to dump the contents in the sink. "How about some hot chocolate? I don't have the ingredients I need to make it right. You'll have to settle for Swiss Miss out of the box."

"That'd be great." He grinned. "Anything to wash this awful taste from my mouth."

She tried to look angry, but her laughter seeped through and gave her away. She filled his mug with water and popped it in the microwave. Two minutes later she set the steaming cup in front of him.

He took a whiff. "Ah . . . this smells considerably better than the sludge you just rinsed down the sink."

She propped her hands on her hips. "Remind me not to hire you to head up my advertising campaign."

"Hey, I'd give your hot cocoa four stars."

Her glare chastised him, but the twinkle remained in those turquoise eyes. "I'm not going to serve my customers a packaged mix, you goose."

Something in the way she delivered that line made Jack think there was still a bit of Kansas remaining in this California girl. Maybe more than she wanted to admit.

She fixed herself a cup of coffee and pulled a stool up to the end of the bar. Pushing a plastic cover aside, she yanked a package of animal crackers from their clip-on display. She opened the package, then slid it toward him. "Help yourself."

They talked and laughed together long after their cups were empty and three crumpled cookie wrappers lay between them. The lighthearted banter felt like a balm, but it also served as a reminder that Vienne Kenney might remember him from his high school days, but she didn't really know him. Not the man he'd become.

He was pretty sure that musical laughter would fade, and fast, once she learned the kind of man he was. And who could blame her. If he lived to be one hundred and never fell again, he'd never make up for the lives he'd hurt on his way down.

But he was going to try. "On second thought, I'd better get out of your hair and let you get back to work. I'd offer to help, but believe it or not, I'm terrible at painting—outside of the artistic kind."

"A likely story," she deadpanned.

"It's true. Ask anyone." He reached for his cup and pushed away from the bar. He rinsed his mug out in the stainless-steel sink and turned it upside down. "And I do appreciate the coffee . . . or the gesture anyway. And I promise to keep my opinions to myself."

"Well, that's a relief. You'll have to come back for some real cocoa after we open."

"I'll do that. Holler if you need anything."

"Anything except painting, you mean?"

He winked and headed for the door. "You might want to lock up behind me."

"Are you kidding? In this safe little Kansas town?"

He heard the door close and lock behind him, and crossed the street, still smiling at her quip. He liked that woman more every minute he spent with her.

He started to turn toward the gallery, but the lights glowing in the downstairs windows of Wren's Nest at the other end of the block beckoned him. He really should go see Wren. Might as well do it while he was in a relatively good mood.

It wouldn't sit well if Wren and Bart heard from someone else that he was back in town. He'd managed to go one whole day without showing his face on Main Street, but Vienne might mention it to someone tomorrow and it wouldn't take three minutes to get back to Wren. He had to come out of hiding sometime. His gas tank was on empty and his cupboards were bare.

He opened the outside door to the dining room of the tiny inn and walked in. The bright yellow and red décor made him do a double take. He'd forgotten about the renovation. He'd gone into rehab not long after Bart and Wren finished remodeling—or rather after Trevor had. His best friend had done most of the work—a fact that had tugged at Jack's guilt strings at the time. But the place looked great, and Jack didn't begrudge Trevor the close relationship he shared with Wren and her husband. Still, that didn't stop the prick of envy that always seemed to come when he realized that Trevor was closer to Wren than he was.

"I'll be with you in a minute." Wren's cheery voice floated from behind the reception desk in the lobby. Her striped tabby cat appeared around the corner and pattered over to rub against Jack's pant leg. He bent to stroke the cat's fur. "Hey, Jasper. How's it going, buddy?"

The tabby's motor revved in reply.

"I'm coming," Wren called again.

"It's me, Wren." Five long strides took him through the dining room. He ducked as he passed under the archway into the lobby, then stood there, waiting for her to acknowledge him.

Wren finished writing something, tucked her pencil behind one ear, then looked up, her pleasant innkeeper's smile firmly in place.

Watching recognition dawn in her eyes, a slow warmth spread through Jack. Though he'd known it since his senior year of high school, it still shocked him a little to realize that this was the woman who had given birth to him.

Wren's hands flew to her face and she gave a little gasp. "Jackson! It's you!" Beaming through tears, she waddled around the desk and threw her arms around him.

He let himself melt into her homey embrace. "Hi, Wren."

She took two steps back and looked him up and down. "You cut your hair." She reached up to brush a strand of hair away from his temple.

He presented his back to her so she could see that his ponytail was indeed gone.

"You look twenty years younger!"

He laughed. "I look like a twelve-year-old boy, huh?"

She placed a hand over her bosom and shook her head. "I forget how young you really are. Well, you look good." She punched out each word so Jack had no doubt she meant it. But her unspoken questions hung between them. *Did you get your life straightened out? Are you right with God?*

"I feel good. It's good to be home." The former was true. The latter he wasn't so sure about yet.

She studied him and seemed to read his mind. "Are you back for good?"

"I don't know, Wren. I'm done with rehab. I'm clean and sober," he added quickly.

"Oh, Jack. I'm so glad."

"Yeah, well, don't stop praying." He smiled so she wouldn't read too much into that comment.

"So, everything went okay?"

"It was hell." He swallowed over the lump that suddenly blocked his throat.

Wren wrapped her arms around him again. "Well, look around you, buddy. You're back from hell now. And welcome home."

That made him laugh. He didn't think he'd ever heard Wren Johannsen use that word. "Thanks, Wren . . . I love you." He'd never said those words to her either. And it was high time.

It took Wren a few minutes to compose herself, but when she let go of him, her face was bright and her eyes sparkling. "So, what's next?"

"I'll open the gallery back up, try to get some classes going . . ." He shrugged. "I have to make a living."

She patted his arm. "I know, I know. You don't have to tell me about that. Well, you let us know if there's anything we can do to help, okay? How's your mom?"

Leave it to Wren to make sure she gave his adoptive mother full credit.

"She's good. I think Florida agrees with her. I spent a couple weeks with her in St. Petersburg right after I got out . . ." He looked at the floor. It was still too hard to finish that sentence.

"I'm glad." She brushed her hands over her apron. "Come have a cup of tea, can you?"

"Sure." He followed her back into the dining room with Jasper close on their heels. He watched as Wren bustled about the little kitchenette pouring tea, pulling a pan of her famous Peaches and Cream Cheesecake from the refrigerator and sliding a healthy slice onto a plate.

Such conflicting emotions he had over his relationship with his two mothers: Twila Linder, the mother who'd raised him—and loved him—from the day of his birth; Wren, who with even greater love, had given him up on that very same day . . . and, he suspected, regretted it every day since.

It simplified things now that Mom wasn't living here in Clayburn. He'd burned too much guilt worrying about hurting either of their feelings. He didn't need that.

There were far more profound things to feel guilty for.

Oh, such regrets she had. If only she could go back . . .

Chapter Seven

*W*ren stood, hands on hips, and watched the door close behind Jackson. *Her son.* The thought never ceased to leave her in awe—and in tears. She knew she'd been forgiven, and she was grateful God had seen fit to give her a relationship with Jackson—belated though it was. And that was her own doing. She certainly didn't fault the good Lord for the delay. But oh, such regrets she had. If only she could go back and—

She brushed her hands together and whirled on one heel, surveying the room for something to occupy her. She'd been dwelling too much on the past lately. It did no good to chew on regrets. Hadn't Bart told her that a hundred times? Dear Bart. What a gift that man was. She bowed her head and breathed a prayer. "Thank you, Lord."

Her eyes fluttered open, and her gaze

landed on the cups and saucers and cheesecake plates Jackson had put in the sink after their brief visit. He was a well-mannered young man. Twila and John had done a good job with him. She couldn't have asked for nicer parents than the Linders to raise Jackson. Oh, Twila had her moments. But then, Wren couldn't exactly be a fair judge about anything involving Jackson's adoptive mother. There were too many comparisons, with each of them somehow thinking the other came out on top.

She squeezed dish soap into the sink and ran the water as hot as it would go. Warm steam, scented with lemon, wafted up and she closed her eyes, waiting for the sink to fill.

Something tickled her neck. She yanked her hand from the soapy water and whirled to swat at the spider she imagined dangling from a thread overhead. Instead she managed to whap Bart, who stood with a clump of suds on his shirtfront, looking bewildered. "That's my reward for nuzzling your neck?"

"You scared the life out of me!" Laughter burbled in Wren's throat, and she took hold of her husband's shoulders, pressing her face against the damp cloth of his shirt. It smelled of Clorox and the peppermint gum he kept in his breast pocket. His long beard tickled her cheek in a pleasant way.

"I just wondered if you were ever coming up to bed."

"In a minute." She pressed closer, letting his whiskers brush her forehead. "Mmmm. How'd you know I needed a hug?"

Bart pulled away, a look of concern knitting his brow. "Something wrong?"

She sighed. "Something's right."

"What's not right?"

"No, no . . ." Why couldn't that man wear his hearing aids? "I said something *is* right. Jackson's back."

"Jackson? When?"

"He stopped by a few minutes ago. I guess he's been back in town for a few days."

"How is he?" Skepticism filtered through Bart's question.

"Good. He seemed . . . different. But in a good way, I think."

Bart cocked his head. "He hadn't been drinking?"

"No. He's done with rehab. He told me he's clean and sober. I didn't ask any more."

"Well, that's something. What's he going to do?"

She sighed again. Couldn't help it. They'd done a lot of sighing together over that boy, with Bart always trying to protect her from the pain of Jack's struggles. It broke Wren's heart that after navigating the difficult teen and young adult years so well, tragedy had caused him to seek consolation in a bottle. "He's planning to open the gallery back up. Start some art classes."

Bart shook his head. "I don't know why he's so all-fired determined to keep that place running."

"Probably the same reason you're so all-fired determined to keep this place running." Wren bit her tongue too late.

Bart looked sheepish. "Well, touché on that one."

She smiled and patted his cheek. In the dozen years she'd been married to Bart Johannsen, she never could stay peeved at him for too long. "I wish we could help him out."

"Knowing you, you'll find a way. 'Course, he might think about doing the same for you."

"Bart . . . He—" She shook her head. Anything she might say would only start an argument. Her husband didn't have a lot of sympathy for the mess Jackson had made of his life. She couldn't make him understand that she felt more than a little responsible for Jackson's problems. Oh, she knew Jack's issues were much more complicated than him coming to terms with her, with being adopted. But that had to play into it.

When he had pulled out in front of that car that afternoon . . . She shuddered, not wanting to think about that terrible day. It hadn't been anybody's fault really. The sun had been blinding at that time of the afternoon. Jackson hadn't seen them. And everybody knew Amy Ashlock had a lead foot. Her own mother admitted she'd had two speeding tickets in the year before the accident. No doubt she was driving way too fast, especially for the rolling hills on Old Highway 40. It was a wonder there hadn't been more accidents along that stretch of highway.

But none of that brought Amy and little Trev back . . .

"Hey, you." Bart's rough, tender hand cradled her cheek. "I see where your mind is taking you. Stop it right now."

She swallowed back tears and put her hand over his. "I know."

"Come on up to bed now. I happen to have just the cure for that frown on your face."

She gave him a knowing smile. "I'll be up as soon as I lock up and turn out the lights."

He patted her backside. "I'll take care of all that. You get yourself upstairs and get that bed warmed up for me."

Wren blushed, but the warmth in her cheeks originated in her heart.

They were just a bunch
of gossipy old women.
But if these good
Christian ladies weren't
willing to look him in
the eye on the street,
how might the rest of the
town receive him?

Chapter Eight

Squaring his shoulders, Jack opened the gallery door, its two-tone chime sounding as he stepped onto the sidewalk. Nearly every parking place on Clayburn's Main Street was occupied. At the post office two blocks over, the flag flapped in the breeze, and a block farther west on Elm the low rumble of the feed mill resounded. He inhaled the faint scent of molasses carried on an easterly wind. Up the street a small group of schoolchildren traipsed after their teacher toward the public library, their voices flushed with excitement.

He'd been back in town for a week now, but he'd purposefully avoided going out during the hours he was likely to run into anyone he knew. But these last gray days of January were starting to get to him, and in spite of all the work he'd accomplished in the gallery, cabin fever had finally set in to the point that venturing out seemed preferable to one more day inside his close quarters. Still, it wasn't easy to think about facing people, explaining his absence, wondering how they'd receive him.

Across the street and down three doors, he noticed gold and red café-style curtains had replaced the newsprint covering the front windows of the soon-to-open coffee shop. Vienne had said she wanted to open on Valentine's Day. It looked like she was ahead of schedule.

An old station wagon pulled into the only empty spot in front of the gallery, and Kaye DeVore climbed out. She seemed not to notice him as she opened the vehicle's back hatch door and helped four children in various stairstep sizes out. While the kids waited on the sidewalk near the curb, Kaye extracted a bundled baby from the car seat.

Jack hurried to the back of the car and helped her with the hatch.

"Oh. Thank you." She kept her head down, fussing to keep the blankets in place over the baby.

"Can I carry that for you?"

Her head came up, and she stared a minute before recognition lit her eyes. "Jack! I didn't realize it was you!" Kaye chattered away like a nervous monkey. "You . . . you cut your hair. I like it."

He shrugged. "Thanks."

"I heard you were back in town. How *are* you?" Her voice held that edge of sympathy he'd come to despise.

He ignored it and forced a smile. "I'm doing well, thanks. You have a new addition to your family."

"Well, not that new. She's almost fourteen months old." Her face brightened and she patted the squirming bundle of blankets in her arms. "This is Harley. I'd show her off, but it's too cold."

The baby had been born months before he'd left for rehab in Kansas City. What else had he missed while he drank himself into oblivion? He shook off the shame. "Where are you headed? Can I carry something for you?"

"Thanks anyway. We're just going across the street." She hiked the baby up on her hip and nodded in the direction of Tot's Togs. "It's good to see you, Jack. You look good."

He shrugged again. Why did everyone feel the need to comment on how good he looked? Had he looked so awful before?

He watched until Kaye and the kids were safely across the street, then started down the sidewalk toward the print shop. He owed it to Trevor to let him know he was back in town. He needed to talk to him about making up some signs to advertise his art classes anyway. It would be a good excuse.

Dana Fremont was at the front desk in the print shop. "May I help you?"

"Hi, Dana. Is Trevor in?"

Dana's eyebrows shot up. "Jack!" Her efforts to hide her surprise were unsuccessful. Aimlessly rearranging the papers on her desk, she scooted her chair back. "Um, just a minute. I'll get Trevor." She disappeared through the door to the pressroom, seeming glad for an escape.

Jack ran his tongue along the inside of his cheek. People's reaction to his reappearance in Clayburn was getting almost comical. But he didn't feel much like laughing. He knew the rumors had to have been flying. He'd left town quietly, on the heels of his mother's move to Florida. But he doubted there were many who didn't know where he'd been these last nine months. Were they expecting him to be the same drunk he'd been when he left town?

The door behind Dana opened, and Trevor emerged from the back. "Well, I'll be . . . Wren said you were back." Jack shook the hand Trevor extended but blanched when his friend pulled him into a one-armed embrace.

Trevor seemed to sense his discomfort and took two steps backward. "I tried to call, but I guess you've changed your number at the gallery?"

He shook his head. "I haven't gotten around to getting the phone hooked up again yet." He nodded toward the pressroom. "You don't have a pot of coffee on back there, do you?"

Trevor eyed him, humor sparking in his eyes. "Since when did you start drinking cof—" He finished the word on a sharp intake of breath and dropped his gaze before meeting Jack's eyes again. "Hey . . . I didn't mean that the way it—"

Jack waved him off. "Don't worry about it." He glanced pointedly in Dana's direction. The receptionist tapped away at her keyboard, but Jack suspected she had one ear tuned to their exchange. "If the coffee shop was open I'd offer to buy you a cup, but . . ." He shrugged.

"It'll be open next week. Ingrid's daughter was in yesterday to put an ad in the paper." Trevor led the way to the break room. "Do you remember her? Vienne Kenney. She was a few years behind us in school."

Jack shook his head. "I don't really remember her, but I met her the other day."

"Seems like a nice gal. Been out in California I guess. Law school."

"Really?" This was an interesting wrinkle. "No wonder she plans to go back."

Trevor's head came up. "She's not staying?"

"She's just getting the shop set up for Ingrid. At least that's what she told me."

Trevor clicked his tongue. "From what I hear, Ingrid's not doing so hot." He dumped out the coffeepot, rinsed it, and filled it with fresh, cold water. He filled a scoop with coffee grinds but paused before depositing them in the filter. "You seriously want coffee?"

Jack shrugged. "I'm trying to learn to like the stuff."

Trevor emptied the scoop and filled another one. "Have a seat."

Jack straddled the old kitchen chair—the same chair with the ripped vinyl seat that had been there since he and Trevor were kids, folding newspapers in Trevor's dad's print shop after school on Wednesdays. He remembered the day they'd delivered the mammoth Heidelberg press Trevor's dad was so proud of. It still sat in the center of the pressroom and by the way it gleamed, it was obvious that same pride had extended to Trevor.

It felt odd to be here again as adults. Awkward, with everything that had come between them. The coffeepot sputtered and started to brew. The aroma mixed with the chemical smells of ink and toner.

Trevor took a chair across from Jack. "So how was . . . Kansas City? Or would you rather not talk about it?"

"It was . . ." Jack tried to think of a word that would encompass it all. There wasn't one. "Let's just say I'm glad I went, but it's not something I'd like to repeat."

Trevor nodded, his Adam's apple working in his throat.

Desperate to lighten the mood and change the subject, Jack tipped his chair and leaned in to punch Trevor's arm. "So I hear you're a newlywed. How's married life treating you?" It had seemed an innocuous question as it formed in his mind, but now that it hung in the air between them, all Jack could think of was that, if it weren't for him, Trevor would soon be celebrating his seventh wedding anniversary with the love of his life.

But Trevor didn't seem to pick up on the implications. In fact, he beamed. "Married life is good. It's very good. Meg will be happy to hear you're back in town."

"Thanks. Tell her hello. I didn't get to know her that well before . . . but she seemed like a great girl."

Trevor nodded. "She is. She's something else." His eyes glazed and he swallowed hard.

Even after more than three years, Amy's presence still seemed to permeate the room. Jack could still see her smile, framed by that pretty olive face. He could still hear her musical laughter. Jack somehow knew Trevor felt it, too.

The coffee wasn't finished brewing, but Trevor jumped up and pulled a pocked Styrofoam cup from a stack on the break table. He pulled the carafe off the warmer, slid another cup underneath to catch the drips, and poured Jack a cup. "You take cream or sugar?"

Jack jumped up and took the steaming cup from Trevor. "I'll take anything you can put in there to kill the coffee taste."

Trevor's laugh was genuine. Jack chuckled along with him, and Amy's memory retreated.

"Listen . . ." Jack settled back in his chair with coffee-laced creamer. "I'm opening the gallery back up, and I want to advertise some art classes. Can I still get an ad in this week's paper, and maybe get some fliers printed up? I don't have my computer set up or anything, but I wrote it out." He dug in the back pocket of his jeans and pulled out the crumpled slip of paper he'd jotted on this morning.

Trevor took it from him. His eyes skimmed the page before he handed it back. "Take this up to Dana and tell her what size of ad you want to run. The deadline is noon today, so you just squeaked in. I'll make sure it gets in this week. When do you need the fliers?"

"Yesterday, actually."

Trevor smirked. "Yeah, you and everybody else."

"No . . . if I have enough interest, I'd like to start the first Monday night in February. But that's probably dreaming. At least by mid-March, though."

"Hey, you know, Amy might be interest—" Trevor put a hand over his mouth. "Oh, man! Where did that come from? I meant Meg . . . *Meg* might be interested in taking that class." He shook his head slowly. "I'm just glad it was you sitting there and not Meg. I'm always afraid I'm going to slip and call *her* by Amy's name."

Jack bit his lip, ill at ease for his buddy. But there was something in Trevor's words that warmed him. *I'm just glad it was you sitting there.* Surely Trevor had struggled with wishing it had been Jack who had died that day. The offhand comment gave him hope that Trevor truly had forgiven him.

When Jack left the print shop half an hour later, he felt almost normal again. He'd broken the ice with Trevor and with Wren. Those were the two he cared most about. He could do this.

He crossed the street and headed back to the gallery. Wren's silhouette was framed in a window of the inn, and he waved as he went by. He couldn't tell if she saw him or not, but he didn't take the time to stop in. He suddenly felt energized to get the gallery in shape for the opening. He would quietly open the doors one week from today, but maybe he could have some sort of grand opening later, draw some of the coffee shop customers that were sure to be downtown when Vienne's coffee shop opened in a few weeks.

The sun eased over the buildings on the east side of Main, but the air was brisk and he pulled the collar of his jacket up around his chin. A cluster of women came out of the beauty salon, headed his way, chattering among themselves. As they got closer, he recognized Clara Berger and a couple of his mother's other friends.

He pasted on a smile and skirted the edge of the sidewalk, making way for the foursome. They were sure to ask about his mom in Florida, and he formulated a reply that would keep the spotlight on Mom and off of him.

He nodded a greeting. But when recognition shone in Clara's eyes, she turned to the group and whispered—or hissed was more like it—something Jack couldn't make out.

Their noisy chatter stopped, and Clara became suddenly preoccupied with the contents of her purse. Hurrying past them, he didn't miss the frenzied whispers that floated back to him. It didn't take a genius to guess what they were twittering about.

He squelched the temptation to turn on his heel and confront their gossip. That would only fuel the fire and give them a new rumor to circulate. He ducked his head lower and stepped up his pace.

They were just a bunch of gossipy old women. But if these good Christian ladies weren't willing to look him in the eye on the street, how might the rest of the town receive him?

His shoulders slumped under the weight of that thought. He'd be lucky to get one customer through the doors of the gallery. And he'd just wasted fifty dollars he didn't have on advertising.

Jerking his collar up higher around his neck, he put his head down and made a beeline for the gallery. He let himself in the front door, quickly locking it behind him. The blinds were pulled down, but in a fit of optimism early this morning, he'd turned the louvers full open. Now he twisted the rod until the thin slats rested flat against each other.

A slatted shadow laid a wide path to the back, and Jack trudged it as though it were an uphill hike. He shut the door between the gallery and the studio and went straight to the far corner.

He reached out a hand but halted when he grasped only empty air. The cabinet wasn't there. He gave a humorless laugh. He'd forgotten Vienne had helped him move the cupboard out to the gallery the other night. But for one blissful second, he'd almost tasted the relief he imagined waited for him there.

His need burned in the pit of his belly. He slapped the wall where the cabinet had been and bit back a curse. He wanted what that cupboard had once offered. Wanted it so badly he envisioned walking the twelve miles to the nearest liquor store in Coyote.

But he had his license back now. And a car. He looked at the clock. *Nine fifty-five.* It would take him ten minutes to get to Coyote. The store would be open by the time he got there. He could have what he needed in twenty minutes. Just one drink.

A familiar anticipation rose inside him. Filled him. His mouth watered and he swallowed, almost tasting the burn of the amber liquid on his tongue. He walked to the back door. Put his hand on the knob and turned it.

Did he dare ask God to keep his secret? He took a risk and shot another selfish prayer heavenward.

Chapter Nine

*N*ine fifty-five. Vienne rolled over in bed and yanked the tassel on the bedroom window blind. She hadn't slept this late since she'd left Davis. The lavender fabric shade—a remnant of her childhood—scrolled up in a puff of dust, and sunlight streamed across the bed.

She crawled out of bed and padded out to the kitchen. Still groggy, she rinsed last night's supper dishes and made a half-hearted attempt at wiping the counters and sink. Between visiting Mom and trying to get the coffee shop ready to open, she'd neglected the house. She knew Mom would understand. Even though she spent very little time here, the dust and clutter were starting to get to her. Maybe she wouldn't mind coming home in the evenings so much if she hadn't let the place turn into such a pigpen.

Maybe she'd go have dinner with Mom

at the Manor tonight and help her with some of the exercises the physical therapist had shown them. Then she'd come home and do some deep cleaning.

The thought held little appeal since she had several days' worth of cleaning to do at the coffee shop. The remodeling was finished, and she'd spent a couple of days training the two college kids who'd waited tables for Mom before the café closed down. Allison and Evan could make sandwiches and salads, refill coffee cups, and bus tables while she played barista. The new counter-service-only would make things considerably easier—not to mention save a fortune in wait-staff wages. But Allison and Evan would be a big help, since they already knew the café's regular customers.

The only thing she was waiting on was the sign for the front. It was supposed to come in tomorrow, and Buddy Rollenmeyer had promised to get a crew together to hang it. It was mostly her fault the sign hadn't arrived yet. She'd gone back and forth about what to call the shop and hadn't placed the order until a couple weeks ago. It was Pete Truesdell who'd ultimately come up with the perfect name for the coffee shop—unintentional though it was. He would have a fit when she told him. Vienne smiled, imagining his reaction.

But the thought of opening day quickly erased her smile. There was a part of her that was terrified of putting the last chair in place and flipping on the neon Open light she'd bought at an auction in Salina last weekend. What if she ran out of food? What if there wasn't room for everyone to sit? She'd be on her own until Allison and Evan got out of class. Things could get crazy.

She tossed the dishrag in the sink and went back to the bedroom to throw on yesterday's work clothes. Leaning to tie her shoes, panic crept in. What if no one showed up on opening day? Jack hated coffee, and Pete wasn't too happy with the café being turned into a "mere" coffee shop.

What if the rest of Clayburn felt the same way?

ripping the steering wheel with clammy hands, Jack watched the clerk unlock the door to the liquor store and flip the sign to Open. The clock on the car's dashboard clicked to ten-fourteen.

A bearded man, the first customer of the day, appeared around the other side of the building. The man walked with purpose toward the front door. Jack recognized the hunger in the man's eyes all too well.

Two beasts warred within Jack.

One wanted desperately to get back on the road. Drive back to Clayburn and forget he'd ever made this trip to Coyote. Forget this liquor store even existed.

The other creature clawed at his throat, wanting only to get out of the car and feed. Get this over with. He'd driven to Coyote for a reason. It was inevitable, wasn't it? Hadn't he always known he'd end up back here eventually? Amazing, really, that he'd made it almost a week before blindly following the road to his old watering trough.

Leaving the car running, he put a hand on the door handle and leaned his shoulder into the door. Putting his left foot onto the gravel, he eased out of the car. He reached in his back pocket for his wallet and slid out a fifty-dollar bill—the last of his cash. But there was only one thing he needed today.

He took a step toward the door, then paused, staring at the flickering neon Budweiser sign behind the plate glass. Was he so weak that the least provocation sent him over the edge? He ran a hand through his hair and took another step.

Was he going to let Clara Berger push him over the edge, ruin almost more than nine months of sobriety? He gave a sick laugh at the thought and retreated to the car, breathing like he'd just finished a marathon. They'd taught him how to handle this in rehab. But everything he'd learned seemed to have been erased from his brain.

He slid behind the steering wheel and reached for his keys. At that moment the customer emerged from the store, brown bag in hand, relief on his face. Jack stared and swallowed hard.

He needed a drink to clear his head, that's all. Just one. He knew when to stop, and he would. He'd handle it right this time.

He waited for the man to get in his car and drive away, then reached for the door handle again. Why was this so hard? He knew what he needed. *Just get out of the car and go get it. You'll feel better. You'll be able to think more clearly.*

"No!" He slammed the ball of his hand hard on the steering wheel. He turned the key in the ignition and put the car in reverse—or thought he did. But the car shot forward, then stopped with a jolt. A loud bang—like a gunshot—split the air inside the car, and something ripped Jack's hands from the steering wheel. A sharp pain shot through his elbow and his face stung, as if someone had slapped him across the face. Hard. The light from the store windows dimmed and everything went dark.

A split second later a puddle of white nylon pooled on the seat around him and a low hiss filled the car. It wasn't until he noticed the haze of fine white powder suspended in gray smoke that Jack realized his airbag had deployed. He looked around, thinking someone must have hit his car. But a quick pan of the parking lot assured him he was the only one here.

Unfortunately, the clerk in the liquor store apparently heard the explosion. He came running and rapped his knuckles on the driver's-side window. "You okay, buddy?" He leaned down and peered through the window. "What happened?"

"I don't know. The . . . the airbag went off."

The clerk pointed to the front of the car where the cap of a concrete barrier poked just above the hood. "Looks like you hit the post. Are you okay?"

"I'm fine." Jack shrugged free of the nylon draped over his torso. He rubbed his elbow and coughed at the fine white powder floating in the air around him. He shut off the engine and rolled the window down, trying to extricate himself from the remains of the airbag that lay heavy on his lap.

"You sure you're okay?" the clerk asked again.

Jack didn't recognize the clerk, but he knew the suspicion in his eyes.

Jack nodded. "I don't know what happened. I was just . . . sitting here, and the airbag exploded in my face."

He'd put the car in reverse. At least he thought he had. But surely he hadn't hit the post hard enough to deploy the bag. He rubbed his elbow again. It was starting to swell.

"Are you going to be able to drive the car?"

"I think so. If I can get this thing up off the floorboard." He clawed at the puddle of fabric spilling from the center of the steering wheel.

"I hear it costs a fortune to replace those things. You're lucky you weren't hurt. You need something before you go? From the store?" The clerk jerked a thumb back toward the deserted liquor store.

Through the plate glass, Jack saw the bottles neatly lined up along the walls, designed to entice. But he'd suddenly lost his appetite for what they offered. He kicked the wilted airbag away from the accelerator. "No. I . . . I'd better get the car to the shop. Get this fixed."

Before the clerk could protest, Jack turned his key in the ignition and eased the car out of the parking lot.

Driving back to Clayburn—fighting the bulk of the deployed airbag on his lap and at his feet—his mind reeled. Yet his thoughts flowed with clarity. He'd learned to pray for a way out of temptation. Instead, today he'd driven straight to it. But God had answered his prayers in spite of that—literally hit him over the head with a way out.

He rubbed his arm. He was going to have a king-size bruise. Something to remember the morning by.

Saved by an airbag. God had a strange sense of humor.

Where he'd get the money to fix the car he didn't have a clue. For now, he chose to just be grateful that he'd been saved from himself.

Slowing down as he came to Clayburn's city limit, he peered through the windshield. The sun was high in a cloudless sky. "Thank you, Lord."

He was grateful. But he couldn't help but wonder if the story would be all over town tomorrow. And who would believe he'd driven all the way over to Coyote and not come back with what he went for? Did he dare ask God to keep his secret? He took a risk and shot another selfish prayer heavenward.

Poor guy.
She'd practically
kissed at him.
Why couldn't she just
tell him the truth?

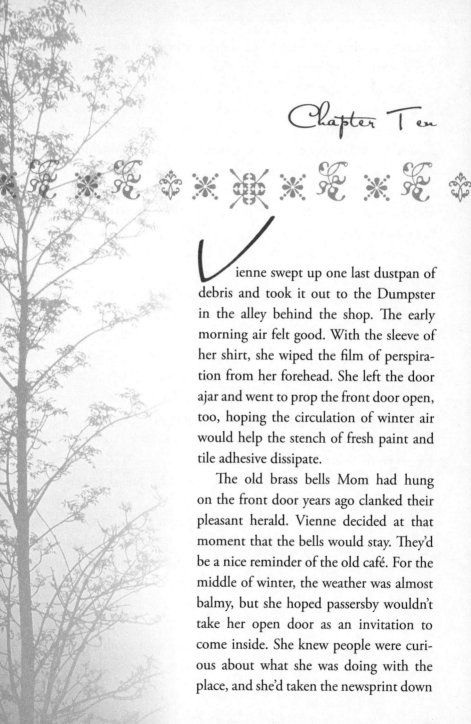

Chapter Ten

Vienne swept up one last dustpan of debris and took it out to the Dumpster in the alley behind the shop. The early morning air felt good. With the sleeve of her shirt, she wiped the film of perspiration from her forehead. She left the door ajar and went to prop the front door open, too, hoping the circulation of winter air would help the stench of fresh paint and tile adhesive dissipate.

The old brass bells Mom had hung on the front door years ago clanked their pleasant herald. Vienne decided at that moment that the bells would stay. They'd be a nice reminder of the old café. For the middle of winter, the weather was almost balmy, but she hoped passersby wouldn't take her open door as an invitation to come inside. She knew people were curious about what she was doing with the place, and she'd taken the newsprint down from the windows last week when she hung the curtains. Let people get a peek over the top of the café curtains if they were that nosy, but that was the only glimpse they'd have until opening day.

It was good to let a little excitement build. She took four steps into the shop and tried to view the space like a stranger might. The steel appliances and espresso machine gleamed behind the smooth granite counters, and a cozy grouping of overstuffed chairs gathered in front of the fireplace. The walls were bare, and she hadn't yet set up the tables and chairs, but things had really come together nicely. People were going to be blown away when they saw the full effect of the place.

Wearing a smug grin, she headed back to get the mop. She'd no doubt have to sweep and mop the floor again before opening day, but it would be good to do it one more time before she moved the tables into place.

"Knock, knock?"

She whirled, recognizing Jack's voice. "Hey, how's it going?"

"Is it time for a coffee break?" He looked hopeful.

"Don't you mean a hot-chocolate break?" She glanced at the giant clock she'd propped on the stone mantel just yesterday. "It's not even nine o'clock. Breakfast maybe, but it's a little early for a coffee break. At least if you're operating on Clayburn time."

"Okay. Hot chocolate it is. And breakfast." He pulled a barstool off the counter and straddled it.

She welcomed the chance to try out the espresso machine one more time before the opening. And she could use a break . . . plus something to eat. She hadn't taken the time to make coffee at home this morning. She'd gotten out of the habit of eating breakfast when she lived in Davis, but then she'd never burned as many calories as she had these last few months.

Rummaging in the cupboards, she came up with another package of the animal crackers she and Jack had shared the other night. She slid a package across the counter with an apologetic grimace. "My food won't be delivered until Monday morning."

He wrinkled his nose at the cookies. "That's it?"

"Sorry . . ."

"Do you have a skillet?"

"Duh. This *is* an eating establishment."

"Duh. Most eating establishments have *food.*"

She grinned. "Point well taken."

He held up a finger. "Hang on. I'll be right back." He slid off the stool and ducked out the door, leaving her standing in the middle of the shop, wondering.

But in less than five minutes, he was back, a bulging plastic grocery sack in tow. He plopped the bag on the counter and pulled out half a loaf of whole wheat bread, a tub of margarine, and a bottle of pancake syrup. He fished three eggs out of the pocket of his jacket and laid them on the counter. "Ta-dah! French toast comin' right up."

She raised an eyebrow. "And I'm guessing those eggs are already scrambled."

Jack laughed, shrugged off his jacket, and came around to the business side of the counter. Vienne handed him a bowl and a whisk. She put the skillet on the stove and turned on the gas.

He held up the bag of bread. "How many slices?"

Her stomach growled in response. "Will you think I'm a pig if I say four?"

"I won't think you're a pig if you say eight. Oh, wait . . ." He did a quick count of the bread bag. "Never mind. There are only eleven slices here. We can each have five and a half."

"Deal."

She started coffee while he cracked eggs and borrowed cinnamon and nutmeg from her spice rack. They worked in silence, but when she started to steam the milk, Jack jumped like he'd been shot.

She burst out laughing. "You don't get out much, do you?"

"What is that thing anyway?"

"The frother? It's where that nice fluffy foam comes from. It's pretty much sine qua non for any decent coffee shop, FYI."

"Sinny *what*?"

"Sine qua non. Essential." She checked herself. Lawyer-speak again. *Shut up, Kenney.* She motioned toward the griddle, where golden squares of egg-dipped toast sizzled. "Hey, don't burn my breakfast."

He whirled back to the stove. A heavenly cinnamon-scented steam rose from the griddle, quickly overpowering the acrid smells of remodeling. She'd have to remember that if the paint smell was still hanging in the air come opening day. French toast would be something quick and easy she could do short-order. In fact, if it wasn't too late, she'd have Trevor Ashlock add it to the menus he was printing up. She'd ordered just a few copies on cheap paper until she could gauge which items proved most popular. Then she planned to have a graphic designer in Salina create a permanent menu.

That thought reminded her that she needed to chalk a basic menu onto the oversized blackboard hanging behind the counter. She pulled her cappuccino cup from the frother and went to add that and "call Trevor" to the long list on the blackboard.

She felt Jack's eyes on her.

"That's a pretty big to-do list. When were you planning on opening?"

She turned around, chalk in hand. "Next Monday. Valentine's Day."

"Ah, that's right. You said that earlier. Appealing to the romantics of Clayburn, huh?"

She shrugged. "I guess."

He sliced a piece of French toast from corner to corner and looked up with an arched brow. "Spoken with the voice of a true cynic?"

She was sorry she'd opened herself up to his question. "Not a cynic exactly. Skeptic maybe . . ." She pulled two dinner plates off the shelf and set them beside the griddle for him.

He studied her. "Not that I'm an expert, mind you, but Valentine's Day *would* be a good advertising opportunity. You could make some of those little heart-shaped cookies with pink frosting and convince all the guys to bring their sweethearts in for coffee . . ."

She turned off the gas under the griddle. "Already have the cookies ordered, but you know, that sweethearts' coffee-date thing isn't a half-bad idea. It could be a moneymaker." She set their hot drinks on the counter.

"Thank you very much." He bowed and placed a plate of golden, steaming French toast triangles in front of her.

"Mmm . . . this looks delicious."

They took their plates to the table nearest the counter and sat down to eat. They hadn't taken two bites when the bells clattered against the glass, and a man poked his head in the front door. "Smells good in here! You open for business yet?"

"Sorry," Vienne hollered. "Not until Valentine's Day."

When a couple of teenagers sauntered in a few minutes later, Vienne told them the same thing. Once they'd gone on down the street, Jack got up and closed the door. "You need a sign."

"I guess I do. Well, it's your fault. You had to go and make it smell so good in here."

He shot her a smile, then pointed to the chalkboard. "I see one of the things on your to-do list is make a menu board. Did you have your heart set on doing that yourself?"

"What do you mean?"

"Well, I happen to know an artist with a little time on his hands." He held out his hands in offering. "I'd do it for nothing, of course. On second thought"—he winked—"I might barter for a hot chocolate now and then."

"That'd be really great, except I don't have any good chalk. The grocery store didn't have anything except white. You're not heading to Wal-Mart anytime soon, are you?"

He bent over his empty mug. "Actually, I'm not heading anywhere anytime soon. My car's in the shop."

"Oh, bummer. Nothing serious, I hope?"

He made a face. "My checking account is going to think it's serious."

"Ouch. Transmission?"

"No, actually, my airbag deployed."

"Really? You were in an accident?"

"No. It was kind of weird. It just . . . exploded." For a minute he looked embarrassed. "About took my head off. And look here . . ." He pushed up his sleeve to reveal a deep purple bruise covering most of his elbow.

She recoiled. "That looks terrible! The airbag did that?"

He nodded and yanked his sleeve back over the bruise.

Vienne shook her head. "Airbags are not supposed to deploy for no reason. You have every right to sue the company. They'd probably settle out of court. We had a case just last year where an airbag deployed and broke *both* of a woman's arms. She had little kids and, of course, had to hire help until she was out of casts. She got something like half a million dollars out of the auto manufacturer."

"We?" He stopped with a fork full of French toast halfway to his mouth. "Hold on. What are you talking about . . . *we* had a case?"

Too late, Vienne realized she'd opened the door to the one topic she didn't want to discuss. "It was a case an attorney I worked for won . . . out in California."

"Oh, that's right." Jack doused his last slice of French toast with syrup. "Trevor said you went to law school."

An odd sense of panic rose in her throat. She picked up his mug. "You want some more cocoa?"

"Not right now, thanks." He gently pushed the cup away. "So . . . you're a lawyer?"

A thousand possible responses went through her mind, but she only shook her head.

"You're still in law school, then?"

She shoved back her chair and took his mug to the sink. She ran water in it, then did the same with her coffee cup. Finally she sat back down across from Jack. "You know, this really isn't something I want to talk about."

He looked surprised. "Sorry." He put his hands up, palms out. "I didn't know it was a touchy topic."

"It's not touchy. I just don't want to talk about it."

"Okay. I'm sorry."

"It's really nobody's business." *Back off, Kenney. He said he was sorry.*

"Hey, I said I was sorry. Subject closed. I won't mention it again."

She opened her mouth and shut it again, realizing she was on the defensive for no reason. Poor guy. She'd practically hissed at him. Why couldn't she just tell him the truth? Now he probably thought she'd been disbarred—or something worse.

She gave a heavy sigh and bent over the counter across from him, resting her elbows on the cold granite. She propped her chin on her hands. "I graduated law school, but . . . um . . . I didn't exactly pass the bar."

Understanding lit his eyes. "Ohhh . . ." He dipped his head, as though embarrassed for her. "I'm sorry."

"It's not *your* fault."

"Well, I'm still sorry for you."

Contempt would have been easier to handle than the kindness his voice held. "Don't be sorry for me."

He raised his hands again in truce. "Okay, I won't."

She hesitated, then propped her hands on her hips. "Well, you could be a *little* sorry." She gave him what she hoped was a ceasefire sort of grin.

He rolled his eyes and she could almost hear him thinking, *Women!* But the smile he returned made up for it.

She reviewed their conversation. She had just told him her humiliating secret, and he hadn't even flinched. It actually felt kind of good to get it out in the open.

Okay, maybe he was writing her off in his mind even as they sat here smiling at each other. That possibility hurt more than she wanted to admit. She was just getting to know Jackson Linder again, and right now he was the only friend she had in the world.

Heart racing, Vienne
ran inside the coffee
shop and grabbed the
receiver of the phone
hanging on the wall
behind the counter.
She punched in the
emergency number.

Chapter Eleven

February

The crane cranked the unwieldy sign up another notch. Vienne held her breath as the flimsy chains swayed and a gust caught the thick sheet of canvas. It snapped in the wind and sailed into the side of the building. Hunched in the bucket of the cherry picker, Buddy Rollenmeyer seemed unconcerned and reached over the side to maneuver the sign into place. Earlier this morning he'd installed the curlicued wrought-iron bracket that would hold the framed canvas.

Another flurry gusted over the building and Vienne shivered. Shielding her eyes with one hand, she looked up into the winter sky. It was a clear gray-blue. No snow in the forecast, but she didn't like the way the wind had picked up.

"Gotcha a new sign, huh?"

She turned to see Pete Truesdell standing on the sidewalk a few feet behind her, hands buried deep in the pockets of his coveralls, weathered neck craned to watch the workmen.

"Hey, Pete." She went to stand beside him. "What do you think?"

"You got a lot done while I was gone."

"Oh? Where've you been?"

"Went to visit my brother out in California. You went to college out there, didn't you?"

She nodded, hoping he wouldn't ask her when she was going back.

"Well, you can have it." He wagged his head in disgust, seeming as anxious to change the subject as she was. "There's not enough money in this universe to get me out there again. Land of fruits and nuts . . . that's what I call it." Pete laughed at his joke—one Vienne had heard no less than a dozen times since she'd been back in town.

She gave a polite laugh, hoping to move off the topic of California.

Pete pointed at the sign. "What's that you're callin' the place? Lat . . . Lat-ee . . ." The crinkles around his eyes deepened as he squinted and worked his tongue over tobacco-stained teeth.

"It's *Latte-dah*. You know, like a latte . . . coffee with milk. You're the one who gave me the idea."

"Me?" Pete glowered at her. "I never heard of such a thing."

"Remember that day you were giving me a hard time for turning the café into a coffee shop?"

"Sure I do, but I don't remember volunteerin' no names."

She smiled. "You said I was opening—and I quote—'some la-di-da coffee shop.' It's a play on words. *Latte-dah*. La-di-da. Get it?"

He doffed his cap and studied the sign again. "Whatever you say, girlie. But your customers are likely to keel over from hunger by the time you explain the blamed thing!"

"They'll get used to it."

Pete scratched his grizzled chin. "Well, I suppose people can just call it the coffee shop. Or maybe Ingrid's place. Why don't you put *that* on your sign? My Velma says you ought to get one of those Internet places to advertise on."

"A website?"

"Yeah, that's it . . . I think." He shook his head. "I don't know diddly-squat about computers, but Velma's gettin' pretty good on 'em now that she's retired. All I know is, she saves a bundle on phone bills to our kids and grandkids with them there e-mails. Pretty slick invention, if you ask me. Velma prints 'em out for me to read, but"—he scrunched up his face—"half the time I can't make heads or tails of them abbreviations the kids use."

Vienne laughed politely, but her smile widened into a genuine one when she spotted Jackson Linder crossing the street, headed in their direction. She waved at him, cheering silently for his well-timed interruption.

"Good morning." Jack rewarded her with a boyish grin that made her stomach do somersaults.

Pete turned to see who she was smiling at. Even in profile, she didn't miss the surprise—and something else—that registered on the old man's face.

"Well, I'll be . . ." Pete extended a hand. "Didn't know you was back in town, Jackson."

Jack shook his hand, then pulled Pete into an awkward embrace. "Yep. I'm back."

Vienne curbed a smile at the good-ol'-boy inflection that had come to Jack's voice.

"It's mighty good to see you," Pete said, still gripping Jack's hand. "You gettin' along okay?"

"I'm good. Thanks, Pete." Jack gazed up at the cherry picker, seeming suddenly eager to change the subject. "This is quite the production, huh?"

"I'd say so." Pete hooked a thumb at the sign. "I was just tellin'

Vinny here that fancy California name is gonna go over like a wet sow in this town. Can *you* make out heads or tails how to pronounce that?"

Vienne gave Jack a look and rolled her eyes. He looked away, but not before she saw a smirk twist his lips. She wasn't sure if it was directed at Pete or at her, but she hoped it was her. In the hours they'd spent together over the past two weeks, she'd grown accustomed to his ornery streak. For him, teasing seemed to be a sign of affection. And she was honored to have Jack Linder's affection aimed her way.

Jack tipped his head and read the sign. "I don't think it much matters how you pronounce it, Pete. As long as the coffee's good. And I hear it's pretty good." He had the audacity to wink at her.

Pete doffed his cap and looked at Jack. "Bein's the place hasn't even opened yet, how would you know that?"

Jack shrugged. "Just a rumor." The grin splitting his face was directed at Vienne.

Pete looked between the two of them and shook his head. He pulled a watch on a chain from the pocket of his coveralls. "I better get over to the beauty shop. Velma's gettin' a perm, and she won't be happy if I'm late pickin' her up. Good luck with your sign there, Vinny." He gave Jack's arm a punch. "And good to have you back, buddy. You hang in there now."

Jack bit the corner of his lip and studied the sidewalk. "Thanks, Pete."

What was that all about? She didn't have time to ponder it for long. A shout from Buddy up in the bucket brought her head up. The Latte-dah sign dangled from the cable, dipping and diving like a kite in the capricious Kansas breeze. Vienne sucked in a breath and held it. Beside her, Jack did the same.

Buddy leaned out over the basket and grasped for the sign, but came up empty-handed. As the canvas swung back in his direction, he lunged again and got a hand on one of the poles that framed the sign.

An updraft bloated the canvas and jerked Buddy halfway out of the bucket—no small feat since Buddy was six-foot-four and probably three hundred pounds.

"Let it go!" Jack shouted.

The boom lurched and the crane operator jumped out of the cab, bellowing directions up to Buddy.

Jack cupped his hands around his mouth and yelled again. "Let go, Buddy!" His voice wavered and his face was drained of color. "That thing is going to drag him over the side if he's not careful."

Vienne tented a hand over her eyes and looked up to where Buddy wrestled with the sign.

"They need another man up there." Jack leaned back and studied the railed balcony that formed a covered porch over the café's entry. "How do you get up there?"

"It's not—" Before she could finish, another gust of wind buffeted the bucket. Buddy held tight to the canvas, but it billowed over his head like a clipper's sail.

The crane operator ran back to the cab. "I'm bringing you down. Hang on." A few seconds later, the bucket lurched and the boom slowly lowered. But another gust sent the bucket swaying. An updraft caught the canvas and Buddy staggered to one side.

"Call 911 and get a fire truck over here! We need another ladder." Jack spat the words and took off toward the crane.

Heart racing, Vienne ran inside the coffee shop and grabbed the receiver of the phone hanging on the wall behind the counter. She punched in the emergency number.

The dispatcher answered just as Jack charged through the front door. "Where's the door to the balcony?"

She covered the receiver. "It's not safe, Jack."

He glared at her. "How do you get up there?"

She pointed to the delivery door. "At the end of the hall. But the flooring up there is rotted through in places."

Jack ignored her and sprinted to the back, shedding his jacket as he went.

"What is your emergency, please?" The dispatcher's voice drew Vienne back to the phone.

"Please send someone to Main Street in Clayburn. I think we need . . . a fire truck . . ." She described the situation.

In a calm voice the dispatcher assured her they'd send someone to help.

Vienne hung up the phone and ran to the front windows. A small crowd had gathered outside the store. It was clear by the tension in their faces that the crisis wasn't over.

A siren blared from the east where the new fire station was. She heard Jack tromping on the floor overhead and prayed it would hold him.

The building had been in poor shape when her mother bought it twenty years ago. Mom had paid to have the main floor brought up to code and fixed enough of the upper level to pass the fire marshal's inspection, but Vienne remembered his warning—oft repeated by Mom—that the upper floor was not safe for occupancy. Mom had put every penny of profit the café made back into the building—just to keep it up to code. But she'd always worried about the state of the upstairs and had once nailed the door shut for fear children searching for the restrooms might wander up there and get injured. But Buddy Rollenmeyer had pried that door open a few months later to install the Internet cable and Mom had left it be, settling instead for an infant safety gate across the stairway.

Vienne jogged to the back hallway. Hurdling the gate, as Jack must have done, she took the stairs two at a time.

She stopped short at the top of the stairs. "Be careful!"

Too late, she rounded the corner to see Jack with one leg out the window. Ignoring her shouts, he climbed out onto the balcony.

Vienne raced back downstairs and outside. A small crowd had gathered on the sidewalk in front of her shop. The lime green fire truck sat beside the crane, its ladder extended, and Doug DeVore—in full fire-fighting gear—was making his way up the narrow rungs.

Vienne's heart stuttered at the sight of Jack stretched out over the railing, helping Doug steady the sign. They managed to get the framed canvas lined up with the bracket, but when Buddy reached for his drill, the sign slipped again.

Jack grabbed for it but stumbled on the balcony's low railing. As if in slow motion, he pitched over the edge. He clawed the air, and one hand finally connected with the bracket that was supposed to hold the sign. It broke his fall, and he hung there, clutching the side of the building with his free hand.

Vienne's heart resumed beating. But only momentarily.

She watched in horror as the large bolt holding the bracket came loose. It made a grinding sound as it lurched from the wall an inch at a time.

With one last, horrible *screech*, the bracket gave way, and Jack swung beneath the metal support, flailing wildly for something to hang on to. His head hit the side of the building and his body went limp. He flopped like a rag doll and slid down the jagged brick wall.

Bits of mortar and concrete showered down behind him. He landed in a heap on the sidewalk. His eyelids fluttered, then closed.

He lay there, completely motionless.

Vienne stood,
rooted to the street,
trying to catch a
glimpse of Jack's face
before they closed
the ambulance doors.

Chapter Twelve

Her body wouldn't obey her brain's instructions. Vienne tried to run to where Jack's still form lay beneath the crane's boom, but she was paralyzed.

People shouted and someone screamed. The crane roared as the bucket was lowered. She managed a halting step forward, her knees like jelly.

Jack lay on his back, unmoving, right where he'd fallen, his face gray and slack. Was he even breathing? She didn't see any blood, but onlookers circled around him, blocking her view now.

She inched her way through, trying to get to him. The sirens crescendoed and faded away as a second fire truck parked in the middle of Main Street. Vienne turned as two men descended from the cab. She heard herself shouting instructions. "He's over here!" She pushed on through the crowd.

"Is someone hurt?"

"Yes, over here." She waved at the fireman, then shouted at the people milling on the sidewalk. "Move back! Let them through."

The younger man—a volunteer, judging by the white shirt and tie jutting above the khaki jumpsuit—sprinted back to the fire truck and grabbed a radio from the cab. She overheard him call for EMTs before he pushed through the gawkers to get to Jack.

Vienne followed in the young man's wake and leaned close to peer over his shoulder. She held her breath again as they worked over Jack. He didn't appear to be breathing, yet the men were calm and methodical as they ran their hands over his limbs. They spoke in low tones to each other, their words indistinguishable. They hadn't started oxygen or performed CPR, so maybe that meant Jack was breathing on his own. That was a good sign.

Oh, Lord, please don't let him die.

Another siren pierced the low murmur of onlookers, and soon two emergency workers parted the crowd with a folded gurney.

An eternity passed before they finally lifted Jack onto the stretcher and rolled it toward the waiting ambulance. Vienne stood, rooted to the street, trying to catch a glimpse of Jack's face before they closed the ambulance doors. But she couldn't see over the tangle of people who'd come out of the shops to stare.

Sirens blaring, the ambulance sped away. She stood in the center of the street, unable to do anything but stare after it and acknowledge the crushing weight in the pit of her stomach. *Don't let him die. Please don't let him die.*

Indistinct bits of conversation drifted toward her from the knot of people still huddled on the sidewalk.

"It was Jackson Linder," a young woman's voice said. "You know . . . from the gallery."

"Are you sure? I thought he'd left town."

Vienne turned to see Erma, who ran the antique gallery next door, talking in a huddle with a younger woman. They didn't seem to notice Vienne.

Erma's brow wrinkled. "What was he doing up there anyway?"

"They were trying to hang a sign. For the new coffee shop." The other woman pointed to the sidewalk in front of the building where crumbled bricks were scattered.

Clucking her tongue, Erma shook her head. "I hope he wasn't drinking . . ."

Vienne's breath caught. *What an odd thing to assume!* A pang of memory made her close her eyes. She was ten years old, standing backstage before the Christmas Eve pageant, trying to keep her clothes-hanger-and-tinsel halo from slipping off her head. She peeked through the curtain to see her father walking in beside Mom. She could hardly believe he'd actually come. His hair was slicked down nice and he even had a tie on. She was naïve enough to take it as a sign that God had answered her prayers and Daddy was "well."

But before they got halfway down the aisle of the sanctuary, Harlan Kenney fell—tripped, Mom always claimed—but Vienne knew better, even at ten. And so did every usher there that night. They'd helped her father to his feet, and tried to hush his cursing, but not before the familiar, ugly words reached her ears—and everyone else's.

The men from church surrounded Mom. Bob Swanson's voice was gentle, but Vienne could tell by the set of his jaw—and the hurt in her mother's eyes—that Mr. Swanson wasn't offering Mom the option to stay.

She started at the weight of a hand on her shoulder. "Vienne?"

She spun to find Doug DeVore standing behind her.

"Is he okay?" she breathed.

Doug pressed his lips in a hard line. "He was breathing on his own. But I'd guess he has a broken bone or two. He fell pretty hard. They took him to Asbury."

Hearing the name of the hospital brought more disturbing memories, most recently Mom's stroke. But the Kenneys had a long history with the hospital in Salina.

"We need you to answer a few questions for us, okay?" Doug's voice was gentle.

She nodded, trying to clear her head. "I'll try."

Frank Marren from the police station joined them.

"Why don't we go inside . . ." She gestured toward the open door of the coffee shop.

They followed her inside, only to find several people milling around in the coffee shop.

Frank took charge. "We're going to have to ask you folks to leave now. Everything's under control, but the coffee shop isn't open for business yet. Not until—" He cocked his head toward Vienne, waiting for her to finish his sentence.

"Monday . . . Valentine's Day. I hope." She looked around. There didn't appear to be any damage to the inside of the building.

The officer asked her a few questions and jotted down her statements. He motioned to the back. "Is that the access to the balcony he fell from?"

She nodded.

"You mind if I take a look around upstairs?"

"No. Of course not. But it's blocked off. You'll have to climb over the gate." She led him to the stairway.

"Do you know if your mom's had the place inspected by the fire marshal lately?"

"We had it inspected before they did the remodeling. Just a couple months ago." He surely wouldn't try to shut her down. She'd *told* Jack not to go up there. She'd told him it wasn't safe.

There goes my opening day. Her thoughts shocked her, shamed her. Jack was injured—maybe dead—and she could only think of her stupid opening? *Forgive me, Lord.*

She expelled a harsh breath. *Forgive me, Jack.*

"Okay. Just checking." Frank Marren touched her arm. "I'd still like to take a look around."

Vienne nodded and led the way up the narrow staircase.

※ ※ ※

*J*ack tried to fill his lungs, but a sharp pain slashed through his right side. Groaning, he raised himself up on the gurney. He leaned on his right arm but quickly slumped back onto the firm pillow. His elbow was still bruised from the airbag injury. Man! This had not been his week.

His vision was blurry, and he blinked against the harsh lights overhead, trying to focus. He was alone in the small curtained room, but he heard voices on the other side of the barrier that closed him away from the main emergency room.

He closed his eyes and let himself drift.

"Jack?"

A deep voice came through the pain-induced fog. He tried to sit up again, but that stab of pain went through him again.

"Here, let me help you. I'm Dr. Unruh."

The ER physician put a strong arm underneath him and helped him sit up on the side of the gurney. "How are you feeling?"

"Like I got hit by a truck."

The doctor wheeled a stool over and sat in front of him. "We're waiting for the technicians to read the X-rays, but it looks like you were lucky this time. Except for a couple of cracked ribs, I don't think the films are going to show any other broken bones. You're going to feel those ribs for a few weeks, though."

Jack shifted his weight and stifled a moan. "Oh, man . . . I feel them now."

"We'll send you home with something for the pain. You can stay on pain medication for a couple of weeks, and we'll see how you're doing after that. If you need to be on it longer, we can adjust the dosage, but this particular prescription can be hard to get off of, so we want to keep you on as low a dose as possible."

A lecture Jack had heard in rehab played in his head. *If you are chemically dependent, you can easily become addicted to certain prescription medicines, even though that particular medication may not have been the substance you abused.*

Dr. Unruh slid off the stool and pushed back the curtain. "The nurse will be back in a minute, and we'll get you ready to go home."

"Thanks." He should probably say something . . . let them know he'd been in rehab.

But the doctor had already disappeared behind the curtain.

Jack glanced at his wrist, then remembered they'd taken his watch off before they took the X-rays. He looked around the room for it, and then for a clock. Nothing. It had to be close to four, though. Who knew how long it would be before they'd let him go. He wasn't letting them keep him overnight . . . that was for sure.

But even if the films showed no broken bones, it didn't change the fact that he was stranded here in Salina without a car. Bart and Wren were the logical ones to call, but they didn't like to drive after dark. And he didn't know who else to call to come get him.

Vienne maybe. After all, he was rescuing her sign when he fell. He still wasn't sure how it had all happened. He remembered reaching for the sign, and everything after that was a blur.

A nurse poked her head around the curtain that screened him from the rest of the unit. "We're just waiting on the techs to read your X-rays. You doing okay in here?"

He managed a nod. "Can you tell me what time it is?"

She consulted her watch. "Four-fifteen."

"I need to make a phone call, if possible. And do you have a phone book I could borrow? I'm not sure of the number . . ."

"Sure. Just a minute." She was back in a minute with a fat area directory and a cordless phone. The Clayburn Café was still listed. He only hoped Vienne was there, and that she wouldn't mind coming to get him.

A dark cloud enveloped him—along with a serious need for a drink. How was he ever going to pay for all this? Between this and the stupid car repairs, he'd be chipping away at his credit card for the next five years. And he'd just paid the dumb thing off. He had a minimum of medical insurance and a sky-high deductible. The ambulance and emergency room services were going to clean him out . . . unless the café had a good policy he could file a claim on.

He didn't relish the thought of asking Vienne, but he wasn't sure he had a choice. He dialed the number and waited while it rang four, then five times. She picked up on the sixth ring. "Hello?"

"Vienne? It's Jack."

"Jack! Are you okay? I've been trying to call you. The hospital wouldn't tell me anything. Are you okay? Did they admit you?"

The worry . . . fear even . . . in her voice filled him with an odd warmth. "No, they're not keeping me. That's the problem, though. That's why I'm calling you. I don't have my car at the hospital. I'm not sure I could drive anyway."

A breathy gasp came over the wire. "Oh! Are you okay? Did you break anything?"

"I'm okay. I'm still waiting for them to read the X-rays, but they think I only broke a couple of ribs."

"Oh, Jack, I'm so sorry. I've been worried sick. You scared me to death!"

The warmth moved through his veins. "I don't suppose I could ask a huge favor? I need someone to come and pick me up. I got here by ambulance and my car's in the—"

"Oh! Of course. I'll be there. Just tell me where to come, and I'll be right there."

"Well, you might want to wait until I call you back. Who knows how long it'll be before they finally read the X-rays . . . and if they do find anything broken, I may have to get a cast—"

"I can't believe all you broke was a couple of ribs. I can't believe you're coming home tonight. When I saw you fall, I thought . . ." Her voice wavered.

"Hey, I'm okay. No big deal. A couple of ribs. I don't think they can put a cast on your rib cage." He knew for a fact they didn't do anything for broken ribs, since he'd cracked three of his falling off the curb in a drunken stupor one night two and a half years ago. He pushed the memory from his mind. That was something he didn't plan on sharing with her.

"Let me come and wait with you. Hang on." He heard her rummaging in a drawer or something. "It's almost four-thirty. You've been there a long time. Are you sure you don't need to stay the night?"

Was she trying to get out of coming to pick him up? "I'm fine."

"If you're sure. Tell me where to come, and I'll be there in twenty minutes."

"Thanks, Vienne. I appreciate it."

He gave her directions, clicked off the phone, and laid it on the tabouret beside the gurney. Looking up, he caught his reflection in the glass covering a medical poster on the wall. He was grinning like an idiot. And the need for a drink had vanished.

Vienne waited as he climbed the steps. But after mounting the first two, he swayed and stumbled.

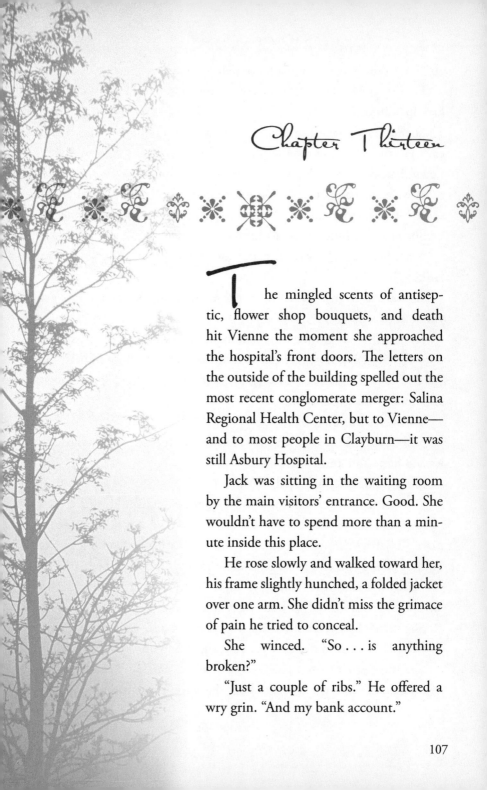

Chapter Thirteen

The mingled scents of antiseptic, flower shop bouquets, and death hit Vienne the moment she approached the hospital's front doors. The letters on the outside of the building spelled out the most recent conglomerate merger: Salina Regional Health Center, but to Vienne—and to most people in Clayburn—it was still Asbury Hospital.

Jack was sitting in the waiting room by the main visitors' entrance. Good. She wouldn't have to spend more than a minute inside this place.

He rose slowly and walked toward her, his frame slightly hunched, a folded jacket over one arm. She didn't miss the grimace of pain he tried to conceal.

She winced. "So . . . is anything broken?"

"Just a couple of ribs." He offered a wry grin. "And my bank account."

"I'm so sorry. Are you in a lot of pain?"

He shrugged. "They gave me something, and I think it's starting to kick in a little."

She let out a breath of relief. "I'm glad it's only broken ribs. I still can't get the image out of my mind of you falling and then tumbling down that wall."

"I wish somebody had caught it on video. Maybe I'd have gotten on some funniest video show so I could pay off the stupid hospital bills."

She glared at him. "It wasn't funny."

Neck held stiff, he gave her arm an anemic punch. "Hey, I'm just kidding."

"It was not funny, Jack. You scared me to death. Come on, let's get you home."

She led the way through the parking lot and stood by the passenger door feeling helpless while he folded himself into her little Mazda. He reached to pull the door closed and sucked in a breath, stifling a moan and holding his midsection.

"Are you sure you're okay?"

Still bracing his ribs with his forearms, he turned, stiff-necked, to look at her. "You know what I am?"

She wrinkled her forehead. "Huh?"

"I'm starving. You wouldn't want to go for pizza, would you?"

"Are you crazy?" She started the car and backed out of the parking place. "I'll drive through for hamburgers if you're really that hungry, but I'm not taking you to a restaurant. You should be home in bed."

"Gee, thanks for the sympathy." His grin quickly turned sober. "Did anybody else get hurt? Did Buddy get down okay?"

She nodded. "Everybody's fine. You were the only casualty."

"Thank God. And did they get your sign hung up?"

She was suddenly overwhelmed with guilt. Jack had been hurt trying to help her, and her attitude about the whole thing had been almost cavalier. She'd been angry that he defied her warnings and climbed to the upper floor of the building. She hadn't considered that he'd acted heroically. And now, when he could have been whining about his own situation, he was more worried about Buddy—and about her.

She pulled to the edge of the parking lot and put the car in park. "Jack, I am so sorry. I feel terrible about this . . . about everything."

He stared at her. "It's not exactly like you pushed me off the balcony."

She giggled, in spite of herself. "I know, but if it weren't for me, you wouldn't be here."

"How do you know? Maybe I would have stubbed my toe at the gallery, and I'd have had to call an ambulance and—"

"Would you stop? I feel responsible." She frowned. "I never should have let you go up there in the first place."

"As I recall, you practically fell all over yourself trying to stop me. We're lucky it's not you with the broken ribs." He grinned that grin she remembered from high school.

"Quit joking about it. I'm serious. I feel terrible."

He eased an arm over the back of the seat and turned to face her. "Don't worry, Vienne. I'm not going to sue you."

She let his comment stew for a few seconds. "Was that some sort of sick lawyer joke? Or is that what you really suspect I'm thinking?"

He opened his mouth as if to protest, but nothing came out.

She eyed him. "It *is*, isn't it? You think I'm worried that you're going to sue me."

He grimaced. "Well, it does sound like you're a little worried about that."

"You know, that's not all they teach us in law school."

"Ah, but it is *one* of the things."

"Well, you can quit worrying. It never crossed my mind. Besides, I'm not a real lawyer, remember?" She bit her bottom lip. For somebody who hadn't wanted anyone to know about her failure, she'd sure done a lot of blabbing about it. Of course she hadn't mentioned that she'd failed the bar *twice.*

He gave her arm a brotherly pat. "Forget I said anything. Besides, you can't get blood out of a turnip. And by the way, you never answered my question. Did they get your sign hung?"

She sighed. "Buddy had to patch up the side of the building first. He's going to try again in the morning—if it's not too windy." She pulled onto Santa Fe Street. "Where to?"

He pointed west. "There's a McDonald's on the way out of town. That's fine with me. Unless you want something else."

"McDonald's it is."

They drove through and ordered burgers and fries, and while they waited in a long drive-thru line, they talked again about the scare he'd given her on the balcony today.

"I really don't even have any memory of falling." Jack shook his head. "It's like one minute I was leaning over the railing, and the next thing I knew I was in the hospital staring up at an X-ray machine."

"Well, believe me, I have enough of a memory of it for both of us."

They got their food and she pulled into a parking space and started doling out burgers and drinks.

Jack took a sip of his Coke but held up a hand when she offered him a box of French fries. "I'm feeling a little sleepy. Maybe you should just take me home. I'm sorry."

"Are you sure? Shouldn't you have something in your stomach with the medication?"

Jack leaned his head against the back of the seat. "If you want to go ahead and eat, that's okay. I'm . . . I'm not feeling well all of a sudden." His words slurred together.

She couldn't tell if the odd cast to his face was just a reflection from the dashboard lights or if he really was a little green. He'd better not get sick on her. "I'll just head back to Clayburn."

He mumbled something she couldn't understand.

She put the McDonald's bags on the console between them and drove home in silence, glancing sidelong at him every few seconds. He appeared to be asleep, his head lolling to one side, his mouth slack. At least his heavy breathing left no doubt he was alive. But she was a little worried. And more than a little uncomfortable.

Clayburn's streets were empty when she pulled into the city limits twenty minutes later. Though the streetlights cast yellow light across his face, Jack seemed oblivious to the fact that they were home. She hated to wake him up.

Except for a couple of cars in front of Wren's Nest, Main Street was empty. She debated parking in the alley behind the gallery. She was pretty sure that was the entrance Jack used for his apartment, but somehow it seemed too personal.

He saved her the decision, stirring beside her. He raised up in the seat but immediately slumped again, crying out in pain and grabbing his side.

"Are you okay?"

"You can drop me off in the alley if you don't mind." He pointed toward the end of the block.

Vienne drove the car around and inched down the narrow alley, trying to find some indication which entry belonged to the gallery.

Jack wasn't much help. He looked straight ahead, his face drawn. Either the pain medication was making him loopy, or it wasn't working, and he was in excruciating pain.

She inched past wide double doors and a brick wall that jutted out into the alley. Past that, she spotted Jack's car parked near a single door with a naked lightbulb mounted beside it. "Is this okay?"

"Any place is fine."

She eased beside his car.

Jack opened the door and swung his right leg out, grimacing. "Man, broken ribs are nothing to sneeze at."

She nodded. "So I've heard. Did they give you some pain pills for later?"

He patted the front pocket of his denim shirt. "Right here. Hey, thanks for the ride. I . . . appreciate it. I'll buy you coffee sometime." He gave a short laugh. "I hear there's a really good place opening up in town."

Even through pain, his sense of humor was intact. She smiled. "I'll hold you to that."

He crawled out of the car and started toward the door. Vienne waited as he climbed the steps. But after mounting the first two, he swayed and stumbled. She held her breath until he'd navigated the last step. He caught the door handle and steadied himself. Fishing in his pocket with one hand, he turned to wave, as if dismissing her. But he made no move to unlock the door.

Maybe he didn't have his keys. She put the car in park and got out. "Can't you get in?"

"I'm not sure." He checked his shirt pocket, then unfolded his jacket and started searching through the pockets.

With no warning, he sat down hard on the top step and put his head between his knees.

"Jack?"

"Those pills must be doing a number on me."

"What's wrong?"

"I'm dizzy," he said to the pavement.

A twinge of panic hit her. She'd never been a good nurse. Even when Mom was recuperating at home after her first stroke, Vienne had felt inept and useless trying to care for her. It was bad enough with Mom in the nursing home with an entire staff to take care of her.

"Did you find your keys?"

Without looking up, he held out his jacket and shook it. Something jingled inside. She poked through his pockets until she found the keys. "Which one?"

No response.

She took a wild guess and jabbed a key in the lock. The latch gave way and she pushed the door open. "Can you get up, or should I call the ambulance?"

His head came up. "No!"

He sounded almost angry, but in the next moment he lowered his voice. "I'll get up. Just give me a minute."

Feeling awkward, she sat down on the step and scooted next to him. "You want to take my arm?"

"Thanks." He linked his arm through the crook of her elbow.

She stood slowly and he rose after her. His weight almost toppled them both over, but she managed to steady him.

She felt for a switch inside the door, but Jack was the one who turned it on. She waited for her eyes to adjust to the light. The room they walked into was mostly taken up with a large worktable covered with empty canvas on stretcher boards and finished art in various stages of framing. Vienne wished Jack felt well enough to give her a tour of the gallery. But he leaned heavier against her by the minute.

"Where's your bedroom?"

He pointed toward a door that stood ajar, revealing a dark stairway. She turned him in the right direction, and they stumbled up the stairs together.

Jack flipped a switch at the top of the stairs. The dim light revealed a small, tidy living room with tall windows that looked out over Main Street. A pass-through on one wall offered a peek into a galley kitchen.

"I'm okay now. Thanks. I'm really sorry, Vienne. I didn't know those pills would affect me that way. I would never have called you to come and get me from the hospital if I thought you'd end up having to play nurse."

Had she spoken her qualms aloud earlier? She was pretty sure she hadn't, but it felt eerily like he'd read her mind. "It's okay. And I'm not leaving until you're in bed."

She cringed inwardly. He was going to think she was putting the moves on him if she didn't choose her words more carefully.

But if he thought anything of it, he pretended otherwise. "Thanks. I'm feeling a little better now. I'll be okay. You go on home."

She hesitated. "You're sure?"

"I'm sure."

"I'll get in touch with you in the morning and make sure you survived the night."

His attempt at a smile looked more like he was about to cry.

"I'll lock the door behind me." She flipped off the light and opened the door to leave.

"Vienne?"

She turned back, waiting.

"Thanks. You're a jewel."

Maybe somewhere inside him there was still a trace of that untainted, genuinely nice kid he'd been.

Chapter Fourteen

The ceiling whirled above him, and Jack held on to the sides of the mattress, willing it to stop spinning. His head pounded as though someone had walloped him with a sledgehammer. Strangely, it felt as if he had a major-league hangover. He despised the memories that fact brought roaring back. He'd thought he was through with this miserable state forever.

He must be having a bad reaction to the pain pills. He desperately wanted to sleep, but between his aching ribs—which the medication hadn't touched—and this unrelenting dizziness, he lay wide awake, listening to the *tick tick tick* of the clock out in the kitchen.

Another wave of nausea crashed into him. He rolled onto the floor and armycrawled to the bathroom. Minutes later he made it back to bed, only to be hit with the jimjams. His extremities trembled worse than they had in detox. His thoughts were muddled, but sleep wouldn't come.

He couldn't remember what he'd said to Vienne earlier tonight, and that only added to his anxiety. *Had he said anything that would incriminate him?*

The stab of guilt the question brought was worse than anything the broken ribs had dealt him. He didn't like keeping things from her, but neither did he want their friendship to be defined by something that no longer applied to him. Or did it? He didn't dare risk ever considering himself "cured."

Maybe she'd heard rumors around town, and she was simply more forgiving than he gave her credit for. But he doubted it. From everything they'd talked about, she was operating on the notion that he was still the nice, clean-cut, sober kid she'd known in high school. Had a crush on in high school.

He smiled at that. She must have been barely fourteen at the time, but still, to think that she'd found something in him that made her pine after him . . . it did a man's heart good. Maybe somewhere inside him there was still a trace of that untainted, genuinely nice kid he'd been.

Though he didn't really remember Vienne from those days, he could imagine her as a teenager. But he saw in her a bit of the same cynicism that had crept into his life. Where had they lost that innocence?

A sudden picture of the double funeral for Amy Ashlock and her little boy answered that question in a way that sent him crawling to the bathroom again.

※ ❀ ※

A drum pounded deep in the jungle and the sun's rays beat down on him in time to the primal rhythms. He ran, the hot breath of whatever was chasing him heavy on his neck. But no matter how many times he turned around, he couldn't see its face.

Jack sat up in bed, the dream as real as the pain that knifed at his rib cage. He raked a shaky hand through his hair. Sweat soaked the sheets, and the room had the faint odor of a sour dishrag. He tossed the tangled covers aside but sucked in a sharp breath when he tried to swing his legs over the side of the bed. His ribs felt like they were on fire.

He needed another pain pill, but his stomach was empty from all the throwing up he'd done last night. The drums started again. No. It was the door. Downstairs. Someone was knocking on the back door. Pounding.

He'd slept in his jeans, but now he pulled on a rumpled sweatshirt and picked his way down the back stairs as if they were a rocky mountain trail. Every step brought a new stab of pain.

He opened the door to find Vienne standing on his stoop. A worried look scarred her pretty face.

She frowned at him. "Are you okay? I've been knocking for five minutes."

"I'm sorry. The pain pills must have knocked me out." He rubbed the space between his eyes and leaned on the doorjamb, willing the world to stop spinning. Whatever was in those pills, he didn't like it. The side effects reminded him too much of a part of his life he'd just as soon forget. "Well, don't stand out in the cold. Come on in." He motioned for Vienne to follow him.

She stepped into the workroom, then held out a paper cup with a spouted lid. "I brought you something hot."

He took it, almost gagging at the thought of a swig of coffee.

She must have read his expression. "It's safe. It's hot chocolate."

Her smile centered him. He took a grateful sip. It warmed him and, surprisingly, didn't threaten to make his stomach revolt.

"It's peppermint mocha. It's kind of an ad hoc concoction, but peppermint is supposed to settle your stomach."

"Thanks." He cast about the room. He didn't dare take her up to his smelly, cluttered apartment. Instead, he led her through the workroom to the front gallery. At least there was a small table and chairs where they could sit.

"Don't you want something to drink?"

She gave a thin groan. "I'm about to float away. I've been practicing with all the different drinks this whole week. I'm up to here with caffeine." She drew a line on her forehead. "I'm no doubt a bona fide addict by now."

He took a sip of the hot cocoa in lieu of a response. Sometimes it almost seemed like she was goading him with her choice of words. How much did she know about his life? How much did he *want* her to know?

She chattered on as though nothing was amiss. "Everything's turning out really good, if I dare say so myself—the drinks, I mean."

"So you're ready?"

"For the opening?"

He nodded.

"Ready as I'll ever be. I've got all the food deliveries set up. And the shop is ready—except for the sign, of course. But I can open without that if I have to." A sheepish expression shadowed her face. "How are you feeling this morning?"

He hadn't been up long enough to take a real assessment. But now he shifted in his chair, pressing the flat of his hand against his ribs for support. "I definitely know I have ribs."

Her smile held sympathy. "I'm sorry."

"That's enough." He reached to put a hand over hers. The warmth of her skin surprised him. "No more apologies from you. It wasn't your fault."

She opened her mouth, looking like she was going to protest but apparently thought better of it. She panned the gallery, and he could almost see her mind scrambling for yet another way to change the topic. Her gaze landed on a wall where he'd hung a few of his later paintings. "Is that your work?"

He reined in a smile. "Depends on whether you like them or not."

She jumped up and went to inspect the paintings. "They're interesting."

"Uh-oh."

She pivoted to face him. "What?"

"*Interesting* is usually a code word for *yuck.*"

"Oh, no. Not at all. I like them. Especially this one." She moved to the landscape hanging near the window.

The morning sun presented the piece at its best, making the oranges and pinks almost glow. Once in a great while he felt he was seeing his work objectively. He had such a moment now. And it made him like Vienne Kenney all the more. "That's a favorite of mine, too."

"I can see why." She took three steps back and studied the painting, tipping her head at various angles, just the way he did when he painted. "You have other art to hang?"

He took another sip of the minty cocoa. "I'm slowly getting things unwrapped. But I need to frame quite a bit of it still."

"Well, if you're serious about doing this grand opening together, you'd better hustle."

He gave a sharp salute, but quickly clutched his elbows to his side. "Oh! Ouch!"

"Do you need another pain pill? Do you want me to go get them?"

He pushed his chair back, forcing a stoic expression. "I've got it. Thanks."

Upstairs, he brushed his teeth and downed a pill. He splashed water on his face and dampened his hair, trying with minimal success to get it to lie flat. Vienne had already seen him at his worst, but she didn't need to think he was always such a slob. He hurried back downstairs, afraid he'd find her gone.

He didn't want her to leave. Her presence brightened up the place in a way no amount of sunshine had ever done.

She did a double take when he sat down across from her at the table again. "Wow, you look worlds better. Those must be some amazing pills they gave you."

"It's all in the hair." He brushed a hand over his still-damp head.

She touched her ponytail. "Then I'm hosed."

"No. You look good." He hadn't really meant to say that out loud, but now that it was out, he didn't necessarily regret it.

"Oh, please."

"Okay. You look like something the cat dragged in."

"Well, now . . . hang on a minute. You don't need to go overboard."

"See there, you should have taken 'good' while I was offering it."

"Okay, okay, I take it back." She grinned.

For a minute he almost forgot how bad his ribs hurt.

What were they
talking about? What
history did they think
was repeating itself?

Chapter Fifteen

"Venti skinny mochaccino, double shot, to go!" Evan bellowed the order over his shoulder.

Vienne pumped chocolate syrup into a to-go cup and poured in two shots of rich, fragrant espresso. "I'm right here, Evan. You don't have to yell."

She was three coffee orders behind, they were already out of biscotti, and the queue was out the door and halfway down the block. She never should have put that coupon in the *Courier*. Thank goodness Evan and Allison had been willing to skip morning classes to be here on opening day.

"Hey, Vinny!" Pete Truesdell squeezed between two gray-haired women in line and leaned the grimy elbows of his coveralls on the glass refrigerated case that held pastries.

"Hi, Pete. I thought you were going to

be my first customer." *Maybe that way you'd be gone by now instead of messing up my shop and scaring off legitimate customers!* She chided herself for the thought even as she plotted ways to ban Pete from the premises. In spite of the tantalizing aromas of fresh coffee and scones, she could almost smell the feedlot Pete had no doubt dragged in on his boots.

"All I want is a cup of coffee. I can pour it myself if you'll show me where the pot is."

Mom had always had a self-serve Bunn on the counter—regular and decaf, side by side. She'd probably lost a fortune on the deal, since payment was on the honor system. But she'd always said it beat paying another server's salary.

Vienne made a shooing motion with her free hand. "Sorry, Pete. You'll have to wait your turn and order at the counter." She put a lid on a grande café latte and called out the order, hoping he'd take a hint and quit butting in line.

"I don't see plain ol' coffee on that there fancy list of yours." He pointed to the blackboard where Jack had penned the beverage menu.

The board was a work of art. Jack had chalked a jaunty Bauhaus-inspired coffee mug in one corner of the blackboard, with the drinks and prices lined up below. She made a mental note to find some kind of fixative that would set the chalk—and the memories of the fun night she and Jack had spent together making posters and putting the finishing touches on the place. "Don't worry, Pete. We have plain ol' coffee. Just tell Evan that's what you want . . . when it's your turn."

She craned her neck and scanned the queue. Another group of women squeezed through the door, craning their necks for a place to sit. This was worse than rush hour on the 80 back in Davis.

She thought Jack would be here by now. But he had plenty to do before his gallery opened. They were still exploring the idea of having some sort of grand opening celebration together in a few weeks.

Allison nudged in beside Vienne, her back to the counter. "Do you know if we have any more bagels in the back," she whispered.

"Why? Are we out up here?"

"There's no more blueberry or cinnamon raisin."

Vienne resisted the urge to curse. She'd ordered twice what she thought she might sell. Just in case. The vendor must have shorted her a dozen bagels this morning, but it was too late now. They wouldn't make another delivery from Salina today. "Can you talk people into trying the cranberry walnut instead? Or the Valentine cookies? Good grief, I don't want to have three dozen of those left over tomorrow. Don't people know this is a holiday?"

"Something's burning!" Evan yelled over his shoulder. "Next, please. What can I get you?"

An acrid scent wafted under Vienne's nose. She sniffed the air and whirled around. "Allison? Do you have something in the toaster?"

The girl squealed and ran to the toaster on the other side of the espresso machine. "These stupid bagels are too fat. They keep getting stuck in the toaster."

No wonder they were out of bagels. Vienne pretended to be intent on the caramel macchiato she was making. Allison would have to deal with the mess herself.

"Excuse me? Vienne?" Frank Marren stood, in full uniform, a few feet behind the woman placing her order.

"Yes?"

Officer Marren took off his cap and fiddled with the rim. "We're going to have to ask you to move the line inside the café. We've got some other merchants complaining that your customers are blocking their doorways."

"But there's no place for them to stand in here." If one more person moved inside, they'd have to start stacking people on top of each other.

"Then I'm afraid I'll have to ask the crowd to disperse."

"The sidewalk is public property, isn't it?" She looked over the top of the café curtains, where she could see a row of heads bobbing beyond the plateglass window. "No one seems to be disturbing the peace."

Marren shifted from one foot to the other and fitted his hat back on his balding head. "I'm sorry, but we have to keep the sidewalks clear for pedestrian traffic."

"Where do you propose we move the line?" Vienne tamped a basket of fresh espresso grounds and blew out a sigh that peppered the counter with the fine black grind. "Allison, toss me that bar rag, would you?"

"I don't care where you move it as long as your customers are not blocking access to the other shops."

She was tempted to tell Marren he could just move the people for her, but a police presence on her opening day probably wasn't the best way to garner business. She turned the frother on and spoke without bothering to meet the policeman's eye. "Okay. Thanks. We'll take care of it."

"I'll count on that." Marren hung back, obviously waiting to see if she was going to obey him.

Vienne finished the coffee drink she was making, then wove her way through the crowd to the front door. "Excuse me, people . . ."

The clusters of people went on talking as though she were invisible. She stepped outside and raised her voice. "Good morning, everyone. Excuse me . . ."

She felt a tap on her shoulder and pivoted to face Jack.

"Not bad for your first day."

She leaned close, lowering her voice. "Except for the fact that the police want me to send everybody away."

"What?"

She told him what Frank Marren had ordered.

"Why don't you just move the line to the alley? Let people come through the back door. The line can form down the hallway."

"You brilliant man! But how do we get them there?"

"You go make coffees as fast as you can. I'll take care of things out here."

She frowned at him. "How are you doing? Should you be up and around?"

"I'm okay." He picked up the tented signboard announcing her opening. He was obviously moving slower than normal.

"You're sure?"

He propped the sign in front of the door and shooed her back inside. "Go . . . go on."

Within minutes there were no more heads bobbing above the café curtains and a neat line snaked from the front counter down the hallway. It made it a tight squeeze through to the restrooms, but at least Frank Marren would be happy.

She heard Jack talking to someone in line, and the next thing she knew, he was beside her with his sleeves rolled up. "What can I do?"

"Oh, bless you. Would you mind clearing off some of the tables and"—she lowered her voice—"see if you can persuade people to clear out of here and make room for the rest of the town?"

"You're not complaining, I hope." He rolled his eyes. "I should have such an opening for the gallery."

"Hey, just put a coupon in the paper for a buy-one-get-one-free painting and you got it."

She handed him a plastic tub from under the counter. "Happy Valentine's Day, by the way."

His mouth opened, then closed. "Oh. Same to you. I forgot that was today." The ornery twinkle in his eyes said otherwise.

Vienne played along, pointing to the menu board he'd decorated for the occasion. "Those pink girly-girl hearts weren't just for looks, you know."

He laughed and went to clear off tables—each with a group clustering around, waiting for him to finish. They wouldn't always be this busy, but what she wouldn't give for the full seating capacity of Mom's café about now.

She made coffees one after another while Evan kept the orders coming and Allison doled out food. By eleven o'clock things finally began to slow down. Vienne headed back to the restrooms to freshen up before the lunch rush started. The door to the ladies' room was locked, so she leaned against the wall to wait, glad for a moment to catch her breath.

Numerous pockets of conversations buzzed from the dining room, the pleasant white noise of success. But when she heard Jack's name whispered at a table near the hallway, her ears filtered out the rest and she perked up to listen.

". . . probably three sheets to the wind, if history is any clue."

Vienne recognized Clara Berger's strident alto and pressed against the wall, sliding a step closer to the dining room.

"Do you really think so, Clara?"

"Broke a couple ribs in the fall is what I heard. Someday he won't be so lucky."

"I wonder why he came back," a shaky feminine voice said. "You'd think he'd want to get as far away from here as possible after that mess with the Ashlock boy's wife and that poor little boy."

Vienne quit breathing.

"Supposedly he plans to reopen the gallery." Vienne didn't recognize the third voice.

"I'll believe that when I see it." Clara's voice dropped to a whisper, and Vienne strained to catch her words. "I hear he's been keeping company with Ingrid's daughter."

"I wondered if there was something to that rumor when I saw him bussing tables this morning," the shaky voice said.

"You'd think she'd have learned a lesson from her mother."

Learned a lesson from her mother . . . ? Vienne held her breath.

"Poor girl." The third woman cooed her sympathy. "I hope history isn't doomed to repeat itself."

What were they talking about? What history did they think was repeating itself? A shadow of memory fell across Vienne, and beads of sweat broke out on her forehead. Her breaths came shallow. For as long as she could remember, Clara Berger had been the queen of gossip in Clayburn.

But Vienne had heard this morsel of gossip somewhere else. That day in the street after Jack had fallen, Erma from the antique store had wondered if Jack had been drinking. Vienne had dismissed it. She knew Jack's reputation from the time they were teens. And he'd given her no reason to think he'd changed. She'd forgotten about the comment in the chaos that followed.

But now it troubled her. And Clara's dining companions today weren't disputing her. Their implications chilled Vienne to her very soul.

Three sheets to the wind . . .

"Hey, you." Jack appeared around the corner, jump-starting Vienne's heart. "Don't tell me you're hiding out back here while I work my tail off? I don't think so."

She couldn't muster the snappy comeback she knew he expected. In fact, she couldn't seem to find her voice at all.

"Vienne? You okay? You look a little green around the gills."

She turned away, unable to look him in the eye. "I'm okay."

The door to the ladies' room opened, and a young mom with two toddlers in tow emerged. Vienne caught the door before it could close and made a clumsy escape.

She punched in the lock and barricaded the door with her body, a cyclone of confusion churning in her brain.

How could Mom still love him after everything he'd put them through?

Chapter Sixteen

Jack knocked on the restroom door again. Vienne had been in there for almost twenty minutes, and he was beginning to think she'd passed out or something.

He pounded again, louder, not caring what the customers in the dining room might think. "Vienne? Vienne, are you okay?"

"I'm fine." Her voice sounded weak. "You can leave now."

What was that supposed to mean? "You've got coffee orders, and Allison doesn't know how to make some of them."

"I'll be out in a minute."

"Okay . . ." He heard the muffled sound of water running.

He went back to the dining room and explained to the waiting customers that it would be just a few minutes before their coffee was ready. He wiped off a couple of tables, keeping one eye on the hallway to the restrooms.

He needed to get out of here. His ribs were killing him, and he was due for a pain pill. He didn't know what was wrong with Vienne, and he wasn't in a very good frame of mind to try to figure it out either.

He threw the bar rag in the sink behind the counter and spoke quietly to Allison. "Vienne will be out in a minute."

"Thanks." Allison's fresh-faced smile glinted before she turned back to the espresso machine to pore over a page of directions.

"I'm heading out now. You guys can handle it from here, right?"

"Where'd Vienne go?" Evan looked around, then checked his watch. "I have to head to class in about an hour."

Jack cocked his head toward the back. "She'll be out in a minute. I think she just needed a break. Pretty good opening day, huh?"

"Crazy, if you ask me," Evan said.

He nodded his agreement. "Tell Vienne I'll come back and help in the morning if it looks like things are this busy again."

"Will do." Evan waved.

Reluctantly Jack left. He crossed the street, head down. Something was bothering Vienne. He'd never seen this side of her, but it worried him. What would make her lock herself in the bathroom while two college kids tried to keep the place afloat? He hoped she wasn't ill.

He let himself in through the gallery door. The electronic chime reverberated in his ears, its tone strident rather than the usual welcoming *ping ping.* He went upstairs to take a pain pill and change into sweats. He felt bad for leaving the coffee shop, but it wasn't like there was anything he could do. Vienne didn't seem to want to talk to him, and he didn't have the first clue about the coffee machine.

He sighed and glanced at the clock. He hadn't planned to waste half the day at the coffee shop. But he still had time to get a couple more paintings framed and hung if he got right to it. The gallery was shaping up, and he was actually starting to get excited about opening it again.

Not to mention that he needed to generate some income in a hurry. Maybe he should reconsider Wren's offer to move in at the inn . . . rent out his apartment for a while. He tried to push the image of his last credit card statement out of his mind. Worry never paid any bills.

The bottle of blue-speckled pills sat on the counter in the bathroom where he'd left it this morning. His bruises had faded, and his broken ribs were healing. His pain wasn't nearly as acute now. Of course, he'd dulled it with constant medication for a week. But he remembered the pain too well to try it without the pills just yet. A few qualms had nagged at him this morning when he'd swallowed the first pill of the day—and qualms of a different sort when he'd realized there were only seven pills left.

He picked up the bottle and stared, unseeing, at the label. The doctor had warned him this prescription could be addictive. He'd been apprehensive when he heard that in the emergency room, but his pain had been great enough then he'd felt the pills were justified.

He rubbed his rib cage. It was wise to be wary. But he needed to take care of this pain, too. Before he could change his mind, he spilled two tablets into his palm, popped them in his mouth, and washed them down with an icy gulp of water from the bathroom faucet.

※ ※ ※

The crowd finally thinned out around four o'clock. Allison was back from her afternoon class and washing a mountain of mugs and dessert plates behind the counter.

Vienne walked through the dining room picking up stray cups and napkins, stealing glances across the street at the gallery. She wished she'd just told Jack what she'd heard those women say so he could put her mind at ease. It was probably nothing. Maybe it wasn't even Jack they were talking about.

But flotsam from the overheard conversation floated back to her.

Broke a couple of ribs in the fall . . .

You'd think she'd have learned a lesson from her mother . . .

They were talking about Jack, all right. And her. And it could only mean one thing. They thought Jack was a drunk.

Like her father.

Why would they think that?

The Jack she remembered from when they were kids was an all-around good guy. The Jack she'd gotten to know recently seemed like a mature version of the same person. A little quieter than she remembered, but nice as they came. Back when she'd had a crush on him, she remembered finding out that Jackson was adopted. It had only added to the mystique of the older boy. In her girlish fantasies she'd sometimes wondered what it would be like to be adopted, to not know who your real parents were. Some days she would have given up knowing Mom to have any father besides Harlan Kenney. The old guilt pressed in, and she shook off its weight.

She couldn't remember all the details, but while Jack was still in high school, he'd discovered that Wren Johannsen was his birth mother. She didn't know how it had affected him. Sometimes stuff like that changed people. Made them bitter. Or made them turn for comfort to places they had no business going. Didn't she know all about that?

A sinking feeling spread through her. Could there be some truth in what Clara and her friends said about Jack? What Erma had implied? It seemed too much to be a coincidence.

"Lord, please don't let it be true. Please . . ."

The thought—the *prayer*—startled her. Mom had always been a big believer in talking to God, and Vienne had done her share of it when she was younger. But where had it ever gotten her? Or her mother, for that matter? In spite of Mom's desperate prayers to the contrary, Harlan Kenney had remained a hopeless, helpless drunk until the day he died.

A memory wrapped itself around her thoughts before she could slough it off. Christmas Eve day, the morning after her father's drunken appearance at the Christmas pageant. Her father had brought home a scrawny Christmas tree—his idea of a peace offering, no doubt—and set it up in the living room.

Mom tried to get her to come out and help decorate the pathetic thing, but Vienne moped in her room, still feeling the sting of humiliation. She had a New Kids on the Block CD playing in a ratty boom box Mom had picked up at a garage sale. She was hoping for a new one for Christmas, yet knew at the same time it would never happen.

"Vinny?" Her dad's voice at the door made her turn down the volume. "Vinny, can I come in?"

She grunted in reply.

He opened the door slowly and leaned against the doorframe. "Vinny . . . about last night . . ."

She scooted back on the bed, reached for her pillow, and hugged it to her, drawing her knees up to her chest. The headboard cut into her back, but she didn't move.

He stared at the shabby carpet on her floor. "I'm sorry, Vinny. I didn't want to miss your show for anything."

She squeezed the pillow tighter. There was nothing he could say that would make things right.

He squatted down on his haunches in front of her door. "I saw you up there . . . on the stage. You looked like an angel." He chuckled softly. "Well, you were supposed to *be* an angel . . . I know that." He looked her in the eye in a way he never had before.

She couldn't turn away.

"Listen, Vinny." He put his head in his hands before he looked up at her again. "Things are gonna be different around here from now on. I mean it this time. You'll see. I'm gonna do right by you and your mom. All that other . . ." He glanced away for a second. But then he reached out and touched her foot, held her gaze. "I'm done with all that, baby. That's all in the past now."

Something in his voice made her believe him.

The next morning—Christmas morning—she woke to the sound of her father singing Christmas carols in the living room. But by the third slurred verse of "Hark the Herald"—accompanied by Mom's hushed, pleading cries—she knew she'd been a fool to ever believe things could be different.

She couldn't remember ever seeing him sober again. He crashed his car a year later, on New Year's Eve. At forty-seven.

It startled her to think of that now. *Forty-seven.* That seemed so young to her now. Mom was five years older. Still, fifty-two was too young to be left a widow with a daughter to raise. Yet Vienne shuddered to think what her life—and especially Mom's—would be like had the man not died when he did. As tough as things had been, their life had *improved* with Harlan Kenney's death.

She still wrestled with guilt over the relief she'd felt getting the news . . . no, not relief. It had been *joy.* A tremor rippled down her spine. What kind of sick person felt joy at hearing her father was dead?

She went to the cash register and counted the day's take. The stack of free coffee coupons was twice as high as the stack of cash. But it would all be cash tomorrow. She hoped.

Counting the bills brought back memories of her and Mom counting the café's drawer each night. They'd struggled to make it after her father's death. It had been a long time before the insurance settlement came through, and cash had been scarce. Mom had worked harder than any woman deserved, just to scrape by. Even so, life had been better without him. It was a harsh thought, but if she couldn't be honest with herself . . .

She tucked the bills into the bank bag and started stacking quarters to roll.

All these years Mom had kept a photograph of Harlan Kenney on the dressing table in her room at home. It was the last picture taken of him before he died, a blurry blown-up snapshot. He was smiling at the camera. But he looked like an old man—his skin sallow and lined, his eyes sunken.

The last time she'd cleaned the house, Vienne had laid the framed photograph on its face. She couldn't stand to look at it. Could barely stand the thought of having that man's image in the same house with her. She knew if Mom could have made her wishes known, she would want the photo on her dresser at the Manor. But Vienne couldn't bear to have to look at it every time she visited.

How could Mom still love him after everything he'd put them through?

She went to the window again, squinting against the afternoon sun, trying to see if there were lights on in the gallery. She ought to talk to Jack. She'd acted like a child, hiding out in the bathroom like that. He probably thought she was a nutcase.

They'd spent hours together since that day he'd come to her back door looking for his UPS delivery. She and Jack had become friends. She dared to hope they were on their way to becoming more. And she didn't think she'd missed the signals that Jack felt the same way about her. But if what those women had implied was true . . .

She didn't let herself form the thought into syllables.

Something snapped inside her. She yanked the string of her apron and lopped it over the counter. "Allison, can you hold down the fort here for a little while?"

The girl gave her a strange look and shrugged. "Sure."

"I'll be back to close for sure." She thought about telling Allison that she would keep an eye on the street to see if they got busy, but she didn't want to admit where she was going. Why, she wasn't sure.

She grabbed her coat off the hook on the way out the back door. A cold wind hit her in the face, and she hurried to her car. She drove around behind Linder's Gallery and parked in the alley.

Jack answered her insistent pounding with a quizzical half-smile. "Don't tell me," he said. "You're swamped, and you need a bus boy again."

She didn't wait to be invited in. "We need to talk."

"Okaaaay." He dragged out the word.

She swept past him and paced the workroom, wondering how to get this conversation started.

Jack pulled two stools from under a worktable and offered her one. "Did I do something . . . wrong? What's the matter?"

She parked herself on the stool and blew out a breath. "This may be nothing, but . . . I've got to ask." She held up her hands, surprised to realize they were trembling.

"Are you okay?" Gentle concern knit his brow.

She despised what she was about to accuse him of, despised even more what she was afraid his response would be. "I . . . I overheard a conversation at the coffee shop this morning. I need to know if it's true."

His eyes took on a wary light, and she could see the path of his tongue as it traced the inside of his cheek. "If what's true?" he finally said.

She shifted on the stool, sliding away from him. "It's stupid, really. It was a bunch of little old ladies. Clara Berger and her coffee klatch—you know them. They're all a bunch of gossips anyway. It's probably nothing." She tried to smile, but her mouth wouldn't cooperate.

She waited for him to say something, lighten the moment like he was so good at doing.

But he just sat there waiting, looking bored. Or angry. She couldn't tell.

"They said you were . . . drunk . . . when you fell the other day."

There. She'd said it. She waited for his reaction—for that smile she loved to light his eyes, telling her she was being foolish. She wanted to see anything but the seriousness that darkened his expression now.

For a long minute he said nothing, then his eyes narrowed. "Is that what you think?" His voice was barely above a whisper. His words were textbook evasion.

Why wasn't he denying it? *Please deny it, Jack.*

She pushed him. "Will you please answer the question?"

"Oh, sorry, Your Honor. I didn't realize you'd asked a question. Not a direct one anyway. In fact, it sounded like an indictment to me." He didn't smile when he said it.

She exhaled. "I don't mean—"

"I'll answer your accusation, Vienne." He rose, picked up his stool, and slid it between them, his eyes flashing. "I was not drunk when I fell off your balcony. There. Are you happy?"

Somehow his denial didn't provide the relief she'd hoped for. "It's not about me being happy."

"Then what *is* it about?" Anger simmered behind his words.

Anger that masked guilt? She'd studied nonverbal communication and diversion tactics in law school, and he was providing her with a mountain of empirical evidence of his guilt.

"Well . . ." Her voice faltered and she trembled inside, afraid of where this line of questioning would lead. "Why would they say that?"

He braced his hands on the rounded sides of the stool and stared at the floor for a long time.

"Jack?" she whispered.

Finally he raised his head and met her gaze. "Those women are gossips, Vienne. They get a charge out of believing the worst of people because . . . I don't know why. Because it makes for a more interesting story, maybe. Or it makes their own faults look mild by comparison." He studied her, as though trying to decide whether to continue.

She waited, and watched.

His stare didn't waver. "Vienne, I'm not going to stand here and tell you those women had no basis whatsoever for the things they said. I wasn't drunk . . ." He blew out a breath. "The truth is, I haven't had a drink—not one drop—in almost ten months. But . . . I've struggled with it. I'll admit that."

An alarm went off in her head. It clanged so loud she could barely hear his voice. But his next words seeped through the din of warning bells, in spite of her determination to blank them out.

"I've struggled with drinking, with alcohol, for a long time." His shoulders hunched forward, as if an invisible weight bore down on him. He didn't meet her eyes. "Something happened. Maybe you already know. Trevor's wife . . . and his little boy . . ." The muscles in his jaw tensed, and his voice broke. "They died in . . . an accident. I hit their car out on Old 40." He jerked his head in the direction of the highway.

It was Trevor's wife who was killed in that accident? His son? What was Jack trying to say?

"For a long time I wished it was me who'd died that day. I'd have traded places with them if I could. I still would. But that's not the way it works. And every day I live with the regret of what I did."

What he *did*? She watched him—his head bowed, jaw tensing. She knew Jack had been involved in a fatal accident, but she didn't know it was Trevor's family who'd been killed. So *that's* what Clara and her friends had been talking about?

Then it hit her. Her breath caught at the base of her throat. She tried to keep her jaw from gaping, tried to swallow against the cotton wad her throat had become. He'd been driving drunk! He'd killed two people driving drunk.

Her heart sank like a stone to the pit of her stomach as the terrible truth obliterated any fragile hope that had remained.

What a fool she was. She slid off the stool, praying her legs would hold her. Blind with shock and anger, she plodded to the door. His footsteps sounded behind her on the wood floor.

"Vienne! Stop. Please let me explain."

The door wouldn't open. She fumbled with the old-fashioned knob.

He reached past her and braced his hand on the door. "Don't walk out on me."

Don't walk out on me. She froze. He was close enough for her to feel his breath on her neck. How many times had she heard her father beg Mom not to walk out on him? And how many times had Mom complied, turned around, and fallen into Harlan Kenney's arms, even though she knew nothing would change, even though she *knew* he'd be drunk again tomorrow morning? And the morning after that?

She would not make the same mistake. She rattled the doorknob. It finally turned in her grip.

Jack touched her shoulder, then slid his hand down her arm. His fingers closed around her upper arm. Something gave way inside her and Vienne closed her eyes, paralyzed by his touch.

So many nights she'd lain awake in the lonely silence of Mom's house, replaying conversations and laughter shared with this man, dreaming of the day when he might touch her in a way that went beyond friendship. In a way that meant she had become as special to him as he was to her.

She swallowed against the wake of those memories, seeing now how shallow they'd been. "Please let go of me."

Slowly he complied.

She pushed the door closed again, pressed her forehead against the cool wood. She would listen. She would hear what he had to say. For now.

Because after today she didn't intend to ever speak to him again.

Vienne wasn't weak
like her mother.
And tears had lost
the power to move
her long ago.

Chapter Seventeen

ienne . . . don't leave without hearing me out." Jack put a hand on her shoulder again, his touch tentative.

She ducked out of his reach and whirled to face him. "How dare you *order* me!"

He took two steps back, his eyes registering shock. "I'm not ordering you. I'm asking. Please." His voice became a whisper.

She shuffled backward and pressed her spine against the door. "Say what you have to say." She fought the urge to plug her ears with her fingers and sing at the top of her lungs. The way she'd done when she was a little girl—to shut out their voices, *his* voice.

"The drinking . . . *my* drinking . . . got out of control." His breaths came heavy. "At first I was in denial, but finally I knew I couldn't handle it myself. So I got help."

Shut up! Shut up! She didn't want to

hear this. She'd heard it all before. A thousand times. And it never changed one thing.

"Vienne, I'm sorry. I guess I figured you already knew all this. This is a small town. It's never been any secret, and I never intended to keep it from you. " His focus shifted, then came back to rest on her. He shook his head. "That's not entirely true. I'd figured you'd heard, but . . . if you hadn't, I didn't want to be the one to tell you. I didn't want to have to see the man I used to be reflected in your eyes. But that's not who I am anymore, Vienne. That's all in the past now."

Liar! The word echoed through her head, despite the softness in his eyes, the earnestness in his expression. *Liar!* He'd deceived her. Nothing he could say would ever change her mind.

"Please. Come and sit down. I'll tell you everything, and then . . . then you can decide."

She couldn't look at him. She'd *already* decided. But she would be fair. She would allow him his day in court.

"Let's go to the gallery. It's warmer in there. I can make you some tea."

Her face felt like marble. "I don't need anything." *Except the truth.* She followed him through the door that separated the two rooms.

Jack pulled out a chair for her and one for himself. He straddled it, drew in a deep breath, and exhaled with a force that riffled a stack of newspapers lying on the table. "Where to start?" He gave a nervous, humorless laugh.

Silence hung between them. She knew he was waiting for her response.

She scooted as far back in the chair as possible, crossed her arms over her breasts, and pressed her lips into a tight line. She would listen, but she had no intention of making this easy for him.

"I guess I'll start with the worst of it and . . . go back from there." He clasped, then unclasped his hands. "I spent nine months in rehab last year. It was my decision to go, but I didn't have much choice. Not really. My . . . my drinking was starting to affect everything in my life. My mom—and Wren . . ." He looked up, a sudden question in his eyes. "You did know that Wren Johannsen is my mother . . . my birth mother?"

She nodded. She'd never really known Twila Linder, Jack's adoptive mother, but it had never been a secret that Jack was adopted. She remembered the story that had appeared in the *Courier* when she was in the eighth grade. Jack had searched for his birth mother and discovered she'd been living right here in Clayburn all along. Back then, she had only known Wren as the short, round lady who ran the inn a few doors down from what was now Jack's gallery.

Wren had made a point of stopping by the café a few weeks ago to welcome Vienne back to town. Apparently she and her husband had recently done some work on the inn, and Wren commiserated with her about the mess of remodeling the café and how long everything was taking.

Vienne had grown to respect the older woman, though she hadn't initiated any contact with her, for fear Jack might think she was chasing him via his mother. How odd that sounded in retrospect. She would be avoiding Wren Johannsen for a different reason now.

Jack cleared his throat. "Anyway, Wren and Mom finally talked me into getting help. I . . . I just couldn't handle what happened to Amy and Trev. What I'd done . . . I still don't understand why it happened." He bit his lip and looked at the floor.

Her last shard of sympathy shattered. "You don't understand why it happened? What part of driving drunk don't you understand? What I don't get"—the words would hardly come—"is why you weren't convicted."

His head came up, surprise—and hurt—in his eyes. "No. No . . . you have it all wrong. It was an accident, Vienne. I never saw the car. The sun was in my eyes. They said Amy was going over the speed limit, but still . . . I felt responsible."

She stared at him, disbelieving. "You *felt* responsible?"

Did he have no conscience, even now? Nausea overcame her. She pushed her chair back, stumbling to her feet. Jack was just like her father. Nothing had ever been Harlan Kenney's fault either.

"You *were* responsible!" she spat.

He reeled as if she'd struck him. "Vienne . . ."

"Do you not understand that if you're driving drunk, you *are* responsible?" She hissed a curse, but it only made her feel like she'd sunk to his level.

In one motion Jack rose, turned his chair around, shoved it under the table. "I wasn't drunk." His voice was leaden with disbelief. He raked his fingers through his hair. "Is that what you think? That I killed Amy and Trev driving drunk? Is that what people in this town are saying?"

He doubled over as if he were in pain. For a minute she thought he might collapse right there on the floor of the gallery. She didn't know how to respond. Was he in denial, or was he telling the truth?

"Can you look me in the eye and tell me you weren't drinking that night?"

He straightened and looked at her. His eyes blazed. "I told you I wasn't."

She didn't flinch. "No. What you said is that you weren't drunk. I don't know if that means you didn't think you'd had enough to be drunk or that you weren't drinking at all."

His jaw tensed. "Where is this coming from, Vienne? What happened? Who have you been talking to, to make you distrust me all of a sudden?"

She could not believe what she was hearing. It was as though Jackson Linder had been present at her house all those nights of her childhood. He was spouting lines from the same script her father had read from every night of his sorry life.

"Why are you doing this, Vienne? Are you going to hold my past against me? An accident?"

"Just tell me one thing. And tell me the truth. When's the last time you went to a liquor store?"

His startled look told her everything. He was guilty as sin.

"Did someone tell you?" He spoke in a monotone, but his face was wet. Whether with tears or with the sweat of anger, she couldn't tell. Nor did she care.

Every time her father had come home sloppy drunk, he'd cry like a baby, knowing it would win him back into Mom's good graces. And she fell for it every time. But Vienne wasn't weak like her mother.

And tears had lost the power to move her long ago.

He'd done everything possible to prove he'd made a fresh start. Couldn't she see that? Couldn't anyone in this stupid town see that he'd changed?

Chapter Eighteen

Vienne stomped through the gallery to the workroom. The back door slammed, and Jack flinched as if she'd slapped him. He'd trusted her. Thought they'd become friends. And hoped for more than that.

He slumped into the chair she'd vacated and rested his head in his hands. That she could have such hatred for him felt like a betrayal. Even if what she'd accused him of were true, how could she be so cruel to throw it in his face after all this time? He'd done everything possible to prove he'd made a fresh start. Couldn't she see that? Couldn't anyone in this stupid town see that he'd changed?

He slammed a fist down on the worktable.

Immediately Jack remembered something he'd learned in rehab. Even now he could still hear the sorrow in the baritone voice of his favorite counselor, Dr. Jim

Boyer. "Jack, I can promise you without reservation that God will forgive every thoughtless act you ever committed while you were drunk. I wish I could promise that the people you love will do the same. I can't do that. Some people will never think of you as anything but the drunk you were when you hurt them. Right or wrong, it's a truth you need to face before you walk out through these doors and try to get back to living your life."

Jack had wondered at the shadows of pain etched so keenly on this gentle man's face. He learned later, from another "inmate," that Dr. Boyer had been a medical doctor, but he'd lost his practice—and his wife—when a young girl died under the shaky, drunken scalpel he'd wielded during a routine tonsillectomy.

"Even though God can give us a clean slate," Dr. Boyer had continued, "there are consequences this side of heaven. There's not a thing you can do but go on trying to prove them wrong. Not one thing."

Jack ached for the man, even before he'd learned the truth behind those sunken eyes.

He half expected people like Clara Berger to hold his past against him. But he hadn't expected it of Vienne. Not her.

He pushed up from the table and kicked the chair behind him. Moving on instinct, he went back to the workroom and headed for the corner. Then he let out a low growl when he realized what he was after was no longer there. Why did his miserable flesh seem doomed to seek comfort in that familiar liquid ambrosia?

Smashing the flat of his palm against the wood-paneled wall, he pushed off and pivoted to take the stairs two at a time. Every step jarred his ribs until they burned, but he didn't care. He'd be feeling no pain soon enough.

The plastic bottle sat on the counter. He clutched it in his fist and pried off the childproof cap. There were five tablets left inside. He tapped three of them into his waiting palm.

❋ 🕷 ❋

Something made Wren turn off the water and lift her hands from the soapy water, stilling to listen. She thought she'd heard the door to the lobby open. She cocked her ear toward the door. There it was again. Someone had come in.

She dried her hands on her apron and started out through the dining room. A muffled crash from the lobby stopped her in her tracks. "Who's there? Bart? Is that you? Is everything okay?" She crept forward a few steps and stuck her head through the archway to the lobby.

Jack stood there, looking at the floor behind him.

"Jack? What happened?" She peered around him to see the wrought-iron plant stand by the door toppled over. The blue-and-white porcelain pot that held an African violet she'd babied all winter was in half a dozen pieces on the floor. "What happened?" she said again.

"Did I do that?" He knelt and scraped the dirt into a pile, nestling the fragile violet in the center. "I'm sorry."

Wren's heart sank to the pit of her stomach. That slur in Jack's voice was all too familiar. She made her voice hard. "What do you need?"

He handed her two shards from the pot and bent to pick up the rest. "I just wanted to talk, Wren."

"What about, Jack?" She didn't care if he heard the wariness in her tone.

"I need to know something."

She glared at him. "Well, I need to know something, too. Are you drunk?"

Slowly he straightened, towering over her. He raised a hand, palm out, looking like a traffic cop in slow motion. "I swear to God."

His irreverent gibe told her all she needed to know. "You come back when you've sobered up." She turned and trudged back toward the kitchen.

His shout stopped her. "Wren! I'm not drunk. I . . . I might—" He came toward her with arms outstretched, looking like a little boy. "I think maybe I took . . . too many pain pills. For my ribs." He patted his side, wincing as if the spot was still tender. "I swear, Wren . . . I promise you, I haven't been drinking. I haven't had a drink since I got back. Not one."

If Jack was telling the truth, she was alarmed at the effect the pills were having on him. The slurred and halting speech was far too similar to the way he'd often appeared before he committed himself to rehab. But she decided to give him the benefit of the doubt. "How many pills did you take?"

"I'm not sure. Three I think."

"Are you in that much pain, Jack?"

His face fell. "Not the kind of pain you think."

"What do you mean? Jack?"

He slumped into a nearby chair and put his elbows on his knees, hanging his head. "Vienne doesn't want anything to do with me now."

Oh, dear. "Now? I don't understand." Wren knew Jack and the Kenney girl had become close over the past few weeks. She'd thought it was good for him. He'd been doing so well, and Vienne seemed to be a positive influence on him. But it was obvious he was hurting now. Had he fallen in love with her so soon?

"I told her . . . about the accident. About my drinking problem. She doesn't want anything to do with me."

Wren's heart raced as fury surged through her. How dare that girl hold Jack's past against him! He had tried so hard. He'd taken all the necessary steps to make things right. *Why, God?*

It broke her heart. She never had understood why the Lord had allowed her son to go through the tragedy of the fatal accident. One split second in time and Jack might be whole and well; Amy and Trev Ashlock might be living happily in their little house in the country. Wren stopped short, thinking of Meg, Trevor's new wife. The broken young woman she and Bart had taken in more than a year and a half ago glowed with confidence now. And Trevor was his old self again, obviously in love with his pretty bride. How could Wren wish that away?

No, there was a reason for the way things happened, and though she might never understand this side of heaven, she could not wish to change what had already happened. Especially when there were redemption stories like Meg's in the midst of tragedy.

But oh, when would it be Jack's turn? Her soul ached for her son. And she couldn't help but wonder if it was her own sin of long ago that had brought this present heartache on Jack. *Oh, Father, I'm so sorry.* But she felt an immediate chastening in her spirit. She'd said those words, sincerely, long ago, and many times since. She'd asked forgiveness and received it. There was no need to go back.

She went to Jack and put a soothing hand on his shoulder. "What happened?" She came around and sat down across from him in an overstuffed chair, one that was not designed with her short legs in mind.

"Vienne and I . . . we've gotten to be pretty good friends. But when I told her about . . . the accident, she accused me of being drunk when it happened."

Again, anger flared up in Wren, but she fought to keep her voice steady. "Why would she say that?" How dare that girl make such an accusation? As if Jack wasn't in enough anguish over what had happened.

"I don't know. Even when I explained, she didn't seem to believe me. Wren . . . is that what people in this town think? That I killed Amy and Trev driving drunk?"

"No! Of course not, Jack. Nobody thinks that. I think everyone knows that your . . . your struggle has been a *result* of the accident. Not something that caused it. Vienne should know better."

"She didn't really want to hear what I had to say."

"Well, I'm disappointed in her." It was an effort to keep her ire out of her voice. "You'd think she of all people would understand."

His brow furrowed. "What do you mean?"

"Maybe you don't remember . . . and maybe I shouldn't say anything . . ." She backpedaled for a brief moment, then decided Vienne didn't deserve confidentiality after the way she'd treated Jack. She bobbed her head. "Vienne's dad was an alcoholic."

Jack's face registered surprise. "She's never talked about him. Where is he now?"

"He was killed . . . in a car accident. Vienne was just a little girl when it happened. She and Ingrid really had a hard time of it."

"Was . . . was he drunk? When he died?"

A light went on for Wren. Bless Jack's heart, he'd understood immediately. "I don't know if anyone knows. But I don't remember seeing Harlan Kenney sober very often. It makes sense, doesn't it?"

He bit his lower lip and stared beyond her.

Wren reached to put a hand on his forehead. "How are you feeling?" She studied him. His day's growth of beard cast a shadow of the bad times, when Jack had been drunk every day. But she loved the clean line of his hair around his ears and neck, and the fact that he'd given up wearing that stupid earring. Her son was a handsome man.

She tipped his chin to peer into his hazel eyes. "You're sure you didn't take a dangerous dose of your pain medication? You're *positive* it was only three pills?"

Again, he nodded. "I just need to sleep for a while."

"Are you still in that much pain?" She thought of what he'd just told her about the pain Vienne had caused and regretted the way she'd phrased her question. "Are your ribs still giving you trouble?"

He rubbed his side absently. "They're getting better."

"Jack?" She put a hand on his knee and made her voice firm. "You're not getting . . . dependent on the pills, are you?"

He rubbed the space between his eyes. "I don't know. Maybe . . ."

"Oh, honey, don't blow all these months of sobriety. Talk to your doctor. Or your counselor, or whoever you need to talk to. Promise me?"

"I will."

She bored into his eyes with hers.

He put his large hand over hers. The contrast between her veined, frail fingers took her aback. Oh, that she could have saved him this terrible cross he bore.

But his voice was strong when he spoke. "I promise, Wren."

And she believed him.

He'd grown into a
handsome man with a
desperate flaw.
A fatal flaw.
The one thing she'd
sworn she would never
tolerate in a man.

Chapter Nineteen

Okay if I head out now?"

Vienne looked up from the espresso machine to see Evan standing at the end of the counter, apron in hand.

It was three o'clock, and a trio of young women with strollers in tow were the only customers left in the shop. They'd long ago finished their caramel lattes and were chatting and laughing by the fireplace.

"Sure, Evan. You go on. Thanks for coming in again."

"No problem."

The second day of business had been busy, but infinitely more manageable than yesterday—only because the free coffee coupon had expired, no doubt.

Vienne's eyes followed Evan out the front door and across the street to where his car was parked, but it was really just an excuse to watch for Jack.

A tiny part of her had hoped he would

just show up and start bussing tables this morning like nothing had happened. But every time she rehashed their conversation—and the harsh words they'd spoken—*she'd* spoken—she realized that things weren't going to be so easily mended. And why would she even want to mend things with him? This had to go down in history as her worst Valentine's Day ever. A pall of loneliness fell over her.

She thought about her old job at Brinkerman and wondered what her friends were doing right now. She glanced at the clock and adjusted for the time difference in her head. They were probably just finishing lunch at that new Thai place they all loved. They'd go buy white chocolate mice from the Candy House and bicycle back to work with sticky fingers. The memory made her smile—and long for warm weather so she could ride her bike again. But imagining herself in Davis with Jenny and their friends from the firm didn't ease the ache inside her. She stood on tiptoe and peered over the café curtains for the tenth time since lunch.

The truth was, she'd barely given California a thought since she'd left there. She'd been busy here, sure. With Mom's therapy and getting Latte-dah up and running, she'd barely had a spare minute to think. But she was thinking now. And she knew in her heart it wasn't Davis or California, or even Jenny and her other friends that she was lonely for.

It was the sweet artist across the street who'd somehow, in a few short weeks, managed to capture her heart all over again the way he had when he was a hunky high school lifeguard. And now it appeared he'd grown into a handsome man with a desperate flaw. A fatal flaw. The *one* thing she'd sworn she would never tolerate in a man.

She sighed and went to wipe off tables. Why did this have to happen? *Why, God?* Her question seemed to hang right above her, hovering just below the embossed tin ceiling high overhead. She, above all people, knew what life with an alcoholic was like. Images of her father floated like ghosts before her. Him, staggering into the middle-school gym at the end of a volleyball game, loud and belligerent, yelling her name when she was on the court, and shouting at the coach to put her in the game when she was on the bench. She'd wanted the hardwood to open up and swallow her that night.

The young women at the corner table got up to leave, tucking babies in strollers and gathering pacifiers and toys from the tables. By the name on the credit card the petite brunette had used, Vienne knew that she was Mike Jensen's wife. Vienne and Mike had been sweet on each other in sixth grade. Of course that hadn't lasted once Mike found out about Harlan Kenney.

She threw the bar rag down on the table. Every day it seemed another disappointment from her past slipped back into her memory banks. What had she been thinking, coming back to Clayburn? She forced a cheerful note into her voice. "Thanks for coming in, ladies."

"Thank *you*," they chirped in unison.

"Really nice place you've got here," Mike Jensen's wife said, maneuvering a double stroller out the front door.

The women's voices faded down the sidewalk, and Vienne went to clean the coffeepots, taking out her bitterness with a Brillo pad and some old-fashioned elbow grease.

A few minutes later the bells on the front door clinked. Vienne dried her hands, put on her how-may-I-help-you face, and went to the counter.

Wren Johannsen stood on the other side, the high counter dwarfing her dumpy figure. The smile that usually crinkled her eyes was absent.

"Hi, Wren. What can I get you?"

"Could I talk to you for a minute, Vienne?"

Not only was her smile absent, but Wren's customary warmth was gone as well. Vienne's thoughts went to Jack. Had something happened to him? Her pulse quickened. "Sure. Would you . . . like something to drink? On the house, of course," she added quickly.

"No . . . thank you. I didn't come here for that." Wren fiddled with the big buttons on her coat.

Vienne came around and led the way to the overstuffed chairs the young women had just vacated. Cracker crumbs and spilled apple juice littered the area, and she stooped to sweep up a handful of crumbs, but Wren didn't seem to notice.

"Please," Vienne said. "Sit down."

Wren plopped into the cushy overstuffed chair, then scooted to the front of the seat until her feet touched the floor. She glanced around the coffee shop. "You have the place looking very nice. I know it was a lot of work."

"Well, thank you." Vienne sat forward in the adjacent chair, anxious to know where this was leading. She was pretty sure Wren hadn't come to compliment her on the décor of Latte-dah. She shot up a prayer that no customers would interrupt them and plunged in. "Is everything okay, Wren?"

"No, Vienne, it's not." Wren looked out toward the sidewalk, apparently unwilling to meet Vienne's eyes. "I don't know quite how to broach this subject. I . . . don't want to interfere, but I feel you need to know a few things."

"Oh?" Swallowing hard, Vienne tucked a wayward strand of hair behind one ear.

"Jack said you had . . . a disagreement last night."

Had Jack run and told Wren about their conversation? She wasn't exactly eager to discuss this with Jack's mother, when she hadn't even worked things out with Jack. She measured her response. "I guess you could call it that."

"He said you accused him of being drunk"—Wren pushed herself up in the chair, her voice taut—"the night of the accident."

"I . . . I asked him if he was. Drinking, I mean."

"Well, he wasn't." Wren pressed her tiny feet to the floor and sat up taller. "He was not drinking that night, Vienne."

Vienne nodded. What had Jack told Wren anyway? "Yes, that's what he said."

"Do you believe him?"

Vienne took in a breath, and held it. She wanted to believe him. Oh, how she wanted that. Slowly she exhaled. "I don't know what to believe, Wren. Jack said he'd been through rehab. That he had a problem with drinking. Forgive me for seeming cautious, but I . . . I know all about that."

Wren's face softened. "I thought about that. Jack did, too. It's understandable that you would"—she held out her hands in truce—"be cautious with someone in Jack's situation. I don't blame you for that. But you hurt him, Vienne. You hurt him deeply."

She opened her mouth, but her words faltered. Jack wasn't the only one hurting. "It was never my intention to—"

"That boy never had a drink in his life before that terrible day." Wren's voice grew more strident, picking up steam. "What happened to Amy and little Trev . . . that wreck . . . was an accident, plain and simple. Jack was at the wrong place at the wrong time. And he couldn't live with himself afterward. He felt so responsible, and he turned to liquor. I'm not saying it's right, mind you. Then . . . well, things got out of control. But that was *after* it happened, Vienne. *After* the accident. Do you understand?"

Vienne nodded, numb, attempting to sort fact from fiction. And what did Wren expect her to do? Jack was the one keeping secrets. He was the one who should be sitting here now, explaining all this.

Wren's bottom lip quivered, and she bowed her head. In that moment Vienne glimpsed her mother in Wren's tortured expression. And her heart broke for the pain both women had endured.

Wren took in a ragged breath, and in that breath Vienne heard her mother. She closed her eyes and saw a much younger Ingrid Kenney, but with a face that wore the same lines her mother's face bore now, in her old age. *He'd* put them there. Every wrinkle, every frown, every word-inflicted wound had been her father's doing.

No doctor would ever admit it, and certainly Mom had never hinted at such a thing, but Vienne knew in her heart that were it not for her father, Mom would still be humming behind the counter at the Clayburn Café and coming home to put tiny, even stitches in her quilts, while old *Mayberry RFD* reruns played on the television.

And the saddest part was that Mom had allowed it. She was a classic enabler, always making excuses for him, always trying to soothe things between him and Vienne.

"Daddy doesn't mean that, Vinny. He's just tired." Or working too hard. Or worried about his job.

She couldn't remember the last time she'd called him Daddy. After he died, she never called him anything. It helped her make believe he didn't exist. But even death couldn't erase the damage he'd done. He'd been gone almost twenty years, and he was still ruining their lives.

She'd tried to forgive him, the way Mom had. She'd heard all the lectures about bitterness only poisoning the one who held onto it. But didn't someone need to *ask* forgiveness before—

"Vienne?"

A slight weight on her knee tugged her away from that place she despised—these wearisome waking dreams about him that she'd never been able to conquer.

Not thinking, she put her hand over the pudgy fingers resting on her knee. The hand was smaller than Mom's. Disoriented, she looked up into Wren's eyes. It all came clear then. The things Wren had said. The things she knew about Jackson Linder now. She pulled her hand away. Not wanting to hurt Wren, but not wanting her to think everything was smoothed over with her and Jack either.

"I'm sorry, Wren . . ." She hesitated. The words sounded lame. She *was* sorry. For making Wren have to defend her son. And for hurting Jack. She'd made a bitter accusation. One that turned out not to be true.

Conflicting emotions warred within her. Her heart ached at the agony Jack must have felt over the accident. But that didn't change the way he'd chosen to handle his grief. His selfishness had caused even more people to suffer. It didn't change the fact that Jack Linder appeared to be poured from the same bottle as Harlan Kenney. And that was something she wanted not even a sip of.

She rose and picked an invisible fleck of lint from the hem of her blouse. "I *am* sorry, Wren. I had no right to jump to conclusions the way I did."

She meant it. She really did. But she couldn't tell Wren the thoughts that roiled in her head. Her misunderstanding didn't change the ultimate truth. The truth about what Jack was.

Wren struggled to her feet and gave Vienne a weak smile. "Thank you for hearing me out."

She nodded and reached to touch Wren's hand. "I'll speak to Jack . . . apologize, I mean. I didn't mean to upset him."

She *would* apologize, and smooth things over with Jack. And maybe they could be friends. But they would never be anything more.

He was good.

She'd give him that.

But was there any

place in this town

she could go and not

have to stare at a

reminder of him?

Chapter Twenty

Vienne closed the cash register hard and plopped the bank bag under the counter. It had been another barely-break-even day. Two vendor bills lay on her desk in the back and it would take her entire profits since she'd opened Latte-dah to pay them. She hoped people were staying away in droves only because they were taking advantage of the weather, and not because of lack of interest.

The digital thermometer on the Clayburn State Bank had hit 55 degrees by noon and, judging by the schoolkids trailing by her window in shirtsleeves, she suspected it'd climbed even higher in the last four hours.

She waited for a couple of high school lovebirds—who'd ordered a Coke to share—to vacate the corner table, then hung a Be Right Back sign on the front door. She grabbed the bank bag and headed for the bank on foot.

Hiding behind an expensive pair of California sunglasses, she gave Jack's gallery a surreptitious glance as she passed by on the other side of the street. There was a banner in the window announcing his opening Monday. The sign hadn't been there yesterday. But no lights shone from inside, and it didn't look like there was anyone in the gallery.

Jack had made himself scarce lately. Except for catching a glimpse of him on the street through the coffee shop windows, she hadn't seen him since Valentine's night, when she'd stormed out of the gallery. More than a week ago now.

She still hadn't decided what she'd say to him when she saw him. Maybe it was best just to pretend they'd never had that conversation, pretend they'd never become friends. She couldn't ignore him forever in a town the size of Clayburn, but she could treat him with the same respectful distance she offered the average fellow businessman and customer.

She'd given Wren her word she'd set things right with Jack, and she'd already let too much time go by. She probably did owe him an apology. Ignoring the sinking feeling that thought provoked, she quickened her steps.

She walked up to the drive-thru window—a small-town privilege she was still getting used to—and put the bank bag in the receptacle. She could see through to the bank lobby, where a grouping of Jackson Linder paintings hung over a reception area. The library had Jack's paintings on display, too. He was good. She'd give him that. But was there any place in this town she could go and not have to stare at a reminder of him?

She looked away and made small talk with the teller through the speaker system. Surely she could do the same with Jack. Be friendly, but detached. Smile, chat about the weather. If she could only manage to look past those hazel eyes, she just might pull it off.

A car turned into the drive-thru lane, and she hopped over the curb to get out of the way. Rounding the corner of the building to the sidewalk, she watched two little girls who appeared to be about kindergarten age. Giggling, they skipped hand in hand, backpacks dangling from their free arms. She turned to watch them, wondering if she'd ever been so carefree—

"Whoa!"

She collided with someone, and looked up to find herself face to face with Jack. Stiff-armed, he gripped her shoulders, obviously protecting himself—and her—from her clumsiness.

"Sorry! I . . . wasn't watching where I was going." So much for being detached.

She took a step backward, and he dropped his hands. She tried to avoid his eyes, but it was a little difficult when he was aiming gold-flecked lasers at her.

"H-hi, Jack."

He didn't respond.

Fine. She started walking.

But he fell in step beside her. "You weren't fair, you know."

She kept her eyes trained on the sidewalk and walked faster. "Excuse me?"

"The other day. You judged me on rumors. And you didn't let me explain myself."

She bit the inside of her cheek. Okay, he had a point. She could at least give him a fair hearing. "I'm listening now. Everyone's innocent until proven guilty, right?"

"So they say." He tucked his hands in the pockets of his jacket. "Okay, here's the truth. I'm going to lay it all out. What you do with it after that is up to you."

She put up her guard, forced a smile.

He appeared not to notice but stretched out his stride. She did likewise, huffing to catch her breath.

"This is the deal." His voice was a hollow monotone. "I got drunk on beer once—one time—at a sleepover at Bryce Manning's house in eighth grade. I puked my guts out and decided I hated the stuff. I never touched another drop until . . . until after the accident. After that I . . . started drinking. And not just beer."

He was pulling no punches here. She tried to nod, to acknowledge that she'd heard him, but he had his head down, his long legs pumping. They traipsed on in silence for a minute, walking right past Latte-dah. Neither of them acknowledged it, and Jack didn't seem to notice the note she'd left on the door. For once, she was thankful there were no customers waiting to get in. She was glad he'd saved her the trouble of figuring out what to say, and she wanted to hear him out.

He skirted around the empty bicycle rack in front of the hardware store and went on reciting facts as if he were reading a deposition. "I told you about the accident. Believe what you will, I wasn't drinking, let alone drunk. And since you seem to need proof, you'll be happy to know there are accounts of the accident in the archives of any newspaper in the county. Four years ago this April twenty-second, if you want to look it up."

"Jack . . . I—"

"Hey . . ." His voice was hard. He lifted his head to meet her eyes. "Let me finish, okay? This isn't easy."

She nodded, chastened, and kept mute, walking briskly to keep up with him.

"I spent most of the next two years drunk out of my mind. I was too hurt, too blind to realize that the place I found to hide from the pain caused even more pain for the people I'd already hurt. It was Trevor and Wren who finally convinced me I needed help." He hung his head. "I killed my best friend's wife and son, Vienne. And he still forgave me."

She could see in the emotion that lit his face how the grace in that act of forgiveness still touched him deeply.

"But Trevor came to me one day and told me—" His voice broke. "He said he could forgive me for the accident, but he was having a hard time forgiving me for letting it ruin my life—and the lives of everybody around me, the people who loved me. Trevor said the accident was . . . well, an accident. But the drinking—I was choosing that of my own free will. That was harder to forgive." His Adam's apple worked in his throat.

Vienne waited for him to compose himself.

He pulled his collar up against the breeze. "After that, I went into rehab—a place in Kansas City. I was there for nine months. It was nine months of pure hell, and I . . . don't *ever* want to go back." His eyes challenged her.

Guilt chided her for making him relive that time—even in his thoughts. "I'm sorry, Jack." As soon as the words were out, she wondered how he would interpret them. She *was* sorry for his pain, but it didn't change anything. It didn't change what he was.

He slowed his pace and turned west. Without questioning, she followed him. A round crimson sun sat atop a hedgerow that bordered a small housing development on the southwest edge of town.

"I'm sure you don't care about all the gory details, but you need to know that I made a commitment before I left Parkside—the rehab center. I was done with the bottle. Done. You don't know me well enough to know this, Vienne, but when I make a commitment, it means something."

There seemed to be a question in his declaration, but she didn't know what it was or how he expected her to respond.

"I was telling the truth when I told you I haven't had anything to drink since then. I . . . I've been tempted. I won't deny that. And . . ." He looked at the ground again. But when he looked up, his eyes were clear and he held her gaze steady. "I did go to the liquor store a couple weeks ago. Things . . . weren't going well, and I . . . thought about buying a bottle."

"And you—"

He held up a hand. "Yes, I went there intending to get a bottle, but . . ." He laughed as if recalling an amusing story. "Let's just say that God intervened. He made a way out of the temptation for me and I didn't fall. I'm still on the wagon and that's where I intend to stay." He held her gaze. "No matter how bumpy the road might get."

Vienne replayed his words in her mind, the pain in his eyes as he'd poured out his story. And she believed him. At least believed his intentions were honest. He wouldn't look her in the eye like this if he were lying. She appreciated the way Jack seemed to be looking to God for help. That struck a chord in her that had been silent for too long.

But just because he was telling the truth now didn't mean he wouldn't fall later. Jack might be naïve, but she knew too much to believe it was that easy. She didn't know anyone—not one person—who'd managed to get sober and stay that way once the demon took hold of them. Most people didn't even try. She admired his intentions. She really did. But intentions weren't worth the energy it took to talk about them.

He walked on, his gaze trained straight ahead.

She owed him some kind of response, but everything she thought to say could too easily be misinterpreted as exoneration. "I . . . appreciate you telling me all that," she said finally. "And I . . . I'm sorry."

He stopped in the middle of the sidewalk. "Sorry for what?" His voice was absent of malice or accusation.

She stood in front of him, hands on hips, breathless from more than the pace they'd been walking. "I'm sorry for jumping to conclusions the way I did. And I'm sorry for what happened, Jack. The accident. What it caused you to turn to. To go through. I . . . I'm glad you got help. I hope it . . . makes a difference."

He nodded. "It already has. I'll always be grateful I got help when I did. I don't know where I might have ended up had things gone on like they were. God was good. He was patient with me."

His implication seemed to be that she should be patient with him, too. But that implied some sort of relationship between them. And she'd already made up her mind.

She glanced pointedly in the direction of Main Street. "I need to get back to work."

He eyed her for a moment, then shrugged. "Sure."

"I'll see you around, okay?"

Unmistakable hurt swam in his eyes. "Yeah . . . I'll see you around."

She steeled herself against his pain and tried for a relaxed gait as she walked away. What Trevor Ashlock had done was commendable. But even after all these years, memories of Harlan Kenney were too fresh in her mind, and she could not muster the same grace toward Jack. As far as she was concerned, he was already in breach of contract.

He had worth in the
eyes of God. His
brain knew that as
fact. But his heart
hadn't quite gotten the
message. And Vienne
Kenney sure wasn't
helping matters any.

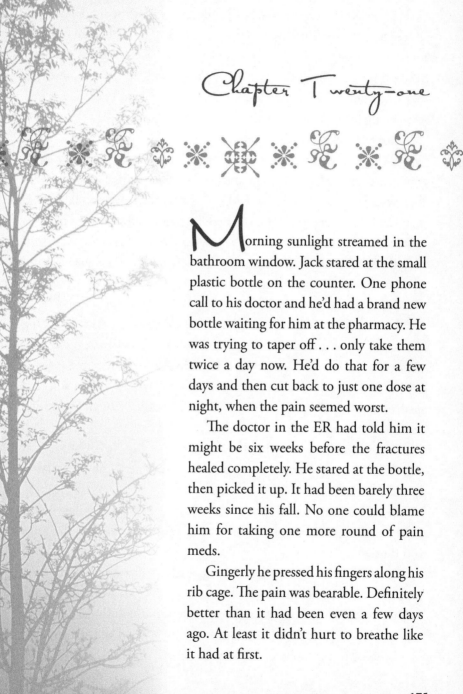

Chapter Twenty-one

Morning sunlight streamed in the bathroom window. Jack stared at the small plastic bottle on the counter. One phone call to his doctor and he'd had a brand new bottle waiting for him at the pharmacy. He was trying to taper off . . . only take them twice a day now. He'd do that for a few days and then cut back to just one dose at night, when the pain seemed worst.

The doctor in the ER had told him it might be six weeks before the fractures healed completely. He stared at the bottle, then picked it up. It had been barely three weeks since his fall. No one could blame him for taking one more round of pain meds.

Gingerly he pressed his fingers along his rib cage. The pain was bearable. Definitely better than it had been even a few days ago. At least it didn't hurt to breathe like it had at first.

He twisted the cap off the bottle and tapped out two pills. It was a couple hours away from his next dose, but he was headed down to finish up some framing and didn't want to forget and let the medication wear off. Besides, after his walk with Vienne last night, he'd come home and dug into some heavy duty cleaning and repairs. He'd overdone it and was paying for it in muscle pain.

Yeah, right, Linder.

He almost had himself convinced. But a familiar check tugged at his conscience. His excuses came into focus, and he recognized them for what they were. He'd abused the pills. Taking them too close together. Taking too many at a time. Taking them for something more than managing pain.

Oh, honey, don't blow all these months of sobriety. Wren's words from the other night rang in his ears, convicting him. He hadn't had a drink in more than ten months, but wasn't he using the pills for the same purpose liquor had once served?

The things Vienne had said, her . . . *judgment*—there was nothing else to call it—angered him, but maybe it had also opened his eyes to the truth. He was fooling himself if he didn't think he was in danger of getting hooked on these stupid pills exactly the way he'd been addicted to alcohol. He put the two tablets back in the bottle. Why did he always seem to seek comfort in a bottle?

He touched his ribs again. They were tender, but he could tough it out. He was getting better every day. He didn't need the pills. It was stupid to risk getting hooked on them.

He took a heavy breath and realized his hands were shaking. Before he could change his mind, he dumped the entire bottle into the toilet and flushed it.

Immediately a sense of panic wrapped itself around him. As if propelled by something outside himself, he dropped to his knees and reached into the swirling water, desperate to retrieve the pills. The water was icy and he pulled his hand out of the toilet bowl and rocked back on his heels. It was too late. They were ruined.

A glare from the light over the medicine cabinet bounced off the full-length mirror leaning against one wall. He turned to see the reflection of a man on his knees, bowing over the toilet. He realized *he* was the man. Fear coursed through him, and he clambered to his feet. Leaning heavily on the sink, he washed his hands and dried them on his jeans.

The pills were gone. Shaking, he tossed the empty bottle into the trash can. But what would keep him from picking up the phone and calling to have that prescription refilled again in a weaker moment?

He'd told Vienne that when he made a commitment, it meant something. What exactly did it mean? Was he a liar?

Give it back to Me.

Jack was learning to know that quiet, steadying voice.

He went in to his bed and knelt beside it. How many times had he given this thing to God? How long would God keep letting him come back with the same confession? He didn't know, but he would keep coming. He couldn't go back to the way things were before. He couldn't.

He covered his face with his hands. "Father, forgive me. I've been flirting with disaster. Thank You for opening my eyes, for showing me where I was headed. Please be patient with me, God. Don't give up on me. I want to lick this thing. Don't give up on me, God."

The peace that swept through him in that moment couldn't compare to any drink, any pill. Why couldn't he remember that? Why couldn't he learn to come to this makeshift altar *first?* Instead of always having to do things the hard way.

He needed to stay busy. That shouldn't be so difficult with all he had yet to do before he opened the gallery Monday. He could forget about the grand opening Vienne had talked about doing together. She was probably just blowing smoke when she brought that up anyway.

He went downstairs and stood for a while in the gallery, admiring the work he'd accomplished over the last two days. Lots of space yet to fill, but it was starting to look like a gallery again. He'd pulled all his old stuff out of storage, cleaned it up, and hung it on the north wall. That filled one wall of the gallery and with the two oversized pieces he'd framed this morning, he had a good start on a second smaller wall. Some of it wasn't what he considered his best work, but it filled the space and made the gallery look like a working studio. It wouldn't do to open up shop and have nothing for folks to look at—or buy.

He'd hung a banner in the front window yesterday, and Trevor had comped him a half-page ad that ran in Wednesday's *Courier,* so he was committed. He'd sold a large landscape through his online gallery, but even though it brought a thousand dollars, that would barely cover the update he'd contracted for his website, let alone shipping the painting out to Oregon. Still, it encouraged him that the website might be a viable way to move art, and it was a plus to get his work seen outside of the state.

He probably should learn how to do the web updates himself. It'd save a bundle, but he'd never fill the gallery if he spent all his time on the computer. What he needed was to get those art classes up and running. That was a way to generate some extra income and still get some painting done. His nerves grew taut just thinking about it.

Would anyone want to take art classes from the town drunk? Would anyone even show—

He felt the check in his spirit immediately and staunched the negative thoughts. It had been so foreign at first, this being down on himself. He'd been a little on the cocky side in high school. Art school had taken a little starch out of him in that regard, but he'd never been one to beat up on himself.

Until the accident. And then he suddenly hadn't been able to see any good in himself. It was something the counselors at Parkside had addressed over and over.

He had worth in the eyes of God. His brain knew that as fact. But his heart hadn't quite gotten the message.

And Vienne Kenney sure wasn't helping matters any.

✳ ✷ ✳

Vienne slammed the phone onto its hook and let out a growl. Evan was sick, and Allison was already ten minutes late. Great. The one day she had customers her help didn't show.

The line was backed up to the door, and it was raining buckets outside. She should be happy about the customers, but the way things were going, she'd probably get sued when somebody slipped in one of the puddles forming on the tile floor. What else could possibly go wrong?

In answer to that question, Pete Truesdell stepped through the door.

Vienne forced a smile and ducked behind the counter, letting the clatter of the ice machine mask her frustrated sigh.

Pete had a couple of good ol' boys from his coverall posse with him. The three of them grabbed the largest table near the fireplace, but when his buddies pulled out chairs and plopped themselves down, Vienne heard Pete set them straight. "It's not like the café, boys. You gotta order up front and carry your stuff to the table yourself."

Pete's friends looked confused, but they followed him to the counter, muttering about the long line.

When their turn finally came, Vienne couldn't help baiting Pete. "Don't want to try a cappuccino this morning, do you?"

He didn't miss a beat. "Think I'll leave that for the boys here. Just give me my usual. Coffee. Black . . . and one of them there muffins in the case. Better make it two. Those are half the size your mom used to make 'em."

And twice the price. He didn't say it, but she could almost read his mind. She hid a smile as she plucked the two plumpest muffins from the tray and handed them over.

"Thanks," Pete grumbled, moving over so his buddies could order.

"How about you gentlemen? What can I get you?"

Pete's buddies ordered black coffee, and after looking over the pastry case, decided they'd just have coffee. The taller man turned to Pete. "We might head out to the Dairy Barn later and see if they've got any more of those biscuits."

Biscuits. These farmers didn't know a latte from a pâté. Why was she wasting her time? And they stank. The rain extracted an array of barnyard odors from their boots and dusty coveralls. They'd probably clear a swath two chairs deep around their table, and then where was she going to put people?

Who are you fooling, Kenney? She was lucky to have ten people in here at any given time. She should be grateful for Pete's business. She pasted on a smile. "Next."

"Hang on there, Vinny." Pete stepped in front of the woman next in line and leaned over the counter. "I don't see the newspaper. You got an extra one back there?"

She'd let the café's subscription to the *Salina Journal* expire. She couldn't afford it, and she didn't have time to read it. Besides, it cluttered the shop. "Sorry, Pete. I don't get the paper anymore."

He rolled his eyes and wagged his head like she was the dumbest fencepost in the field. Ignoring him, she turned back to the patient woman at the counter. She was finishing up the woman's brevé white chocolate mocha when the barnyard stench grew stronger again. She turned to see Pete heading her way.

Before she could stop him, he came around behind the counter and leaned to whisper in her ear. "Can you turn that music off? We can't even hear ourselves think over there."

Okay, that was the last straw. How much thinking could they really be doing if Mozart could drown it out? She inhaled through her mouth to avoid smelling anything. "I suppose I could turn it down a little."

He frowned. "That's better than nothing, I guess."

She handed the woman her mocha, turned the music down half a notch, and started on the next order.

At eleven Allison called to say she had to make up a missed test. At noon the girl still hadn't shown up. By now the crowd had dwindled, and Allison's absence merely meant Vienne wouldn't have to pay her for those hours.

Pete and his buddies were still hogging the table by the fireplace. She'd conceded to customer's complaints last week and put out a couple of air pots for free coffee refills. Now Pete's Posse was draining them dry single-handedly. Since no one was waiting for a table, she couldn't very well ask them to leave.

"Hey, Vienne?" Pete pointed out the window and down the street. "Did you see ol' Jack's got his gallery open for business again?"

"I saw that."

"Doesn't look like he's gettin' much business, though."

She ignored his comment, but she'd noticed. She remembered how afraid she'd been that no one would show up on her opening day. But then, art galleries didn't operate the same way eating establishments did. She was about to suggest that Pete take his gang over to visit the gallery, but one look at them changed her mind in a hurry. She wouldn't wish this crew on her worst enemy.

Pete and his buddies were sprawled out at the table like they owned the place. Buddy Number One—Mitch, she'd heard Pete call him—jabbered over a splintered toothpick mysteriously attached to his lower lip. Buddy Number Two had one leg propped on his knee, exposing hairless lily-white ankles. Good grief.

Did the city statutes have some definition of loitering—or disturbing the peace—that would apply to these guys? If Allison ever got here to take over the cash register for a few minutes, she just might be tempted to run over to city hall and check out her options.

A screech of chairs on the tile signaled that Pete's Posse was finally leaving. She acknowledged his good-bye with a brief wave. No need to encourage them.

The minute they were out the door, she grabbed a bottle of disinfectant and doused their table. She'd have to get Allison to sweep up the mud clods their boots had scattered over a ten-foot radius. They'd each left a quarter tip on the table. She rolled her eyes and slipped the coins into the pocket of her barista's apron. At this rate she'd be able to retire in sixty or seventy years. If there wasn't so much truth to it, it'd be funny. She let out a sigh, and some of her frustration seeped out with it.

She heard the back door open, and a minute later Allison appeared, aproned and ready to pitch in. "Sorry, Vienne. Hope I didn't put you in a bind. The stupid prof wouldn't let us make up the test any other time."

Vienne held up a hand. "Hey, been there, done that. I understand. Can you watch the front while I go make a supply list?"

"Sure." She tipped her head, studying Vienne. "So where'd you go to college? I remember your mom saying something about law school . . ."

Oh, boy. Here we go. "Yes. I went to law school. UC Davis. In California," she added, seeing Allison's blank look.

"Cool. So you're a lawyer? Wow. I bet it's frustrating having to work here. When will you go back to your practice?"

She chose to sidestep the "you're a lawyer" assumption. "At this point, I don't have any plans. Mom . . . well, things are taking a lot longer than anyone thought. I'll stay as long as I need to. Get the coffee shop launched . . ."

A shadow crossed Allison's pretty face. "I'm so sorry about your mom. Is she getting better? How long has it been now?"

"Three months since she had the stroke. That was in November. She's . . . hanging in there, I guess. But she still has a long way to go."

Allison shook her head and clucked her tongue like an old woman. "Wow. I didn't realize it'd been that long. I feel bad I haven't gone to visit her. Between school and work I have no life. Would she be up for company?"

Vienne brightened, knowing this cheery, talkative girl would be good for Mom's spirits. "Oh, please do go see her. She'd love a visit. But I'll warn you, she really struggles to communicate—and she'll probably cry when she sees you. But just pretend you don't notice. Just talk to her.

Tell her what's going on in your life. She can understand you fine, she just can't . . . find her words yet."

It was wearing Vienne out to try to keep up that one-sided conversation with Mom every night. It would be wonderful to have an "accomplice."

Allison studied Vienne with something like pity in her expression. "How are *you* holding up, Vienne?"

"I'm fine." Her throat filled unexpectedly, and she turned her back to Allison and grabbed a bar rag. She rinsed it under the gooseneck faucet, running the water as hot as she could stand it. After a minute, she wrung the rag out in the sink and started swabbing down countertops that were already perfectly clean.

Allison apparently took the hint and went to straighten tables and chairs. But an hour later hunkered over the cluttered desk in Mom's office, Vienne was still pondering the girl's question. As she tried to compose a grocery list that wouldn't break the bank, yet would keep Latte-dah in business, she wondered. How *was* she holding up?

She might have answered that more positively, were it not for the whole mess with Jack. Why couldn't she just quit thinking about him? They'd ended on a reasonably gracious note after their walk the other night. He'd been a little defensive, and she'd been noncommittal. But she thought they'd left things on friendly enough terms that she could face him without feeling uncomfortable when he came in for coffee or when they ran into one another on the street.

She'd mentally checked him off her list of close friends and possible dates. And yes, she was disappointed to have to do so. But it wasn't the end of the world.

Yeah, right, Kenney. Then why do you feel like somebody ripped your heart out and put a stone in its place?

He'd already jumped in with both feet . . . might as well finish it. Not like he had anything else to lose with this woman.

Chapter Twenty-two

March

"Hey, Jack, how's it going?"

Jack leaned to peer around the canvas propped on the easel in front of him. Meg Ashlock, Trevor's wife, stood in the doorway, bundled against the cold front that had moved into the state last night.

"Hi, Meg. What are you up to?" He'd met Meg shortly before he went into rehab. He hated to guess what she thought of him. He'd been at his worst back then. He hadn't gotten to know Meg well, but even so, she held a special place in his heart now because she'd brought happiness back to Trevor's life.

She stuck out a gloved hand. "Trevor said you were back in business. Welcome home."

He dipped his head. "Thanks. It's good

to be back." He still wasn't sure about that statement, but it seemed to be what people expected him to say.

"I'm here to sign up for your art class. Trevor showed me the ad."

"Oh?"

Meg's expression turned sheepish. "I hope it's not too late. I was worried you'll fill up right away when the paper came out. Any chance you still have a spot?"

Meg was a New York native, new to small-town life. She obviously hadn't been in Clayburn long enough to know that her place in the class was assured. "I don't think that'll be a problem." He gave a wry smile. "You'll be number one on the list."

"Great!" Meg reminded him of an eager puppy being offered a treat.

He slid off the stool, propped his paint palette on the seat, and went to the front desk. "I have some forms in here somewhere." He rummaged through a file cabinet drawer until he came up with a rumpled sheet of paper. He laid it on the desk in front of her. "I may have to change a few things, depending on how many sign up, but you can fill this out for now." He only hoped he wouldn't have to call her later and tell her the class was cancelled for lack of interest. "You're an artist yourself, aren't you? You could probably *teach* this class."

"Oh, no way. I have a lot to learn." She peeled off her gloves and rubbed her hands together to warm them before taking a pen from the mug on the counter. She printed her name in neat, square letters.

"Is it cold enough for you?" He was becoming a master at small talk.

"Oh, I'm used to it. This is what New York winters are always like. I was beginning to think Kansas was some kind of tropical paradise."

Jack laughed. "Yeah, right. Well, we knew it couldn't last."

Meg laid the pen down and scanned the gallery. "You've got the place looking nice. You have some new stuff up, too."

"It's mostly old stuff, actually. Just something to fill the walls. I sold almost everything before I closed down last spring." He didn't mention that while she and Trevor were on their honeymoon, he'd had a liquidation sale of sorts—sold his work at 30 percent of what he was used to getting, just to collect enough cash to get by on while he was in rehab. "When I left I . . . lost the other artists who had their stuff here on commission."

She nodded, understanding clear on her face. Meg probably empathized more than most. She'd had a tough life before coming to Clayburn. Somehow it put him at ease to know that. She wouldn't judge him as harshly as others did. The way Vienne did.

Meg glanced toward the easel in the corner. "So what are you working on now?"

He shook his head. "It's a landscape. At least it's supposed to be. I'm struggling a little bit with this one."

"Kind of hard to get back in the swing of things, huh?"

He shrugged. "I don't know . . . Oils are relatively new to me. I did a couple of canvases I was pretty happy with earlier this month." He pointed to the duo hanging on the far wall. "I don't know why I'm clutching with this one." That wasn't altogether true. He glanced out the window and down the street to Latte-dah. He had a pretty good idea why his work was suffering, why he couldn't seem to concentrate on anything for more than two minutes.

Meg followed his line of vision to the coffee shop. "You've got a prime location right across from Latte-dah. You'd think Vienne's new place would bring some outside money to Clayburn." She laughed. "Trevor says it's a good thing *we* live out in the country. We'd go broke if I was within walking distance of a good latte every day."

He cleared his throat. "I'm not really a big fan of coffee."

"Are you kidding? You apparently haven't tried their cinnamon cappuccino. Oh my goodness, it is to die for." Her forehead creased. "I just hope Vienne can keep it going here. Trevor said he's been in there a couple of times, and it was pretty dead."

"That's too bad." He tried to act disinterested, but Meg's comment surprised him. Was Vienne really struggling to get business? It seemed like there were usually cars parked on the street in front of Latte-dah, but he'd been so worried about his own sad financial affairs that he hadn't really paid attention to how she might be doing. He shot up a quick prayer for her. He'd have to go over there now and then for lunch or a cup of hot chocolate. And surely Pete and his retired buddies needed someplace for their coffee breaks. Maybe he could encourage them to frequent Latte-dah, drum up some business for Vienne. Maybe that would help him back into her good graces.

Meg finished filling out the form and they made small talk, but as soon as she was out the door, Jack covered his paints, grabbed a jacket, and headed across the street. He had a sudden hankering for a big ol' venti or grande or whatever she called her big-gulp-size hot chocolate.

A minute later he pushed open the door of Latte-dah. At the clank of bells against the door, Vienne looked up from the bakery case, where she was spritzing the glass with a bottle of Windex. Recognition sparked in her eyes, but her expression didn't hint at what she was feeling toward him.

An elderly woman working a crossword puzzle at a table by the window was the only customer within sight. Jack hung his jacket on the coatrack beside the door and went to the counter.

Vienne quickly finished polishing one section of the glass case and came to wait on him. He waited for her to crack some joke about his love of coffee.

"What can I get for you?"

So it was going to be all business. She'd been cool toward him since they'd talked that night two weeks ago after she literally ran into him at the bank drive-thru.

"I'll have a large hot chocolate, please." He tried to win her over with a smile.

She didn't bite. "To go?"

"No. For here, please. Um . . ." He looked at the floor before meeting her eyes again. "I'm not sure how this works, but can I buy you a drink, too? Do you have time for a coffee break?"

Her face softened and, for a second she looked as if she might say yes. Then her shoulders sagged, and she donned her poker face again. "Thanks, but . . . I'm kind of busy."

He glanced around the shop. The woman in the corner had gathered up her things and was shuffling toward the door.

"Yeah, I can see things are really hoppin' around here." He puffed out one cheek with his tongue, but his expression was wasted on her.

She turned and grabbed a carton of milk from the refrigerator and poured it into a metal pitcher.

He stood at the counter and watched her make the hot cocoa. Some kind of classical music played on the CD player, but neither of them spoke until she placed the steaming, oversized mug in front of him. "That'll be $4.57."

He fished his wallet from his back pocket and slipped out a five-dollar bill. "Keep the change." He could have had the full meal deal at the Dairy Barn for five bucks. But this wasn't about the money or the drink. This was about making some headway with her.

"Thanks, and have a nice day." She put the money in the cash register and dismissed him with a pat smile. She picked up her spray bottle and a roll of paper towels.

Something inside him snapped. He glanced around to make sure no one else was in the shop. "Hey!"

She turned and looked, first at him, then at the door, as if she thought he might be talking to someone else.

"Listen, I don't know what your deal is, but I sure don't like it."

She took two backward steps, her eyes widening. "Excuse me?"

He had her full attention now. He plunked his mug down on the counter. The cocoa sloshed over the rim, burning his hand.

She tore off a piece of toweling and handed it to him.

He took it and wiped his hand, then sopped up the mess on the counter.

"Here . . ." She reached for a bar rag. "I'll get it."

He glared at her. "You know, I thought we'd worked things out the other night. For a while there, we had a pretty nice friendship going. You're new in town, I've been gone awhile. I was enjoying your company, and I could have sworn you were enjoying mine. I'm not too thrilled with being demoted to average customer." He exhaled. "'Thanks,'" he mimicked her. "'Have a nice day'? What's that all about?"

She arched her brows but said nothing. Instead she stared at him, almost daring him with those turquoise eyes, as if she couldn't wait to hear what outrageous thing he might say next.

He'd already jumped in with both feet . . . might as well finish it. Not like he had anything else to lose with this woman. "Do you mind telling me what's going on in that pretty head of yours? Is this about you still thinking I'm the town drunk?" Immediately he regretted his dismal attempt at humor.

Her mouth fell open. She shook her head.

He shook his head. "I'm sorry. That was uncalled for."

She nodded—whether in agreement with his statement or acceptance of his apology, he wasn't sure—and blew out a puff of air. "Jack . . . I—"

He waited.

But she shook her head again and turned to the sink, plunging her hands into the basin of soapy water.

Unbelievable. So she was just going to ignore him? He stormed behind the bar counter and leaned against the counter beside the sink, crossing his arms over his chest. "If you want me to leave, say so. But I don't think it's too much to ask for you to tell me where I stand with you."

She tossed the dishrag behind the faucet and flicked the water off her fingers into the sink. Hands still damp, she whirled to face him, her face flushed the color of ripe peaches. Her chin quivered, and tears sprang to her eyes.

Jack stood there in shock, arms at his side.

Vienne swiped at one cheek before turning away from him.

Instinctively he reached out to hold her, then stopped himself. He wanted to take her in his arms, wipe away her tears. But something told him that would be exactly the wrong thing to do right now.

Compromising, he gently touched her arm. "Vienne? What's wrong?"

She stiffened, then shook her head, bowing over the sink.

"Do you . . . want me to leave?" Dumb question. She'd made that pretty clear the other day.

She took a stuttering breath and swiped at her cheeks again. "No. You don't have to leave. I . . . I don't even know where to begin." All the anger had drained from her eyes, and what he saw there now was something akin to sorrow.

"Whatever it is, you can tell me. I can take it." He wasn't sure that was true, but he would risk being wounded to know what was making her so sad.

"It's not you. It's . . . me."

"Will you come sit with me? Just for a minute?" He looked around the room. "I think I can find us a table." He risked taking her arm.

She didn't flinch. In fact, the corner of her mouth turned up in a tiny smile, and she met his eyes for a brief second before looking away.

"I'll even help you wash dishes before I go." He was beginning to sound desperate, but anything to keep that smile on her face.

She sniffed and rolled her eyes. But her grin widened a bit. "There are like . . . two dishes in the sink. Business stinks."

"Is that why you're crying?" *Oh, please, Lord, let that be all it is.*

It was all he
could do to resist
wiping the tears from
Vienne's cheeks.

Chapter Twenty-three

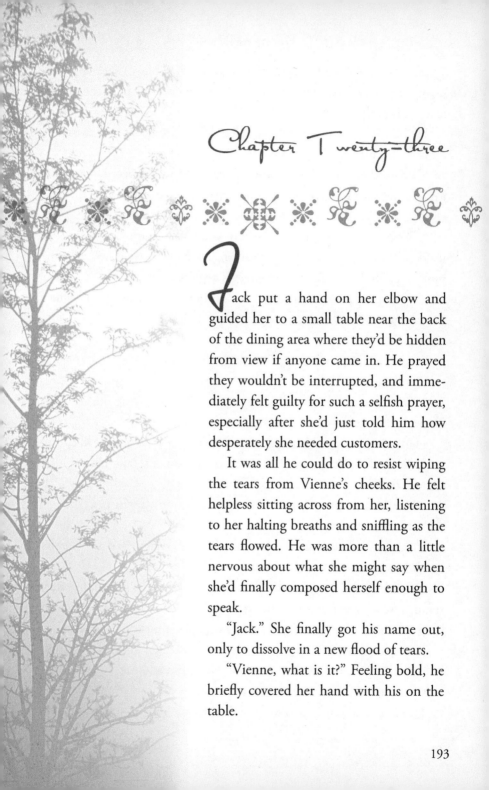

*J*ack put a hand on her elbow and guided her to a small table near the back of the dining area where they'd be hidden from view if anyone came in. He prayed they wouldn't be interrupted, and immediately felt guilty for such a selfish prayer, especially after she'd just told him how desperately she needed customers.

It was all he could do to resist wiping the tears from Vienne's cheeks. He felt helpless sitting across from her, listening to her halting breaths and sniffling as the tears flowed. He was more than a little nervous about what she might say when she'd finally composed herself enough to speak.

"Jack." She finally got his name out, only to dissolve in a new flood of tears.

"Vienne, what is it?" Feeling bold, he briefly covered her hand with his on the table.

193

She shook her head, even as the words trickled out. "I feel silly even saying anything because . . . well, maybe you never saw us as more than just . . . friends."

He pulled a paper napkin from the holder on the table and twisted it between his fingers. Where was she going with this?

She breathed in deeply again. "I just . . . I need to concentrate on my mother, and on getting the shop solvent. I don't have time for other . . . commitments in my life right now."

"Vienne . . . good grief, I'm asking you to tell me what's going on inside of you, not go shopping for an engagement ring." Seeing a line of pink creep up her neck, he immediately regretted his words.

She looked as if she might start crying again. But she regained her composure and even managed a feeble grin. "I know that. I just mean—"

"Can I ask you something?" He knew he was taking a risk.

She shrugged.

"Wren mentioned something about your father having the same"—he swallowed hard—"struggle that I've had."

Her jaw tensed, and her eyes glazed over with what looked like fear.

Jack held up a hand. "If you don't want to talk about it, I understand."

"What did Wren tell you?" Her voice was almost a whisper.

"That your dad was . . . an alcoholic."

Vienne rolled her eyes and gave a humorless laugh. "It's not like the whole town didn't know that already."

He shrugged. "I didn't know. But I'm sorry, Vienne. I think I understand now why you reacted the way you did when you found out I'd been in rehab. I can see why it might make you a little . . . gun-shy."

She opened her mouth, then hesitated as if trying to decide whether to go on. "My dad made our lives hell. For Mom and me. I-I will never go through what my mother went through. Never."

He let that sink in for a minute. "I don't blame you. I understand . . . I think that's wise. I guess I'll just have to prove to you that I'm serious about my recovery."

She didn't respond.

"Vienne, I'm never going back to my addiction. I promise you that." His voice faltered at the sudden vision of the pills swirling down the toilet. "Maybe you don't know me well enough yet, but I don't make promises idly. I'll do whatever it takes, for however long it takes, to earn back your trust. To earn back the trust of this town."

She pressed her lips into a thin line, and he was afraid the tears would come again. She took a deep breath. "I wish you the best, Jack. I really do."

An ache started in his chest and spread as the resolve in her eyes deepened. "So this is . . . farewell and good riddance? We're back to 'thanks and have a nice day'?" He'd dared to hope she'd smile and dispute him.

Instead she bit the corner of her lip and said nothing.

He must be a glutton for rejection. He was tempted to get up and walk out. Tempted, honestly, to go find a bottle and salve the sting of her rebuff. He combed a hand through his hair, feeling the old yearning for the relief the bottle offered. But he wouldn't do it. He knew now that any relief it might offer would only last until the liquor evaporated. No. If he knew anything, he knew that he was strong enough now—and he cared enough for this woman—to not run away. He would tough it out. Whatever happened.

He straightened and met her eyes. "Tell you what . . . can we start over?"

The bells on the door rattled against the glass. Vienne looked from Jack to the door and back. She dipped her head in apology and started to rise.

"Wait . . ." He put a hand over hers on the table.

She sat back down, waiting.

"Please . . . can we be friends again? *Casual* friends? Fellow Chamber of Commerce members? No strings."

A shadow of something—suspicion, perhaps?—darkened her face for a brief moment. But then her smile broke through it. "Sure. I think I can handle that."

He resisted the urge to pull her into a grateful hug. He needed to go slow with her. But he would win her over. If it took him fifty years, he'd earn back her trust and her friendship.

And maybe, someday, her love.

※ ❀ ※

Vienne poured coffee for the well-dressed elderly man at the counter. From the corner of her vision, she watched Jack cross the street to the gallery. Did childhood crushes always die this hard, or was her attraction to Jackson Linder in the present? The slight slump of his shoulders told her she'd hurt him more than he let on. It hadn't been easy to brush him off when her emotions made her long to be so much more than "just friends." But she knew better than to trust her emotions.

Reluctantly, she made change for the fifty-dollar bill the customer handed her. Now she'd probably need to run to the bank and get some smaller bills to get through the rest of the afternoon. The man smiled, showing even white teeth. He thanked her, and she wondered for a minute if she should know him. He looked vaguely familiar, though she couldn't think why she should know him. But she'd been amazed how many people from her childhood still lived in Clayburn. Mom's next-door neighbors were the same people who'd lived there when Vienne was living at home.

The man took his coffee to a table by the window, removed his suit coat and hat and placed them on the seat of an adjacent chair before settling in over his newspaper.

Vienne started a fresh pot of decaf brewing while she relived the conversation she'd just had with Jack. Something about the look on his face when he'd promised her they'd just be friends—casual friends—made her suspect that his idea of "casual" was considerably different from her own.

She'd be friendly to Jack. It wouldn't be fair to do otherwise. But she'd keep her distance, keep her guard up.

"This used to be the Clayburn Café, didn't it?" Her lone customer's voice disrupted her thoughts.

"That's right." She answered in a tone she hoped wouldn't invite small talk and turned back to her work. She wasn't in the mood for conversation. She wanted to replay her conversation with Jack, try to sort things out.

But the man rose and ambled over to the counter, coffee cup in hand. "So, are you the owner of . . . Latte-dah, is it?" She looked up to see him perusing the framed license that hung behind the counter. "Clever name."

Well, *that* was a new one. "Thanks. My mother is the owner."

"Ah . . . Ingrid?"

"Yes. You know her?" She studied him, looking for something familiar in his face that she'd missed before.

He nodded. "How is she?"

Carafe in hand, Vienne paused. "I'm sorry . . . should I know you?"

The man smiled, and again Vienne had the feeling she'd seen him before. "I lived here years ago. I doubt you were even born yet. But I remember Ingrid—your mother. Beautiful woman. As is her daughter." He made a courtly bow.

Something about his manner made Vienne uneasy. She ignored his transparent attempt at flattery and took the carafe around to the low table where the air pots sat in need of a refill. He seemed not to notice and followed her, waiting while she filled the pots, then pumping a stream of coffee into his mug before heading back to his table.

Vienne set the carafe in the sink, then scrubbed it with hot soapy water. But she kept an eye on the man while she worked.

He sipped his coffee in silence, reading the paper and gazing out the window occasionally. Twenty minutes later, after two refills from the air pot, he brought the saucer and empty cup to the counter. "Say, I see the inn across the street is still open for business."

"It is. I'm sure they'd have a vacancy if you need a place to stay. About the only time they fill up is during the Smoky Hill River Festival in Salina, or sometimes if there's a basketball tournament going on there."

"Does Wren Manchester still run the place?"

"You mean Wren Johannsen?"

"Of course . . . Johannsen. Manchester is her—the name I knew her by. So Wren's still in town?" He gazed across the street, a faraway look in his eye.

She nodded. "She's run Wren's Nest as long as I can remember."

He grunted and continued to stare across at the inn. He was attractive and friendly enough, and had an air of wealth about him. But something about him left Vienne feeling a bit unsettled.

She was relieved when he finally donned his suit coat and hat and left the shop. She moved to the window and watched to see if he would go across to the inn. But instead, he got into a fancy maroon car parked in front of the flower shop next door. He backed the car around and drove south toward Old Highway 40.

Maybe she should mention it to Wren—that someone had asked after her by her maiden name. She shook off the thought as soon as it came. It was probably nothing. Probably just an old friend back in town.

Being back in this little Kansas community had reminded Vienne how jaded and suspicious of people she'd become. Living on the West Coast could do that to a person.

No. She would mind her own business. She didn't want to worry Wren. The truth was, she'd gone out of her way to avoid Wren recently.

Sure, after Wren confronted her, she'd kept her promise and had apologized to Jack. But she doubted Wren would be very happy with her intentions to steer clear of him. Not that she would ever voice those thoughts to anyone, let alone Wren.

But somehow Vienne got the feeling Wren could see right through her. And at the moment she needed a serious transformation of her heart before she was ready to be so transparent.

Why had he come back? Why now?

Chapter Twenty-four

*J*ack looked up from his painting to realize that it was almost dark outside. He slid off the stool and stretched. It was about time for Vienne to pass by on her daily jaunt to the bank.

Since that first time he'd caught her at the bank and they'd walked together, he'd been tempted to stop her again and invite himself to walk with her. But he knew that would be pushing it. She'd agreed to a casual friendship. And barely that. He needed to take it slow.

He covered his paints and put his brushes to soak. The evening stretched out in front of him. An evening with nothing worth watching on the television and nothing productive to do unless he came back down here to paint.

Sometimes he thought he'd go crazy with boredom. It was no one's fault but his own. He reminded himself it would get better once his art classes started next week. That would fill two nights a week. Trevor had said something about a city basketball league starting up. Maybe he'd get on a team.

He went to the front desk and rummaged through a stack of mail. Somewhere in here was a postcard about a meeting of the local art association sometime later this month. He'd been active in the group a few years ago . . . before rehab. Odd how his life had once been marked by "before" and "after" the accident. Now the demarcation line had shifted to rehab. Before rehab. After rehab. He supposed it was an improvement.

He tucked the art association postcard under the phone, to remind himself to call and make a reservation for the next meeting. It would be good to get involved again. Something else to fill his time. Every hour he could fill was one less hour his mind, his flesh, could tempt him.

He sighed and took a swig from the lukewarm water bottle sitting on his desk. It didn't begin to quench his craving. Would this terrible thirst for the forbidden ever leave him? In rehab he'd heard too many testimonies to the contrary to feel very hopeful. Still, he was encouraged that he'd been home for over a month now, and except for his flirtation with the pain medication, he hadn't fallen.

Thank You, Father. It's only because of You.

He'd managed without so much as an aspirin since the day he'd flushed the pills. Since that day, he'd begun every morning on his knees beside his bed. He ended each day likewise. It was a precious time, and he knew there was strengthening in those moments spent with God. Still, he awoke every single morning knowing that only God's grace kept him from yielding to temptation.

Outside, the streetlights began to flicker on and movement on the sidewalk across from the gallery caught his eye. He smiled. Vienne. With a pink wool scarf swaddling her neck, she walked with purpose, a bank bag swinging from her right hand. She must return by way of the alley each night because he never saw her walk back by on Main Street.

He smiled to himself, remembering her comment about "accomplices in the alley" that first night she'd made him Swiss Miss in the coffee shop. No, she probably didn't come up the alley. Maybe she walked on home from the bank. Or to the Manor to visit her mother.

He wondered how Ingrid was doing. He hadn't asked Vienne about her mom for a while. It was thoughtless on his part. There was so much he didn't know about Vienne. So much he wanted to discover. But he needed to be careful. He didn't want her to think he was prying. Or that he was attempting to be more than "casual friends." This wasn't going to be easy.

He walked to the front door to lock up and checked the clock again as he passed the reception desk. It was seven-thirty in St. Petersburg. Maybe he'd call his mom later. He hadn't talked to her in over a week, and he knew she worried about him. As much as he loved his mother, he was grateful she was in Florida. She didn't need to witness his struggles, and he didn't need her spoiling him and pandering to his every wish. The long-distance relationship had been good for them both.

His eye fell on the foil-wrapped African violet on the corner of his desk. He'd purchased the plant at the flower shop the other day to replace the one he'd knocked over at Wren's. He needed to take it over to her before he ended up killing it, too. He always had a standing invitation to hang out at Wren and Bart's. But he wasn't in the mood for trying to be upbeat tonight. And Wren would sense his unrest in a heartbeat.

As much as he loved Wren, he could think of someone else he'd rather hang out with. He pushed the thought from his mind. No use entertaining that fantasy.

He poured the rest of his bottled water into the little pot and willed the fragile flower to hang on for another day or two.

He rose, tossed the water bottle into the trash can, and went to his easel. He stood there for a long time and studied the still life he was working on—a nice combination of colors. Pale yellow and airy greens, punctuated with scarlet. For some reason he'd been unable to view his work objectively lately. But he liked this painting. It gave him a sense of . . . peace.

He turned off the lights in the gallery. Then he climbed the stairs to his apartment to fix something for dinner.

※ ❀ ※

Wren pulled the warm sheets and towels from the dryer and shook them out, trying to smooth out the wrinkles. She'd be happy when the weather would let her dry the linens on the clothesline again. They smelled so much fresher that way.

Lopping the folded sheets over one arm, she wove her way behind the front desk and down the hall to the room their most recent guests had vacated this morning. She would never complain about beds to make and bathrooms to clean. It meant business was good. And it hadn't always been so. But oh, her shoulders did ache after a full day spent doing laundry and making up beds.

Bart would help her if she would only ask, but frankly, his bed-making skills left more than a little to be desired. She prided herself on crisp hospital corners and drum-tight sheets you could bounce a dime on. No, she'd make the beds, thank you, and let Bart knead the knots from her shoulders every night. That was a fair trade-off in her eyes.

She worked her way around a queen-size bed, tucking the contour sheet in just so. She whipped the top sheet out with a snap and let it float down over the bed. Amidst the soft *whoosh,* a faint chime from the lobby made her pause to listen. Was that the desk bell? They didn't have any reservations tonight, but they had been getting a lot more drop-ins since they'd started advertising in the *Journal.*

She left the guest room and scurried down the hall. Sure enough, a dapper-looking gentleman stood at the desk, hat in hand.

"I'm coming! I'm coming!" These short legs would only go so fast. She sure hoped the heavenly body God had in mind for her included long, shapely legs.

Pulling a ballpoint pen from the bun on top of her head, she hurried around the front desk. She affected her business voice. "Good afternoon. Welcome to Wren's Nest. Are you needing a room for the night?"

The handsome, silver-haired man in front of her wore a knowing grin. Oh, dear, had she forgotten a reservation?

"Hello, Wren."

She leaned away and looked at him again, trying to put a name with the familiar face. When it came to her, her knees nearly buckled. "Marcus." She gripped the counter and willed her legs to hold her.

"It's been a long time."

"What . . . what are you doing here?" Her question sounded rude to her own ears, but she had no reason to be anything else toward this man. She wanted nothing to do with him.

"I simply wanted to talk to you."

Anyone else might be swayed, but Wren knew his winsome smile masked a devious heart. Her throat filled and she choked back tears. She didn't want to be here. Didn't want to face the old feelings that were suddenly as fresh and raw as they'd been more than three decades ago.

He took a step closer. "Come on, Wren. Is it so surprising that I'd want to look up an old friend while I'm in town?"

Wren backed away, matching him step for step, keeping her distance. She'd hoped never to lay eyes on Marcus Tremaine again. And now he stood here, defiling this place that had been a sanctuary for her and Bart. Her chest heaved. She struggled for breath. *Father, give me the words to make him go away.* "Please leave. I have nothing to say to you."

Where was Bart? Part of her pleaded inside for him to come and rescue her. Part of her wanted to weep at the thought of Bart being forced to meet this man, to have a face to put with a name neither of them had spoken since she'd confessed her secret to Bart the day he asked her to marry him.

"I want to know about our son, Wren."

Wren opened her mouth to protest, then let the words die in her throat. Willing her voice to steady, she forced herself to meet his gaze. "What are you talking about?"

"Wren . . ." Marcus shook his head in that condescending, scolding way she remembered all too well. His smile faded. "I have a right to know."

She'd given herself away. And it was obvious Marcus knew something. Why else had he come back after all these years? But she refused to budge.

"You know very well what I'm talking about, Wren." His voice took on the syrupy tenor that, once upon a time, had persuaded Wren of his affection.

But his devotion had turned out to be feigned. Their . . . affair—there was no other name for it—had ended in heartache that still colored Wren's life. Marcus had told her lie upon lie until she'd finally stopped believing him capable of the truth. Why had he come back? Why now?

Anger tightened her chest. How dare he march in here and ruin what she'd rebuilt after he'd nearly destroyed her. She rose to her full five-foot-two-inches. "I have nothing to say to you. Please leave . . . before I call the police." Her breath caught. She didn't know where that threat had come from.

Marcus gave a musical laugh and reached across the desk to cover her hand with his. "Wren . . . dear Wren . . . please. I'm not here to make trouble. I simply want a chance to know our son."

She yanked her hand away, loathing his touch. And inside, she wept. *Please, God. No. Don't ask this of me. Of Jackson. Not now.* "How . . . how did you find out?"

"I was working on my family genealogy. Came across an old story in the *Courier* about a mother and son reunited after an adoption. A woman I . . . *knew* once. It could only have been me, Wren. Does he still live here?"

She bit her tongue, tempted to try to deceive him again. All those years ago she'd allowed the newspaper to publish the feature. She'd thought perhaps it would be healing for Jackson and for her. And perhaps even for other women who'd gone through similar circumstances.

Even though the *Courier* was only a small-town weekly, for a while she'd worried that Marcus—wherever he was—might see the story and put two and two together. But she'd stopped worrying long ago.

And now, here he stood. Jackson's father.

She saw the resemblance so clearly in Marcus's still handsome face. Would other people in town see it, too? She should never have allowed that article to be written.

"It's . . . it's not for me to say." She fiddled with the ballpoint pen, then tucked it back in her hair. "You have no right coming back here . . . showing up after all this time." She fingered a thread of white hair that had come loose from her bun. She wondered how she must look to him after all these years . . . then hated herself for caring.

He leaned over the desk. "I'll find him, Wren. With your help or without it." His words were meant to be menacing, in spite of the smile and the honeyed voice with which he delivered them. If only she could have seen that so clearly thirty years ago.

"He's my only son, Wren. A son deserves to know his father."

"Jack had a father." Wren forced her voice to steady. "A wonderful father. More of a man than you ever thought—"

"Jack." A wistful smile turned up Marcus Tremaine's mouth.

Her face must have revealed her trepidation.

"Ah, yes . . . I know, Wren. Jackson Linder. I noticed a little gallery down the street. Linder's Gallery, I believe it's called. So our son remained here in Clayburn? And apparently he inherited his father's artistic bent."

Wren's spirits plummeted as though weighted by a cinder block. Oh, the weight of regret. She'd betrayed her son even before his conception.

And now she'd done it again.

When she reached
for the lock, her heart
leapt to her throat.
A man stood on the
sidewalk, just beyond
the door.

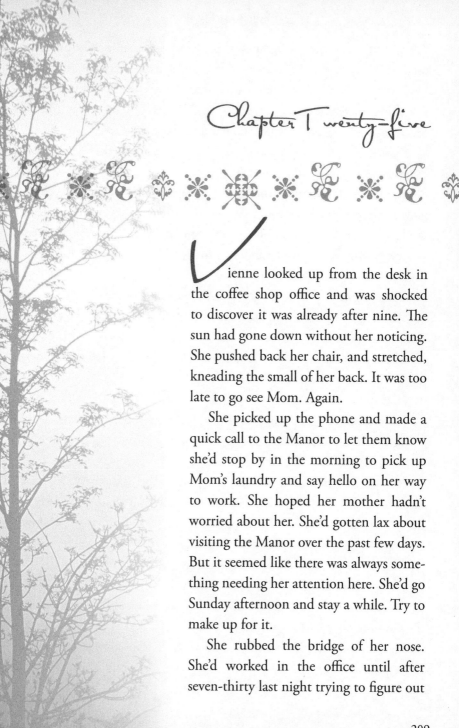

Chapter Twenty-five

Vienne looked up from the desk in the coffee shop office and was shocked to discover it was already after nine. The sun had gone down without her noticing. She pushed back her chair, and stretched, kneading the small of her back. It was too late to go see Mom. Again.

She picked up the phone and made a quick call to the Manor to let them know she'd stop by in the morning to pick up Mom's laundry and say hello on her way to work. She hoped her mother hadn't worried about her. She'd gotten lax about visiting the Manor over the past few days. But it seemed like there was always something needing her attention here. She'd go Sunday afternoon and stay a while. Try to make up for it.

She rubbed the bridge of her nose. She'd worked in the office until after seven-thirty last night trying to figure out this stupid tax stuff, and she wasn't sure she'd made an inch of progress tonight. She might have to break down and have an accountant take a look at it. But she hated to guess what that would cost. Of course, at the rate things were going, all Latte-dah would be able to show was a hefty loss. Maybe they'd actually get some money back.

Sighing, she rose and pushed her chair up to the desk. She was too weary to think about it anymore tonight.

Out in the dining room the lights from the bakery cases cast a yellow glow across the darkened room. She flipped them off and went to check the lock on the front door. She watched her own reflection in the glass as she approached the door, but when she reached for the lock, her heart leapt to her throat.

A man stood on the sidewalk, just beyond the door.

She staggered backward, certain he'd already seen her. Her pulse throbbed like a bongo drum in her ears. Her reflection dissolved to reveal the man on the other side of the glass. He lifted a hand to knock on the glass, and she exhaled in relief.

Jack.

He smiled an apology and motioned for her to open the door.

Still clutching her throat, she turned the key in the lock and let him in. "You scared the living daylights out of me!"

He touched her shoulder and laughed softly. "I'm sorry. I didn't mean to. Really. But I saw the lights on over here and wondered if everything was okay." He looked beyond her to the back of the store, as if he expected to see someone else here with her.

"I'm fine. I'm trying to figure out this stupid tax stuff."

He wrinkled his nose. "Good luck with that."

"Yeah, thanks. You'd think a law school degree would prepare you to file a simple tax return, you know?"

He laughed. "Only the IRS could make it too complicated for a lawyer."

She affected a wounded glare, aiming to get back at him for practically giving her a heart attack. "I'm not a lawyer, remember."

"Sorry." He winced, chagrin darkening his eyes. "I'm sorry, Vienne. I . . . wasn't thinking."

Now it was her turn to wince. "Hey, I was kidding . . . forget it. It's no big deal." The words were barely out before she was aware they were true. Something had happened to her over the last few months that had completely transformed her thinking. She didn't give a flying buffalo that she'd failed the bar. She understood now that *she* was the only one in Clayburn who would have been impressed by her fancy law degree. She smiled to herself.

"What's so funny?"

"Nothing." She hadn't realized her smile had reached her face. She pressed her lips together and shook her head.

"Okay . . . well"—he turned toward the door—"I'll leave you alone. Just wanted to make sure you weren't being robbed or kidnapped or held at gunpoint for a blueberry scone."

Her smile returned. "Not unless you count being held hostage by the IRS."

He reached for the door handle. "Lock the door behind me."

She gave a sharp salute. "Yes, sir."

"Sorry." Chagrin shadowed his features. "I know you're a big girl. I have no idea where this bossy streak comes from."

The lump that came to her throat caught her off guard. "It's okay. It's . . . kind of nice actually." It was true. Having someone to worry about her touched her in a place she hadn't been touched in a while. Until now, she hadn't realized how much she missed Mom's mother-hen routine.

Jack opened the door and stepped out onto the sidewalk. He stood motionless for a minute, then pivoted to face her. "Have you been outside tonight?"

She shook her head, not sure where he was going with that.

"A warm front came through this afternoon." He stuck a hand out the door like he was checking for rain. "It feels like spring out here. You wouldn't want to go for a walk, would you? I bet some fresh air would clear your head . . . might even help those tax forms make sense."

The invitation enticed her more than she expected. She needed the exercise desperately, and she could actually hear crickets chirping in the flowerbeds next door. It was all she could do to refuse the offer.

But it was Jack. And long evening walks weren't something one did with casual friends or "fellow Chamber of Commerce members." She'd made up her mind not to get involved.

He stood there waiting, with a winsome smile and a hopeful expression.

She felt her guard slip a notch. Why not? It was just a walk. A much-needed break from work. And she wouldn't feel safe walking alone after dark, even here in Clayburn.

"Sure." She answered before she could talk herself out of it. "As long as there's not an engagement ring in your pocket." She winked so there'd be no mistake that she was kidding.

He rewarded her with a smile that made her question her rash decision.

"Let me get my jacket." She'd keep it short. Just a quick stroll around the block and keep the conversation light. Talk about the weather.

A sliver of pumpkin-colored moon was suspended over Clayburn. The balmy evening air smelled of damp earth and the newborn spring. They headed south down Main at a brisk pace. Before they'd gone two blocks, Vienne shed her jacket and tied it around her waist. The crocuses and daffodils in the planters in front of the firehouse poked up green heads under the streetlights and her spirits lifted with them.

"It won't be long till winter is a memory." Jack's voice carried a wistful tone.

"You sound like you'll miss it."

"Oh, no. It's not that. It's just . . . I've got a lot to do in the next few weeks."

"Getting ready for your art classes? I saw the ad in the paper."

"Yes, that, and I volunteered the gallery for a show in April—for the art association in Salina. Funny how I'm seeing all the stuff that needs repairing now that I've committed."

She shook her head. "I know how that goes. Do you have room to hang a show with all your other art?"

"I'll have to take a lot of mine down, but that's okay. What's up now isn't my best stuff anyway. But I need to worry about the classes first. They start a week from Monday."

"Do you have quite a few signed up?"

"Just five right now."

"That's not a bad start, is it? Five?"

He shrugged. "I was hoping for at least eight. For the sake of tuition, I wish I had room for ten or twelve." He gave a crooked smile. "But I'll take what I can get."

"Wow . . . can you fit that many in the gallery?"

He looked sheepish. "No. It'd be a tight squeeze with eight. But we could make it work." With a hand on the small of her back, Jack steered her to the right as they crossed Main and turned down Pickering Street.

She quickened her pace, relieved when his hand didn't linger, and keenly aware that they'd already gone far beyond her self-imposed once-around-the-block limit. Well, too late now. Besides, it did feel wonderful to stretch her legs and breathe in the evening air.

"So how do you teach something like art?" she said, picking up the thread of their conversation again. "Isn't that something you're either born with or you're not?"

"Oh, I wouldn't say that exactly." He thought for a minute. "A God-given gift helps, but a lot of skills can be taught, too. But I'd venture to say most of the people who've signed up already have some artistic talent. You don't usually sign up for an art class unless you've shown some promise."

"I'm not so sure about that."

"What do you mean?"

"Well . . . maybe fine art is different, but I sure didn't have any talents in the legal field when I started law school."

He gave her a look. "I don't believe that for a minute. Why else would you start something that time consuming and expensive? There must have been some spark there."

"Not a flicker."

"I don't get it then. Why did you go to law school? . . . If you don't mind me asking."

She felt her defenses rise, but after all, she was the one who opened the door to this topic. For someone who didn't like to talk about her failures, she'd sure managed to open her big mouth a lot around Jack Linder.

The soles of their shoes thumped out a pleasant cadence on the brick sidewalks of Clayburn's older neighborhoods. They passed a two-story home with every window alight. Vienne heard the muffled laughter of children from within and tried to imagine a different sort of life in Clayburn from the one she'd known.

"Why did I go to law school?" She peered up at Jack from the corner of her vision. His expression held genuine interest and a deep kindness that held a mysterious sway with her. "I really don't know," she said finally. She grinned up at him, feeling oddly like she was about to leap from a cliff. "You may have noticed that I have something of a chip on my shoulder."

"No!" He feigned shock. "You? Surely not!"

She gave him the punch in the arm he deserved, but quickly turned serious. She felt a sudden longing to be understood on this. Or maybe she just wanted to understand herself. "Living in Clayburn wasn't the best experience in the world for me. My father's reputation was—well, you know." She shrugged and scuttled away from that topic. "Money was always tight. There was never enough for nice clothes like the other girls wore. I couldn't get involved in the activities at school because I had to help out at the café in my spare time." She stopped in the middle of the sidewalk. "I'm sorry . . . you don't want to hear my sad sob story."

"No, please . . . I like hearing your story." Jack's expression remained full of kindness. He started walking again, but at a more leisurely pace.

She followed. "Life probably wasn't as horrible as I thought back then. Especially after my father died." In spite of the voice inside that warned her to shut up, to go home and lock herself away before it was too late, she kept talking. "Mom and I had our differences, but we only had each other. And we were close. I . . . ." A lump clogged her throat. She swallowed it, but renewed guilt hit her for the way she'd neglected Mom the last few days. "Sometimes I'm afraid she'll never come home."

Jack touched her arm briefly. "I'm sorry, Vienne. That must be so hard."

She forced a smile over the tears, angry with herself for breaking down in front of him. Again. Yet somehow, at the same time, she wanted to throw herself into his arms and absorb the comfort she knew he would offer. How had they moved to such intimate conversation in ten blocks' time? She should have followed her first instincts and said no to this walk.

They strolled in silence for a while until Vienne heard the river in the distance. They'd almost walked the distance to the small park that bordered the banks of the Smoky Hill. The night sky was black, but a myriad of stars winked at them from above. She stopped again and turned toward the faint lights of town. "I really need to get back."

"Sure. Of course . . . it's getting late. You warm enough?"

She nodded, but she untied the jacket from her waist and slipped her arms back into the sleeves, wrapping the front tightly around her torso.

She never should have come.

She shivered. She
had to get Mom out
of this place. How
could anyone live here
and not eventually
lose their sanity?

Chapter Twenty-six

✦ ❀ ✦ ❀ ❖ ✶ ❀ ❀ ✦ ❀ ✶ ❀ ✶ ❀ ✶ ❀ ❖

W ell . . . good night." Jack closed the door of Vienne's car and stepped away. She started the engine and backed from the alley behind the coffee shop onto Elm Street.

He waved, but she didn't see him . . . or pretended not to. She looked his way one last time before disappearing into the darkness. She'd clammed up on the walk back to the coffee shop, and he wasn't sure why.

Heading back to the gallery, he tried to think what he might have said to upset her, but he drew a blank. Maybe, like she'd said, she was just worried about her mother.

He let himself in the back door and walked through to the gallery, turning off lights and checking locks before going upstairs to watch the news. He flipped on the TV on his way through the living room and went to his computer in the small office beside his bedroom. Maybe he'd have a few more e-mails from people interested in his art classes. It had been Trevor's suggestion to allow registration by e-mail, and Jack had forgotten to check yesterday.

He checked his in-box and waited while fifteen e-mails downloaded. That was at least a dozen more than he usually got. The spammers must have detected his new e-mail address already. But he was surprised to find that only half of the posts were spam. He had a note from Mom saying she finally had her Internet up and running in her apartment in St. Petersburg. He added her to his address book, relieved that he could communicate with her via e-mail now. Their brief phone calls had been too fraught with emotions for both of them. Mom wasn't convinced he was "cured"—as she put it. And outside of inviting her to come take a look for herself, he'd run out of ways to convince her he was getting along well.

He scrolled down the page. There was a confirmation of his reservation for the art council dinner meeting next week, and a note from another possible student for his art class, along with an inquiry about future sessions. Good. The class might fill up after all.

A newscaster droned from the TV in the living room. Jack leaned back in his chair and laced his hands behind his head. Things were coming together. He was starting to feel like a seminormal person again. During the counseling he'd received in rehab, he'd come to realize that nothing would ever take away the sorrow and regret over the pain he'd caused Trevor. But he'd been forgiven—by God and by Trevor—and their friendship had been restored. And now that Trevor had a beautiful wife to love, the guilt had diminished somewhat and God had softened the anguish.

Jack breathed deeply. It seemed that even his physical pain had lessened—without pain medication. He clicked the mouse and opened up the last e-mail. It was from one of the online galleries where he listed his work—probably a bill for the month's listings. But as he read further, his hopes soared. It was a notice of sale. He'd sold one of his largest land-scapes. And it brought full price! Twenty-five hundred dollars. Fifteen hundred dollars after the gallery took their 40 percent.

He let out a whoop. If he hadn't learned to move slowly for the sake of his ribs, he might have jumped up and down. But instantly humbled, he turned his elation into a prayer. *"Thank You, Father. And forgive me for every minute I spent doubting You."*

He'd scarcely said "amen" when a twinge of worry edged into his thoughts. His car repairs, the emergency room bill, and a minimum payment on his credit card bill would eat up fifteen hundred dollars faster than he could get it to the bank.

Still, God had never yet failed to provide for his needs. He could trust. *Help me to trust You, Lord.*

He printed out the e-mail and studied the information again. The buyer was listed only as T&T Enterprises, no address given. Paid with a money order. He didn't recall making a sale to that name before, but it was always nice when the buyer was corporate—a chance for his work to hang in public and serve as a free billboard. Interesting. He'd have to inquire of the online gallery about it. But for now he was going to celebrate.

He headed upstairs to the fridge for some Rocky Road, this morning's splurge from the ice cream aisle at the IGA—and almost as effective as pain pills.

✳ ✖ ✳

Vienne moved through the lobby of the Clayburn Manor with a purposeful gait. She heard Flossie's strident voice before she saw her, standing at the reception desk jawing at the poor woman sitting there. Vienne put her head down and veered to the right, lest Flossie spot her and take her hostage with a running monologue of the latest Manor gossip. Or worse, try to hold her hand like she'd done the other night.

She shivered. She had to get Mom out of this place. How could anyone live here and not eventually lose their sanity? And yet, Mom had seemed unusually cheerful the last time Vienne visited. Her gibberish was a little less jumbled and she only cried once, when Vienne left to go. Maybe the therapists were making progress after all.

"Hello there. Yoohoo! Hello! Kenney!"

She glanced behind her to see Flossie shuffling at top speed down the hall to catch up with her.

"Hi, Flossie." Vienne gave a little wave over her shoulder and lengthened her stride.

Snoop that she was, Flossie had actually proven to be a good source of information, and there were days Vienne appreciated the details she shared about the goings on in the Manor. But today wasn't one of them.

She pushed open the door marked 215 and all but dove in to her mother's room.

Mom was dozing in the vinyl chair by the window, but her head jerked up when Vienne closed the door. A knowing expression came to her mother's lined face. She knew exactly what Vienne was up to.

Vienne couldn't help but smile. She gave an exaggerated sigh and wiped the back of her hand over her brow. "Whew! I made it past the gauntlet."

"Foss-eee?"

Vienne nodded, feeling sheepish.

Mom giggled, musical laughter that sounded more like her old self than she had in a long time. It was contagious. Vienne's giggles only made Mom laugh louder. Since the stroke, any overt show of emotion was likely to get out of control, even to the point of hysteria. But tonight Mom seemed in control of herself. Her shoulders shook and her eyes twinkled, but she didn't fall apart.

"That's not very nice of me, I know"—Vienne glanced back at the door—"but that woman would talk my ear off if I stopped for two seconds. Does she do that to you?"

Mom started shaking her head up and down, and reached up to tug at her own ear. Vienne could have sworn she winked. They got tickled again, and as their laughter intertwined, Vienne's spirits mounted. She'd talked *at* her mother from the day they'd moved her from the hospital to the Manor, but tonight was the first time she felt they'd actually had a "conversation" of sorts.

Her mother must have felt it, too, for she beamed and reached out for Vienne with her left hand. Vienne took it and held it in hers. "We should do your therapy." She transferred Mom's hand to her own left hand and opened the drawer of the bedside table. She rummaged through the clutter until she found a bottle of lotion. Gently she removed the sweat-damp washcloth the aides put in Mom's grip in an attempt to keep the muscles from atrophy. She didn't like the odd bent that hand had to it since the stroke.

As she massaged her mother's hands and fingers with the soothing lotion, she started to talk about her day. "The shop was a zoo this week, but the cash drawer sure doesn't reflect that. Still, we made almost three hundred dollars more than the week before." She stroked a thumb along Mom's soft, veined wrist. "Who knows what makes the difference. It's anybody's guess . . ."

She looked up to see her mother watching her, pure love gleaming in her eyes. Vienne swallowed hard and went back to work massaging Mom's hand and wrist. Maybe if this were done more often, Mom would regain more use of her right side. She'd talk to the physical therapists. She could start coming right after supper each evening to work with Mom a little longer. Double up on the therapy sessions.

Her shoulders sagged at the thought of coming here for more than her usual quick good night and laundry pickup after a full day's work. But it was the least she could do for this woman who'd worked so hard to give her a chance at life. A chance Harlan Kenney had all but stolen from them.

Mom's hands tensed in Vienne's lap. She looked up to see concern knit on her mother's brow. "What is it? Do you want to tell me something, Mom?"

Ingrid Kenney raised up in the chair, her weak leg causing her body to list to one side.

"Are you okay? Here let me help you." She propped a bed pillow under her mom's arm.

"Ahhh . . . yuuuu . . ." The drawn-out syllables turned into low groans.

Somehow Vienne understood. "You're worrying about *me*?"

Mom's head flopped like a rag doll in the affirmative, and Vienne detected a spark of triumph. Mom had made herself understood.

Vienne gathered up the frail, warm hands, enfolding them in her own. "Don't you worry about me. I'm fine. I've got lots of help. Evan and Allison are doing a great job."

Her mother beamed and Vienne's heart sang. They were having a conversation, she and Mom. They'd understood each other, and they'd both been energized by the exchange.

For the first time in weeks, Vienne felt full of hope.

She wanted to keep the conversation going. "Jackson Linder's helped out at the shop some, too. He came and bussed tables for me the first day. And I've got these big boards with the menu on them . . . he chalked those out for me. You should see them. They're works of art in themselves."

Mom nodded her approval and pushed out a word. "Zhak."

"Yes, Jack. You remember him, right? From the gallery."

Mom nodded more vigorously. "Zhak." She flung out her left arm in the awkward way she'd adopted since the stroke, trying to point at something on the windowsill. Several greeting cards were lined up there, among the fading plants Mom had received while she was in the hospital. Vienne had watered them faithfully for the first weeks, but the wilted, yellowing leaves testified to her recent neglect.

"Zhak." Mom thrust her index finger at a little vase of still-fresh daisies that sat among the plants. Vienne hadn't noticed it before. She got up and went to read the florists' card stuck in a plastic holder.

Keeping you in my prayers . . . Jackson Linder.

Vienne studied her mother's face. "Jack . . . sent these?"

Mom nodded vigorously. "Zhak."

"Mom, do you know . . . about Jack? Why he closed the gallery?"

Again, Mom nodded.

"He was in rehab, Mom."

Mom nodded her understanding. Her eyes filled with tears, and her mouth worked the way it did when she was struggling to get a word out. "Youuu . . . daaadd-ee. Har-leee." Her face crumpled and the exaggerated sobs came.

Vienne hurried to put an arm around her. "It's okay, Mom. It's okay—" After all these years, Mom still mourned her husband and lived with regret for what might have been.

But her mother pushed away from her and placed her left palm along Vienne's cheek.

"What is it?"

"Zhak?" The concern was clear in her eyes.

"How's Jack?"

Mom nodded, her eyes wide with anticipation.

Not wanting to worry her, Vienne had never told her mother about Jack falling from the balcony at Latte-dah. She understood that Mom's question now was about how Jack was doing since rehab.

"I think . . . he seems to be doing well. The gallery is open again and he's starting some classes."

"G-gooood!" Mom beamed her approval.

Vienne looked past her at the daisies on the windowsill. Jack had sent flowers.

Something about Mom's concern for Jack, her obvious affection for him, caused Vienne's spirits to mount.

But just as quickly, it reminded her of the way Mom had always stood up for Harlan Kenney, always been his champion—regardless of how he'd hurt and humiliated them. Mom's love for the man had been blind and irrational.

She would never understand it. And after all these years, she and her mother were still suffering the repercussions of that foolish love.

This was going
to be a challenge—
for different reasons
than he'd originally
thought.

Chapter Twenty-seven

*J*ack paced from the workroom to the gallery and back again. He glanced at his watch and paced some more. His students would start arriving in fifteen or twenty minutes. Everything was ready—borrowed easels and stools in place, supply lists printed and copied, and everything set up for his demonstration. So why was he a nervous wreck?

He went to the utility sink in the workroom and ran the water cold. He searched for a cup, then remembered he'd taken them up to his kitchen, trying to tidy up the studio. He drank from his hands, attempting to lubricate his parched throat. He'd rehearsed his introduction in his head a dozen times. He knew exactly what he wanted to share with his students tonight, but a part of him was terrified the words wouldn't be there when he needed them.

It wasn't like he hadn't done this before. Shoot, he'd done it drunk—and received compliments on his classroom presence. But could he do it sober? Sadly, he'd known people who were a sight more interesting when they were liquored up. He just prayed he wasn't one of them.

The front door chime sounded and he heard footsteps on the wood floor. His nerves kicked into overdrive. Guess he'd find out soon enough. He closed the door to the workroom behind him and went to greet his first student.

He relaxed a little, seeing an elderly man standing in the middle of the gallery, hat in hand. Jack didn't think he was a student, since Doug DeVore was the only male who'd signed up for his classes. Not to mention the man wasn't exactly dressed for painting. His overcoat was unbuttoned over a navy suit and a wide tie in shades of maroon and teal.

The man studied the large painting near the front window. It was a new piece and one Jack was proud of, but it was still difficult to have people peruse his work in his presence. Since reopening the gallery, he'd regretted having to sell his better stuff before going into rehab. Then again, it had offered incentive for getting new work finished and hung.

He approached the man, stopping just near enough to announce his presence, yet not so close as to interrupt his viewing.

The man seemed lost in the painting. A good sign.

Jack cleared his throat. "Good evening. May I help you?"

The man looked up, holding Jack's gaze a moment too long, and making him feel uneasy. "I'm just browsing," he said finally.

"Of course. Um . . . the gallery is actually closed tonight. I have an art class starting in a few minutes. But you're welcome to look around."

The man nodded and moved to the next painting. Jack busied himself adjusting easels that would only have to be readjusted when his students arrived. He was relieved when Trevor and Meg Ashlock showed up arm in arm.

Jack met them at the door. "Come on in, you two." He winked at Meg. "Did you actually talk this guy into getting a little culture?"

Trevor held up his hands, shaking his head adamantly. "You know better than that. The only painting you'll see me doing is on Sheetrock with a gallon bucket of semigloss."

Meg rolled her eyes. "Not to mention there's some basketball game he wants to see on ESPN tonight. Sorry, Jack. He's just dropping me off." She stood on tiptoe to kiss her husband.

Jack looked away while they kissed like a couple of honeymooners. But it did his heart good to see his friend so happy again. And Meg, too. They were obviously head over heels for each other.

"Things going okay, Jack?" Trevor's attempt to make the question seem offhand was convincing, but his eyes betrayed concern.

With a twinge of guilt, Jack saw again how selfish his escape to the bottle had been. He put a hand on Trevor's arm and gave a smile he hoped was reassuring. "Things are going well. I'm doing good. Thanks, Trevor."

"Good . . . good. Well . . . see you later, buddy." He clapped Jack on the shoulder, then kissed Meg one more time. "Good luck with the class, babe. Don't let the instructor be too hard on you." He winked and headed for the front.

The elderly man had made the rounds through the gallery, and now he followed Trevor to the door.

"Thanks for coming in." Jack waved to the man's back, regretting that he'd neglected his customer while he joked with his friends.

The man turned, tipped his hat in acknowledgment, and started to leave. But then he closed the door behind Trevor and turned to Jack. "You have some nice work here. Would you have a card I could take with me?"

"Sure, sure . . ." Jack pulled one of his old business cards from a stack on the counter and handed it to the man. He pointed to a line on the card. "Our regular hours are on there. And you can see some work from other galleries at my website. Let me know if I can help you."

"I'll do that. Thanks. Sorry to interrupt." He acknowledged Meg with a nod.

"No problem at all." Jack followed him to the door and turned the Closed sign around in the window once the man was out of sight.

Meg frowned. "I hope we didn't interrupt a sale."

"I doubt it. He has my card. Most people look more than once before they buy." He panned the room. "Well, you have your choice of seats. Take your pick."

They both turned at the ping of the door chime. Doug DeVore walked in. Meg gave a comical lift of her eyebrows and quickly claimed a seat front and center.

Jack held back a smile. "Come on in, Doug. I probably shouldn't warn you that you're going to be sadly outnumbered tonight. I've got four women signed up—and you."

Doug laughed. "Hey, that's the story of my life. I'm outnumbered six to two in my own home."

"How's Kaye doing? And the kids?"

"Everybody's great."

The three of them made small talk as the other students drifted in. His butterflies came back big time when Clara Berger came through the door. He excused himself and went to greet her. "Can I help you?"

She slipped her glasses down her nose and eyed him over the frames. "Well, I want to sign up for the art class. Isn't that what this is all about?" She looked past him at the students chatting in the gallery.

"Oh . . . Of course. Sure. Let me get you a registration form." He hadn't expected any new registrants tonight, and certainly not Clara, but he found an extra form in a file cabinet and handed it to her.

"My friend Myrt is coming, too. You know Myrtle Hawkins, of course."

He didn't, but Clara didn't leave room for him to squeeze a word in.

"Myrt's parking the car." She cocked her head toward the street and moved closer, though the whole room couldn't help but hear her stage whisper. "The woman won't park next to another vehicle. Doesn't want her fancy Lincoln dinged, you know."

Just then the door opened again and a plump, heavily made-up woman sashayed in, wheezing to catch her breath.

"Good evening." Jack slid a second form on the counter beside Clara. "You must be Mrs. Hawkins."

She beamed.

"You ladies fill out the registration, and we'll get started in just a minute." He raised his voice until he'd captured everyone's attention. "If everyone could find an easel, we'll get started."

He waited while people found their seats.

"Excuse me . . . Jack!" From her perch at the reception desk, Clara snapped her fingers.

"Yes?"

"What are you looking for on this line where it says 'experience'?" She cleared her throat and waited until everyone's eyes were on her. "I've won several ribbons at the state fair for my acrylics, and I recently received an award of merit from the Coyote County Craft Council. Is that the type of thing you're looking for?"

He looked away, only to catch the barely perceptible rolling of Doug DeVore's eyes. He had to bite his cheek to keep from laughing. When he'd composed himself, he told Clara, "You could certainly list those accomplishments if you like, Mrs. Berger. I was really wanting to know whether you've taken art courses before, or workshops, that sort of thing."

Clara scribbled madly on the form, and Jack fully expected she'd soon be asking for an additional sheet on which to list her voluminous artistic accomplishments.

He looked out over the eager faces assembled in his studio, and excitement buoyed him, making him forget all about being nervous. He'd forgotten how rewarding it was to share his knowledge with others. "We won't do any actual painting tonight, but I promise we'll get our hands dirty next week. You might want to dress accordingly. I have some smocks if anyone needs to borrow one, but an old shirt will work fine." He looked pointedly at Clara and Myrtle, who, coiffed and bejeweled, were settling in at their easels, as if they were warming a church pew.

"Now . . ."

Meg grinned at him from a front row seat, obviously aware that he was having trouble keeping a straight face. He looked over her head.

This was going to be a challenge—for different reasons than he'd originally thought. He took a deep breath and tried to think serious thoughts. "If you'll take a look at your handouts, we'll go over some of the basics."

The evening flew by, and he didn't realize it was nine o'clock until he saw Trevor slip in the door.

Jack glanced at his watch. "I guess that's all the time we have for tonight. I'll see you all back here same time next week. Don't forget to pick up the supply list on your way out, and please try to have all your supplies by then."

As Clara slithered into her coat, she craned her neck and peered through the plate-glass window. "Too bad the coffee shop isn't open. We could all go have a latte."

The murmurs of agreement around the room sparked an idea. Jack could hardly wait until morning to run his scheme by Vienne.

Jack stepped inside. Rats. She'd mostly managed to avoid him for the last two weeks.

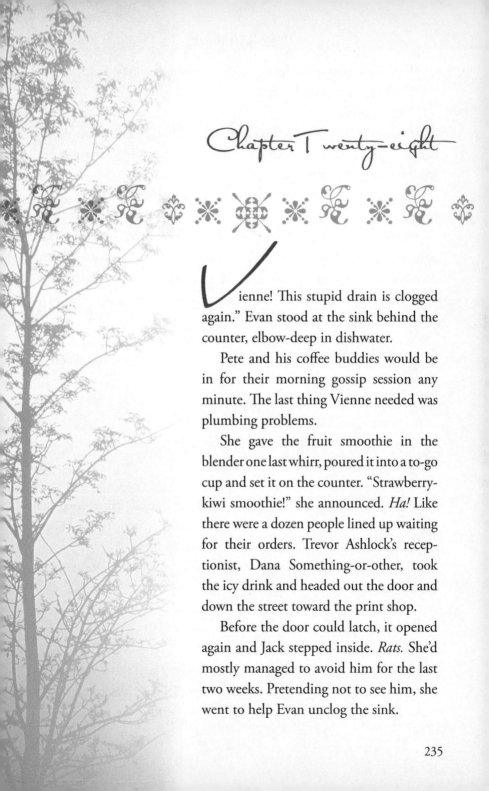

Chapter Twenty-eight

"Vienne! This stupid drain is clogged again." Evan stood at the sink behind the counter, elbow-deep in dishwater.

Pete and his coffee buddies would be in for their morning gossip session any minute. The last thing Vienne needed was plumbing problems.

She gave the fruit smoothie in the blender one last whirr, poured it into a to-go cup and set it on the counter. "Strawberry-kiwi smoothie!" she announced. *Ha!* Like there were a dozen people lined up waiting for their orders. Trevor Ashlock's receptionist, Dana Something-or-other, took the icy drink and headed out the door and down the street toward the print shop.

Before the door could latch, it opened again and Jack stepped inside. *Rats.* She'd mostly managed to avoid him for the last two weeks. Pretending not to see him, she went to help Evan unclog the sink.

"You're sure you didn't let any coffee grounds go down there?"

"No." Evan wagged his head

"Banana peels?"

"Come on, Vienne, I'm not a complete idiot." Evan threw up his hands in mock defense, flicking soapsuds in her hair in the process. "Sorry 'bout that, boss."

She gave him a look and nudged him out of the way. "Here . . . let me see."

Probing the bottom of the sink, she came up empty-handed. She refused to pay a plumber ninety dollars an hour to unclog a sink. "Evan, do me a favor, would you? Run to the IGA and get some of that extra-strength drain cleaner? And see if they have a decent plunger while you're at it. That one you tried this morning is a hundred years old."

"Got it." Evan stripped off his apron and turned, then hooked a thumb toward the front counter. "Oh . . . want me to take this order first?"

She risked a glance Jack's way.

He waved and flashed a smile. "No rush."

"I got it," Vienne told Evan. "You can take a twenty from the cash register. Hurry back."

"I will."

Evan got the cash and jogged to the back door. Vienne dried her hands and, reminding herself of all the reasons she couldn't get involved with Jack Linder, went to the counter to wait on him.

"Sorry about that." She glanced over her shoulder. "We've got a backed-up sink."

"Bummer. You want me to take a look at it?"

"Are you a plumber?"

"Not by trade, but I'm pretty good with—"

"Jack." She offered a half-grin. "I'm kidding. I sent Evan to get some Drano. But if that doesn't do the trick, I might let you have a go at it. My luck, this'll be the day the health department decides to pay a visit."

He winced. "That would not be good."

"No," she agreed, moving to the cash register. "And thanks for the offer. I'll let you know how it turns out. Now what can I get you? A nice latte maybe?" She bit her cheek to keep from smiling.

"Maybe another day," he deadpanned. "I'll just have a Coke. Actually, I came in to talk to you about something, but"—he eyed the sink behind her—"is this a bad time?"

She kept her sober expression. "I can't do anything with that until Evan gets back, but . . ." She glanced about the empty shop. "I'm kind of swamped with customers right now."

Jack rolled his eyes. "I can take a hint."

She laughed. "Let me get your Coke and I'll be right there."

She fixed his drink and took it to the high-top where he'd perched. She untied her apron and slipped it over her head, then raked the rubber band from her ponytail and shook out her hair. "So what's up?"

Jack took a long sip from the straw, then tented his hands on the table in front of him. "I have a proposition for you. After class last night my students were saying that they—"

"Oh, that's right . . . how'd that go?"

He nodded. "Good, I think. I had seven students and nobody walked out on me. Anyway, everybody was saying they wished the coffee shop was open so they could all go out for drinks together afterward."

She cocked her head and folded her arms. *If he thought she was going to open . . .*

"Wait . . . I know that look." He shook a finger at her. "Hear me out."

She eyed him with suspicion but kept quiet.

"Here's what I was thinking: since you're usually here one night a week doing the books or cleaning or whatever, what if you stayed open that one night. There probably wouldn't be that many people besides my class, but I just had another one enroll this morning, so that's nine of us, counting me"— he shrugged—"well, assuming everybody comes for coffee . . . But if word got out that you were open that one night, people might decide to make a night of it. And since you're here anyway—" His voice gathered steam. "I'd help you bus tables and clean up afterward, whatever. But I think it could be good for both of us."

She considered what he'd proposed. "How late would I have to stay open?"

"Well, class is from seven to nine, but maybe I could move it up half an hour. Would that help?"

"I guess it doesn't really matter. Really, later is better. That way I can go see Mom in between the regular closing and opening back up."

She could tell by the boyish enthusiasm on his face that he was surprised she was saying yes so readily. But it was actually a good idea. She may not make a ton of money, but like he'd said, she was here anyway. And it would be one way to foster goodwill with a community who hadn't been too impressed with Latte-dah up till now. She shrugged. "I think it could work."

Jack beamed. "Great! I'll tell everybody Monday night." He snapped his fingers. "Better yet, I'll send an e-mail to everyone so they can plan ahead. You're okay to start next week?"

"Sure. We'll try it for a week or two . . . see how it goes."

"That's fair."

"So tell me about your class. Sounds like you had a good turnout."

"I'm pretty pleased. I wouldn't mind adding a couple more, money-wise. But it's a good number as far as the hands-on stuff. I couldn't do it justice if we had too many more."

The doorbells clattered and two middle-aged women came in, chattering away. Vienne wanted to tell them to go away. Jack would probably leave now, thinking he was intruding. Reluctantly she excused herself, grabbed her apron, and went to wait on these rarest of creatures—customers.

To her surprise, ten minutes later—with the ladies settled in front of the blazing fireplace sipping lattes—Jack was still there.

One beer couldn't
hurt. It'd be a
good chance to prove—
to himself—that he
had a handle on this.

Chapter Twenty-nine

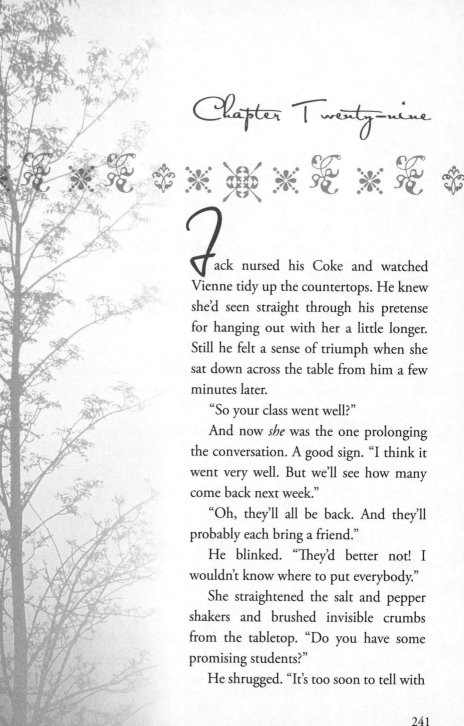

*J*ack nursed his Coke and watched Vienne tidy up the countertops. He knew she'd seen straight through his pretense for hanging out with her a little longer. Still he felt a sense of triumph when she sat down across the table from him a few minutes later.

"So your class went well?"

And now *she* was the one prolonging the conversation. A good sign. "I think it went very well. But we'll see how many come back next week."

"Oh, they'll all be back. And they'll probably each bring a friend."

He blinked. "They'd better not! I wouldn't know where to put everybody."

She straightened the salt and pepper shakers and brushed invisible crumbs from the tabletop. "Do you have some promising students?"

He shrugged. "It's too soon to tell with

most of them. But Meg Ashlock is very talented. Shoot, she could probably *teach* the class."

"Trevor's wife?"

He nodded. "I understand she worked as a graphic designer in New York. I saw some of her work a year or so ago and it's pretty impressive."

She eyed him playfully. "Doesn't that worry you? To be training your competition?"

He laughed. "Maybe it should. But no . . . I figure God has room for more than one artist in Coyote County."

"I'm not sure I could say that if somebody else tried to open another coffee shop here." She frowned. "Not that anybody would be that stupid."

"Well, your situation is a little different. People have to come to Clayburn to enjoy the fruits of your labor. You can't exactly sell lattes online."

She smiled. "Oh, don't I wish. Anything to eliminate the dishwashing, floor-mopping aspect of this job. Not to mention the money-losing aspect."

He laughed and shook his head. "Nothing would surprise me anymore. Who knows what technology might come up with next?"

She looked skeptical.

"Okay, maybe not lattes online. But then, I never thought I'd sell my art online either. Stranger things have happened. There was a place in Kansas City when I lived there where you could order groceries—milk and bread and eggs—over the Internet and have them delivered to your door the same day. It was pricey, but still . . ."

"That's crazy."

"I actually have my art posted in several online galleries."

"Really?" She tipped her head. "Do you sell much that way?"

"I haven't had great luck with it in the past. People might see my work online initially, but then they'll usually visit a brick-and-mortar gallery to see the real thing before they decide to buy. But the Internet market really seems to be opening up. I've sold a couple of pieces straight through my website recently."

"Wow, that's great."

"Every bit helps. Oh, by the way, you'll never guess who showed up for my art class."

She shook her head.

"Clara Berger. And her friend . . . Myrtle Something-or-other . . . ?"

Vienne smiled knowingly. "Myrtle Hawkins, I bet. They come in here together sometimes."

Jack nodded. "That's her."

She gave a little laugh. "That ought to keep things interesting."

"I'm halfway suspicious that my mom signed her up to spy on me long-distance." He rolled his eyes. "Bless Clara's heart—and this isn't very nice to say—but I'm telling you, the woman just might drive me to drink."

No response.

"Vienne . . ." He put a hand on her arm. "Hey, I'm kidding."

She glared at him. "Don't even joke about that." She gave a sheepish grin. "And that *wasn't* very nice."

He wasn't sure if she meant his comment about Clara, or his quip about drinking. "Sorry, bad joke."

"Very bad. Extremely bad." Her furrowed brow couldn't hide her smile.

It was a warm, open smile. A very nice smile. And right now, it was doing strange and wonderful things to his insides.

❋ ❋ ❋

Smoke from the bar wafted through the restaurant. Jack coughed discreetly as he trailed the hostess down a narrow hallway lined with taxidermied specimens. He was glad the art council had reserved a meeting room in the back. It gave him a few extra minutes to gather his wits about him.

He thought about seeing everyone again and clenched and unclenched his hands, then wiped damp palms on his khakis. It didn't help matters that he was half an hour late. He figured most of them knew the reason for his absence of nearly a year. Unlike too many in his hometown, these people would welcome him back as if nothing had happened. Still, of all nights to have a flat tire.

"Here you go, sir." The pretty hostess opened the door to a back dining room and held it for him.

"Thanks." He swatted at the grass stain on his pants leg to no avail.

"The others have their food already, but Carla will be with you in a moment to take your order."

"Oh, no . . . that's okay. If I could just get . . . a Coke?"

"Are you sure? I'll be glad to bring a menu."

"No, that's okay. Just something to drink will be fine." He ran two fingers under the collar of his button-down shirt. Something to drink sounded pretty good right now. He pushed the image of an ice-cold beer from his mind. He could almost taste the smooth, amber liquid, feel the calming powers as it worked its way through his veins. One beer couldn't hurt. If he knew this crowd, he'd be the only one not drinking. It'd be a good chance to prove—to himself—that he had a handle on this.

Don't even go there, Linder.

"Could I get you something from the bar?" The hostess smiled up at him, as if she sensed his nervousness.

"No—" He shook his head, but somehow, before he knew what took hold of him, his mouth was saying the opposite of what he intended. "You know . . . on second thought, you could bring me a beer, if you don't mind. Bud Lite."

"Sure thing." She turned and hurried back toward the main dining room.

"Thanks." Jack watched her, feeling like he'd just stepped out of an airplane without a parachute. In a few minutes Carla Somebody-or-Other was going to come and set a beer in front of him. And then what was he going to do?

You're going to sip it slowly, make it last all night. That's what.

He knew better. Knew the rap here. Before he finished the first beer, Carla would come back and set another one in front of him. Or one of the guys would offer to buy him a drink. A shot of whiskey or a vodka tonic. The beer would have him nice and loosened up, so it'd be easy to say yes to something a little stronger. Just one. He'd intend to have just one. But that wasn't the way it had ever worked with him. He couldn't stop with just one. He knew that about himself.

It had taken nine months in hell to learn that about himself. And two years before that in a place worse than hell.

Was he going to throw that away just because he was nervous about walking into this room? Was he willing to take the risk that tonight he'd be strong enough to say no after the first drink?

No. Trembling, he sucked in a breath and turned away from the doorway that led to the meeting room. Before he could change his mind, he took a step toward the restaurant's front door. Each step was like slogging through molasses.

Fear gripped him like the teeth of the grizzly bear staring down at him from the hunter's gallery on the wall. What if he ran into someone from the art council on his way out? How would he explain why he was leaving?

Get out. Get out now.

Jack was beginning to know that Voice better than he knew his own. He lengthened his stride and raced through the restaurant. He pushed through the wide front doors and jogged through the parking lot, gulping in the cool night air. He stood beside his car, panting to catch his breath.

Several minutes passed before he opened the door and slid behind the wheel, feeling like a failure of the worst sort. He'd come so close. So close to throwing it all away. So close to risking his sobriety. He leaned over the steering wheel, feeling sick to his stomach.

You did the right thing.

"I did." The sound of his voice in the silence of the enclosed car startled him. But it was true. He'd done the right thing. He'd had no business ordering that beer. But he hadn't drunk it. He hadn't put himself in a position to be further tempted.

He had escaped. There was nothing to be ashamed of. He'd done the right thing. *Thank You, Lord. Oh, God, thank You.*

A windstorm of thoughts battered him as he drove back to Clayburn. He was still weak. He knew that now. He'd gotten a little too self-confident—

Self. That was the problem. Always it came back to that. He'd trusted himself and forgotten to ask God to give him strength. He'd let down his guard.

But he'd learned something in the process—about himself, and about God's patience and grace. And blessedly, he'd learned before he made a mistake he might have regretted forever.

He might have to avoid the art council meetings . . . at least when the venue was a bar. Maybe someday he'd be strong enough that the temptation wouldn't have a grip on him, but he wasn't there yet. He might take three steps forward and one step back, but with God's help, he was going to make it.

A bubble of hope rose inside him and he smiled up at the night sky. Through the windshield, the lights of Clayburn twinkled in the distance, and he drove through the darkness toward their warmth.

Who'd want to come in for lattes and scones with these geezers holding court and spouting quotes from The Farmer's Almanac every weekday morning?

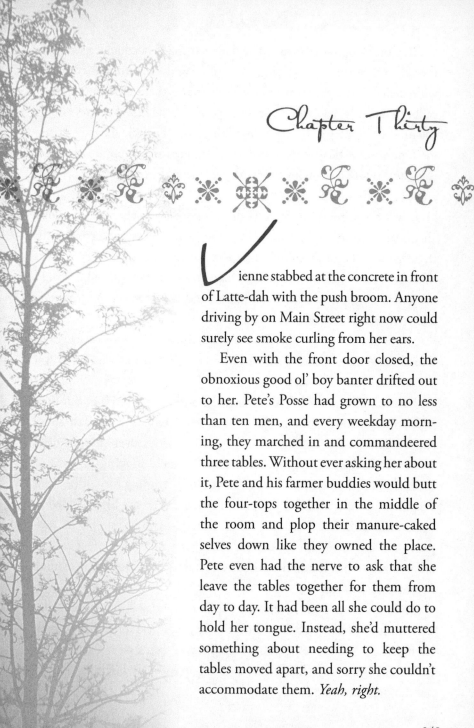

Chapter Thirty

Vienne stabbed at the concrete in front of Latte-dah with the push broom. Anyone driving by on Main Street right now could surely see smoke curling from her ears.

Even with the front door closed, the obnoxious good ol' boy banter drifted out to her. Pete's Posse had grown to no less than ten men, and every weekday morning, they marched in and commandeered three tables. Without ever asking her about it, Pete and his farmer buddies would butt the four-tops together in the middle of the room and plop their manure-caked selves down like they owned the place. Pete even had the nerve to ask that she leave the tables together for them from day to day. It had been all she could do to hold her tongue. Instead, she'd muttered something about needing to keep the tables moved apart, and sorry she couldn't accommodate them. *Yeah, right.*

This morning they'd roosted at their self-made headquarters next to the air pots since ten, slurping free coffee and drowning out Handel with their half-baked farm market reports and their lame junior-high-caliber jokes. She had half a notion to go put some nice, loud rock-and-roll on the CD player. If Pete was still there when people started arriving for lunch, she'd do just that. And then, unless they were ordering up soup and sandwiches with the works, she would personally escort him and his buddies to the door.

It was no wonder she couldn't drum up a regular clientele, let alone an upscale crowd. Who'd want to come in for lattes and scones with these geezers holding court and spouting quotes from *The Farmer's Almanac* every weekday morning? Once in a while Pete's buddies would order French toast or even a sandwich. And they *had* started tipping a little better. But no way were they earning their keep.

She could not go on like this for much longer. She'd seriously entertained thoughts of putting the place on the market. But who'd buy it if she couldn't prove solvency?

Besides, she wouldn't do that without talking to her mother. Mom was making some progress with her rehab, and the last thing she needed was to be bogged down with worries over the business. But something had to give. Vienne was actually looking forward to Monday night, when Jack's art class would be coming for coffee. That was the kind of crowd she'd hoped to attract when she first decided to open Latte-dah. She'd ordered some fancy pastries from a Salina supplier, and a new Wynton Marsalis CD that would be perfect for the artsy crowd. Allison had promised to help her do some extra cleaning Monday afternoon.

She'd thought about advertising the new Monday evening hours, but decided it would be wise to see how the first night went before she made it official. For now, she just hoped and prayed Pete and his gang didn't get wind of it. So help her, if they showed up Monday night and started rearranging furniture . . .

She beat the broom on the sidewalk and carried it back into the shop.

"Hey, Vinny?" Pete beckoned her over to the table.

She resisted rolling her eyes, propped the broom against the doorframe, and went to see what he wanted.

A chorus of "How's it goin', Vinny?" went up from the table. Pete had them all calling her by that odious nickname. Another burr under her saddle.

"What do you need, Pete?"

He pointed to the table where the air pots sat. "The pump pot's dry over there. Could you get us some refills when you get a minute?"

She blew a wisp of hair away from her face. "Sure. I'll get right on it."

The door opened and Mike Jensen's wife, Heather, came in, pulling a stroller backward through the door. Looking out the window, Vienne saw two other moms, one with a baby in a frontpack, making their way across the street. The library story hour crew. She'd almost forgotten that was today. And Allison had class until eleven.

She hurried to get a pot of coffee started for Pete's crew and called out a greeting to the new customers. They usually ordered light and only stayed forty minutes or so, until story hour was over and they had to pick up their preschoolers. Occasionally they came back with toddlers in tow for lunch. That meant major cleanup, but it was good business, and the young moms were surprisingly good tippers. Most of them could probably still remember when they'd waited tables at the Dairy Barn for minimum wage.

Heather Jensen ordered cappuccino and a cinnamon roll, then turned to look around the shop. "I think there's going to be about a dozen of us today. The library had a big promotion for story hour and we invited some of the new moms."

Vienne gave an apologetic smile and looked pointedly toward Pete's table. She lowered her voice. "The men's coffee klatch should be leaving in a few minutes. If you want to wait by the fireplace, I'll take care of everybody's orders and then we can move some tables around."

"We can just take that nice long table when they're finished. If we can scoot one more table over, it'd be perfect for our group."

Vienne hesitated. So much for nicely clustered tables and ambiance. "Okay . . . Sure, we can do that." Beggars couldn't be choosers. At least she had customers.

Pete and his friends chugged a whole pot of coffee and finally filtered out of the shop. When the last farmer left, Vienne grabbed a dustpan and started in on the dried chunks of mud their boots had left behind.

But Heather waved her off. "Don't worry about that, Vienne. Seriously, we're used to a little mud, and you may as well sweep up the mud and cracker crumbs at the same time."

"Um . . . I don't know if you saw who was sitting here before you, but . . . well, it may be . . . worse than mud."

Heather giggled and wrinkled her nose. "Okay . . . maybe you could sweep the worst of it up."

The other moms who'd come in laughed at that and pulled back the chairs so she could sweep. When she was finished, they settled in at the table, which now stretched almost the width of the dining area.

Vienne straightened and stood at the end of the row of tables, broom in hand, surveying her shop. Hmmm . . . With the tables pushed together that way, it left room for another shorter row of tables behind it. Or a grouping of two or three fourtops. It wasn't the classiest look, but at least she could avoid letting Pete think he'd swayed her by making it clear it was the story-hour moms she was leaving the tables up for.

She didn't mind catering to these young moms—especially if their little group continued to expand. Six of them were lined up to order now, and another six sat around the table, minding babies and chattering like chipmunks. This was at least a little closer to what she'd envisioned when she'd first dreamed up Latte-dah.

A wave of longing sluiced over her. If she were honest with herself, she was a tiny bit jealous of these women who, judging by the light in their eyes, had somehow managed to find happiness without ever having left Clayburn.

"One day at a time. That's the secret. You hear me? I wake up every mornin' and I say to myself, 'Just git through this day.'"

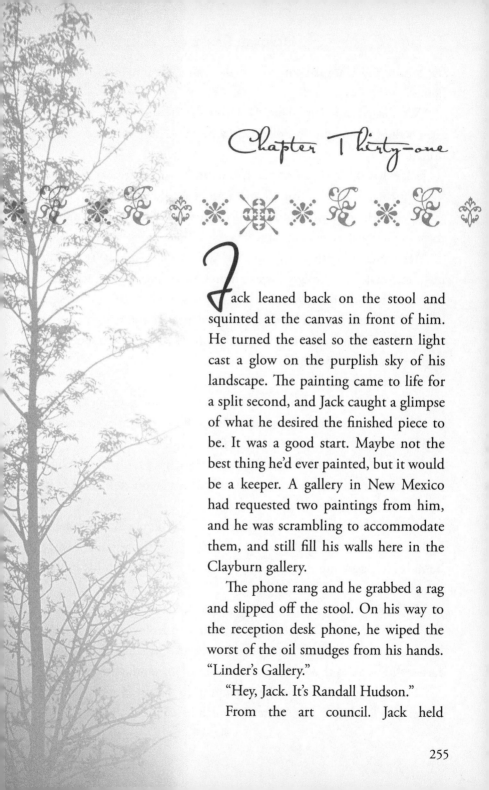

Chapter Thirty-one

*J*ack leaned back on the stool and squinted at the canvas in front of him. He turned the easel so the eastern light cast a glow on the purplish sky of his landscape. The painting came to life for a split second, and Jack caught a glimpse of what he desired the finished piece to be. It was a good start. Maybe not the best thing he'd ever painted, but it would be a keeper. A gallery in New Mexico had requested two paintings from him, and he was scrambling to accommodate them, and still fill his walls here in the Clayburn gallery.

The phone rang and he grabbed a rag and slipped off the stool. On his way to the reception desk phone, he wiped the worst of the oil smudges from his hands. "Linder's Gallery."

"Hey, Jack. It's Randall Hudson."

From the art council. Jack held

his breath and slumped into the desk chair. "Hey, Randall, how's it going?"

"We missed you last night. Did you forget we had an art council meeting? I thought you planned to be there." He sounded a little miffed.

Jack exhaled. "Well, I *had* planned on it, but . . . I had car trouble." That much, at least, was true. "I apologize. I should have called."

"Yeah, well, we were wondering if you're still willing to hang a show there in your gallery next month."

"Yes, I meant to call you about that. We're talking in May, right? I'm planning on it. I . . . I might have to hunt down some display racks. You may want to come out and take a look at the setup here before you sign off on it. Space is kind of limited, but I'm definitely willing."

"Well, we're counting on it if it's still okay. We don't have many other options. I told the council I'd give you a call."

"You can plan on it."

Randall hesitated on the other end. "How're things going for you, Jack?" The trepidation in Randall's voice told him the man knew why he'd been out of the loop over the last few months.

Jack had assumed word would get out. He'd never really tried to hide it. But neither had he made any announcements before he'd checked in to the clinic in Kansas City.

He wondered what had been whispered about him in his absence last night—and was grateful all over again that he'd left the restaurant when he did. He wasn't quite ready to air his dirty laundry with his professional peers.

Holding the phone between his shoulder and his ear, he deliberately misinterpreted Randall's question. "It's been a little slow getting the gallery back up and running, but it's coming. I started teaching some classes earlier this week so that's taking a hunk out of my work schedule."

"Hey, I hear you on that. I'm trying to do that here, too. Well, we missed you last night. Just wanted to touch base."

"Thanks, Randall. Sorry again about missing the meeting. You let me know when you're ready to hang that show."

Jack hung up and sat there, staring out onto Main Street. Well, that wasn't so hard. He probably hadn't missed anything except for certain temptation and the possibility of blowing nine months of therapy.

He stared at the stack of bills skewered on the spindle by the phone. Sometimes he wondered if he'd ever bail out from the debt he'd piled up while he was in rehab. One more consequence of his mistakes. No. He corrected himself—his *sin*. He pulled a receipt for his last frame order from the top of the pile and checked the due date. He had thirty days to pay it. He'd better sell something. Several somethings.

Pete Truesdell went by on the sidewalk in front, hands deep in the pockets of his coveralls. No doubt on his way to Latte-dah for morning coffee. He had quite a crew getting together over there these days. Vienne had to be happy about that. Jack waved.

Pete pulled his hand from his pocket and waved back. He passed the gallery's entrance, then did an about face and came back to the door. He stepped through, doffing his cap as he crossed the threshold. "Mornin'."

"Hey, Pete. Headed for coffee?"

"You got it. But I saw you weren't busy and thought I'd stop in and say hi."

Jack came around the reception desk and extended his hand.

Pete shook it. "I've been wondering how you're gettin' along." He pivoted on the worn heel of his boot, looking the gallery over. "Looks good in here. For what I know about art anyway."

"Well, thanks. It's coming . . . slow but sure."

"My Velma thought about signing up for your art class, but I think she chickened out. She doesn't much like getting out anymore . . . since she had her surgery."

"Is she doing okay?" Jack scrambled to remember what kind of surgery Pete's wife had had.

"She's doing good. Better than they expected, I think. We're just grateful they caught it when they did. But I didn't come here to talk about Velma." He put a warm hand on Jack's forearm. "How is ol' Jack doin'?"

Jack knew what Pete was asking, and unlike with Randall Hudson, he didn't mind opening up to Pete. "I'm doing pretty good, Pete. It's still day-to-day, but I think I just might make it."

Pete shook his head. "It's bound to be that way the rest of your life, son . . . day-to-day."

Jack studied Pete, a thousand questions running through his mind. The old man sounded like he knew . . . firsthand.

As if he'd read Jack's mind, Pete nodded. "Yep. I know what you're goin' through. 'Course you had a sight more reason to pickle your problems than I ever did. I'm sorry for you on that. I really am. It was a hard thing that happened. But every fella's got his own reasons."

Jack nodded, his throat constricting.

Pete took a step back and looked him in the eye. "I want you to know somethin', Jack. I been stone-cold sober myself for thirty-two years now. Thirty-two years and five months as of April first." He chuckled. "Appropriate, huh? April Fool's Day. The day I had my last drink."

"You?" Jack whispered. "I . . . didn't know."

"I know you didn't. Not many here do. And I'd appreciate it if you'd keep it that way." He looked at the floor and scuffed the toe of his boot along the hardwood. "Velma . . . she don't like me talkin' about those days. I put her through the worst kinda hell."

"I'm sorry . . ."

Pete put up a weathered hand. "No. It's me should be sorry. I shoulda said something earlier. Probably shoulda said something before you left for that treatment center. But . . . well, comin' to Clayburn was a fresh start for us. I figured I owe it to Velma to keep my trap shut and let her have her dignity back."

"I never knew," Jack said again, still trying to wrap his mind around this truth about Pete. "Thirty-two years, huh?"

"And five months."

"You still count the months?"

Pete's mouth hardened into a line and he nodded. "Wish I could tell you something different. And don't get me wrong . . . there's sometimes days on end go by that I don't give the bottle much thought. But then I'll get down"—he jabbed two fingers at his own forehead—"and that hunger'll hit me right between the eyes, fresh as it ever was."

Jack's spirits sank. Would he still be fighting this battle thirty-two years from now?

Pete thumped a stubby finger in his chest. "In thirty-two years I've never backslid once. Not once."

A spark of hope rekindled in him.

"If the temptation comes to you, that's one thing," Pete said. "The good Lord makes a way out at times like that."

Jack nodded slowly, remembering the airbags at the liquor store.

"But you can't walk into temptation your own self and expect to win. No sir, Jack, that dog don't hunt."

"I'm learning that, Pete." He told him about what had happened at the restaurant in Salina last night.

Pete listened, nodding and muttering understanding as if he'd been there himself. And maybe, in a sense, he had.

Jack frowned. "If it was just . . . the drinking . . . If that's all I had to concentrate on . . . But the bills are piling up and I still don't have the gallery up to full speed. And I need to spend some time with my mom, but I don't have time or money to make a trip to Florida." He held up a hand. "Sorry. I didn't mean to unload on you."

Pete clapped a hand around his arm. "Hey, that's what friends are for. You go ahead and pitch everything you've got at me."

"Man, Pete . . ." Jack shook his head. "Thirty-two years . . . That's a long time to fight a demon."

Pete's eyes misted over and he pulled Jack into a brief, awkward embrace. "I don't mean to discourage you, son. I only told you all that because I'm just about the stubbornest old cuss you'll ever meet, and if I can get through this, you can, too."

Jack nodded, unable to speak over the knot in his throat.

"One day at a time. That's the secret. You hear me? I wake up every mornin' and I say to myself, 'Just git through this day, Pete. Just git through today. 'And when I lay down at night, I say thanks to the man upstairs for helping me do just that." He looked heavenward.

Jack nodded. "I've been getting down on my knees every morning. It helps a lot."

Pete chuckled again and splayed his fingers over his knees. "If I got down on these ol' knees, I may not get up again. But you keep that up. That prayin'. It's a good thing. It'll help."

"Thanks, Pete. I won't say anything, but . . . well, you'll never know how much it means that you trusted me with this. It . . . gives me hope."

"I'm pullin' for ya." Pete slapped his cap on the knee of his dusty coveralls before placing it on his head. "I better get on over for coffee. I'm bettin' the boys are there already, and I don't want Vinny to think I'm not comin'."

He winked. "She don't let on, but I think she enjoys the company."

Tonight there
would be a rare
touch of class
in Clayburn.

Chapter Thirty-two

ith the breakfast crowd gone, Vienne propped open the door to the coffee shop and watched two robins flit and preen in a puddle at the curb. The morning air was still brisk and heavy with last night's rain, but as she stood in the doorway, the sun climbed above the tops of the buildings on the east side of the street. Its warmth and light reflected off the plate-glass windows of the shops across Main Street. The window displays brimmed with Easter baskets and tulips and daffodils.

The weather had finally turned nice enough that she could ride her bicycle to work. She'd forgotten how exhilarating it was to ride with the sun on her face and the breeze in her hair. She'd stretched her trip home each evening, biking around town, soaking up the beauty of springtime.

She took in one last breath of the crisp

air before going back inside. People would start coming in on coffee break in about an hour. She slipped Vivaldi's *Four Seasons* into the CD player, then prepared to make up the day's sandwiches. She'd ordered extra meats and cheeses, and two new desserts so she'd have some nice things in the case tonight when Jack's art class came for coffee.

She was more excited about the prospect than she'd let on. Not so much for the possibility of a little extra income—though that would certainly be appreciated. But because she was eager to see Latte-dah the way she'd envisioned it all those nights she'd worked designing the floorplan, refinishing the parquet floor, and painting the walls and counters.

Tonight the coffee shop would be an artsy hangout with music and laughter, and conversation about something besides cattle futures and grain commodities, with people who would appreciate her creative beverages and the ambience Latte-dah had to offer. Tonight there would be a rare touch of class in Clayburn.

It was too warm for a fire in the fireplace, but she'd bought a few chunky vanilla candles that would give a nice glow and make it smell like she'd just taken sugar cookies from the oven.

She assembled sandwich ingredients on the counter and sliced a fresh loaf of whole-wheat bread the bakery in Salina had delivered early this morning. Now that she had a routine down, her days had taken on a pleasant rhythm. If she didn't let things like Mom's recovery, or mounting expenses, or Pete and his annoying crew get to her, she found she actually enjoyed her days. She hadn't thought about law school or bar exams, or even California for a long time. And good riddance to them all.

Two women came in for lattes, and she washed her hands and fixed their drinks before returning to wrap the sandwiches and arrange them in the refrigerated display case. Kneeling by the case, she swept a few crumbs from the pastry case into her palm.

The bells on the front door jingled and she rose to find Jack smiling at her from the other side of the counter. It was becoming more and more difficult to ignore the way her heart always responded to his presence. She smiled, remembering Jack's promise that they'd just be casual friends, "fellow Chamber of Commerce members." Except none of the other Chamber of Commerce members seemed to have this effect on her blood pressure.

She brushed the crumbs into the trash can and turned to greet him, trying hard for breezy. "Hey, Jack."

"Good morning. You busy?" He was still smiling.

She wished he wouldn't do that so much around her. "Not too bad. Why, what's up?"

"I have a proposition to make."

"Now hang on just a cotton-pickin' minute." She put her hands on her hips, but she couldn't stop the smile that tugged at her mouth. "I'm staying open late tonight, thanks to the last proposition you made me. Maybe we should see how that goes before you—"

He held up a hand. "I know . . . I know. But this one isn't that involved."

"Okay, I'm listening." She walked to the cash register. "You want something to drink?"

"Sure. I'll take a Coke. Please."

"Coming up." She drew a Coke from the fountain and came around to hand it to him.

He fished in his pocket, but she demurred. "This one's on the house—unless this proposition is going to cost me an arm and a leg. Then you can pay me." She grabbed a bottle of water and followed him to the table in the back that had become "theirs" by default over the past couple of weeks.

Jack took a swig of pop. "Okay. Here's the deal. I sort of promised to hang a show next month for the art council in Salina. But the more I look at the gallery, the more I realize I just don't have the space." His gaze trailed pointedly around the perimeter of Latte-dah. "And the more

I look around here, the more I realize this would be the absolutely perfect place for that show."

"Okay, I'm listening." Through the window, she spied Pete and his friend, Mitch, making their way across the street. *Great.* She rolled her eyes and gave a little snarl.

"What's wrong?" Jack looked over his shoulder, following her line of vision.

"Pete," she huffed. "That's what's wrong."

"Pete Truesdell?"

"Yes," she said through clenched teeth. "That man comes in here and parks his carcass in those filthy boots"—she hooked a thumb at the neatly arranged tables Pete would soon take over—"and he and his posse guzzle coffee like camels and—"

"Whoa . . . whoa . . ." Jack leaned back in his chair and eyed her like she'd just shot somebody. "Whatever happened to 'the customer's always right'?"

She shook her head. "Not that customer."

"Vienne, Pete and his 'posse'—" He parroted the word back to her, using the same inflection she had. She didn't like the way it sounded.

"Those men are your bread and butter," he continued. "If it weren't for people like him, this little town would have died long ago." He swallowed and his voice turned gentle. "You know, maybe if you'd see Pete as a valued customer, he'd rise to the occasion."

She slanted a dubious glance at him.

"Think about it, Vienne. You do an awful lot of complaining about how slow business is to be griping about the business you *do* have. How many friends has Pete brought in here . . . introduced to the place?"

She opened her mouth to protest, but Jack held up a hand, not giving her an inch. "Okay, granted, they may not be quite the clientele you had in mind, but I was always taught the first rule of business is 'beggars can't be choosers.'"

She cocked her head and narrowed her eyes. "I thought it was 'the customer is always right.'"

He grinned. "That's rule number two."

The bells jangled against the door, and Pete and Mitch clomped in.

Feeling chastened—and rightly so—Vienne leaned out of her chair to peek around the counter. "Good morning, Pete."

Jack winked at her and gave her a smile that went a long way to smoothing her ruffled feathers. He tipped back on his chair and waved. "Hey there, Pete." Turning back to Vienne, he touched her hand. "You go on. I can wait."

"It won't take but a minute." She rose and slipped behind the cash register. "Will it be the usual this morning, gentlemen?"

The old man looked behind him, like she might be talking to someone else. It hammered home Jack's point. Had she really been so cool toward Pete that he didn't even believe it when she was friendly to him? Regret pinched her, and she resolved to do better.

A few minutes later, with Pete and Mitch settled in with hot coffee and complimentary day-old muffins, she came back to the table. "So . . . you want to hang an art show here? What exactly would that involve?"

Jack studied the high walls of the coffee shop again. "Well, a lot of nail holes in your walls, for one thing. But you have paint left over, don't you? I promise I'd come and repair the holes and paint over any dings in the wall as soon as we took the show down." Jack laid out his plan for hosting the art show at Latte-dah. His enthusiasm was contagious, and the potential for what a show like this could mean for the coffee shop wasn't lost on her. Watching Jack now—his eyes bright and clear with anticipation, his business savvy apparent—she saw him in a way she hadn't viewed him before. And the contrast was startling.

It struck her—to her shame—that from the day she'd learned of Jack's struggle with alcohol, she had looked at him through the specter of Harlan Kenney, projecting all her father's faults onto Jack. After the night she'd brought Jack home from the hospital and helped him up to his room, she'd imagined in him not just her father's drunkenness, but his laziness, his mean-spirited nature, his immaturity. She'd believed that if she became involved with Jack, eventually he would show his true colors, and she would have been duped exactly the way her mother had.

Mom had given up so much—everything, really—because of her tragic marriage. Ingrid Penner had been an honor student, traveled the world while she was an exchange student in Sweden. She'd been on her way to a college degree and a promising career. Her marriage to an alcoholic had destroyed all that, and would have destroyed her, if Vienne's father had lived long enough to finish her off.

Vienne didn't want to live out the rest of her life alone, but that was preferable to making a mistake like her mother's. If she married, if she ever let a man into her life, he would have to be—

She stopped short. He would have to be *like Jack.* She'd gotten to know him again over the past months, and when she lined up everything she knew about Jackson Linder, what she saw was a man of integrity. The kindest man she'd ever known. Just look at how he'd stood up for Pete.

And he'd been honest with her about his struggles long before he owed her any explanation whatsoever. She stole a glance at him, and a lump formed in her throat. How unfair she'd been in her judgment of him. Of Pete. Of anything to do with Clayburn, if she were honest.

She'd allowed so much bitterness to take root in her heart. And it colored the way she viewed everything. The way she treated everyone. Why could she see that so clearly all of a sudden? *Lord . . . I'm so sorry.*

"So, what do you think?"

At the timbre of Jack's voice, she slipped from her reverie, tucking her discoveries away to examine them more closely later. She squinted, trying to imagine Latte-dah with its walls full of paintings. "What kind of art are we talking about?" She narrowed her eyes playfully at him. "This isn't some kindergarten class project, is it?"

He laughed. "No. It'd all be professional stuff. Everything would be framed. Some of it will be better than others, of course, but I don't think there'd be anything that was just terrible."

"Nudes?"

Jack grinned. "Not that kind of terrible. But . . ." He scratched his head. "Hmmm . . . I suppose that's always a possibility."

She shook her head. "I can just hear Clara Berger if she has to stare at a Rubenesque nude—no matter how tastefully done—while she chokes down her cucumber sandwich." She gave in to a grin, picturing the scene. "You know, that might almost be worth it."

Jack threw back his head and laughed. "Okay. I'll tell them we can't allow nudes. No Rubenesque ones anyway. Not in a fine establishment such as Latte-dah." He sobered and gave her a boyishly hopeful look. "Does that mean you're in? There'd be an opening, of course, and I could just about guarantee a good crowd. We'd want you to cater it—or we can arrange something . . . whatever works best for you. But it would be win-win—a great venue for us, and a way for you to get some people in here who might go home and tell their friends about it. The advertising the council does will be essentially free advertising for Latte-dah . . ."

She tried to curb her excitement. It sounded like a win-win proposal, an answer to her prayers, even. "I'd need all the details before I said yes, but it actually sounds like a good idea."

He pumped a fist in the air. "Yes!"

She laughed. "You sound like Evan when he gets a good tip."

Jack backed toward the door, waving. "See you tonight? You *are* still planning on us around nine, right?"

She pointed to the pastry case. "I didn't make forty-kazillion sandwiches for nothing."

"Great!" He turned and stepped outside.

The door bells jangled as Jack let himself out. She watched him jog across the street. Seconds passed before she remembered Pete and Mitch were still here. She rose and went to their table. "How's everything over here. You gentlemen need anything else?"

Pete gave her a quizzical look. "What are you so cheery about this morning, Vinny?"

"Oh . . . nothing . . ."

Pete gave a knowing grin and looked toward the door where Jack had just exited. "If I were a bettin' man, I'd say spring is in the air in a big way around here."

She felt herself blushing and looked past him to the sun-drenched front window, trying to pretend she didn't have a clue what he was talking about. "It's a beautiful day, isn't it? Can I get you a refill, Pete?"

"No . . . better just let me get it myself, like usual. I'd hate to tax your brain too much when you obviously have other things on your mind." He nudged up the bill of his cap with one thumb and winked in Mitch's direction.

If she wasn't
flirting with him,
he didn't know
the definition of
the word.

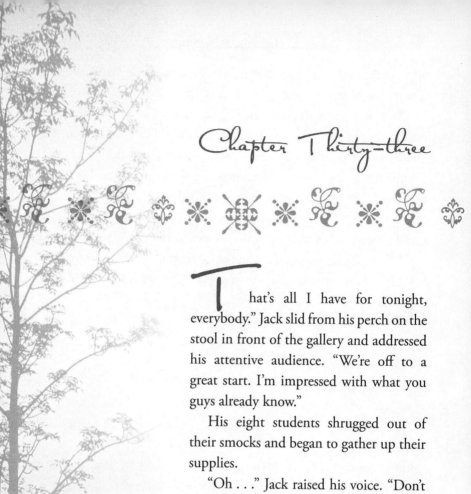

Chapter Thirty-three

That's all I have for tonight, everybody." Jack slid from his perch on the stool in front of the gallery and addressed his attentive audience. "We're off to a great start. I'm impressed with what you guys already know."

His eight students shrugged out of their smocks and began to gather up their supplies.

"Oh . . ." Jack raised his voice. "Don't forget the coffee shop is open late tonight. Vienne Kenney is keeping it open especially for us, so I hope you can all come. And tell your friends. I know she'd really appreciate any business we can give her."

A low murmur went through the group, and Jack wondered if he'd just inadvertently started a rumor that the coffee shop was in danger of going out of business. He started to issue a disclaimer, then decided against it. Anything he might say now would only reinforce people's suspicions. If he heard the rumor repeated, he'd have to confess to Vienne that it was his fault.

He waited until the last student was out the door, then locked up the gallery and went across the street. It looked like everyone but Doug DeVore—his poor lone male student—had gravitated to Latte-dah. Vienne was at the espresso machine using whatever it was that made all the noise. The frother, he thought she called it.

He went to her side and waited for her to look up and notice him, for fear if he startled her, that thing would spew hot milk all over them both.

"Oh. Jack. There you are. Thanks for sending everyone over."

"Hey, thank you for staying open for us. Can I help? Take orders or something?"

"Oh, that'd be great . . . if you don't mind."

"I'll just write them down."

"Works for me."

Clara Berger was next in line at the counter. "Well, you're just a 'jack' of all trades, aren't you?" She tittered like a third-grader at her own joke.

Jack laughed along good-naturedly. "What will it be tonight, Mrs. Berger?"

She squinted at the menu board he'd chalked. "Oh, dear. You'd better give me something decaffeinated, or I'll be up all night."

Vienne hollered over her shoulder. "I can make your caramel macchiato decaf, Clara."

"Oh, wonderful!" Clara clapped her hands, obviously having the time of her life. She took a ten-dollar bill out of her black patent-leather pocketbook and laid it on the counter. "Keep the change."

"Are you sure? It's only $4.57."

"I'm sure." She mouthed the words silently to Jack, cocking her head pointedly at Vienne.

Oh, dear. He'd definitely started a rumor. And now he was bilking little old ladies out of their money in Vienne's name. He could hardly wait to tell Vienne.

"You can sit down, Mrs. Berger. I'll bring your drink out when it's ready." He turned to Vienne and hollered, doing his best Evan imitation. "Venti caramel macchiato decaf!"

Vienne whirled around, laughing. "Hey, not bad. You looking for full-time work?"

"We'll see how tonight goes. If the tips are good enough . . ." He muffled a snort. He was as bad as Clara, laughing at his own jokes. And this was one poor Vienne wouldn't get yet.

It took them about twenty minutes to get everyone served, but when Vienne finally handed him the peppermint mocha he'd ordered, he looked to see that his class was clustered around two tables, visiting like long-lost old friends. Trevor and Meg were head to head at a table-for-two. He could tell from snippets of their conversation that she was telling him all about what she'd learned in class tonight. He felt a strange sense of pride at that.

He turned to find Vienne cleaning off the counters. He came up behind her and yanked her apron string. "Here, let me help with that."

"Nonsense. Go sit with your class. Thanks for helping, though." She looked out over the group. "I'd say this was a success, wouldn't you?"

He nodded and took a sip of his cocoa. "From my end it sure was. Look at them." Clara and Myrtle were giggling at some story Brenda Deaver was telling, and at the end of the table, the three other women were deep in their own conversation. "Was it worth your while money-wise?" He leaned close. "I'll have you know you got a five-dollar-and-fifty-cent tip from Clara."

"No way!" She put a hand to her throat, hamming it up. "How did you manage *that*?"

He frowned. "It's a long story. One I'd probably better explain. Do you want something to drink?"

"I've got water." She grabbed a water bottle off the back of the counter and lowered her voice. "Now, what's this about Clara's tip?"

He led her to "their" table, thankful it was somewhat secluded at the end of the counter. "Um . . . I sort of launched some scuttlebutt about you," he said when they were settled across from each other. He told her about the unfortunate wording of his invitation tonight.

To his relief, Vienne just laughed. "If I'd known I could make a mint in tips just by starting a rumor that we're going under, I'd have done it long ago."

They sipped their drinks in silence for a few minutes. The way Vienne watched her customers, it was obvious she was proud of the coffee shop. She had reason to be. The candlelight and the soft glow of the pendant lights that hung from the pressed tin ceiling showed off the building in its best light. Some nice jazz music came from the stereo speakers. He wished it were only seven o'clock instead of going on ten. It was a weeknight and Clayburn would be rolling up the sidewalks any minute.

She leaned across the table. "So . . . the art class went well?"

He wasn't sure what had gotten into her tonight, but her aloof manner was gone, and in its place was a warmth that made him like her far too much to be just friends. "It went very well. Everybody seemed to have a great time, and thankfully I think there's still a little bit I can teach them before the students surpass the instructor."

She gave him an appreciative smile. "I doubt there's any danger of that." She held his eyes and her smile faded. "I've been wondering . . . how are you doing, Jack?"

He knew immediately what she meant, and her bluntness took him aback a little. He tightened his grip around the warm mug and slowly shook his head, seeking his heart for an honest answer. "I'm doing well," he said finally. "It's . . . one day at a time. I'm beginning to think it may always be that way." He thought again of his conversation with Pete and the courage it had given him. He wanted to tell her, but he wouldn't betray Pete's confidence.

"If it's none of my business, just say so. But . . . are you going to AA or something like that?"

He wondered at her interest. This seemed like the last topic in the world she'd wanted to talk about before. And frankly, he wasn't in the mood to talk about it tonight. He'd been enjoying just spending time with her, laughing together. It felt like a step backward to talk about it all now. He didn't want to go backward with her.

But if she was asking questions, he wanted to be open with her. "No AA. I have . . . a counselor I can call if I need to talk, but so far I'm managing on my own—with God's help, of course." He shook his head. "I couldn't do it on my own. I get on my knees every morning, Vienne, and ask God to get me through the day . . . clean and sober. He's answered my prayers in some pretty neat ways."

She nodded. There was something in her eyes he couldn't quite read—a longing perhaps. But the harshness, the judgment he'd seen too often in her face were absent. He dared not read too much into it.

He tried for humor again, wanting to get back to the easy place they'd been with each other minutes ago. "So . . . no AA, but I am going to have to join WW if I don't watch it."

She crinkled her nose. "WW?"

"Weight Watchers." He patted his belly. "I think I've gained twenty pounds since I discovered how ice cream soothes the soul."

She laughed, the stern arch of her brow relaxing. "Ah, but ice cream doesn't cloud your mind. Besides, it looks good on you."

"Ha! You're nice to say so."

"I'm not just saying that. Men look better a little on the hefty side."

"Hefty? Excuse me? Now I'm *hefty*?" He feigned a pout.

She flushed that gorgeous shade of peach that made the gold highlights in her hair stand out. "I did not say *you* were hefty."

"Oh, I think you did."

She swatted his arm, laughing. "Stop!"

If she wasn't flirting with him, he didn't know the definition of the word. He couldn't imagine what had brought about this sudden change of heart, but he was loving every angle of it.

She was his mother.
There had been too
many times in his life
when she hadn't been
able to protect him.
Well, now she had
that power.

Chapter Thirty-four

April

Wren slipped on oven mitts and pulled the heavy quiche plate from the oven. She set the pan on the counter to cool, inhaling a fragrant whiff of cinnamon and peaches. She sometimes wearied of baking the same thing for every church dinner, but if she carried anything other than her famous Peaches and Cream Cheesecake into the church kitchen, she had to listen to the good-natured complaints that followed.

She rummaged in the cabinet for her good cake-taker. The trick would be to keep Bart out of the cheesecake until Sunday. He'd had quite a time keeping his blood sugar down of late. The last thing he needed was a slice of this delicacy. She looked down at the apron stretched taut over her plump figure and amended that thought. It was the last thing either of them needed. She felt a little guilty leaving it sit on the counter to tempt her husband, but it would get soggy if she covered it before it cooled.

She heard the lobby door open, and flipped off the oven and untied her apron strings. "Be with you in a minute," she hollered.

She came around the corner and stopped short. She saw him before he saw her.

Marcus.

She went numb. He wasn't going to let this die. Guilt weighed heavy. She hadn't yet told Bart that Jack's birth father had showed up in Clayburn. She'd wanted to. She'd started to on a couple of occasions. But somehow the words just hadn't come.

She knew Bart had noticed she'd been acting strange. She could never hide her true feelings from her husband. But he hadn't pressed her, and she'd held her secret in.

She had to put an end to this. Whatever Marcus was up to, it couldn't be anything good.

She marched into the lobby. "Hello, Marcus."

"Wren! I'm glad you're here. Can we talk for a moment?"

She folded her arms over her bosom. "I'm listening."

He gestured toward the sofa and chairs near the fireplace. "May we sit for a spell?"

He was all manners and charm. Didn't he know she knew better than to fall for that by now? Brushing a flyaway strand of hair from her face, she moved reluctantly to the sitting area and took the chair that would place her farthest from him, no matter where he chose to sit.

He took one corner of the sofa, but sat on the edge and leaned forward, looking intently into her face.

She heard the whine of the weed-eater in the side yard and prayed Bart wouldn't come in until Marcus was gone. Hopefully forever.

She fiddled with her wedding ring, refusing to meet his eyes. "Please say what you came to say, Marcus."

"You know why I'm here, Wren. I want to know our son. But I want your . . . blessing before I contact him."

Her *blessing*? That didn't sound like the Marcus of years ago. Unless she considered the cunning deceit with which he'd manipulated everyone around him—including her. She checked her thoughts. She herself had had a dramatic change of heart in the thirty-five years since she'd last seen Marcus. Thanks be to God, she wasn't the same naïve, thoughtless woman who'd had a child with another woman's husband.

Her throat filled at the sorrow for what she'd been all those years ago. Perhaps, over the years, Marcus had softened as well. She hoped so.

Still, even if he'd had a change of heart, it didn't change anything. Not as far as she was concerned. And certainly not where Jackson was concerned. She set her jaw. "I can't give that blessing. Jack has been through too much. This is not the time for another upheaval in his life."

Alarm shadowed Marcus Tremaine's face. "What do you mean, he's been through too much? What happened?"

She felt as if she were in the grip of two forces that were pulling her from limb to limb. Marcus's concern seemed genuine. But then she'd fallen for that from him before. Still, something about him seemed different.

But this surely wasn't the time to light one more stick of emotional dynamite under Jack. And should this be *her* decision to make? Jackson was a grown man. Shouldn't he have something to say about whether he met his birth father or not?

Yes. She was his mother. There had been too many times in his life when she hadn't been able to protect him. Well, now she had that power. Jack shouldn't have to suffer for the mistakes of her past. She could protect him from that at least. *Oh, Father . . . give me words to say that will make him go away. Jack doesn't need this. Not now.*

She steeled herself and turned to face Marcus. "Jack has . . . he's been dealt some hard things in the past few years. I'm begging you, Marcus. Leave him be. He's in a tough place right now. Maybe in a year or two when he's stronger. Maybe then I'll talk to him, tell him about you. And let him decide if he wants to meet you. But if you care anything for him, you won't interfere in his life right now."

"Wren?" Bart's voice came from down the back hall. "Wren, can you help me out here? That dad-blamed weed-eater conked out on me."

At the sound of Bart's footfalls coming down the hall, Wren's pulse surged. She'd hoped this day would never come. Bart knew all about Marcus, of course, but the two men had never met, and she'd thought that part of her past was buried. She didn't want to have to dig it up and parade it before the man she loved with all her being.

"Please go, Marcus." She didn't have to force the desperation in her voice. "Give me a number where I can reach you and I'll call you . . . later on. When Jack is stronger."

"Is he sick? Wren, you owe me an answer. Tell me what's going on with our boy."

"He's not a boy, Marcus! And he's certainly not *ours*. He's a grown man. A good man. He's made a life for himself. You didn't want any part of him when you could have been a father to him." Her voice wavered, then fractured, betraying her. But she'd waited thirty-five years to tell Marcus Tremaine what she thought of him, and she wasn't about to hold back now. "I gave you a chance to be a father to Jackson, and you threw it away. Now leave us alone. You . . . have no right . . ." She dropped her head into her hands, overcome with this sorrow being resurrected from her past.

Strong hands pressed into her shoulders, and she felt the familiar tickle of Bart's beard on her forehead. She looked up to see him, red-faced, peering into her eyes. Marcus stood off to one side, his face a sedate mask that she couldn't interpret.

Struggling out of the chair, she slumped into the haven of Bart's arms. She clung to him, feeling the vibrations of his deep voice against her cheek.

"What's going on here?" By the tenor of his voice, Wren knew Bart's question was addressed to Marcus.

She pulled away but took her husband's hand. "Bart . . . honey, this is Marcus Tremaine."

A shadow crossed Bart's face as the name registered. "What are you doing here?" His voice dropped, but Wren heard the veiled threat behind his words.

Marcus shifted from one foot to the other. "Wren can tell you if she so wishes."

"Wren?" Bart's voice was gentle but cautious, as if he were afraid she'd betrayed him.

"He wants . . . to meet Jack."

"Why?"

"I—" For once, Marcus seemed at a loss for words. "He's my son," he said finally.

"No." Bart shook his head in a wide arc and spouted the word again. "No. You'll not see him. Jack does not need this right now."

Marcus narrowed his eyes in a way that made Wren shudder—and remember a time she'd worked hard to forget. He turned his glare on Bart. "I hoped to have Wren's blessing before I made contact with our son. It seems she's chosen to withhold it. But if I want to see my son, I *will* see him." Marcus straightened his shoulders and buttoned his jacket. "And don't think for one minute that you can stop me." He brushed past them both and strode to the door.

When it slammed behind him, panic rose in Wren. "He's going there, Bart. He's going to Jack's."

Bart went to the window and parted the curtain. "No," he said after a minute. "He's driving off . . . in a red Lexus. He turned around in Trevor's lot. He's heading toward the highway."

Relief flooded her. But it was only momentary. This was the second time Marcus had come to Clayburn. How long would it be before he'd go to Jack—with or without her blessing?

Bart crossed the room, holding out his arms to her. She met him halfway, and he pulled her close, stroking her hair. "What do you suppose brought him out of the woodwork after all these years?"

She heaved a sigh. "It's not the first time he's been here, Bart."

He pulled away, a million questions in his eyes.

"I should have told you." She hung her head. "I'm sorry. I . . . I didn't think he'd carry through with any of it." She told him then about the first time Marcus had come to see her. "He somehow came across that article . . . in the *Courier*. He has it in his mind now that he wants to meet Jack."

Bart set his mouth in a hard line, pausing for a minute before he spoke. "Do you think he wants . . . a relationship with Jack?"

She shook her head. "I don't know what he wants. Why couldn't he just leave well enough alone? Why did he have to show up now, of all times?"

"I don't know the answer to that." Bart kept his voice even, but Wren knew by the shadow in his eyes that he was deeply disturbed by the encounter with this man from her past.

Bart had always held Jack at a bit of a distance because of Marcus Tremaine. Understandably. And yet she longed for her husband to get to know Jack the way she had. To share the chance she'd finally had to be, if not his mother, at least his friend.

Bart gave Wren a look that left no room for argument. "I don't want you speaking to that man again. No good can come of this. And I think you need to tell Jack."

"No!" She put a hand to her throat. "No, Bart. Not yet. Please. He doesn't need one more thing to worry about right now."

"What if Tremaine makes good on his threat?"

Wren shook her head. "I don't think he will. If he truly wanted to talk to Jack, he would have gone there first. I think . . . it just set him off to have you . . . forbid him."

She saw the hurt in his eyes. She hadn't meant to accuse him. Bart had only wanted to protect her, and she was grateful for his intervention. But she did not want Jack to have to deal with this. Not yet.

A thread of fear knotted itself around her heart and pulled taut. She'd have to tell him. Soon. It was time Jack knew the whole truth. But not quite yet. Not when he'd only now begun to live free from the shadow of tragedy.

Jack couldn't shake
the feeling that
something . . . . odd
had just transpired.

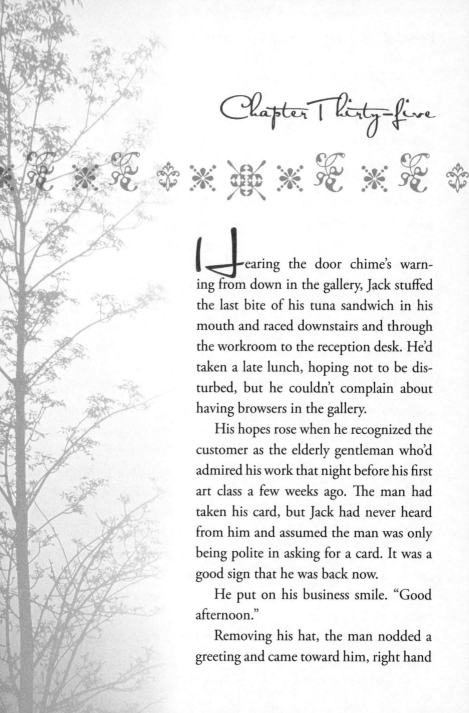

Chapter Thirty-five

Hearing the door chime's warning from down in the gallery, Jack stuffed the last bite of his tuna sandwich in his mouth and raced downstairs and through the workroom to the reception desk. He'd taken a late lunch, hoping not to be disturbed, but he couldn't complain about having browsers in the gallery.

His hopes rose when he recognized the customer as the elderly gentleman who'd admired his work that night before his first art class a few weeks ago. The man had taken his card, but Jack had never heard from him and assumed the man was only being polite in asking for a card. It was a good sign that he was back now.

He put on his business smile. "Good afternoon."

Removing his hat, the man nodded a greeting and came toward him, right hand extended. "I was in your fine gallery the other day. I'm Marcus Tremaine."

"Yes, of course . . . I remember. Nice to see you again." Jack shook his hand.

Tremaine studied him, seeming poised to speak. But he only continued to hold Jack's gaze.

After a few uncomfortable seconds, Jack averted his eyes and took a step back. "Well . . . make yourself at home. Let me know if you have any questions about any of the pieces. As I think I told you, I do have work in other galleries. You can view that online if you have Internet access, or I'd be happy to show you some facsimiles. You have my card, I believe."

The man nodded.

Jack started toward his easel set up in a corner near the reception desk. People seemed to enjoy watching him work, and even though he preferred to work in solitude, he often painted while customers browsed. He was nearly finished with the piece on the easel and the gallery in New Mexico had requested it, in spite of the fact they'd yet to sell the two smaller canvases he'd shipped last month. But they'd moved his work well—before he'd gone into rehab—and he was grateful for their continued interest.

He'd no sooner settled onto his stool with palette in hand, than Mr. Tremaine moseyed over. "Have you had the gallery for long?"

"About eight years now. Clayburn is my hometown . . . I came back to open the gallery after I finished at The Art Institute in Denver. My degree is in commercial graphics, but I was fortunate to find some success selling my paintings." Jack fingered the bristles of a favorite paintbrush and affected his tour guide voice, recounting a bit of the gallery's history while he painted.

"This building was the old Montgomery Ward catalog store for years."

The old man nodded. "Yes . . . I remember."

Jack looked up. "Really? You're familiar with Clayburn, then? I apologize for giving you my spiel. You probably could have done it better justice."

"Oh, no, not at all. I found it interesting. And enlightening."

Jack gave him a quizzical look, but Tremaine made no move to explain. "Do you live around here?"

Tremaine pulled a handkerchief from his breast pocket and coughed into it. "Oh, I've been all over. Lived in Chicago for many years."

"And how did you come to know about Clayburn?"

Oddly, the man seemed taken aback by the question. "I-I lived here . . . many years ago."

"Is that right? Well, welcome back. I don't suppose the town has changed all that much since you lived here." Though the occupants of the homes and the signs on the storefronts in this tiny town might transition from year to year, the only noticeable change any native might notice would be the new savings and loan out on the highway coming into town, and the Come 'n' Go that had gone in on the opposite edge of town a couple of years ago.

Tremaine shook his head. "Things have changed more than you might think. I notice the little inn is still here, though."

"Oh, yes. It's a landmark. They struggled to keep it open for quite a few years, but they're doing pretty well now, I think. If you need a place to stay, Wren and Bart will take good care of you. Maybe you know them?"

Tremaine bent his head and moved toward the north wall of the gallery. "I know . . . Wren." He bent to inspect a small still life hanging low on the wall.

But Jack got the feeling Tremaine wasn't really interested in the art anymore. He was just an old man reminiscing about days gone by, maybe retracing his family's history. Something about the man struck Jack as sad, in spite of his dapper appearance and the maroon Lexus parked outside, hinting at affluence.

"I'm sure the inn would have a room open if you're in town for a while. . . ."

With a slight nod, Tremaine waved him off. He set his hat back on his head and started for the exit. With his hand braced against the door, he turned. "You have a nice place here, Mr. Linder. It . . . it looks like you've done well for yourself."

Jack dipped his head. "Thanks for coming in. I hope you'll come back soon."

The man gave a curt nod and pushed open the door.

Jack watched him get in his car and back out. He set back to work on his painting, then realized that Marcus Tremaine never had told him where he was from. Jack couldn't shake the feeling that something . . . *odd* had just transpired.

✳ ✵ ✳

As soon as Vienne put out her Closed sign Saturday afternoon, Jack and four of his friends from the art council invaded Latte-dah. While she cleaned up the kitchen, the five of them lugged in box after box, unloading the paintings from a van parked in the alley.

Once the boxes had been unpacked and the paintings stacked carefully along the perimeter of the dining area, Jack climbed a tall ladder he'd lugged over from the gallery. He perched there for two hours, measuring and marking, and pounding nails into Vienne's freshly painted walls.

She had a brief bout of second thoughts, but once the paintings started going up, she caught the excitement from the crew hanging the show.

The gallery-like walls transformed Latte-dah. The varied hues in the paintings echoed the rich colors in the floor tiles she'd worked so hard to lay last fall. Everywhere one looked, there was something interesting to hold the eye. She would have clapped her hands and jumped up and down for joy, had she not been trying to appear halfway sophisticated for Jack's sake.

The woman and three men on the art council who'd come to help hang the show deferred to Jack on every decision, their respect for him evident. His eye for design amazed her, as he arranged and rearranged the framed canvases along the walls, grouping them for the best effect.

Vienne lost herself in the paintings. There were a few amateurish offerings, and a few that weren't exactly her cup of tea, but most of the work was polished and professional. She wouldn't have minded owning a couple of them, including the wonderful winterscape Jack had contributed.

She knew she would enjoy looking at these walls every day. And so would her customers. She could almost hear the buzz Monday morning when the breakfast crowd started coming in. She made a note to scoot the tables in just a bit so people could walk around and get a good look at the show.

She made complimentary coffees for the crew while they worked, and when they were finished and the mess had been swept up, two of Jack's friends bought a second drink for the road.

Corinne, a designer from Topeka, beamed as she sipped a cinnamon latte. "I can't wait to bring my husband here some Saturday. You have a great little shop here, Vienne."

Jack winked at her, and she easily read his thoughts: *See? Already we're making good on your half of the win-win I promised you.*

Jack's friends helped him cart the boxes upstairs for storage until the show was over. When they'd left, he helped Vienne put the tables and chairs back in place. With everything set aright, Vienne went around behind the order counter and admired their handiwork. Even the little placards that gave the artist's name and the asking price were works of art—neatly penned calligraphy on cardstock the color of café au lait.

She felt Jack watching her and turned to see him wearing a wary expression.

"Well? Are you having second thoughts?"

"Yes. Take it all down." But she couldn't hold a straight face for a split second. "Jack, I love it!"

"Really? Do you?"

She frowned, as a new thought struck her. "I think I might *cry* when you guys come to take it down!"

He looked surprised, then raised his eyebrows. "If you're serious about that, you could probably talk most of these artists into leaving their stuff on display here. I could handle the sales if anyone wanted to purchase something. Just like we're handling it for this show."

Vienne's mind swirled with possibilities. Jack came around to stand beside her, and she instinctively knew he was trying to see the room through her eyes.

He turned a smile on her. "It does look pretty nice, doesn't it?"

"Gorgeous," she breathed.

"And look"—he winked—"not a Rubenesque nude in the bunch."

She laughed, and pointed to a rather childishly rendered horse portrait. "I should have specified no horses, either."

"Hey!" His eyes wore a wounded scowl. "That's my masterpiece you're talking about."

She felt her face freeze in horror.

Jack broke into fits of laughter. "Gotcha!"

"Oh! You!" She grabbed the flyswatter hanging conveniently under the counter and whapped him with it.

His eyes went wide. But he laughed and grabbed it from her. She tried to wrest it away from him, but he playfully grabbed her wrist and held tight. "Say uncle."

She giggled. "Huh-uh. No way." She tried to twist out of his grasp. But she didn't try as hard as she could have. "I'm not giving up that easy." His closeness was hard to ignore. His hands over hers, their knees bumping as they played a tug-of-war.

All at once Jack let go and stared down. "Ewww . . ."

She followed his line of vision to the plastic swatter. "What?"

"Look at that." His mouth twisted in revulsion. "There's a dead fly stuck on there."

She dropped the nasty swatter like a hot potato.

Jack caught it before it hit the ground and gave her backside a swat before she knew what hit her. "Gotcha again!"

She squealed. "You!" And the game was on again.

She finally made him call a truce and they stood, breathing hard and smiling at each other.

"Hey . . ." His smile faded and he looked at her . . . like he wanted to kiss her. Her palms went clammy, imagining what that would be like. She held her breath.

As though sensing her hesitation, he took one step backward. He laid down the flyswatter and motioned eastward. "You want to go for a drive? We could get something to eat in Salina."

For once, she didn't balk at his obvious desire to draw out any time they spent together. But she'd promised herself she wouldn't skip her visit with Mom tonight. The extra therapy seemed to be having an effect and even the physical therapist mentioned that he was starting to see some real progress. And frankly, she was grateful for an excuse. "Thanks for asking, but I promised Mom I'd visit after we finished here."

He shrugged. "I understand. Maybe another time."

He didn't put a question mark behind it and she didn't commit.

But she had to fight off daydreams about his invitation the rest of the evening. Jackson Linder was making the thought of being stuck in Clayburn for the rest of her life downright appealing.

She'd never stopped
believing in God,
but she'd been mad
at him for most of
her life.

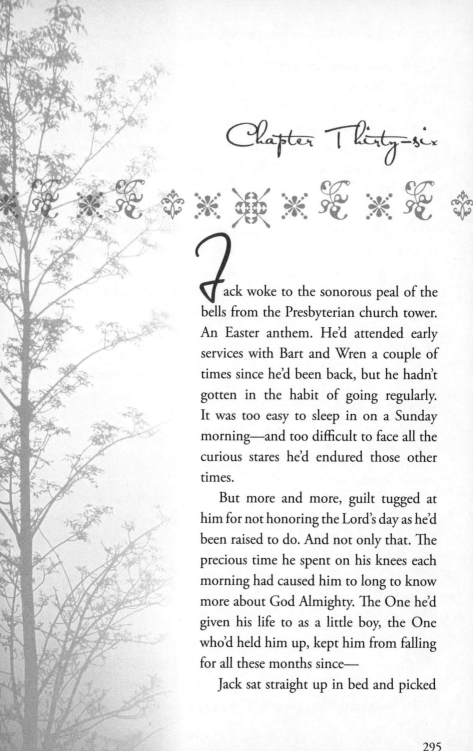

Chapter Thirty-six

*J*ack woke to the sonorous peal of the bells from the Presbyterian church tower. An Easter anthem. He'd attended early services with Bart and Wren a couple of times since he'd been back, but he hadn't gotten in the habit of going regularly. It was too easy to sleep in on a Sunday morning—and too difficult to face all the curious stares he'd endured those other times.

But more and more, guilt tugged at him for not honoring the Lord's day as he'd been raised to do. And not only that. The precious time he spent on his knees each morning had caused him to long to know more about God Almighty. The One he'd given his life to as a little boy, the One who'd held him up, kept him from falling for all these months since—

Jack sat straight up in bed and picked

up his watch from the nightstand. The tiny number on the calendar confirmed his hunch.

Today was his anniversary.

One year ago today, on a rainy night in April, he had checked into the rehabilitation center in Kansas City. He had been sober for one year now. How like his heavenly Father to arrange for his anniversary to fall on Easter Sunday.

He thought of Pete, still counting the years after thirty-two of them. He whispered a prayer for this good man. It made him weary to think about the rest of his life, the possibility that it might always be such a struggle. And yet if every one of those years were as good as this past one had been, compared to the three before that, he didn't care if he had to scrape a mark for each minute onto a sandstone post.

He slid from the bed and hit his knees. Resting his elbows on the mattress, he covered his face with his hands. "Father God, I praise Your holy name for bringing me through this past year." Tears swallowed the rest of his prayer, seeping through his fingers and dampening the sheets.

Twenty minutes later, freshly showered, he stood in front of his tiny closet, trying to find something suitable for church. He hoped Clayburn Community Christian Church didn't mind if he didn't have a proper suit for Easter Sunday morning.

He wondered if Vienne would be there. Ingrid had always been active in Clayburn Community, so he assumed that was where Vienne had grown up going to, though he knew she hadn't attended church since she'd moved back.

It crossed his mind to call her and invite her to go with him, but given that she'd declined his invitation to dinner last night, he decided he'd better not push his luck.

He pulled a white button-down shirt off its hanger and tried to shake out the wrinkles. Deep in thought, he pushed each button through its buttonhole from the bottom up, then fastened the cuffs.

He wondered where, exactly, Vienne stood with the Lord. He'd been open with her about how much he depended on God to keep him from temptation. She had always seemed to respect his faith and he'd heard her speak of God a few times in a way that seemed to indicate she believed in Him.

Slipping the only necktie he owned through his collar, he went to the mirror. Could he even remember how to knot the stupid thing? *This is where a wife would come in handy.* He aimed a wry smile at his reflection.

There was certainly nothing he'd seen in Vienne's life that made him think she didn't believe in God, but she wasn't vocal about her faith, and it had begun to concern him.

Because as much as he'd tried to safeguard his emotions, shield himself from being hurt, he was growing to love Vienne Kenney deeply. And suddenly it seemed important that he know exactly where she stood in that regard.

※ ❀ ※

Vienne stared at her reflection in the full-length mirror in her bedroom in Mom's house. The silky fabric of her skirt skimmed her hips and grazed her calves. It was a far cry from lacy white gloves and an Easter bonnet, but it seemed like she ought to dress up a little today. She couldn't remember the last time she'd worn a skirt. She curtsied and smiled into the mirror. The chartreuse and coral made her feel rather pretty and feminine. Maybe she'd wear this to the art council opening next week—and lose the barista apron for one night.

Easter services at the Clayburn Manor didn't start until after lunch, since the pastor performing the service had his own church's Easter sermon to preach. But she'd arranged to go early and eat with Mom in the dining room.

She wasn't crazy about dining with the other residents, but Mom seemed to enjoy the interactions.

Vienne ran a little water over her hairbrush and attempted to tame her flyaway curls. She was beginning to accept that her mother might never be able to come home again. But if Mom was to become a permanent resident of the Manor, she wanted to do all she could to help her come to peace with that reality.

Mom *had* made progress. The doctors said she'd probably always be bound to her wheelchair. And her speech was still slurred and muddled. But as she'd learned to control her emotions more, she was able to make herself understood. She and Vienne had developed a shorthand between them—an ability to read each other's facial expressions, to say much with few words—borne of the years they'd struggled together to make it.

Now that Vienne had managed the coffee shop on her own for two months, she had a new appreciation for the years Mom had toiled in the café. She didn't know if she could keep this up for years on end the way her mother had. She wasn't sure—if Mom couldn't come back—that she even wanted to keep the shop. So many things she had to decide.

Then there was Jack. Against every shred of resolve, against everything she knew about life with an alcoholic, she'd let down her guard and allowed Jack to slip into her affections. She was falling for him. Hard. This, too, made her understand her mother better—the blind devotion she'd always had to Harlan Kenney.

And that she understood scared her to death.

Sighing, she slipped into a pair of sandals and stepped out into the carport. It was a glorious morning and she eyed her bicycle with longing as she climbed into the Mazda. One bad thing about wearing a skirt. Maybe if she got home from her visit with Mom early enough, she'd change clothes and take a nice, leisurely bike ride.

The drive to the Manor gave her a front-row seat for an Easter parade of little boys in three-piece suits and pastel bonneted girls swinging grass-filled baskets, as church parking lots emptied onto Main Street and everyone headed home for Easter dinner. At the Baptist church, congregants milled about the lawn in all their Easter finery.

The air still carried the scent of Saturday's fresh-mown lawns, and she rolled down the car windows to enjoy every whiff of it.

Cruising past Trevor's print shop, headed south, she caught sight of Jack with Trevor and Meg Ashlock crossing the street to Wren's Nest. They were still dressed for church, Jack's shirtsleeves rolled past his wrists. He tugged at his tie while he walked, joking with Trevor about something, that gorgeous Jack-smile lighting his face.

Vienne waved, but none of them saw her. She swam against a wave of loneliness and allowed herself to entertain a little daydream of how it would feel to be a part of that close-knit group of friends. To be with Jack.

That thought shook her to her senses. She trained her eyes on the road and drove on to the Manor.

Mom was waiting in the lobby when she got there. Vienne looked pointedly at the wheelchair. "Did you wheel yourself down here?"

Her mother nodded broadly, pride clear in her eyes. The physical therapists had rigged the wheelchair so it could be maneuvered with only one arm, but it was no small feat for Mom to have gotten all the way to the lobby.

"I'm impressed." She leaned to give her a hug. "You look nice this morning . . . all spring-y." Mom was dressed in an aqua sweater set and pearls, and it looked like she'd had her hair done in the Manor's beauty shop yesterday.

She reached her good hand to tug at the hem of Vienne's skirt. "Youuu t-toooo . . . Veeee."

"Thanks, Mom. Here . . . let me take it from here." Vienne wheeled the chair to the dining room and found a place for them to sit.

They'd barely finished their ham and green bean dinner before the nurses' aides started moving residents into the multipurpose room for the worship service.

Vienne helped her mother in the bathroom before wheeling her into the large, sunny room. She parked Mom's wheelchair at the end of a row of padded folding chairs and took a seat beside her. She reached for her mother's hand and squeezed it. Mom turned to her with a crooked smile, and Vienne was flooded with love for her.

A noisy children's choir—from the First Presbyterian Church, according to the printed program—filled two rows in front of them. The little girls were decked in now-chocolate-stained dresses in Easter-egg pastels. The boys fiddled with clip-on ties and wiggled in their seats like so many jumping beans.

Vienne looked over their heads at the front of the room where a portable pulpit stood beside a wobbly standard that held the microphone. On the wall behind it two framed paintings decorated the space. She recognized one of them—a red barn in the snow. Jack's work. It had been on his easel that first night she'd helped him move a cabinet in the gallery. She'd liked it unfinished. It was stunning now.

She didn't remember the paintings being here before, but then she'd never spent much time in this room. She wondered if he'd donated them. That would be so like him.

The young pastor came to the lectern, and she turned her attention to him as he gave a brief welcome before launching into the sermon. His voice rose in increments to counter the screaking of chairs on the tile floor, the constant murmur of three nurses' aides flitting about the room, and the involuntary moans and gibberish from some of the less lucid residents. Most of the folks from the Manor seemed more interested in watching the children than in hearing the sermon.

The pastor concluded his message—the familiar story of Jesus Christ, who'd died for the sins of the world, and risen in glory that long-ago Sabbath morning—and the little choir filed to the front of the makeshift chapel to line up in three crooked rows.

Listening to their cheery voices carried Vienne back to her own Sunday school days. *Jesus loves me, this I know.*

Mom had always been adamant that they be in church on Sunday mornings. Of course her dad was usually sleeping off a drinking binge by that point in the weekend, but no matter what, Ingrid and Vienne Kenney were in the car headed for Sunday school at ten till nine.

She had good memories of that hour each week. Even some of the kids who wouldn't talk to her at school were nice to her in Mrs. Wilkins's Sunday school class. She still remembered most of the Bible stories the teacher had read to them, having the students act out the parts of Joseph or Daniel or Miriam.

The summer Vienne turned six, she'd asked Mrs. Wilkins to pray with her to "invite Jesus into her heart." She hadn't quite understood then how Jesus could get in her heart if He was up in heaven. But her memories of that moment—the freedom of being a brand-new person, being loved more than she'd ever imagined—were suddenly as fresh in her mind now as they'd been that long-ago Sunday morning.

"God's gift of new life is for everyone," the pastor had said. "Even today in this twenty-first century."

Did she still believe that?

The question haunted her long after she said good-bye to her mother and drove back to the house.

Eager to enjoy the rare, warm afternoon, she changed into jeans and a T-shirt, and started a load of Mom's laundry, then headed out on her bike ride. She turned north on the route she usually biked—a winding loop through the neighborhoods of Clayburn. The sun warmed her face as she pedaled, and she reveled in the feel of the wind in her hair. Somehow her thoughts always seemed clearer out here on the bike.

She rode for an hour and found herself headed east on the outskirts of town. She soon came to the little park by the Smoky Hill River where she and Jack had walked that night.

Riding along the bumpy lane that led down to the river, she made a mental list of the things she needed to do before the art council opening next week, but her mind kept returning to the little Easter service and the memory it had prompted of the day she'd prayed with Mrs. Wilkins.

For a while, that overwhelming love had stayed with her. She had prayed at night in her bedroom and felt God right there with her. She'd had a joy inside her that didn't depend on whether her father went on one of his rants, or if nobody sat with her in the lunchroom.

But then God stopped answering her prayers—about feeling happy again, about her father's drinking, about the way the kids at school treated her.

About passing the bar. About Jack.

The thoughts shocked her. She steered the bike to the edge of the lane and squeezed the handbrakes, dragging the toes of her tennis shoes in the sand until she stopped. She'd never stopped believing in God, but she'd been mad at him for most of her life. Mad, and not speaking. Childish. Especially when she considered that it wasn't God's fault her father had been a drunk. It wasn't God's fault that people had treated her and Mom with disdain because of her dad.

It certainly wasn't God's fault she'd failed the bar. Even the second time.

She leaned the bike against a tree and picked her way down the bank to the river's edge. The water lapped at the banks, flowing without restraint after the winter melt.

All these years she'd stubbornly held on to her bitterness, projecting what she felt for her father onto God. Onto Jack. Even onto dear Pete. She'd found reasons to be bitter toward almost everyone she knew. Even her mother, who'd sacrificed everything for her.

All Mom had ever done was love the man she'd married. She couldn't have known that Harlan Kenney would fall into the clutches of alcohol. And yes, Mom should have sought help. She shouldn't have tolerated the things he inflicted on them. But she had been loyal to her husband. She'd agonized over his soul. And she'd loved him with all her being until the day he died. And even beyond.

If Mom could love a man like Harlan Kenney that way, couldn't Vienne risk loving a man like Jackson Linder? A good man who'd suffered tragedy, and made some of the same bad choices her father had.

But that was where the similarity ended. Jack had put his trust in God, and done the hard work of setting his life aright.

She looked up at the cottonwood trees that drank from the Smoky Hill, their branches suspended over the water. Dressed in only a light jacket of spring leaves, the ancient trees whispered overhead, as if they had secrets to impart.

Jack was a man of integrity, who knelt over his bed every morning, placing his life in God's hands.

And that was the secret. She got it now. It wasn't about trusting Jack or even trusting herself. Jack trusted God's power to make new creatures from the old. To change lives. And he had demonstrated his willingness to *let* God change him.

Could she do the same?

Oh, but God had begun working in her spirit long before today. She recognized it now. With clarity, she traced His hand in bringing her back here to Clayburn—to where she'd begun. She'd come so far since November. So far.

She thought of the other day, watching Jack in the coffee shop. God had broken through the hardness of her heart, shown her how prideful and judgmental she'd been.

But now she saw a bigger picture. And it was all about Him. The God who'd been there all along, waiting for her to come running back to Him.

Oh, God, I'm so sorry. She bowed her head and blinked back tears. "I've been so far away from You, Lord," she whispered. "I've been so bitter. Please forgive me."

A melody wove itself through her lips, a wandering, made-up tune at first. But gradually, the tune permeated her mind, her spirit, and she recognized the Easter anthem the children's choir had belted out at the close of the service this afternoon.

The joy on their faces had been so clear, so sweet. She remembered feeling that way all those years ago.

Christ the Lord is risen today. Alleluia!

She knelt in the soft earth at the water's edge. "I want to come back, God. I want to know You the way I did when I was a little girl."

The banks of the river became an altar, and Vienne willingly placed every fragment of her being upon that altar, and vowed—like Jack had—to make that surrender anew each day.

Love's redeeming work is done. Alleluia!

Peace rippled over her like the waters of the Smoky Hill, and her heart soared—the joyful heart of a six-year-old girl.

Something didn't
fit. The more she
thought about it,
the more it niggled
at her.

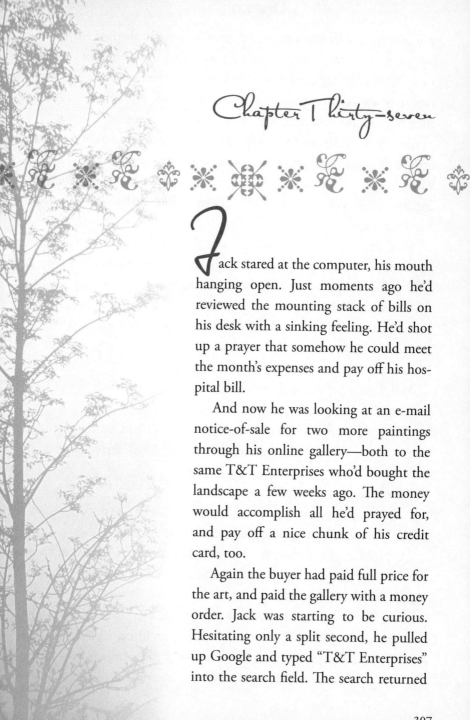

Chapter Thirty-seven

Jack stared at the computer, his mouth hanging open. Just moments ago he'd reviewed the mounting stack of bills on his desk with a sinking feeling. He'd shot up a prayer that somehow he could meet the month's expenses and pay off his hospital bill.

And now he was looking at an e-mail notice-of-sale for two more paintings through his online gallery—both to the same T&T Enterprises who'd bought the landscape a few weeks ago. The money would accomplish all he'd prayed for, and pay off a nice chunk of his credit card, too.

Again the buyer had paid full price for the art, and paid the gallery with a money order. Jack was starting to be curious. Hesitating only a split second, he pulled up Google and typed "T&T Enterprises" into the search field. The search returned millions of hits. Overwhelmed, he scrolled through the first fifty or so, but gave up after pulling up a dozen manufacturing firms and investment sites. Nothing rang a bell for him. None of the companies were typical prospects for the purchase of art. None had area addresses . . . but then he wouldn't expect sales to be local through an online gallery.

Finally, he shut off the computer. Maybe when the money order arrived, it would hold more information. It didn't really matter. Money was money, and he certainly wasn't going to question God's way of meeting his needs. Still, he was always curious to know where his paintings had found a home.

He glanced at the clock. Tonight was the opening for the art council show at Vienne's, and he wanted to make sure the caterers had gotten hold of her. He picked up the phone and dialed the coffee shop.

"Latte-dah. This is Vienne." Her voice was noticeably louder, and he heard the growl of the frother and the chatter of customers in the background.

"Hey, it's me. Is this a bad time?"

"Hi, Jack. Can you hang on one sec?"

"Sure."

The *ching-ching* of the cash register was followed by her friendly barista voice. "Thanks, and come again. Okay, Jack. Sorry about that. What's up?"

"Are things busy there? I can call back . . ."

"No. I'm good now. But I've had people crawling out of the woodwork. That must have been some ad campaign the council did."

"Good! I'm glad to hear it." He smiled to himself. His idea to hang the show at Latte-dah had worked out better than he'd hoped. "Are you hearing good comments about the art?"

"No. They're all too enamored with my amazing lattes to notice the art." She spoiled her deadpan delivery with a very unladylike snort. "Yes, silly. The art is a big hit. Not to mention"—her voice dropped to a secretive tone—"the artists are bringing their friends and family in for coffee and lunch, and I'm making money hand over fist. I gotta hand it to you. You're brilliant."

He loved the smile in her voice. "I am, aren't I?"

"Don't let it go to your head, Linder."

"Yeah, I'll try not to. Seriously, though, hand over fist? That good, huh?"

She laughed. "By comparison, yes. I'm not going to be jetting to Paris anytime soon, but I might actually break even this month."

"I'm glad."

"Thank you, Jack. I . . . I'm truly grateful."

He tried for an aw-shucks nonchalance. "It was nothing."

"Well that's not true, but"—the smile was back in her voice—"I appreciate your modesty. It's a refreshing change from that guy with the big head I was talking to a few minutes ago."

He laughed and his heart swelled. He pushed his chair back from the desk and carried the phone to the front window, hoping he might catch a glimpse of her through the coffee shop window.

No such luck. But just looking down the street and knowing she was mere seconds away, made him feel more connected to her. He had it bad for this woman.

"Oh, and by the way," she said, apparently oblivious to the emotion that had him by the throat right now, "the caterers called and they'll be here at five-thirty. Any chance you can come over and help them unload? I'm going to have my hands full around then."

He pulled his head out of the clouds. "Sure, I'll be there. And I'm glad the caterers got hold of you. That's why I was calling. Listen, if you need me to come over sooner, I can."

"Not unless you just want to. You probably have plenty to do."

He looked out over the gallery. He'd spent all day yesterday polishing the hardwood floors to a sheen, washing the windows, and tidying the reception desk for tonight's opening. The gallery walls were full of art. He'd given Meg Ashlock part of one wall to hang some of her watercolors. She and Trevor had agreed to play hosts at the gallery so he could keep it open late and take advantage of having so many art connoisseurs in town.

At least that was the plan. If nobody but the artists themselves showed up for the opening, it could be a bust.

Not really though. Vienne had already declared it a success. And that made it so in his eyes.

※ ※ ※

Vienne recognized the elderly man at the counter. He'd been here before, a few weeks ago. Asking about Wren Johannsen. She frowned, slightly wary. "What can I get for you today?"

He ordered coffee, black. But instead of taking his mug to the table as he'd done before, he stepped back from the cash register and looked around the shop.

"You have a nice display here."

"Thank you. Are you here for the opening tonight?"

His quizzical expression told her he didn't know anything about it.

"This show is put on by the art council over in Salina," she explained. "Their opening is here tonight. I just thought that might be why you were in town."

He shook his head. "No, actually . . ." He looked over the heads of the diners at the art displayed around the room. "I came to inquire about a local artist. Jackson Linder." He glanced around the room again. "But I don't see his work displayed here."

Vienne brightened and pointed. "We do have one of his paintings here—that still life over by the window. But Jack's gallery is just across the street. He has some wonderful work there, if—" Something in his face made her stop. She smiled an apology. "You probably know all about the gallery if you're looking for Jack's work."

He rubbed the brim of his hat with his thumb. "I haven't yet had the pleasure of visiting the gallery. But I hope to. I wondered what you could tell me about the artist."

"About Jack . . . Jackson?"

He nodded. "You seem to know him well."

She grappled for words. How would she describe Jack? She smiled to herself. She doubted "kind, honest, handsome, gorgeous eyes, and a killer smile" were quite the descriptors this man was looking for.

She hesitated, not sure how much she should tell him. But if she could help Jack make a sale, what was the harm? And people did like to know something about the artist whose work they were investing in. "Jack is very talented. He studied at The Art Institute of Colorado— commercial graphics, but he's never really worked in that field." She recited the meager professional facts she knew about Jack. "I happen to know he's in the gallery today. I'm sure he'd love to show you around, if you're interested."

"Does the gallery do pretty well? Financially?"

Vienne was taken aback by such a personal question. She gave him a pleasant but firm smile. "I really wouldn't know about that."

"Does Jack—Mr. Linder—have a family?"

"No . . . he's . . . single." For some odd reason, she felt almost as though she were betraying Jack, even with the vague answers she'd provided. And she was uncomfortable with the direction the man's questions were taking. "I'm sure he could answer your questions better than I can."

He nodded, his eyes seeming to acknowledge that he knew he'd crossed a line with her.

She looked out the window, ready to direct him across the street to the gallery. She did a double take when she recognized Jack crossing the street toward the coffee shop.

She turned back with a smile. "Well, speak of the devil. Here comes Jack now."

He followed Vienne's gaze, then quickly turned away from the window. His face blanched and he grabbed for the counter, steadying himself. He cast about the room, almost as if he were looking for an exit.

Vienne's suspicion turned to concern, and she wondered if he might be ill. But a few seconds later, she thought perhaps she'd imagined his odd reaction. He appeared perfectly composed, and ambled over to the wall to study the painting of Jack's that she'd pointed out earlier.

Just then Jack came through the door. He paused to admire the fireplace, where she'd arranged candles in the hearth and a fresh bouquet of pink alstroemeria on the mantel for tonight, then headed quickly toward her.

"Hey, that looks nice," he said, beaming. "Looks like you've got everything under control here."

She came from behind the counter and nodded pointedly past him, toward the gentleman. She leaned close and lowered her voice. "There's someone here to see you."

Jack followed her gaze. Just then the visitor turned and strode toward them, his posture erect, hand outstretched to Jack.

Vienne gestured between them. "Jack, this gentleman was asking about your work . . . I'm sorry, I didn't get your name—"

But Jack took the man's hand and shook it. "Yes . . . yes, we've met. Good to see you again . . . Mr. Tremaine, isn't it?"

Vienne looked from one man to the other, confused. "I'm sorry, I didn't realize—"

"Is your gallery open, Jack?" Turning his back to her, the man—Tremaine—pointed across the street. "I'd like to take a look around if I may."

"Certainly." Jack brightened. "You're more than welcome to come over. We have a nice show up in the gallery right now. Some new pieces since you were in last."

"Ah, good." The man nodded.

"We're hoping for a good crowd tonight. Did Vienne tell you about the opening?"

Tremaine started for the door. "Let's head on over there, if you're ready." Again, he addressed Jack alone, and Vienne got the impression he was purposely ignoring her.

Fine. She could take a hint. She caught Jack's eye and gave a little wave behind Tremaine's back before moving behind the counter again.

A group of women came through the door as the two men exited, and Vienne spent the next few minutes making coffees. But once the guests were settled in with their drinks by the fireplace, she replayed the strange encounter with this Mr. Tremaine as she worked at the sink. She was certain the man had told her he'd never been in the gallery before. Yet Jack had clearly referred to the last time he'd been in . . . she'd assumed he meant the gallery. Something didn't fit.

The more she thought about it, the more it niggled at her. Tremaine had purposefully avoided eye contact with her once Jack came in. Jack had seemed pleased enough to see the man, and eager to show him to the gallery. Obviously, Tremaine was interested in Jack's art. A wealthy art collector, she hoped. These artsy types could be eccentric. But he hadn't known about tonight's opening, and he'd barely given the other art in the coffee shop a second glance.

She walked to the door and shaded her eyes, looking down the street to Linder's. The glare on the gallery's plate-glass window prevented her from seeing inside.

But something wasn't right. She could feel it.

He leveled his gaze at Jack. "Have you ever heard the phrase 'Things are not always as they seem'?"

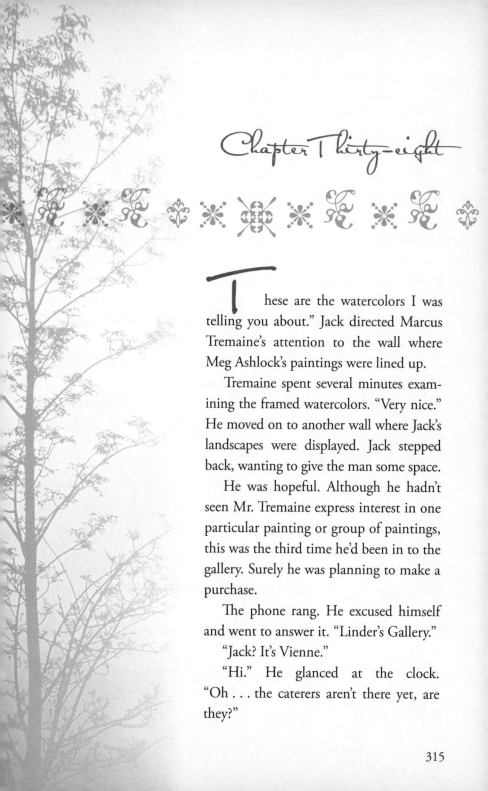

Chapter Thirty-eight

These are the watercolors I was telling you about." Jack directed Marcus Tremaine's attention to the wall where Meg Ashlock's paintings were lined up.

Tremaine spent several minutes examining the framed watercolors. "Very nice." He moved on to another wall where Jack's landscapes were displayed. Jack stepped back, wanting to give the man some space.

He was hopeful. Although he hadn't seen Mr. Tremaine express interest in one particular painting or group of paintings, this was the third time he'd been in to the gallery. Surely he was planning to make a purchase.

The phone rang. He excused himself and went to answer it. "Linder's Gallery."

"Jack? It's Vienne."

"Hi." He glanced at the clock. "Oh . . . the caterers aren't there yet, are they?"

"No, it's not that. I . . . uh . . ."

He waited, wondering at the hesitation in her voice.

"This might sound odd but . . ." Her voice dropped so low he could scarcely hear her.

He cradled the phone closer to his ear.

"I know that man is over there right now and . . . I just thought I needed to tell you that something seems . . . I don't know . . . a little fishy."

He glanced over at Tremaine, who was working his way around the northwest corner of the gallery. "I'm . . . not sure I understand." What in the world was she talking about?

"That man . . . Mr. Tremaine? He told me when he first came in to the coffee shop a little while ago that he'd never been in your gallery before."

Tremaine moved around to the wall nearest his desk.

"Is that right?" Jack hoped Vienne could tell by his clipped responses that Tremaine was within earshot. "I wonder why?"

"I don't know. Maybe it's nothing, but he asked if there was any of your work in the show over here . . . Then he started asking a lot of questions about you."

"Oh, really? Like what?"

"He wanted to know if the gallery was doing well. He asked if you . . . had a family. It's none of my business, Jack. Maybe you know him, but it seemed odd."

"Yes, it does. That's interesting."

It was silent on her end for a moment. "I'm sorry if I sound like a paranoid wacko, but I felt like I should call—"

"No, not at all. I'm glad you did."

"Okay, I'll let you go now. I just thought you should know."

"I appreciate that. I'll . . . uh . . . get back to you later today. Why don't you call me when the caterer gets there?" Vienne hung up and the phone went dead. But he held the phone to his ear a minute longer, his mind churning.

Why would Tremaine be snooping around asking questions about him? And why would he have lied to Vienne about never having been in the gallery? It didn't make sense.

The dial tone buzzed in his ear. Reluctant, he hung up and returned to where Tremaine was standing. Uncertain how to proceed, he decided to pretend nothing was amiss. There was certainly no physical threat from the man. He would simply act as if he didn't know the things Vienne had told him. And maybe she *had* misunderstood. "Is there something in particular you're looking for that you don't see?"

"No . . . no. I'll just look around a bit more, if you don't mind." The man moved to stand in front of another painting, but Jack got the distinct feeling he was only pretending to look at it.

Jack had to force himself not to pace. He looked at the clock again. Five o'clock. Trevor and Meg would be here soon. If Mr. Tremaine was still hanging around by then, he wouldn't feel right leaving them here while he went over to Latte-dah to help Vienne set up. Not until he figured out what this man was up to.

Jack moved to his desk and turned on the computer. Might as well get a little work done while he waited. He settled in his chair and pulled up the file that contained his art sales so he could record the sales tax. Looking at the invoices for the most recent purchases, the T&T Enterprises notations caught his eye. He looked across the room at Marcus Tremaine, then back at his computer screen. Tremaine. T&T . . . Was it possible . . . ?

He pushed his chair back and strode to where the man was standing. "Mr. Tremaine, I . . . I have a question for you."

Surprise registered on the older man's face. "Certainly . . ."

"You aren't by chance—" Jack glanced at the floor and back at Tremaine. It was a wild guess. How would he explain it if he were wrong? But he had to know. "You wouldn't by chance be here representing T&T Enterprises, would you?"

Tremaine's brow knit into a frown. "I'm sorry. T&T . . . what was that?" Either he was a whale of an actor, or he truly didn't have a clue what Jack was talking about.

"Never mind. I'm sorry . . ." Jack shook his head. No. Something was going on, and he was going to find out what it was. "Have you purchased any of my art before, Mr. Tremaine?"

The man bit his lip and twisted his hat in his hands. "Why . . . would you ask that, Jack?"

Something clicked. He'd found it odd earlier, at Vienne's, when this rather proper man referred to him as Jack. He remembered Tremaine had called him "Mr. Linder" that day he'd come in here and introduced himself. The way he said it just now seemed a bit too . . . familiar.

"Mr. Tremaine . . . I have to ask. This is the third time you've been into my gallery." Jack held up a hand. "I—I'm flattered that you seem to admire my work. And certainly there's no law against . . . browsing. But—" He took a sigh and plunged into the deep end. "I get the feeling there's something else that brings you here. Forgive me if I'm mistaken."

Tremaine stared at the hat in his grip, his silence confirming for Jack that something was amiss. Jack's patience evaporated, and he fought to keep an edge from his voice. "You were asking about me. Earlier, in the coffee shop."

Tremaine's eyes widened. "That young woman told you." There was no animosity in his tone. It was simply a statement.

"This isn't about her. It's about why you're here. What is it you want to know about me? And why?"

The man's mouth twisted. Whether in guilt or embarrassment, Jack couldn't tell. But Tremaine made no effort to answer.

"If you have questions, Mr. Tremaine, you can ask *me*. Do you understand?"

Still silence.

"I don't know what is going on here, but I need to go. I'm going to ask you to leave now. Please."

Jack started for the door, grabbing his phone as he passed by the desk. If Tremaine refused to leave, he wouldn't hesitate to call the police. This had gone far enough.

He pushed open the door and held it, praying Tremaine would leave without incident.

The old man scratched his head, then clutched at his temple, as if a sudden headache had come on. He blinked as though trying to clear his vision and walked to where Jack stood.

He leveled his gaze at Jack. "Have you ever heard the phrase 'Things are not always as they seem'?"

Jack backed away,
staring at
Marcus Tremaine,
certain he'd
misunderstood.

Chapter Thirty-nine

ienne kept one eye on the door, wondering what was going on with Jack. Thirty minutes had passed since she'd talked to him, and he hadn't called her back.

The caterers arrived and were hauling coolers and boxes in through the alley door. Jack had said to call her when they got here, but she hated to interrupt if he was in the middle of a sale.

"Here . . . let me get that." She relieved one of the caterers of a long, shallow box.

"Truffles," the bearded man said. "You can just set them on the counter until I get the trays in."

"Got it." She set the box down and glanced out the window. Cars were beginning to fill up Main Street—an unusual sight for Clayburn. Where was Jack?

She hadn't been able to tell from his truncated responses on the phone earlier whether he knew why that man had been asking about him. But she sensed that Jack was suspicious, too.

She helped the catering staff arrange forks and napkins on the long bank of tables they'd set up near the back. But when Jack still hadn't shown up fifteen minutes later, she excused herself and walked to the window and looked down the street. The sky was darkening, and the streetlamps took turns flickering to life. Lights blazed through the gallery windows and she could see several people inside. Probably Trevor and Meg.

Everything seemed to be fine. Between Latte-dah and Linder's, Main Street looked positively festive. Pansies nodded in the flower boxes the Lions Club had built on the street corners, and even some of the shops that were closed had kept their lights on in hopes of luring future customers.

It was almost six o'clock. Evan and Allison should be here to help any minute. People would start showing up for the opening soon. But she was ahead of schedule.

She lit the candles in the fireplace and stood back to admire the effect. Perfect. Everything was ready to go—except for Jack.

If he still wasn't back by six, she'd give him a call. Or march over there and get him. She wasn't about to preside over this opening by herself.

※ ❀ ※

*J*ack backed away, staring at Marcus Tremaine, certain he'd misunderstood.

Tremaine took a halting step toward him, but Jack stopped him with an upheld hand.

The man bent his head, suddenly looking years older. "I can see you're not convinced?"

Jack shook his head, unable to find his voice. He reached for the desk to support his weight.

Tremaine lifted his shoulders, expelled a sigh. He gave Jack a pleading look and took another step toward him. "It's true. I *am* your father, Jack." He stood motionless, as though he knew it would take a while for the truth to soak in.

Jack released his breath and backed away. "You mean, you and—"

"Wren," Tremaine finished. His eyes held sorrow. Or was it guilt? "She . . . didn't tell you, then?"

He knew—because Wren had told him—that his birth father was a married man who'd wanted nothing to do with Wren once he'd discovered she was pregnant. Wren hadn't told him anything more, and he'd never given it much thought. John Linder had been a good father to him. Jack had carried his surname proudly, and he still missed the man who'd been felled by a heart attack far too early in life.

Now he stared at Tremaine, tried to discern his own features in the lined face of the old man. He'd never dreamed of this moment. Not the way he'd dreamed of finding Wren. As a teenager, he'd often imagined being reunited with his birth mother. His high school girlfriend had helped him search.

He'd found Wren. And he loved her. Perhaps not the way he loved Mom and Dad, but she'd become dear to him.

He hadn't cared to know more than the little Wren had shared with him. On the rare occasions when Jack thought of the nameless man whose DNA he carried, he hadn't held a very high opinion of him.

But now, here he stood. The man whose genes had contributed to so many things that Jack Linder was. In spite of the bowed shoulders and the silvered hair, it wasn't difficult to see that his athletic build had come from his birth father. And the square angles of his jaw. Jack rubbed a hand along his stubbled chin. Had he also inherited his artistic abilities from Tremaine? His sense of humor?

A chilling thought immobilized him. Could he blame this man for the gene that had rendered him an addict? He dismissed the thought as quickly as it had come. Even if he were genetically predisposed to this addiction, counseling had taught him that he alone was responsible for how he dealt with his temptations. He'd discovered what his triggers were, and, for him, it had all begun with a tragedy that had nothing to do with heredity or DNA.

But a thousand other questions fought for prominence, and he was bereft of answers as they piled one atop the other.

What could he possibly say? What did Tremaine want from him? *Tremaine.* That would have been his surname, had things been different. What might his life have been like? He knew nothing about the man. Where he lived, what he did for a living.

His breath caught. Did Tremaine have other children? Perhaps he had half siblings. It was too much to take in all at once.

He swallowed against the parched lining of his throat. "Why . . . have you come here? What do you want from me?"

The man reached for the back of a chair and steadied himself. He seemed to grow more frail. "Perhaps I shouldn't have come. But, after all these years, I . . . I didn't want to have regrets. And maybe . . . if there's something you need, maybe I can make up for the years I wasn't there."

The door opened, and Trevor and Meg burst in talking and laughing. Their attention went to Tremaine, and their voices immediately stilled. The *ping* of the warning chime reverberated as the door settled back into place.

Trevor stepped forward into the silence that hung between Jack and Tremaine. "I apologize for interrupting. We could come back later, Jack."

But Trevor must have seen something in his face, because he looked from Jack to Tremaine and back, concern creasing his brow. "Jack? Is everything all right?"

Jack nodded, numb. "Can you guys watch the gallery for a while?"

"Sure thing," Trevor agreed. But his voice held a question.

Jack turned to Marcus Tremaine—his . . . father. The thought sent another jolt through him. "Would you mind if we went for a short walk?"

Tremaine gave a slow nod and took a step toward the door.

Jack held it open for him. Before he stepped out onto the sidewalk, he turned to Trevor. "Could you call Vienne for me and let her know I'm going to be late? Have her talk to Randall if she has any questions. Oh, and . . . tell her I'm fine."

He caught Marcus Tremaine's eye briefly, and they set out walking. Jack turned off Main at the end of the block, wanting as much privacy as the streets could offer. As they headed west on Ash Street, Jack's mind reeled.

Jack glanced briefly at Tremaine, who trudged silently beside him. "I'm not sure what you want from me . . . why you came."

"I simply wanted to meet you. To know you. I . . . I have regrets in my life, Jack. You are one of them." Tremaine held up a hand. "Forgive me . . . that didn't come out right. What I mean is that I regret . . . the way I handled the situation with Wren . . . with you. It . . . was complicated. There were—"

Jack frowned. "Wren has told me everything I want to know."

Tremaine nodded. "I have no intention of interfering in your life."

Jack slowed his gait to match the older man's. "Then why are you here?"

A deep sigh. "I'm not sure I can answer that question . . . even for myself. I guess . . . I wanted to know that you are all right. That you've made your way. That Wren is . . . taken care of."

Jack clenched his jaw. It was an effort to speak with civility. "I'm sorry, sir, but it seems a little late for that."

"Yes . . . I suppose it does."

Jack exhaled, and concentrated on a crack in the sidewalk beneath their feet. A dandelion had pushed its way through, reaching for the last gasp of sunlight. Jack reached into his heart for something that would satisfy this man.

And send him on his way.

"I've had my share of problems," Jack said finally, working to keep his voice steady. "But I hope you understand that I blame you for none of them. I was blessed with a happy home and good parents. God has been good to me, and I . . . after a few bumps in the road . . . I have a good life."

Tremaine swallowed hard, and Jack thought he saw a sheen to his eyes that hadn't been there before. "I'm glad. I'm glad for you." He cleared his throat and nodded behind them toward the gallery. "Judging by what I've seen, you've done all right for yourself. Your grandfather—my father—was a talented artist. He painted only for his own pleasure, but he was gifted. As you are."

Jack took advantage of the subject at hand. "Forgive me, but . . . I'll ask you again. I . . . I need to put my mind at rest about something. Did you buy some of my paintings? Anonymously?"

Tremaine stopped in the middle of the sidewalk and met Jack's gaze. "I did not. I am many things, Jack. But I am not a liar."

Jack opened his mouth to point out that he had, indeed, lied to Vienne. Or at least deceived her. But he felt a check in his spirit. Nothing would be accomplished by arguing that point. And for some reason, he believed the man on this. It had not been Marcus Tremaine who'd purchased those paintings.

He wondered if perhaps Tremaine had it in his mind to seek a relationship with him. But that didn't seem to be the case, and Jack was grateful. Perhaps the man was simply trying to right some old wrongs.

If anyone knew the agony—the impossibility—of righting wrongs, outside of God's grace, Jackson Linder did. And he would somehow find it in his heart to offer the same forgiveness to this man that he'd been afforded himself.

Even if Tremaine couldn't quite find the words to ask for it.

"Whoever bought them paid full price. Never even tried to make a counteroffer. And they paid with a money order . . . with no address. There's just something weird about the whole thing."

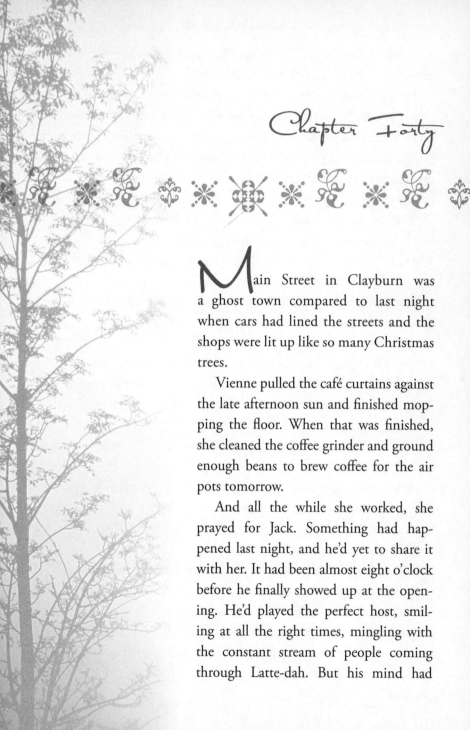

Chapter Forty

Main Street in Clayburn was a ghost town compared to last night when cars had lined the streets and the shops were lit up like so many Christmas trees.

Vienne pulled the café curtains against the late afternoon sun and finished mopping the floor. When that was finished, she cleaned the coffee grinder and ground enough beans to brew coffee for the air pots tomorrow.

And all the while she worked, she prayed for Jack. Something had happened last night, and he'd yet to share it with her. It had been almost eight o'clock before he finally showed up at the opening. He'd played the perfect host, smiling at all the right times, mingling with the constant stream of people coming through Latte-dah. But his mind had been somewhere else. Something had happened with that man Jack called Tremaine. And Jack was troubled by it.

He'd thanked her before he left, promising to come and help her clean up this afternoon. The caterers left the kitchen area spotless, and she'd done most of the work last night before going home. Maybe she should have called Jack and told him not to bother, but she was selfish enough to want to see him. And curious enough to hope he would tell her what was going on.

The roar of the coffee grinder must have masked the clatter of the bells, because when she glanced up, Jack was standing at the counter.

He pointed back to the door. "You really ought to keep that locked when you're in here by yourself."

She smiled and rolled her eyes, remembering another conversation they'd had . . . what seemed a lifetime ago. "In this little Podunk town?"

But his expression remained sober, and he didn't banter back the way she'd hoped for. "I'm serious. Anybody and their dog could walk in here and take whatever they wanted." His tone wasn't gruff, just serious.

She eyed him. Did this have something to do with last night's encounter?

When he looked away, she took the hint and finished grinding the coffee. Its heady aroma filled the room.

Jack brushed his hands together. "What do you need me to do?"

"I think the floors are dry now, if you want to put tables back."

He nodded and grabbed one of the overturned chairs off a table.

She hurriedly stored the ground coffee and went to help him.

They worked together in silence for a few minutes before she risked conversation. "I thought the opening went really well, didn't you?"

He looked at her and smiled, a little more himself than when he'd first come in. "It was a great success. Thanks, Vienne . . . for everything you did."

She waved off his thanks and dragged a table across the tile. She didn't want to have to ask him what had happened with Tremaine. She wanted him to volunteer the information. But he seemed lost in thought.

When the dining room was put back together, Vienne went from table to table, straightening salt-and-pepper shakers and making sure the napkin holders were filled. Jack came to sit at the table where she'd stopped.

"Do you have a minute?"

She pulled out a chair and sat down. "I have all day." *Finally.*

"I wanted to talk to you . . . about something that happened last night."

For the next hour he poured out his heart to her, telling her about meeting his birth father, and the conflicting emotions the encounter had stirred in him. "Am I a heel that . . . I didn't really feel anything for him? Except maybe pity."

She touched his hand briefly. "He wasn't really your dad, Jack. It takes more than biology to be a father." An old ache started in her heart. Didn't she know that? "You . . . you were blessed to have a father like the one who raised you." She forced a smile, not wanting to get maudlin on him. "He did a really good job, too."

That smile she adored bloomed on his face and she had to reel her heart in . . . stop her imagination from running away with her.

"I'm still curious about those sales—the paintings," he said. "I'm not sure why I had such a strong feeling that it was him buying those pieces. The T&T, for one thing, I guess. Tremaine . . . T&T . . . it made sense. At first I thought maybe the guy was buying them as an investment. No harm in that, but I'm not that big of a name outside of Kansas. And it was a little odd that he was practically stalking me. When he started asking *you* questions, that was the last straw."

"Do you still think he's the one who bought them?"

Jack shrugged. "Maybe . . . but I don't think so. I think I believe him when he said he didn't know anything about it."

"What were the paintings? Something you had in the gallery here?"

He nodded. "They were fairly new. Landscapes. But they were big ones. And whoever bought them paid full price. Never even tried to make a counteroffer. And they paid with a money order . . . with no address. There's just something weird about the whole thing."

"Don't you keep records of who buys your work?"

"If I can. When they sell from out-of-state galleries, I don't always know. It depends on how good of records that gallery keeps. But—" He looked sheepish. "I kind of get attached to my art. Sometimes it's hard to let them go. You want a painting to go to a good home, you know?"

She smiled and made a pouty face. "They're your babies."

He gave a short laugh. "Yeah . . . something like that." He pulled a napkin from the napkin holder and twisted it into a rope—an endearing habit of his, but she was going to have to start charging him for the crazy things if he was going to hang out here.

"Is there any way you can get more information about the buyer? Doesn't the online gallery keep a record? Surely they'd have the address."

He shook his head. "It's really not that big of a deal. I did like those pieces though . . . both of them. But"—he tendered a wry grin—"it's not like I'd trade them for the money I got for them."

She smiled. "Good point. Which ones were they?"

"They were oils. The barn in the snow . . ." He looked at her. "You might remember it. It was on the easel the first night I met you, actually. You admired it." He winked at her. "Or at least you claimed to."

She ignored his teasing and wagged her head. "That wasn't it."

"What do you mean?"

"That painting with the barn . . . in the snow? That one is hanging in the Manor. Unless you did another one just like it . . . ?"

Jack's forehead furrowed. "No. That's the only snowscape I've done recently." He described the painting in detail.

Vienne nodded. "That painting is hanging in the multipurpose room at Clayburn Manor."

Jack cocked his head. "You're positive?"

She nudged her chair back and tugged at his sleeve. "Come on . . . I'll show you."

She had to admit
the old guy had
started to weasel his
way into her heart.
Even more so now,
seeing how touched
Jack was.

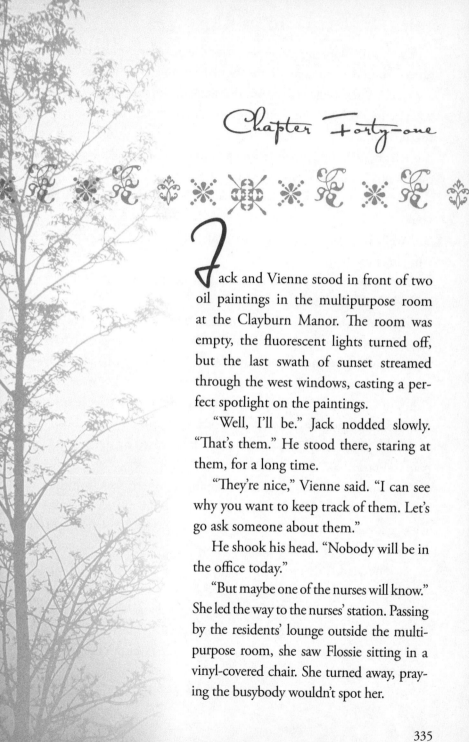

Chapter Forty-one

Jack and Vienne stood in front of two oil paintings in the multipurpose room at the Clayburn Manor. The room was empty, the fluorescent lights turned off, but the last swath of sunset streamed through the west windows, casting a perfect spotlight on the paintings.

"Well, I'll be." Jack nodded slowly. "That's them." He stood there, staring at them, for a long time.

"They're nice," Vienne said. "I can see why you want to keep track of them. Let's go ask someone about them."

He shook his head. "Nobody will be in the office today."

"But maybe one of the nurses will know." She led the way to the nurses' station. Passing by the residents' lounge outside the multipurpose room, she saw Flossie sitting in a vinyl-covered chair. She turned away, praying the busybody wouldn't spot her.

The harried-looking nurse who stood bent over the counter at the nurses' station wasn't one of the regular evening shift nurses. As they approached, she glanced up from the chart she was reading.

"Excuse me." Vienne pointed in the direction of Mom's room. "I'm Ingrid Kenney's daughter . . . Room 215 . . . ? We're wondering if you can tell us something about those paintings hanging in the multipurpose room . . . the two large ones in the front?"

The nurse looked from Jack to Vienne and back again. "But aren't you . . . ?"

"Well, yes." Jack gave a modest bob of his head. "We're wondering who donated them."

The nurse seemed puzzled. "I . . . I just assumed *you* did."

Jack shook his head. "No. It wasn't me."

The nurse shrugged. "You've got me, then . . . I just started working here a few weeks ago, but they've been here as long as I have. I don't know where they came from. You'd have to ask Mrs. Whitely— the administrator. She'd probably know." She gave Jack a meek smile. "They're very nice—the paintings. My parents have a couple of your watercolors. Beautiful landscapes. They're very proud to own them."

"Well, thank you," Jack said, clearly embarrassed by the praise. "I'm glad to know that."

The woman laughed. "Well, I'm hoping to inherit them someday."

Vienne's heart swelled with pride for Jack. She turned to him. "I'll try to get away a little early tomorrow and catch Mrs. Whitely before she leaves for the day. I'm really curious now."

Jack nodded. "Me too."

They thanked the nurse and started back down the hall, but at the doorway to the multipurpose room, he stopped and touched her hand. "Is it too late to stop by and see your mom while we're here?"

"Oh . . . I know she'd love to see you. I didn't want to say any—"

"Vienne! Yoo-hoo! Vienne Kenney!"

At the strident voice behind them, she and Jack did an about-face.

Flossie Cameron shuffled down the hall toward them, waving like a newly crowned Miss America.

"Oh, dear," Vienne said under her breath.

Jack grinned. "A friend of yours?"

Flossie caught up with them, red-faced and out-of-breath. She looked Jack up and down, and for a minute, Vienne was terrified Flossie would make some comment about Jack being her boyfriend.

But she circled Vienne's wrist with a cool, crepey hand and leaned in close. "I couldn't help overhear you asking about those paintings." She gestured toward the multipurpose room on their right.

Vienne felt Jack tense beside her. Why did this woman have to get in everybody's business?

But Jack fell for it, moving close to speak to her. "Do you know something about them?"

Flossie propped one fist on her ample hip. "Well, I should think so. I was here the day they hung them."

Vienne looked from Flossie to Jack, and back. "You were, huh?" She'd just about had it with this know-it-all.

Flossie scuffled past them through the doors of the darkened room. "Hang on. Let me get the lights. They're right over here." She flipped a row of switches.

Light flooded the room, and a fluorescent buzz wafted overhead.

"These the ones you're talking about?" She went and stood in front of Jack's paintings.

"Yes." Vienne eyed Jack, who just shrugged.

With a Vanna White flourish, Flossie indicated the winter scene with the barn. "That one there . . . now that's halfway decent. At least you can tell what it is. This other one . . ." She clucked her tongue. "Any monkey with a paintbrush could have slopped that together."

Vienne caught her breath, not daring to look at Jack. She cast about for a way to shut the woman up, but Flossie wasn't finished.

"Look over there." She pointed to a wall by the kitchen doors, where a small gallery of amateur artwork hung, most of it unframed or matted with construction paper. "They try to pawn this schlock off on us 'cause they think we're old and blind—and apparently stupid, too." She rolled her eyes and turned to Jack, gesturing toward the paintings. "Seriously, you look at those. Am I right?"

"Well, now." Jack winked at Vienne. "I doubt I could do any better."

Vienne snorted and bit her lip to keep from laughing. Jack kept a straight face, but she didn't miss the hilarity dancing in his eyes.

Flossie stood there shaking her head.

When Vienne finally got control of her silent giggles, she put a hand on Flossie's arm. "You said you were here when they hung the paintings? Do you know who donated them?"

She looked at Vienne as if that were the dumbest question of all time. "Sure I do. It was Velma Truesdell and her husband." She scratched her head. "His name's not coming to me right now . . . Steve maybe? Or is it Paul? Just a minute . . . it'll come to me."

Jack touched Flossie's arm. "Pete? Was it Pete and Velma Truesdell?"

"Pete! That's it." Flossie stabbed at the air with her index finger. "I knew it would come to me. Oh, yeah, they used to have a big farming operation east of town—maybe still do. I lose track of things being shut up in here. But that's who it was all right."

Jack pressed Flossie. "So you think Pete donated these to the Manor?"

Flossie harrumphed. "I *know* he did." She made a furtive sweep of the room with her eyes. "I heard him tell Mrs. Whitely—you know her, Vienne." She turned to Jack. "She runs the place. Anyway, she was wanting to put up placards and put a story in the newspaper about it. Ol' Truesdell, he had a fit. Said he didn't want any publicity. Said he just wanted the residents to enjoy the art. Ha! He's probably just trying to get 'em out of his house so he didn't have to look at 'em." A gleam came to Flossie's eye. "Shootfire, maybe he's the one who painted 'em—or, more likely, one of his grandkids."

"Or some monkey with a paintbrush," Jack whispered to Vienne.

She lost it again.

But Flossie didn't seem to notice. "He probably figures he and Velma will be moving in here soon enough, they might as well start moving their junk over here, too. Probably got a good tax write-off for that donation, too. The old codger always was a tightwad." She cackled at that.

Jack didn't respond, and Vienne turned to see him staring at his paintings, a faraway look in his gaze.

"Thanks, Flossie. We appreciate the information." She tried to say it in a way that dismissed the woman, but Flossie never had been one to take a hint. She rattled on about some "fool nurse" who'd had the nerve to send her to her room before eleven o'clock.

Vienne muttered uh-huhs and pretended to listen, but she put a hand on Jack's arm and whispered, "Let's come back and see my mom another time."

He nodded, murmured his thanks to Flossie, and let Vienne lead him outside.

When they got in Vienne's car in the parking lot, he sat beside her with a stunned look on his face. "I don't get it. Pete bought the paintings? That doesn't make sense. I know they were sold online . . . and I don't think Pete even owns a compu—" A knowing look came to his eyes. "Velma! Pete said Velma's gotten really interested in computers since she was laid up after her surgery."

"So you think Velma bought them online?"

"That has to be it."

"But T&T Enterprises—"

"Truesdell and Truesdell. T&T . . . Pete's farming operation was probably incorporated."

Vienne frowned. "But why wouldn't he just come in and buy the paintings? The pieces he bought were on display in your gallery here, weren't they?"

Jack nodded slowly. "They were, but—" He swallowed hard and his voice quavered. But he looked Vienne in the eye. "If he'd bought them straight out from me, I would have seen through him in a minute."

She shook her head. She still didn't get it.

"Pete bought them to help me out, Vienne. Pure and simple." He gave a low chuckle. "He's probably of the same opinion as that woman . . . any monkey with a paintbrush could've painted them."

Vienne giggled, but Jack was solemn. "That old guy bought those paintings out of pure . . . love . . . for me. He knew I'd never accept it as an act of charity, so he found a way to do it without me knowing. And he made a nice donation to the Manor in the process. I'll be . . . a monkey's uncle . . ." He gave her an ornery wink.

Vienne got the joke and laughed even harder. "But hey, don't forget it was a tax write-off."

A soft smile lit Jack's face. "That may be, but Pete Truesdell is anything but a tightwad."

Vienne thought of the quarter tips Pete and his posse left beside the remains of their long coffee breaks and begged to differ, but she had to admit the old guy had started to weasel his way into her heart. Even more so now, seeing how touched Jack was.

"You know," he said, "after I found out who Marcus Tremaine was, I suspected he was buying my paintings to . . . well, to buy me off. To make himself feel better for his own failures. I hated the way that felt. But with Pete . . ." He shrugged. "It's different somehow. Pete—he's earned the right to do something like that." Jack looked over at her. "Does that make any sense at all?"

She reached across the car and put her hand over his. "It makes all the sense in the world, Jack. All the sense in the world."

He took a risk
and reached out
to brush a wayward
curl from her cheek.

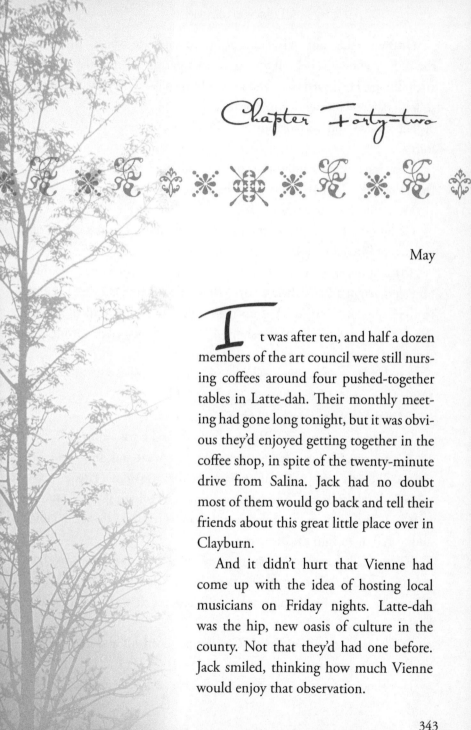

Chapter Forty-two

May

It was after ten, and half a dozen members of the art council were still nursing coffees around four pushed-together tables in Latte-dah. Their monthly meeting had gone long tonight, but it was obvious they'd enjoyed getting together in the coffee shop, in spite of the twenty-minute drive from Salina. Jack had no doubt most of them would go back and tell their friends about this great little place over in Clayburn.

And it didn't hurt that Vienne had come up with the idea of hosting local musicians on Friday nights. Latte-dah was the hip, new oasis of culture in the county. Not that they'd had one before. Jack smiled, thinking how much Vienne would enjoy that observation.

He drained his mug of hot chocolate and got up to take his dishes to the sink. Vienne was behind the counter preparing the next day's sandwich fillings. He leaned close and lowered his voice. "Sorry this is taking so long. We're winding down, I promise."

She smiled and waved him off. "Don't worry about it. I'm in no hurry."

He came around behind the counter and grabbed a plastic dishpan from the sink. "I'll have everybody bus their own table."

"You don't have to do that, Jack."

He ignored her and took the tub over, plunking it in the center of the row of littered tables.

Three of the women who'd ridden out together from Salina took his hint and scraped back their chairs. They piled their plates and mugs in the dishpan, then gathered up their belongings and headed out to their car parked in front of the shop. A chorus of good nights from the remaining members ushered them out.

Randall Hudson and two of the guys Randall worked with at Design Depot also pushed back their chairs.

"Hey, Jack. We're going for pizza. Wanna come?"

He looked at his watch. "Thanks, but I think I'll pass tonight."

"Come on. It's been forever since we just went out and shot the breeze. There's a new place out on Santa Fe that stays open late."

Jack shook his head. "You guys go ahead. I'm going to help clean up here." He gathered up crumpled napkins and silverware from the table and tossed them into the dishpan.

Vienne called across the pastry case. "Hey, you don't need to stay on my account." She waved a hand in the direction of the door. "Seriously . . . Go on if you want to. There's not that much left to do here."

"Yeah, man, come on." Rick Cressler punched his shoulder. "Let's go. The night is young."

Jack shook his head. "You guys go on." He gave Rick a look.

Rick glanced from him to Vienne and back again. His smile and his wiggled eyebrows said he got it. Jack prayed Vienne didn't see the big thumbs-up Rick gave him.

Rick followed the other guys out the door. "Thanks for everything, Vienne. Nice place you've got here."

Before the guys were in their cars, Vienne came around to the dining floor where Jack was pushing tables back in place. "Jack . . . if you want to go, go. It won't take me ten minutes to clean this up." She hooked a thumb toward the street. "Hurry . . . before they get away."

"Vienne, I don't want to go with them." He met her eyes. "I know these guys. They'll just end up at some bar getting sauced. I don't really need that temptation."

Her mouth dropped open. "I'm such an idiot. I . . . wasn't thinking. I'm sorry." She closed her eyes and slumped into a chair.

He touched her arm lightly. "Hey. Don't worry about it. It's no big deal."

She opened her mouth, then closed it again.

"What? You were going to say something?"

She studied him for a minute, as if deciding whether to risk something. "I . . . I just wondered if . . . if you're still tempted. Is it still a struggle for you?"

He gave a slow nod, choosing to misinterpret her question. "Oh, I'm tempted all right."

He didn't miss the fear that crept into her eyes. "I'm sorry."

He smiled softly. "It's not what you think."

"Oh?"

He came around the table and pulled out the chair beside her, straddling it backward. He took a risk and reached out to brush a wayward curl from her cheek. "I still struggle from time to time. But . . . not about going to a bar with the guys. At least not tonight. That's not what's tempting me tonight."

She frowned. "I don't get it."

He touched her cheek again, let his hand linger on the softness of her skin. She didn't move but held his gaze with those turquoise eyes.

"I'm tempted right now, Vienne Kenney, to take you in my arms and kiss you. *That's* my temptation tonight." His gaze lingered on her mouth. "It's what's been tempting me for some time now, actually."

Her eyes turned smoky, and she put her palm over his hand on her cheek. A slow, easy smile came to her face. "Well, you know . . . I've had the same temptation . . . for some time now." Her eyes twinkled with silent laughter.

Oh, this woman . . . Softly, he traced the curve of her lips with one finger. Surely she could hear his heart thumping in his chest. "Are you . . . giving me permission?" he whispered. "For that kiss?"

She scooted to the edge of her chair and leaned in. "I'll do better than that." Placing her hands on either side of his face, she closed her eyes and drew him toward her. He met her halfway, gently matching his lips to hers. He pulled away after a minute, wanting to memorize her face, to remember this moment for the rest of his life.

But what he saw was tears. Her shoulders shook and she wept silently.

His chest tightened. "Vienne? What is it?" He lifted her hands and kissed each finger, entwining them with his own. "What's wrong?"

"I'm scared, Jack. Because . . . I want to love . . . I want to love you so badly. But . . . I'm terrified. I don't want this to end up . . . like it did for my mom."

"I'm scared, too, Vienne. I'd be lying if I said I wasn't. I've prayed, so many nights, asking God to make me worthy of you." He exhaled an audible breath. "I've asked him to change our feelings for each other if He doesn't mean for us to be together."

Her gaze stayed intent on his.

He scooted closer, put his arms around her, in spite of the chair back between them. "I promise you I will do everything in my power to never fall again. But . . . I'm human." He thought of Pete Truesdell, wanted desperately to tell her Pete's story. But he wouldn't violate that trust. Still, there were other stories he *could* tell. "I won't kid you. You and I know this isn't a battle that's easily won. But I know guys who've managed to get off of a lot stronger stuff than the bottle. And they've gone on to do amazing things. To make something of themselves."

He told her about Dr. Boyer, his counselor in Kansas City. And some of the lectures he'd heard in rehab from men and women who'd battled demons far worse than his.

Her eyes stayed glued to his. They said clearly that she wanted to believe every word he was telling her. His confidence grew.

"Here's the thing, Vienne. In all the victory stories I know, there's a common denominator. It's always God who makes the difference."

She nodded and the crease in her brow softened. "I know."

"Without Him, I wouldn't have an ounce of faith that I could do this. With Him . . ." His voice caught and he struggled to keep it steady. "With Him I have all the hope in the world."

Her chin quivered and her eyes shone, but she held his gaze.

He thought of Pete's thirty-two years of sobriety and recited his own numbers. "It's been fourteen months and twenty-two days since I had a drink, Vienne. It's getting to be a habit. A good one."

She bowed her head, and a single tear spilled onto his hand, still clasped over hers. He wiped it away with his thumb and untangled his fingers from hers. "Hey . . ." He tilted her chin. "I understand your fears, believe me. And . . . well, you should be cautious. We both need to make sure we're hearing from God on this. Take it slow. This isn't something to rush into."

She touched his face. "That terrifies me, too."

"What do you mean?"

She gave him a sheepish grin. "I don't *want* to take it slow with you, Jack. What if God asks us to wait . . . for a long time?"

He squeezed her hand, his pulse revving. "If He asks us to wait for two days, that's a long time, as far as I'm concerned. But I'll do it. If He asks us to wait for ten years, I'll wait. Because you're worth the wait."

"You, too, Jack. I mean that." She leaned forward until her forehead rested on his shoulder. When she raised her head again, she wore an expression he couldn't decipher. She tilted her head to one side. "I'm wondering . . ."

He waited. "What is it?"

"Do you think . . . just once more that you could give in to . . . that temptation?"

"You mean this one?" He cradled her face in his hands and kissed her slowly, like he meant it.

Dear Reader

I f you've lived long enough to be able to read this book, you probably, like Jack and Vienne, carry some baggage from your past—mistakes you've made, sins you've committed, bad habits you've picked up, maybe even addictions that you've found difficult to break. And even aside from the troubles we bring on ourselves, we've all experienced circumstances beyond our control that have caused pain or even changed the course of our lives.

Jesus Christ gave His very life to save us from all these things. That doesn't mean it won't be a struggle to put the past behind, to shed those bad habits and to heal from the pain of hurtful childhoods or willful mistakes. How grateful I am that God is patient with us, not willing that any of us should be lost forever.

If you've been hurt, if you've struggled with sin, or an addiction of any kind, I hope you won't close the cover of this book before you lay everything at the feet of Jesus, allowing Him to begin working (or to continue working) in your life. May He help you forgive anyone who's been the cause of your pain (yes, even if they don't deserve it). May He allow you to experience the freedom that comes only from a personal relationship with God, through Christ. May He be with you one day at a time, as old habits fall away to be replaced with the wonderful newness of life God desires for His children to enjoy.

Therefore we do not lose heart.
Though outwardly we are wasting away,
yet inwardly we are being renewed day by day.
For our light and momentary troubles are
achieving for us an eternal
glory that far outweighs them all.
So we fix our eyes not on what is seen,
but on what is unseen.
For what is seen is temporary,
but what is unseen is eternal.

—2 Corinthians 4:16–18

Discussion Questions

1. In *Leaving November*, Vienne Kenney has escaped the hometown where she always felt second-class because of her father's alcoholism. She's sought to become "somebody" by getting a law degree.

Have you ever sought validation by striving for outward things to make you feel worthy? A degree or title? A bigger home or fancier car? A prestigious address or a lucrative occupation? If so, have these things accomplished what you hoped they would, and given you a sense of worthiness? If not, why do you think that is? What happens to the temporary sense of worth such things can give when they are suddenly taken away from us, the way Vienne's future in the legal profession was when she failed the bar exam for the second time?

2. Jackson Linder comes home from nine months in rehab, *still* struggling with his desire for a drink. Have you ever suffered from an addiction that held you in its grip for months or years after you stopped the addictive behavior? Maybe you're struggling with an addiction or a bad habit right now. How do you continue to have hope in the face of ongoing temptation? What have you found that helps you in your struggle? If you've overcome a past addiction or bad habit, what secrets can you share with those still struggling?

3. While she felt humiliated about failing the bar two times, Vienne

comes to realize that she really isn't cut out to be a lawyer. Her reasons for seeking a law degree had nothing to do with the way God had gifted her or with God's leading in her life. Instead it was all about trying to find self-worth.

How do you feel about Vienne "wasting" her law degree? Have you ever sought after something, only to realize once you attained it, that it wasn't what you wanted after all? How did you deal with that realization? Is it possible Vienne's education wasn't wasted after all, in spite of the fact that she's now running a coffee shop? Explain.

4. As Vienne becomes friends with Jack, she almost doesn't realize that she is falling in love with him. Have you had a similar experience? If so, what did you find to be the pros and cons of falling in love with someone who was a friend before they were a romantic interest? How did your story end?

5. The downside of Vienne's falling in love with Jack is that when she discovers Jack has struggled with an addiction to alcohol, she realizes he has the one fault she promised never to abide in a man (because of her father's alcoholism).

If you were in Vienne's shoes, how would you handle the situation? Would you break off all contact with Jack? Would you do as Vienne grudgingly did and try to remain friends, while putting aside thoughts of romance? Or are there other possibilities? Read Colossians 3:1–15 and 1 Peter 4:8 and discuss how these commands might apply to Jack and Vienne's situation.

6. Forgiveness is a large theme woven throughout *Leaving November*. Vienne is faced with forgiving her father (who never repented). Then she must forgive Jack's past. Jack has been forgiven of a great mistake (even though it was unintentional). Now, he must forgive his birth father, as well as forgiving Vienne for her judgment of him.

Forgiveness is difficult, especially when there is no remorse. Have you struggled to forgive someone in your life? In what situation(s)? What do you think it means to "forgive and forget"? Read Psalm 103:8–14. Is it possible to ever truly forget a wrong that was done to us? Why or why not?

7. Like Jack, Wren has to deal with events from her past that color her present life. How do you feel about the way Wren handled Marcus Tremaine's reentrance into her life? Do you think Wren gave Jack enough information about his father? Why or why not?

8. Jack's confrontation with his birth father left him feeling conflicted about what his response should be. What do you think about the way Jack handled his father's attempt to be a part of his life? How could Jack have handled it differently?

9. Jack's addiction to alcohol began as an escape from his shame and sorrow over the accident he inadvertently caused. Do you view Jack's addiction any differently knowing this? How do you think the circumstances might have changed the methods counselors used to help Jack recover?

Discuss some of the recovery techniques Jack used to remain sober. How did you feel about the way his recovery was portrayed in the book? Did you trust that Jack had his addictions under control by the end of the book? Why or why not? If Vienne were your daughter, would you be comfortable with her having a romantic relationship with Jack? Why or why not?

10. Vienne felt quite a bit of animosity toward Pete Truesdell. What reasons did she give for this, and did you think her feelings were justified? Is it possible there were other reasons Pete irritated Vienne that she wasn't willing to admit? What might those reasons have been?

11. Pete reveals to Jack that, for thirty-two years, he's struggled with the same addiction Jack is struggling with. How did that make Jack feel? When you're in the midst of a trial or temptation, is it helpful to know that others have the same struggle? Why or why not?

Read Romans 5:1–5 and Romans 12:15. In what ways can you find something positive in your own trials, knowing that someday you may be able to offer comfort to those who are walking in your shoes?

DEBORAH RANEY had dreamed of writing a book since the summer she read all of Laura Ingalls Wilder's *Little House* books and discovered that a little Kansas farm girl could, indeed, grow up to be a writer. After a happy twenty-year detour as a stay-at-home wife and mom, Deb began her writing career. Her first novel, *A Vow to Cherish,* was awarded a Silver Angel from Excellence in Media, and inspired the acclaimed World Wide Pictures film of the same title. Since then her books have won the RITA Award, the HOLT Medallion, and the National Readers' Choice Award; she was also a finalist for a Christy Award. Deb enjoys speaking and teaching at writers' conferences across the country and serves on the advisory board of American Christian Fiction Writers. She and her husband, artist Ken Raney, make their home in their native Kansas and love the small-town life that is the setting for many of Deb's novels. The Raneys enjoy gardening, teaching married couples in their church, watching their teenage daughter's ball games, and traveling to visit three grown children and grandchildren who live much too far away.

Deborah loves hearing from her readers. To e-mail her or to learn more about her books, please visit www.deborahraney.com or write to Deborah in care of Howard Books, 3117 North 7th Street, West Monroe, Louisiana 71291.

Yesterday's Embers

by Deborah Raney

Prologue

Thanksgiving Day

You sure you guys'll be okay?" Doug Devore leaned over the sofa to give his wife a kiss.

Kaye turned her head away and his lips landed on her left ear. She wrinkled her nose and put a hand over her mouth. "Sorry, but you better not kiss me. My luck, I'm probably already contagious." She looked down at six-year-old Rachel, asleep in the crook of her arm.

The car horn tooted from the garage and Sarah appeared in the kitchen doorway. "C'mon, Daddy! Hurry up! Landon's bein' bossy and Kayeleigh says she's gonna walk to Grandma's if you don't get the lead out."

"You tell Landon to cut it out, and tell Kayeleigh to hold her horses and quit sassing." He gave Kaye what he hoped was a desperate frown. "You sure you don't want me to stay home with you?"

She narrowed her eyes at him. "Don't even think about it, buster." She turned her pretty face to the hearth, where the first fire of the season crackled like brittle leaves underfoot. "But, hey, thanks for the fire."

Oh, what he wouldn't give to call Kaye's mother and bow out of Thanksgiving for all of them. Just sit here by the fire with a good book, watch the game later without Kaye's brothers giving their obnoxious play-by-play. But that would never fly. Kaye's mom had no doubt been cooking for days. Besides, if he stayed home, Thanksgiving dinner was likely to be a sleeve of stale saltines and a can of Campbell's tomato soup that he heated up himself.

With visions of the usual dinner-table mayhem, Harley in her high chair flinging soup all over the kitchen—and Kaye too sick to supervise—he reconsidered. "I'll bring a couple of plates home for you two."

"Uh-huh . . . that's what I thought." Kaye laughed and he knew she'd read his mind.

He reached down to brush a wisp of hair off Rachel's forehead. "Man . . . She feels hot."

His wife gave a knowing nod. "I don't think this little angel is going to be eating anything anytime soon."

Kaye had been up all night with Rachel while Doug managed to play possum through the sounds of his daughter's retching. A twinge of guilt nipped at his conscience now.

Kaye tugged on his sleeve. "Make sure Harley wears a hat if the kids take her outside."

"I will." He grabbed his jacket off the back of a kitchen chair and started for the garage.

"Hey, you . . ."

He turned back at the sound of Kaye's voice.

She winked. "I like lots of whipped cream on my pumpkin pie."

The door to the garage opened again and Sadie, Sarah's twin, popped her head in. "Da-aad, hurry up. Harley's fussin' . . ."

He gave Kaye a hopeful grin. "You *sure* you don't want me to stay?"

Kaye pulled Rachel closer and cocked an eyebrow at him. "And clean up vomit?"

He stuffed his arm through the sleeve of his coat. "I'm going, I'm going." Talk about the lesser of evils . . .

His wife's soft laughter followed him out the door.

Chapter One

December 2

The parade of taillights smoldered crimson through the patchy fog hovering over Old Highway 40. Mickey Valdez tapped the brakes with the toe of her black dress pumps, trying to stay a respectable distance from the car in front of her.

They'd left the church almost twenty minutes ago and the procession was still barely two miles outside Clayburn's city limits. The line of cars snaked up the hill—if you could call the road's rolling incline that—and ahead of her, the red glow of brake lights dotted the highway flickering off and on like so many fireflies. Cresting the rise, Mickey could barely make out the rows of pewter-colored gravestones poking through the mist beyond the wrought iron gates of the Coyote County Cemetery.

She smoothed the skirt of her black crepe dress and tried to focus her thoughts on maneuvering the car. But when the first hearse turned onto the cemetery's gravel drive in front of her, she lost it. Her sobs came like dry heaves, producing no tears, and for once she was glad to be in the car alone.

The line of cars came almost to a standstill as the second hearse crept through the gates.

The twin black Lincolns pulled to the side of the gravel lane, parking one behind the other near the plots where two fresh graves scarred the prairie. The drivers emerged from the hearses, walked in unison to the rear of their cars, and opened the curtained back doors. Mickey looked away. She couldn't look at those two caskets again.

When it came her turn to drive over the culvert under the high arch of the iron gates, she wanted desperately to keep on driving. To head west and never turn back. But Pete Truesdell stood in her way, directing traffic into the fenced-in graveyard. Mickey almost didn't recognize Pete. He sported a rumpled navy double-breasted suit instead of his usual coveralls. How he could see through the tears gushing down his cheeks, Mickey didn't know.

Her heart broke for the old man. He must be related to the family somehow. Seemed like everybody in Clayburn was related to at least one other family in town. Everybody but the Valdezes.

Pete waved her through, halting the car behind her with his other hand.

Maybe if she just sat in the car until the procession left the cemetery . . . She didn't want to walk across the uneven sod. Didn't want to risk the kids seeing her, risk breaking down in front of them. What would she say? What could anybody say to make what happened be all right?

She wondered if Doug DeVore found any comfort in the knowledge that his wife and daughter had left this earth together.

But on Thanksgiving Day? What was God *thinking*?

She'd never gotten to know Kaye DeVore. Not really. She always seemed so happy-go-lucky. She and Mickey exchanged pleasantries whenever Kaye dropped the kids off at the day care, but it was usually Doug who delivered the children each morning and came for them at night. The DeVore kids were always the last to get picked up. But Mickey had never minded staying late, waiting for Doug or Kaye to come. She loved those kids.

Especially Rachel. Sweet, angel-faced Rachel, whose eyes always seemed to hold a wisdom beyond her years. Now Mickey made herself look at the tiny white coffin the pallbearers lifted from the second hearse. But she couldn't make it seem real that the sunny six-year-old was gone.

How Doug could hold up under this tragedy was more than Mickey could imagine. She dreaded facing him whenever he brought the other kids back to the day care center.

Maybe he wouldn't. She'd heard that Kaye's mother was planning to move in and help Doug, at least for a while. Thank goodness for that. Six kids—She corrected herself. Only five now. But five kids had to be a handful for anyone. The DeVores had gone on vacation in the middle of April last year, and the day care center had been deathly quiet without Rachel and her lively twin sisters and little Harley. It would be deathly quiet now.

Deathly. Even though she was alone in the car, Mickey cringed at her choice of words.

She jolted at the sound of someone tapping on the hood of her car, and looked up to see Pete motioning her through the gates. She put the car in gear and inched over the bumpy culvert. There was no turning back now.

Also available in the Clayburn series

What if you could start all over again? What if you had a chance to walk away from mistakes in your past and reinvent yourself? *Remember to Forget* is an unforgettable story of second chances that holds the promise of starting over, of creating a new life in God's care.

1-58229-643-X